THE ALWAYS REALMS

THE DAY AFTER ALWAYS

BOOK TWO

BY

CHARLES EARL HARREL

The Saga Continues

Charles E Harrel

March 2024

THE ALWAYS REALMS

The Day After Always
Book Two

Additional information and story references can be found in the *Glossaries*, *Appendix*, and *Cast of Characters*.

ISBN: 978-1-962168-60-1

To all those who helped with this novel,
believed in it, and prayed for it to make a difference:

Thank You!

Contents

Till the sea runs dry, till the moon don't shine, till the rain
clouds are all left behind. Till the wind don't blow.
Till the stars don't show.
I'll praise His name till the day after always.

—Song lyrics by Paul Dee Allen (1988)

MAP OF CENTRAL HEAVEN

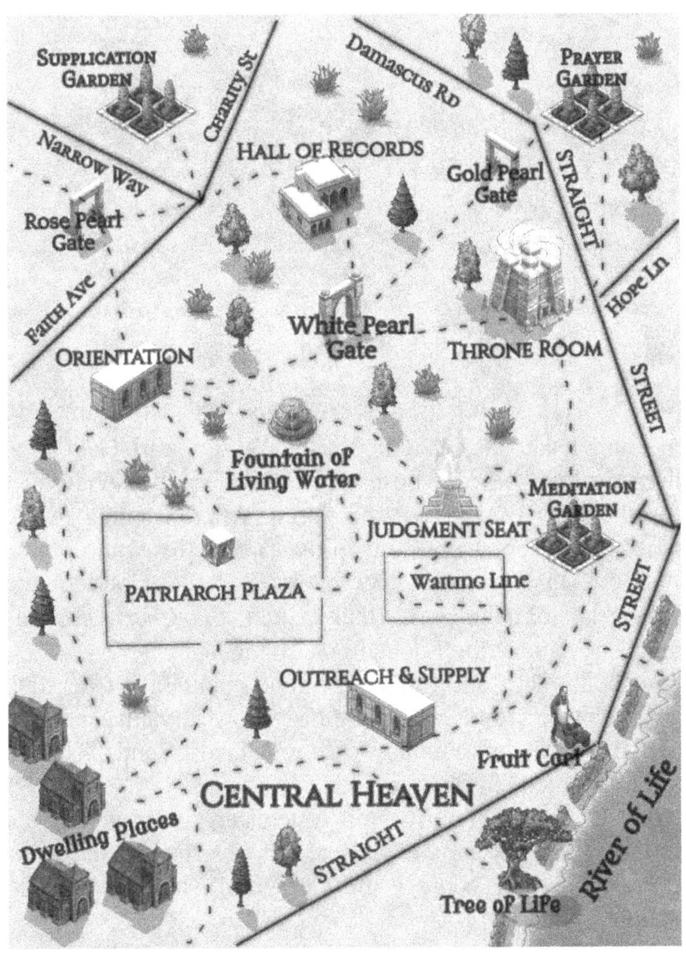

The locations and landmarks in Central Heaven are speculative. Notwithstanding, several are based on Scripture, others inspired by tradition.

"But as it is written, Eye hath not seen, nor ear heard, neither have entered into the heart of man, the things which God hath prepared for them that love him" (1 Corinthians 2:9).

CHAPTER 1

THE RETURN

Jesse Walt and the three envoys had just returned to heaven from Eskaonus, arriving at the White Pearl Gate. The guardian angel, elChesed, whose name means mercy of God, met them as they arrived through the portal. After listening to the emissaries share about what transpired during their outreach to confront evil and restore the knowledge of God to the Eskaonites, he told the group that Uzziel, *the Cherubim*, was waiting to see them at the Fountain of Living Water.

Annabelle, Seth, and Lundy gave one final hug to Chesedel, the name he preferred to use among his fellow servants, and then transported over to the fountain. Jesse remained behind. "There's a question I wanted to ask about—"

"Yes, I know. You're still interested in how heaven accounts for the passage of time. Let's discuss the eternity-timeframe issue after you see the Cherubim. Best not to keep him waiting."

"Okay, later it is. Aren't you joining us?"

"Indeed, I wouldn't miss it." And Chesedel disappeared into thin air. Jesse decided to walk to the meeting. He still liked the old method of traveling, namely, using one's feet. This popping in and out of places wasn't his first preference. Although Jesse hurried, he arrived last at the fountain.

The Fountain of Living Water was a popular heavenmark that lay between Patriarch Plaza and the Judgment Seat. This eternal wellspring sprayed twelve jets of water high into the air creating a refreshing mist. Saints often gathered around the fountain to drink from the life-giving waters. Others would wade in the pool surrounding it or splash water at one another, reveling in the festive spirit always present. Any saint could enjoy the blessings of the waters of life, freely given by God.

Uzziel stood by the south side of the pool, nearest Patriarch Plaza. His long golden hair waved in the gentle breeze that seemed to be ever present in Central Heaven. He scanned the vicinity with a watchful eye. His celestial wings were folded behind his back. His flaming sword, usually gripped in his left hand, remained in its scabbard. "Gather around, Beloved. I see you're all here except Maximus. I had a feeling he might stay in Eskaonus for the time being. You can explain those circumstances later. First, let me say we appreciate your willingness to serve. Your efforts and dedication led to the defeat of evil, bringing unity to the divided realms. Most of all, the inhabitants have discovered their forgotten heritage of faith. I realize there were sacrifices, lives put in jeopardy, even some lost, yet in the end, the populace embraced a new hope, divine truth, and a restored purpose." In a gesture of admiration, he opened his palms and bowed.

"The other reason I requested your presence is to ask you to speak during the next rally at Patriarch Plaza." Uzziel walked up to the pool. He cupped his hand, withdrew a palm full of water, and took several sips before tossing the remainder into the air where it dissipated. He stared upward as if pondering his next statement. "Jesse, you're scheduled as the main speaker. In fact, I want each team member to share about their experiences on Eskaonus and why outreaches to other places in God's vast kingdom remain expedient for eternity."

"When is this meeting?" Jesse asked.

"People are gathering now," elChesed replied. "You have enough time to visit your dwelling places prior to the rally."

Time, hmm, will I ever get an explanation? Jesse turned to consult with his three colleagues, but they had already vanished. Uzziel departed soon thereafter, leaving Jesse and his guardian angel by themselves.

Chesedel moved closer. "Time in a timeless eternity is an interesting concept. And rather complicated." Jesse pressed for clarification when the angel added, "Fortunately, there's an individual who visits here on occasion. He may be able to explain the matter."

"Who is it?"

"Albert."

"Albert who?"

"Einstein."

"Wasn't he an agnostic?"

"No, far from it. In fact, he has a Jewish heritage. His parents were Ashkenazi Jews. Albert was observant until about twelve years old. Sadly, he didn't remain interested in Judaism long enough to participate in his bar mitzvah. Yet the seed of faith remained planted in his heart."

"They say he was a wise intellectual."

"Indeed. Where do you think he gained his wisdom? God is the author of all such knowledge." Chesedel stepped sideways to lean against a marble pillar near the pool. "Einstein determined time was relative. In other words, the rate at which time passes depends on one's frame of reference. And ours is eternity." The angel righted himself and wandered over to the fountain to take a drink. "Much better than the silty water on Eskaonus, wouldn't you say?" Jesse smiled, recalling the journal entry where he noted the water tasted like mud. "Concerning Einstein, next time he is up this way, I'll arrange an appointment for you. Although heaven's dispensation of time is far more advanced than Albert ever imagined, his theories might help you understand this whole forever thing a little better."

"Great, that would be useful. This no night, never-ending day, and forever and ever timeframe is a head-scratcher."

"I understand. All new arrivals ponder it, as do most long-term residents. I believe you referred to the concept as *the day after always*. Actually, your phrasing is somewhat correct."

"Do you know all my private thoughts?"

"Most, it comes with the job, but I also read each of your log entries. Since we constructed your journal from heavenly scroll paper, anything written thereon also appears in the Hall of Records. I didn't tell you beforehand because I didn't want you to feel restrained about the things you recorded while off-heaven. Actually, your journal was our only source of information. When you traveled to a different time and space, I could no longer hear your thoughts or prayers. According to Uzziel, this is normal for most outer-realm communications."

"I figured somebody in heaven kept track of what I wrote. I just—"

"Good. Thanks for understanding. Sorry for being abrupt; the Cherubim has summoned me. See you at the gathering. Don't be . . ." Chesedel vanished in mid-sentence.

"If time is relative," mused Jesse, "how can I be late?" He wandered along the many footpaths, unhurried, enjoying the view, until he reached his housing complex. Once he arrived, he climbed the stairwell to the tenth floor and entered his room. Nothing had changed.

His assigned living quarters were modest. The place contained a comfortable bed, a hardwood writing desk with four-legged stool, and a chest of drawers. It had no windows, no bathroom, and only one entry door. All the units on his floor and throughout the entire housing complex were much the same. Jesse had barely sat on the bed when Seth popped through the wall. His friend occupied the room down the hallway on the left.

"Dude, it's time to go. We're giving the rap this span, er, cycle. Ah, you know what I mean. Guess I'm still hooked on using terms from Eskaonus. At any rate, we better book it. Don't wanna miss the introductions."

Jesse wasn't so sure. He didn't mind reporting the mission results but wasn't looking forward to sharing about his leadership failures. While Seth tapped his foot impatiently, Jesse gathered his heavenly white robe and leather sandals on the bed. He was about to change into them when he decided to stay with the outfit given to him by the local mender from the Upper Realm. Before leaving, he removed his journal from his pocket and placed it on his writing table.

"Hey dude, you may need that. Better bring it along." Jesse nodded, returned it to his front leg pocket, and then he transported away with Seth to the plaza.

CHAPTER 2

PATRIARCH PLAZA

Patriarch Plaza was a large area in Central Heaven with unlimited seating, located adjacent to the Judgment Seat and below the Fountain of Life. Citizens of heaven packed the courtyard. The gathered were visiting, excited about the meeting, wondering which patriarch would be the speaker. Jesse and his three colleagues sat in the front section, quietly waiting for the rally to begin.

Gabriel, messenger of God, strode to the podium and greeted the saints. "Welcome to our current residents and each new arrival." Those already seated, stood to their feet and joined the audience in applause. Shouts of *Shalom* and *Maranatha* filled the plaza. "We have a surprise for this meeting. Instead of one of our regular patriarchs, we have ambassadors who recently returned from a special assignment." He glanced at the guests in the front row. "Would you four please join me on the podium?"

The advocates rose, walked the steps to the platform and formed a half-circle behind the archangel. Everyone in the crowd took their seats in anticipation. Some looked bewildered, but most smiled, excited about the unexpected change of venue speakers. Surprises were commonplace in heaven and always greeted favorably and with expectation. "If you don't know them already, allow me to introduce you to Jesse Walt and his band of envoys. Jesse, the podium is yours." The archangel stepped aside.

Jesse hesitated, peered at his feet, bit his lower lip, and

shuffled in place as if pondering what to say or how to say it. Chewing on his bottom lip was a habit he did unconsciously when he became nervous. Before the silence grew awkward, Anna moved forward, assuming Jesse was concerned about being put on the spot, especially if he had to address his personal struggles in front of the saints. "As our team leader prepares his address, let me say a few words. My name is Annabelle Altshuler. We just returned from a lost world called Eskaonus."

"While we drink living water and reside in nice abodes, not every person in God's kingdom is as fortunate. His realm, or perhaps I should say realms, are vast, unending domains. More than I first realized." Her voice rose with intensity and passion, her tone, heartfelt. "Some places are fighting spiritual and physical battles, facing untold evils, and their lives are in peril. Most of all, they lack the knowledge of Yahweh. They are struggling and need our help. We should do more than float on celestial clouds, and I speak ironically because I don't see any clouds up here." With misty eyes, she turned to face Lundy. "Reverend, can you please continue. I'm too emotional right now?"

"Aye, Annabel, me be happy to." Lundy strolled to the podium. "My name is Lundy MacBain. I've been in heaven a long time." He paced around the podium like he did during his church services on earth. "You know, laddies, I've been a minister all me life. Lived in Scotland 400 years ago, earth time I reckon. One day, I encountered a mob of agnostics who didn't care for me preaching, and that's how I became a martyr. Not a bad way to get to the hereafter." He continued circling the platform. "As for my purpose, it's ministry. Always has been. It's what I was called to do. On Eskaonus, I received an opportunity to continue my calling and use my earthly education to translate several ancient scrolls, which allowed the Eskaonites to rediscover their heritage. I even confronted a couple evil doers and knocked a bit of sense into their noggins with me lecture stick, so to speak." The crowds grinned, enjoying Lundy's unique style of humor. He leaned on the podium like he did when he preached from the pulpit, read his audience, and allowed for a dramatic pause before proceeding. "You know us preacher folks, if you give us a wee bit of time, we'll take it all. I might even decide to receive a missionary offering."

Laughter erupted, followed by a saint yelling, "Preach it, brother!"

"Aye, there's more to this amazing story, much more. Meet me in the Garden of Meditation later, and I'll give you a full update. If Jesse's journal is published somewhere, get a copy to read. You'll be surprised at what's out there in eternity. Okay, lads and lassies, time to turn this lecture over to the kid."

Seth shuffled forward. "Hey, you dudes, my name is Seth Cahir. Yeah, I was part of the gig to Eskaonus. Wow, what a trip, I mean adventure, I mean outreach. You catch my drift, right? Anyhow, I'd been living in heaven since the 70s. Found God in the Jesus People Movement. Thought I had learned everything there was to learn, faced every hardship out there, except I was wrong. God has more on the ticket. And Annie nailed it. Heaven is more than hanging around being a forever resident. God has lots for us to learn and experience. As for me, I discovered two important rules. My best buddy, Maximus Gallius, shared them with me."

His mind wandered to Max who stayed behind in Eskaonus. Perhaps it was his second chance at life. Perhaps the Eskaonites needed a former Roman centurion to lead their military. Maybe it was both. Either way, Seth believed providence played a part.

After the memory lifted, he continued: "Rule Number One says to always expect the unexpected, and Rule Number Two is about facing our fears to overcome them." Seth wiped moisture from his eyes as he remembered the circumstances. Choking back the emotion, he tried to finish. "One cycle, or span, or day, or whatever . . . you dudes get the gist, right? When you travel off-heaven, these two rules may save your life or those of your friends. Trust me; I've been there, done that." He turned to face Jesse. "I said what I had to say. Your play, JW. Time to hit the ball out of the park."

Jesse smiled at Seth's consistent use of clichés. Seth returned to his spot with the others. As he passed by, Jesse whispered, "Max would be proud of you, recruit. Ya done good." Next, he gave Seth a hard slap on the back. "It's what Max would have done if he were here." Seth covered his face to hide the tears reforming in his eyes. "I miss him too, kid." Jesse strode to the podium, gazed at the huge gathering, and pulled out his journal to refer to it. He flipped through several entries. The throng sat in silence and waited. Jesse cleared his throat twice and began:

"My name is Jesse Walt. I came up recently in the Arrival, what theologians call the Rapture. Heaven was not exactly what I expected, and I didn't understand how one accounts for time here. Still don't." The audience nodded in agreement, indicating that many of them didn't either. "Once I got situated to my current surroundings, I attended a lecture right here." He pointed his finger at the four corners of the plaza. "It was my first one. Seth, who has been here longer than me, suggested it. I sat down front like you on the first row." More nods. "I listened to patriarch Abraham give a speech about this life. What I remember most is what he said at the end." He paused and looked again at the journal. "That we may be asked to do as he did, to leave the familiar, the safety of our abodes, and journey to an unknown place to carry out God's purposes. Abraham reminded us that we're not redeemed to have an eternal vacation but to further God's outreach to lost worlds, wherever they might exist."

"One of those places turned out to be Eskaonus. I have no idea where it is, how it exists, or in what dimension. However, the world was real, and the inhabitants needed help to understand truth and defeat evil. So, our group volunteered, left our immortality behind, passed through the White Pearl Gate, and portaled to this mysterious place."

"Perhaps you assume life is the same wherever it's found—that individuals fit into the same mold, follow the same customs and laws, embrace the same plan of salvation, and sing worship songs from a hymn book. Well, they don't. Maybe you think spiritual warfare and physical conflicts no longer occur in eternity. Well, they do."

"I discovered the hereafter has new challenges and offers opportunities for continued ministry, and for me, a second chance to become the leader God redeemed me to be. Redemption, after all, has an ongoing purpose, and eternity, an everlasting timeframe. The latter I'm still trying to figure out."

"Here's the deal: If a cherub asks you to minister to a

different world, I hope you'll say yes. Your life will be enriched, and you might rescue a society facing peril." Having finished, he bowed to the audience to show respect and rejoined his cohorts. As the colleagues discussed their presentations, Gabriel returned to the podium.

"Dear Saints, you have much to ponder. May you have an ear to hear. Thank you for attending our lecture series. Please check with Orientation for the next meeting. Hope to see you then. Godspeed." Faster than a blink of an eye, Gabriel vanished.

Afterwards, Jesse decided to head across to the River of Life. As soon as he cleared the plaza, he began to jog. Running was an activity he enjoyed on earth when he desired to be alone. Jesse increased the pace and then switched to a sprint. He passed Outreach & Supply and approached Straight Street. On the side of the road, Holley Rossie stood waiting. She was a former nurse practitioner and recent resident of heaven.

"Excuse me, Jesse. May I have a word?"

"Sure thing, Holley, what is it?"

"I must apologize for not going to Eskaonus with you."

"Apologies aren't necessary. There's no condemnation in heaven. We all have the freedom of choice in regard to serving."

"Agreed. Still, when I heard your story and later talked with Seth, I realized my healthcare knowledge was the reason Uzziel chose me for the outreach. A medic would have been advantageous, considering the dire conflicts you and the Eskaonites faced."

"Well, we did encounter several—"

"I'm merely saying I've prayed about it, and if you ever require an associate with medical experience for another outreach, I volunteer."

"I don't make those decisions, Holley. The management does."

"Understood. I only wanted you to know I'm willing." She stepped forward and threw her arms around his neck. "Thank you, Jesse. Your speech at the plaza challenged and inspired me." He noticed tears running down her face before she vanished, disappearing into thin air.

He crossed Straight Street and continued on toward the river. In the distance, Jesse spotted Uzziel and Chesedel standing beneath the Tree of Life. Chesedel waved at him and shouted, "Come and join us."

Jesse wandered over to their location. "Meeting you here is interesting. I just finished speaking to the crowds at Patriarch Plaza and decided to take a walk to unwind a bit. First, I run into Holley, and now, you two."

"No such thing as coincidences in heaven," replied the Cherubim. "We believe you were destined to meet us at the life tree. Chesedel and I are discussing a world called Camayah. The Lord would like to send a team of emissaries there."

"And I suppose I'm part of the pack?"

"If you choose to help, you are."

"Hmm, I see. Guess you better give me the lowdown."

"I'd be happy to explain the situation," Uzziel replied. "Camayah is an advanced civilization where science and technology have become the official religion. Other belief systems are forbidden, unlawful. The followers of such prohibited factions are persecuted, hunted down, and imprisoned. Any sympathizers are reprogrammed. The procedure takes away their will, turning them into mindless drones. Spiritual leaders are usually terminated."

"Doesn't sound good."

"It isn't. And there are other issues," added elChesed. "The pursuit of pleasure has become the mainstay for the populace, except for the believers who seek compassion, not carnality. Unfortunately, their numbers have been dwindling. Worse yet, deception runs rampant and the sick are mistreated, even killed."

"Consequently, we need a leader to take a group to Camayah and determine the best course of action to resolve the various situations before their entire culture slides into peril. The first priority is to locate and protect the few believers who remain faithful." Uzziel moved closer and focused on Jesse's face; his empathic stare seemed to pierce Jesse's heart and soul. "You are under no obligation because serving is always a choice. However, if anyone from the group leaves heaven and portals to this planet, they must leave their immortality behind and become mortal again."

"Just like last time when we traveled to Eskaonus."

"Correct." Uzziel took two steps backwards and unfolded his white wings, which arched high over his head. "So, if you're interested in participating, you should stop by your room, change into appropriate clothing for Camayah, and then join your new partners at Outreach & Supply."

"Who's on this team?" But the angels had disappeared, vanishing into the unseen realm. *Here we go again.* He pictured his living quarters in his mind and instantly arrived in his room.

CHAPTER 3

OUTREACH & SUPPLY

After arriving in his room, Jesse stood silent for a few moments, wondering who the new members might be. He felt a little apprehensive about leading a different group to another world and facing more dire circumstances. Not that he was afraid, he wasn't. However, if push came to shove, Jesse didn't want a repeat of the leadership failures he had endured on Eskaonus.

Glancing around, he noticed the outfit Uzziel mentioned, laid out on his bed. It looked like a silver jumpsuit—similar to the clothes the Robinson family wore for the "Lost in Space" television series during the 1960s. *Well, the angels did say it was a futuristic place.* The suit appeared old, wrinkled in spots, with faded streaks running down the legs. The knees were reinforced with patches. *What happened to making all things new?*

He slipped out of the Eskaonite clothing he wore to the rally and put on the strange silver ensemble. He couldn't decide if it was made out of aluminum foil or some other metallic fabric. At least it's comfortable and flexible. When he finished changing, he placed his white robe and sandals into the middle drawer of his dresser. On the top of his desk he spotted a different satchel, slightly smaller than the one he'd left for Ottaar on Eskaonus.

The satchel was shaped like a grocery cooler bag, similar to the ones sold in stores on earth, except it had one long handle instead of two. It was made of the same silvery fabric as his jumpsuit. He assumed it was a replacement carrier for his journal. Inside, he noticed another ink pen, exactly like the one he gave to the mender. *Nice!* He stuffed the pen and journal into one of the interior pockets. *Still room for more.* An idea floated through his mind as he packed. He rolled up his Eskaonus clothes, tucked them into the carrier, and closed the flap. There was just enough space for one more item that he planned to procure at Supply. Maybe the clerk angel would have a suggestion like he did last time. With one last glance around his living quarters, he transported to Outreach & Supply where he hoped to meet the new collective.

The building was located between Patriarch Plaza and Straight Street. Upon entering the facility, he found Holley Rossie at the counter dressed in the same type of silvery outfit. *Apparently, Holley is one of the members.* She and the clerk angel were talking. "Well, young lady, what can I get for you?"

"What do you recommend?"

"Since you were a medical professional on earth, I suggest a doctor's kit."

"Actually, I was never a doctor, only a nurse practitioner. I spent most of my time in the emergency ward."

"Perfect, then our standard-issue doctor's kit will come in handy." The angel floated up to the fifth shelf, grabbed a silvery bag with a shoulder strap, and returned to the counter. "Inside this satchel is a complete medical kit with antibiotics, various medications, diagnostic equipment, first-aid supplies, and a procedural manual. With this medkit, you can become the MD you always desired but never had the chance. Your former experience, plus this amazing healing kit, will enable you to handle most medical situations, even minor surgeries. And there's a compartment for personal items."

The angel slid the doctor's satchel across the counter to Holley. She peered inside, pulled out the containers, read the labels, and stacked them on the counter. She opened the scroll-like manual and scanned the chapters. After rerolling the scroll, she returned everything to the medical bag. "This is like a dream come true."

"It's what we do up here. Who's next?"

"We are." Jesse craned his neck around to see who had spoken. Behind him were Seth, Lundy, and Anna—dressed in silvery outfits like his.

"So, you guys are on the team?"

"Correctamundo, JW." Seth grinned, his freckled face beamed with excitement. "You're stuck with us dudes again."

"Not stuck. I'm glad Uzziel recruited you. I couldn't have asked for better colleagues."

"Wonderful reunion!" The angel looked slightly perturbed. "But since the Cherubim asked me to get everyone outfitted as soon as possible, I need somebody to be next."

"If you dudes don't mind, I'll go."

"Ahh yes, you're the one who took the *tijvah* last time. How did the little corded rope work out for you?"

"It was totally awesome. Worked like a charm, I mean, as advertised."

"Great. I have an even better item this time." He rushed to a nearby display counter and removed a silver-colored satchel and returned. "Inside this bag is a portable, two-person, all-terrain hoverboard, solar and battery powered. It's extremely fast. Some find it hard to balance. Whereas an individual like yourself, an experienced Malibu surfer from earth, shouldn't have any difficulty. And the unit folds in quarters and fits into this handy carrying case, shoulder strap included."

"Dude, I mean angel sir, how did you know?" Seth inspected the board, unfolded the sections, tested its stability, refolded it, and stuffed the hoverboard back into its satchel. "This is mint. I'll take it."

"Figured you would, next . . ."

Annabelle stepped forward to the counter. "Greetings, Precious One."

"I appreciate the honor but only God is truly precious." He pointed in the direction of the Throne Room. "Hmm, I remember you. You're the musician with the glifstring. What did you think of it?"

"It was delightful, very anointed. I decided to leave it on Eskaonus."

"I understand all of you left items there. No matter, our loss is their gain. Would you like another musical instrument?"

"Oh yes."

Reaching under the counter, the angel clerk pulled out a

silver satchel with a shoulder strap. "I think you'll like this." He opened the carrier and took out a brown flute with gold inlays and elegantly carved patterns. "This is a nyeflute. Songs played on it will cause certain effects, such as sleepiness, temporary blindness, confusion, and invisibility. Certain tunes instill confidence, encouragement, and alertness. Other than one exception, the player of the flute is unaffected. Depending on the result intended, you may want others to cover their ears. And it comes with a tablature guide. The instrument is similar to a Boehm flute, although slightly shorter in length. For obvious reasons, be sure to learn the arrangements prior to playing them out loud."

Anna held it reverently, running her fingers across the designs, studying the tone holes. "I love it. May Yahweh bless you."

"He always does. And by the way, my name is Abdiel. It means servant of God. This is where I serve Him. Who's next?"

Lundy shuffled forward. "What ya got for an old Scotsman like me?"

"Ahh, Reverend MacBain, I assume the Gospel of John came in handy?"

"Aye, it did. A great scroll of Scripture it is. The Eskaonites will learn much by reading it."

"Glad to hear it. Since you are an experienced linguist and translator of documents, I have something to assist with your upcoming endeavor: a binder of programming scrolls. It's what earth people call a coding book, except this one has universal cyphers. With it, you or a tech-savvy person should be able to understand complex codes and program most data devices, including mainframe systems. It comes with a strapped carrier, silver of course, to match your outfit."

"Right up me alley. Thank you, Abdiel." Lundy slung the bag over his shoulder and went to the rear of the line to talk with Annabel.

"That leaves you, Jesse Walt. You're the team lead, right?"

"Yes sir."

"I assume you're taking your journal again. According to elChesed, it doesn't count as an item. Therefore, let me recommend a set of communicators." Abdiel disappeared for a moment and returned with five walkie-talkies and stacked them on the counter. "These little gadgets are fully powered, pocket sized, and can transmit and receive on any band or frequency. Voice activated, five separate channels. Since they're long-range transceivers, you'll be able to stay in touch with your party at great distances." Being familiar with police two-way radios, Jesse forwent the inspection. He packed the units into his satchel and slung the strap around his neck, letting it come to rest at his side.

"What about the big guy, Maximus Gallius, the former Roman centurion? I don't see him here with the rest of you."

"It's kind of a long story. He's . . . uh . . . still on assignment."

"Assignment, you say. Interesting. I'll keep him in my thoughts. Alright, if there's nothing else, I have other duties to attend."

"Abdiel, I was wondering if I could have a spare outfit."

"What size?"

"Extra-large."

"Sure. No problem. In fact, I'll throw in two suits: one extra-large, one medium. I better give you an additional carrier, too. Always best to have contingency plans." Since Jesse's bag was full, he asked Lundy to add the extra items to his.

A final check confirmed Jesse and his crew were outfitted and ready to depart. "Okay, fellow travelers, let's gather at the White Pearl Gate and portal out of here."

"Hey JW, I'll be there in a flash. I gotta dip by my pad and see if there are additional items I should bring." Before Jesse could reply to Seth, Anna and Lundy decided to do likewise, and all three vanished into the unseen realm. Jesse gestured with his hands as if to say, I have no idea why they left. Holley shook her head, indicating she didn't either. After a moment of awkward silence, the two walked to the portal and waited for the others to return.

Jesse and Holley were talking with Uzziel and elChesed when the three stragglers arrived at the gate. With everybody now present, the angels took turns embracing each person and offering words of encouragement. The Cherubim gave the same charge as last time. "Hold hands as you pass through the gateway, so you stay together. Remember what you have learned here in heaven, acknowledge God no matter what, use wisdom, don't quit or lose heart, and most of all, trust the Holy Spirit to guide your paths."

Chesedel added, "All of heaven will be praying for you." He leaned over and whispered in Jesse's ear, "Say hello to Maximus for me."

Surprised, Jesse raised his eyebrows and took a step backwards. "How did you know?"

"Remember, I'm your guardian angel; I can hear your thoughts, at least in this domain. Your little detour to Eskaonus was not unexpected." Chesedel propped himself against a pillar as he spoke. "Be sure to write updates in your journal so we can monitor your progress." He righted himself and gave Jesse one more hug of encouragement. "Uzziel and I wish you all Godspeed."

As soon as the angels departed, Jesse explained to the others about the detour to visit Max in Eskaonus. Seth, Anna, and Lundy sensed their itinerary might change, and like Jesse, had packed their old Eskaonite clothes. Holley was supportive of the side excursion, glad for the opportunity to actually visit the realm, yet concerned about her lack of proper clothing. She declined the invitation to join Jesse's team on their first trip to Eskaonus and regretted her decision. Fortunately, heaven is a place of second chances, and this was hers.

The group grasped hands and nodded they were ready. As they marched past the gate's two white pillars, a bright light flashed, thunder sounded, and they were gone.

MAP OF ESKAONUS

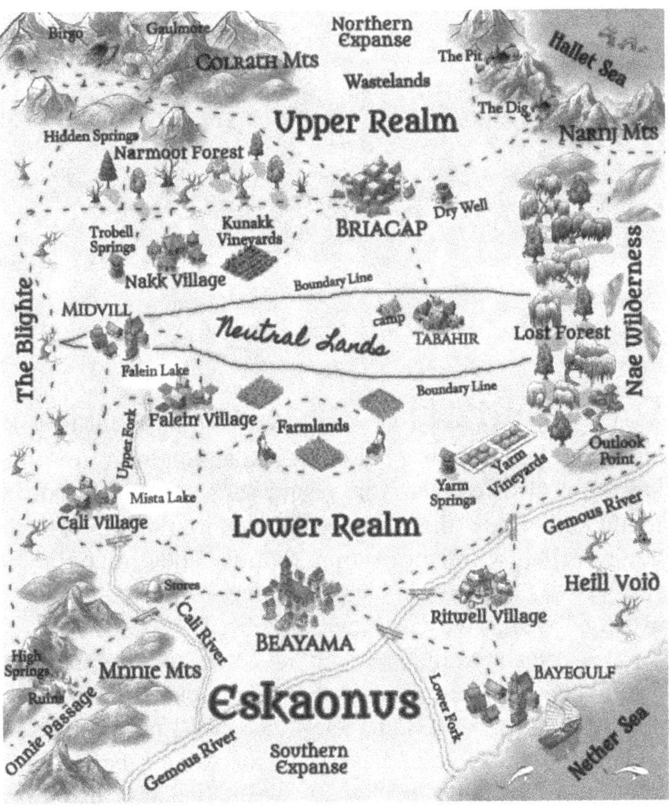

Eskaonus is a fictional world or place. The cities, villages, and landmarks are imaginary.

"For by him were all things created, that are in heaven, and that are in earth, visible and invisible, whether *they be* thrones, or dominions, or principalities, or powers" (Colossians 1:16).

CHAPTER 4

DETOUR TO ESKAONUS

The group of five arrived at Outlook Point in Eskaonus, the same place the original team landed, and like the first time, they were disorientated, dizzy, and nauseated. "Oh man, what a ride! Don't think these dimensional portal jumps or whatever they're called will ever become routine. They're cool but totally wild." Seth checked his hands and feet to make sure none were missing. "Well, JW, what now?"

Jesse scanned the area. "Same cottlepine grove. Our shelter is still standing." He conducted a quick count to make sure each member was present. On their first visit, Lundy went missing. Apparently, the reverend lost hold of Anna's hand and landed miles away in Briacap. "Good, we all made it this time." He noticed Holley bent at the waist, holding on to her knees, trying to adjust to the dizziness. Seth and Jesse helped her to stand upright. A few moments later, her vertigo eased. "You're gonna be okay, Hol. The effects will pass shortly." She forced a hopeful grin.

The landscape appeared earthlike with several major differences. There was no sun, just an aurora borealis glow with yellowish bands. The foliage grew lush as it fertilized with steroids, and the trees, a type of evergreen pine with oak-shaped leaves on their branches instead of needles, towered skyward. The locals called them cottlepines. Jesse leaned back to view the horizon and determined it was midday, what the Eskaonites refer to as midcycle.

Shouts came from inside the shelter as five wary individuals scrambled forth. "I'm not sure where these silvery phantoms hail from," remarked the apparent leader to the others, "but during the rumbling noise, they appeared out of nowhere." Two of the militia had longbows notched, and the other three held their spears at the ready. "Halt! Come any closer and we'll release our arrows."

"Hey dudes, Max and I made those bows. Put them shooters away."

"Do you mean Captain Maximus of the Militia?" asked Chepho. "Is that you Seth? Why are you wearing such strange clothes?"

Jesse stepped in front of Seth. "You mean these tattered spacesuits. Long story." Jesse motioned for his fellow travelers to gather around him. "Give us a moment to change into proper Lower Realm outfits before we talk shop. We brought them with us."

"I didn't," Holley interjected.

"Hey Chepho, you're still the Militia Chief, right?" Jesse asked.

"No, Lady Saephira promoted me to Militia Lead after your group departed."

"Good decision. Belated congratulations. I wonder if you have something Holley can put on to cover her silver outfit, an extra coat perhaps."

"We sure do," replied one of the militiamen. "She can have mine."

"Great. Don't want to shock anyone else." As they changed into their Eskaonus clothing, Jesse explained they had come from the high province, their code word for heaven, for another important undertaking. He didn't offer any specifics. "Where is Max? We would like to talk with him."

"He's in Beayama," the lead advised. "Saw him at firstlight on the practice field, working with the new recruits. If you hope to reach the city prior to darkout, you'll have to ride kacks." Kacks were four-footed creatures with long-haired manes used by the locals as mounts and pack animals. "You can borrow three of ours. We can acquire replacements in Ritwell Village to finish our scouting patrol." Jesse thanked Chepho for his generosity and dashed to the shelter to unhobble three mounts.

After changing into local attire, Seth took one kack, the other four rode double: Lundy behind Anna and Holley behind Jesse. They packed their satchels into side carriers and traveled the two leagues between Outlook Point and Beayama, arriving by latecycle. As they approached the city gate, a watchman called out, "Identify yourselves!"

"Jesse Walt and party. We ask permission to enter the city."

"Is it really you, Jesse?" Captain Gelr of the Safeguards leaned against the tower ledge to take a closer look. "I haven't heard a varmint's hide or hair from you in sixty cycles."

To Jesse, it only seemed they were gone for a few hours or what he used to call hours. In heaven, time was relative, but in Eskaonus, hours were called spans and days, cycles. "Is Seth with you?" asked the captain.

"I sure am, dude, I mean commander." Seth trotted his kack a little closer. "How's my *tijvah* working out?"

"Perfect, your little corded rope is beyond strong. It can hold twenty stones or more and never break. The length remains the same no matter how much I cut off." Gelr untied the cord around his waist and showed it to Seth. "See, I didn't lose it. What about Annabelle and Lundy? Are they here, too? And who is this new person?"

"Yes, they all came." Jesse replied, taking over the conversation from Seth. "We can visit later, and I'll introduce you to our newest partner. Right now, though, we need to contact Max."

"Not sure where he is currently. I saw Captain Maximus and Lady Narleen earlier on dayrise. He had just finished a training session with our militia recruits at the practice field. Did you know she and the captain are married and have living quarters in Residential Hall? You can probably catch both of them at the banquet later." Jesse turned around to explain to Holley about the two meal times: breaking fast at dayrise and the prominence of the nightrise banquet. "I believe Ottaar, our lead mender, is in town. She'll be offended if you don't stop by and see her. Would you like an escort?"

"No, we remember the way. We'll head there first."

The party rode past the town square, veered left, and stopped at the mender's home. They dismounted, leaving their kacks out front. Several street vendors noticed their presence, but most went about their business as usual. Seth bounded up the steps, stopping on the porch. "Come on dudes, let's go. Ottaar probably has some good eats inside."

"Shouldn't we knock?" Holley asked.

"No, Hol, it's cool. The mender's place is always open, dayrise or nightrise. We are all tight here." Seth waved for Holley to come join him on the porch. Moving closer, he whispered into her ear, "It might be best if you avoided yarm berry products. Until you build immunity, it can be a real downer. Last time I chomped one handful too many of those pinkish treats and got yarm poisoning. The whole party did. Without Ottaar's antidote, we would have been tarkk bait."

Holley wondered if Seth had exaggerated the situation or if there were actual dangers involved. Either way, the exchange piqued her medical interests. Perhaps this mender person could elaborate. "Thanks Seth, I'll be careful." *What's a tarkk?*

As Seth and Holley visited outside, Jesse pushed the door open and entered. Ottaar sat at her large table with papers spread clear across it. A kettle of tea simmered on the stove, giving off a steady stream of steam. "Good dayrise, Mender of the Realm."

Recognizing the voice, Ottaar turned around, almost dropping her ledger on the floor. When she spotted Jesse standing in the doorway, she arose and hurried over to give him a big hug around his neck. After releasing him, she responded with the standard Eskaonite greeting and then added, "Dayrise will bring what it brings." They both laughed hysterically at the mender's favorite saying.

Anna and Lundy entered next, followed by Seth and Holley. "Delightful, you're all here. I hoped I'd see you again. Welcome." Standing behind Seth, Ottaar noticed a young woman with short ginger hair and brown eyes. She wore a militia coat that partially covered a tarnished silver outfit. "And who is this precious one?"

"Her name is Holley Rossie. She's an experienced medtech, a mender like you," advised Jesse.

"Well now, this is wonderful. Good dayrise, Mender." She

offered Holley a smile and deep curtsy, which Holley returned. "So why are you here?"

"To see Max," responded Jesse.

"I can send the captain word and request an audience or better yet, you can join me as honored guests for dinner. He and Lady Narleen will be there, as well as other leadership."

"That works. Besides, if he's unaware of our arrival, it would be fun to surprise him."

"He'll be overjoyed to see you. Maximus has missed everyone." Ottaar opened her front window blind and peeked outside to see if any militia were passing by. "Would you like me to notify Lady Saephira? We should inform her of your return."

"I'm pretty sure she's been advised. We talked with Captain Gelr at the gate, and I assume he told her already."

"No doubt." Changing the topic, Ottaar said, "Looks like you've ridden hard to get here this cycle. Feel free to relax until we leave for the Great Hall. There are fresh clothes in the guest rooms upstairs and soaproot for washing. The banquet starts in about a span. While we wait, I would love to talk with your mender and compare treatments."

"I would enjoy doing that." Holley set off for the exit. "Let me get my medical satchel from the side carrier and I'll be right back."

"You can freshen up first if you would like."

"No, I'll do it later. I'm excited to learn more about your healing methods and to share mine."

"Join me at the table once you're ready. In the meantime, would someone move those kacks to the rear?"

"Aye, let the Scotsman handle the animals. And while I'm at it, I'll bring in our gear." On the way out, Lundy stopped by the stove, poured himself a spot of Anatora tea, took a couple sips, then moseyed outside.

Holley returned with her bag as the others headed to their rooms. She sat at the table, opened her medkit, and a discussion on doctoring procedures ensued. Ottaar and Holley were still visiting when the others returned, wearing clean garments.

"Almost dinner time and this dude is starving. Let's go, Doc."

"Oh, I'm sorry. I got so involved learning about healing potions on Eskaonus I forgot about changing into appropriate attire. Give me a minute, Seth."

"Take your time, Mender Holley. I'll wait and walk with you." Glancing at Seth and the others, Ottaar added, "You guys know the way. We'll meet everybody there shortly. I have extra torches in a barrel outside. Better take them with you. It'll be darkout soon."

CHAPTER 5

BANQUET TIME

As twilight approached, the travelers filed into the Great Hall for the usual evening meal, which in Eskaonus was called a banquet. In addition to banquets, people used the hall for public events such as exhibitions and business meetings. It contained a large dining section, side conference rooms, and two kitchens. Although community meals were occasionally hosted in the hall, most of the time, the residents feasted at home.

The party waited for Ottaar and Holley before entering the Great Hall together. They were greeted by a unit of safeguards who watched the entry, spears in hand, each sporting a friendly smile. Inside the entryway stood Lady Saephira, Captain Maximus and Lady Narleen who were holding hands, and Captain Gelr. Their faces beamed.

As the group approached the first hallway, Saephira exclaimed, "Welcome honored travelers! Your efforts saved our realm, both realms in fact. We will always be . . ." Not waiting for her to finish, Max and Narleen rushed forward. Max embraced Jesse, arm to arm, in the comrade's greeting. Narleen hugged Annabelle, giving her a kiss on the cheek and then curtsied to Lundy and Seth. Captain Gelr approached Holley and introduced himself as Captain of the Safeguards, a part of the military tasked with guarding entryways into the city.

"You are just in time. We are about to serve the banquet,"

explained Saephira. "Jesse, you are dining with Lady Narleen and me at the center table. Your colleague, Max, of course, will join us. Please follow me." For a brief moment, Jesse felt Saephira's right hand brush against his as they made their way to the raised platform. He wasn't sure if the touch was intentional or inadvertent.

Ottaar invited Holley and Lundy to join her at the mender table, where three of her trainees were sitting. Gelr asked Anna and Seth to follow him to the leadership council table. As soon as the people were seated, Lady Saephira addressed the crowds. "I apologize for the limited seating this nightrise. Once word spread the wayfarers had returned from their high province, our whole town desired to be here. Perhaps our guests will stay longer so there will be time for everyone to greet them. We owe them our bond for their efforts to save the Lower Realm from wickedness and reveal our lost heritage." When she finished, the kitchen staff began setting out platters of food, starting with the center table.

The dinner consisted of entrees of roasted tarkk fillets, dishes with stuffed river eel, and several trays containing sliced antaloop roast. Servers brought out baked kin loaves, platters of maize mixed with odd-looking vegetables, bowls with various types of yarm berry puddings and desserts, pitchers of slightly fermented yarm, and kettles holding steaming-hot Azollie tea. Mindful of Seth's warning about pink berries, Holley avoided the desserts, although she did try a few sips of yarm.

As the meal proceeded, Jesse asked, "What happened after we departed the Copper Rail in Tabahir?"

"Negotiation teams from the Upper and Lower realms met as per the agreement," replied Narleen. "After a rough start, the deliberations ended fairly well. Other than a handful of disturbances by disgruntled guardsmen, the truce held. Sixty cycles have passed since the conference occurred."

Saephira continued Narleen's update, adding more details: "During the peace negotiations in Midvill, we renamed the Disputed Lands to Neutral Lands, ending our long-running boundary dispute. The representatives discussed combining the two realms into one, named Middle Realm, but they tabled the idea for the time being. We decided that Senior Commander

Bolgog would become the leader of the Upper Realm, and I'd remain the leader of the Lower Realm. Our two realms agreed to put aside our differences and work towards being allies. Open trade is now allowed within the cities and villages, without fear of reprisal for products once considered contraband. Amnesty was granted to all. Other issues are to be decided at the next meeting in thirty cycles."

"Tell me, sir. Why did you return to our land?" Max asked.

"I wanted to see you, of course, and reconnect with our Eskaonite friends." Jesse swung his hand in a wide arc around the hall, pointing to the assembled diners. "However, there's a more pressing reason."

"You can speak freely here, sir. What matter is so pressing?"

Jesse glanced at Lady Saephira, analyzing her demeanor. She seemed as confident as he remembered, her blue eyes focused, her smile compassionate. Lady Narleen's face, however, showed concern. He chewed on his lower lip, pondering how to word his request, unsure if he should present it in front of the two women leaders. "I would appreciate your assistance with an endeavor."

"I'm a soldier, sir. Spit out the specifics. What you say will be held in utmost confidence."

"Okay, here it is: We have a new mission to a place called Camayah. It's an advanced world where science and technology have become the official religion. Other belief systems are forbidden. The followers of such prohibited factions are persecuted, hunted down, and imprisoned. If they don't submit, they're terminated. Most of their spiritual leaders have already been eliminated. Apparently, deception runs rampant and unrestrained pleasure has become society's main goal. Other issues are sketchy at this time. We are tasked with resolving the various situations before their entire civilization slides into chaos."

"I agree, sir. Sounds like a necessary outreach. And I would like to help. Normally, I wouldn't hesitate to volunteer, except I'm wed now and need to stay here with my spouse. Furthermore, I have a commission in the Militia, and they depend on me. Sorry sir, I cannot go."

"Yes, you can, and you should," Narleen retorted. "These envoys are your friends and comrades. We both owe them our bond."

"Nar, I can't leave you behind."

"You won't have to because I'll be going with you, if such things are even possible."

"No, I forbid it. It would be too dangerous. And who would assume command of the Militia?"

"Since when are you afraid of a little danger? Besides, I am the vice-leader and technically, I outrank you. If I decide to go, my dear spouse, it's my choice, not yours. Regarding temporary command, Militia Lead Chepho or Captain Gelr can handle things if you request a leave." Lady Saephira leaned slightly backwards and balanced her open hands like a scale, as if to indicate she had no qualms with either officer being a replacement.

Max ignored the gesture. "Narleen, I will not risk losing . . ." His voice cracked as he choked down a swallow, the words sticking in his throat. "You don't realize—"

"What I do realize is . . . I cannot bear another separation. At our betrothal, I pledged to always stand by your side. And I'll not break that promise." She stared at Max with stern yet tender eyes before turning to address Jesse. "My spouse and I will discuss this matter. We'll give you our decision later."

"Narleen—"

"The matter is tabled, Captain. Let's enjoy these nice desserts before darkout."

Lady Saephira remained silent as her vice-leader and militia captain debated the issue. She was likewise concerned about the hazards and half-agreed with Narleen about not being separated from one's spouse. If Jesse had asked her to volunteer for a perilous undertaking, she'd be hard pressed to say no, considering all he had done for her and the Lower Realm. The man had earned her respect and trust, and in some ways, her heart as well. Concerning the issues raised, Saephira would discuss those matters with Narleen in private once her emotions settled.

Jesse considered apologizing for stirring up a hornet's nest, but as soon as he opened his mouth to withdraw the request,

Narleen raised her hand to silence him. “We will let you know at firstlight.” She faced her spouse again. “Maxie, can you please pass me the yarm berry pudding?”

At the mender’s table, Holley and Ottaar discussed medical diagnoses and treatment practices while the three mender trainees listened in, occasionally asking questions.

Holley opened her medkit and pulled out an IV. “We use this device to provide blood transfusions, add fluids, and inject medications.” Next, she removed a hypodermic needle. “With this little glass tube, we administer antibiotics and vaccinations.” The conversation went on and on as she withdrew various items from her doctor’s kit and elaborated on their purpose. The mender trainees were amazed at the terminology and innovative treatments. So was Ottaar, except she never let on she only understood half of what Holley explained.

“I see why Jesse brought you. Your knowledge is invaluable. Perhaps you could stay here for a time and teach us these new mender methods.” Ottaar appealed to her trainees who hardily agreed.

“I would love to not only share remedies but learn more about your practices. However, I think we’re leaving in the morning.”

“If you’re departing at firstlight, then let me supply you with Helixzon healing salve. I have extra bottles in my office. Perhaps I can also add a package of healing leaves.”

“Excuse me for interrupting. Are ye talking about leaves from the life tree?” inquired Lundy. “On our last visit, we left you a dried pip. It’s a seed found inside fruit from the Tree of Life. I assume you planted it, and if so, where?”

“I carried the pit up Onnie Pass, accompanied by a militia escort, and buried it by the ancient ruins near High Springs. It sprouted immediately and grew into a tree about four paces high. Multicolored leaves developed on the branches and purple blooms appeared. We waited to see if any fruit would follow. It didn’t. So, I picked a haversack of leaves, and we departed for Beayama. I plan to return in one or two periods and check on the tree’s progress. The following cycle, I made tea from the leaves. The drink seemed to cure almost any injury or infirmity. In fact, it works better than my best potion or healing salve."

"Aye, it's a tree of life for sure. Exactly like the one in heaven, me thinks. I would like to stay and see it, but alas, we must depart at dayrise." Following Lundy's comment, the conversation turned to recent events and questions about the Gospel of John he'd given to Lady Saephira to share with the Eskaonites.

Nearby, Captain Gelr and a squad of his safeguards listened to Annabelle as she talked about the importance of embracing one's destiny. Seth tried to appear interested but kept looking across his shoulder at the rear table. Finally, he pushed his plate aside and stood up. "Sorry Anna, I gotta say hello to my fishing buddies. It might be my last chance. You two have a nice rap session, I'm dipping. Catch you dudes later." Seth excused himself, trotted to where Calrin and Raydoo were sitting, and slid into a chair.

After Seth departed, Gelr shuffled over to take his empty seat. While the safeguards talked among themselves, Gelr and Annabelle continued their conversation. They reminisced about their first meeting and how he changed his destiny by rejecting the evil Lord Eddnok, thereby helping Lady Saephira save both realms. Smiles and quiet giggling ensued. The captain and Anna seemed to enjoy one another's company.

At the rear table, Seth and the teens talked about fishing. They rehashed the events from that fateful day at Mista Lake when Seth saved Calrin from a school of attacking tarkks.

"We plan to go tarkkie fishing on the morrow," stated Raydoo. "You should join us."

"I agree. Now that you understand how to use a harpoon correctly, you won't lose my lucky one," Calrin said with a smirk on his face. "And because you overcame your fear of water, we can use a boat this time. Rule Number Two, remember?"

"Yeah, I recall. Good rule, but JW says we have to bug out soon. We just stopped in to check on Maximus. I'll have to take a raincheck." Both Raydoo and Calrin shrugged their shoulders, wondering how one checks the rain. The conversation continued, most of it small talk and more teasing. For dessert, Seth consumed three helpings of yarm berry pudding.

The banquet finally ended. One by one, servers cleared the tables and people grabbed their torches to head home. Since it was already darkout, a period of pitch blackness after midnight, they needed torches to see. When Jesse's party arrived at the mender's place, Anna went directly upstairs to her room and pulled out her nyeflute to practice fingering positions from the tablature scroll. Because she hadn't learned what each tune could do, which according to Abdiel caused unique effects, she was reluctant to play the flute out loud.

Holley stayed for a bit longer and visited with Ottaar. The mender gave her two bottles of Helixzon salve, two pieces of Netherute, and a small bag of healing leaves harvested from the life tree. She tucked the items into her medkit and climbed the stairs to her room. She fell asleep as soon as her head hit the fur-covered pillow. Jesse peeked into the quarters that Seth and Lundy were sharing. Seth lay curled up in his bed and Lundy was snoring. Since his crew had settled in for the night, he entered the last guestroom and lit a candle. He removed the journal from his satchel, opened to his last entry, reread it, primed his pen, and started writing the next log.

Entry Twelve

We detoured to Eskaonus. Since these entries are duplicated in the Hall of Records, I suppose heaven already knows about our side trip. Located Max and gave him an overview of our assignment to Camayah. I asked him to join our efforts. Although his support would be invaluable, my request created more conflict. Narleen, his wife now, and Max got into a heated discussion. She doesn't want him to go anywhere without her. And here's another concern: If Max does volunteer and Narleen insists on going with him, can she make the portal jump with the rest of us? No doubt I'll find out soon enough. Like Ottaar the mender often says, "Dayrise will bring what it brings." In other news, the alliance is doing fine. I'm glad Holley is with us. Her doctoring skills may be necessary before this mission concludes. Guess that's about it for this entry.

Jesse closed his journal and tucked it into his carrier before lying down on the bed. Tired from the long day, he drifted off to sleep.

At firstlight, the collective arose and scrambled downstairs wearing their silvery jumpsuits in preparation for the transport to Camayah. Sitting at the mender's table were Captain Maximus and Lady Narleen. A sliced loaf of freshly baked kin sat on a platter between them. Max's plate was empty; Narleen's plate contained a half-eaten piece, which she had pushed aside as if she wasn't hungry. Both were sipping cups of hot tea. Ottaar hovered by her stove, cooking what smelled like bush varmint stew.

Max spoke first. "It seems we are both going on this little outing. Got any more of those worn-out, silver outfits?"

"Aye, laddies, I have two stuffed in my satchel, along with an extra carrying pouch."

Max took the jumpsuits and handed the smaller one to his spouse. "Nar, you can have the silver tote too." Getting a tepid response from Narleen, he turned to Jesse. "Sir, I assume we're allowed one item, like last time."

Jesse hesitated with the answer, giving Seth an opportunity to respond first. "Exactamundo. Wait till you see my hoverboard, bro. It's totally cool."

"Show me later, recruit." Max checked the sword he always wore at his side. "My item will be the Gladius. What about you, Nar? Are you bringing the glifstring Miss Anna gave you?"

"No, I'm leaving it." She unstrapped the musical instrument and placed it on the table. "I decided on a sling." Her comment was sharp. Apparently, some tension lingered from last night's discussion with her spouse. Speaking to Jesse instead of Max, she added, "I've been target practicing and can hit a cottlepine at a hundred paces. Will I be able to find small rounded stones where we're going?"

"I think so. Not sure you'll need a weapon, though. Not sure about a lot of things at this point, my Lady. We'll know more once we arrive in Camayah."

Narleen and Max entered a side room and changed into silver jumpsuits. She packed their old clothes into her satchel, in case they needed them later. Together, they said their goodbyes to Ottaar and thanked her for breaking fast with them. "Okay Jesse, Max and I are ready. What now?"

"Everybody form a circle and grab a hand."

"And remember to hold on tight, real tight," Anna instructed. "We don't want to lose anybody." Lundy nodded in agreement, knowing he had released his grip on their first transport attempt to Eskaonus, ending up in a different location.

"Will you do the honors, Preach?"

"Aye, just think where ye want to be and you're. . ." A slight shaking vibrated the floor, followed by the sound of distant thunder, and the collective disappeared into thin air.

MAP OF CAMAYAH

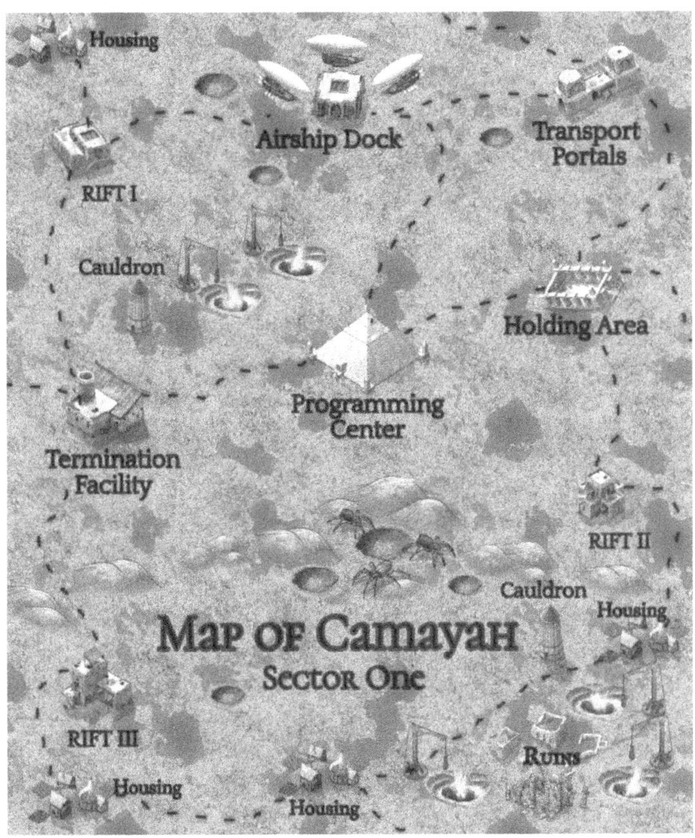

Camayah is a fictional planet. The locations are imaginary. However, all tangible planets, whether known or unknown, were made by God.

"Through faith we understand that the worlds were framed by the word of God, so that things which are seen were not made of things which do appear" (Hebrews 11:3).

CHAPTER 6

ARRIVING IN CAMAYAH

A bright light flashed, followed by the sound of distant thunder, and seven travelers dressed in silvery jumpsuits appeared, seemingly out of nowhere. They had materialized in an area filled with crumbling structures and surrounded by huge pits of flaming fire.

Jesse again checked to see if everyone arrived. All were present. Holley seemed to fare better this time but not so with Narleen. She was kneeling on the ground, bent at the waist, experiencing a bout of dry heaves and vomiting. Max knelt beside his wife, trying to comfort her with reassuring words. Seeing the situation, Holley rushed over, getting there before Jesse.

"Max, let me help her. Medical is what I do best." She pulled the medkit from her satchel and tucked it under her arm. "How are you feeling?"

"Not sure. As soon as we arrived, I became sick, my gut started churning, and I had to empty my stomach. I feel a little better now."

"Are you well enough to stand, my Lady?"

"I'll try." Narleen rose to her feet and took three steps. "The ill sensation seems to be passing. Hope so anyway." She wiped the leftover dribble from her mouth.

"Max, let Holley see to your spouse. She can do more for her than we can. In the meantime, I need you and Seth to travel west and scout the terrain." Pointing to the reddish sun dropping below the hills, Jesse added, "I assume this way is west." He opened the five-unit transceiver set from his satchel, removed one device and handed it to Seth. "Take this radio and report what you find. I've already set the dial to channel one. I'll keep mine tuned to channel five. No talk buttons to push since the units are voice activated."

"Sure thing, JW."

Still standing next to Lundy, Anna inquired, "What about us?"

"You two do the same except in the opposite direction." He indicated east, or what he assumed was east. "This radio is set to channel two. Contact me on channel five after you do a preliminary search. I'm staying here with the doc and Lady Narleen." Anna grabbed the radio in one hand and Lundy in the other, and they hurried off to explore the area. Seth had already traveled twenty feet when he realized Max wasn't following, so he stopped, wondering whether to wait for Max or proceed without him.

"Max, she'll be okay," reassured Jesse. "It was probably the transport. The first time is always a doozy. I'm sure the effects will ease soon. Seth is waiting for you. We have to know the lay of the land before it gets too dark to see." Feeling more confident about Narleen's condition and Holley's doctoring, Max caught up to Seth, and they both took off at a jog.

While Holley diagnosed Narleen's condition, Jesse decided to hike to the ruins and snoop around. "I'll be right back, Hol. Here, keep this walkie-talkie handy. It's already set to channel three. I'm on five. Contact me if her condition doesn't improve." Holley tucked the device into her bag and continued with her health queries.

"You said you felt nauseated, my Lady. When did the symptoms start?"

"Six cycles ago, maybe more. It mostly happens at firstlight and latecycle."

"You mean you've been having nausea every morning for a week, my Lady." She returned the medkit to her satchel.

"I would prefer if you dropped the title. Please call me Narleen." She walked over to a crumbled section of wall a few feet away, sat cross-legged, and rubbed her sore stomach.

Holley followed and plopped down beside her. She put a hand on Narleen's shoulder. "My diagnosis is morning sickness. I believe you're at least six weeks pregnant."

"What does pregnant mean?"

"It means you're gonna have a baby."

"Aah, I wondered if I might be with child. Maxie and I wed two periods ago and we've been sharing sheets."

"Does he know yet?"

"No. Please don't tell him. He would insist I return home or remain in a settee all cycle."

"You have my pledge. Your medical condition is confidential. At some point, though, you should inform him."

"I will, but not now. He needs to focus on the mission and not get sidetracked worrying about me. And I don't want this morning sickness to hinder me from participating."

"Alright, I can give you medication for the nausea. I'm sure there are antiemetics in this doctor's kit somewhere. They'll provide temporary relief. And one more thing."

"Yes . . ."

"Congratulations!"

"Thank you, mender." Narleen smiled, wiped a tear from her left eye, and gave Holley a warm, heartfelt hug.

The radio crackled: "Anna calling team lead."

"Go ahead Annie."

"Not much this way, Jess. We passed one of those strange fire pits. The crane is idle. No workers present. Looks like the mining operations, if that's what they are, have shut down for the day. Lundy veered south to scan for signs of life. All he saw were rocks, dirt, miles of barren land, and depressions in the ground, which could be caves or fissures. No vegetation or water."

"Copy that." His reply was instinctive. He paused for a moment, remembering how often he'd used the same code as a police officer to acknowledge radio messages. "You and the reverend better head on back. Please be careful."

"Okay, will do."

A few minutes later, the radio sounded again: "Seth to JW. Got your ears on?"

Seth's CB jargon made him laugh. "Yeah, I'm listening. What did you guys find?"

"A bunch of dirt, a flaming pit, and a crane-like machine with a hanging bucket. Max spotted a footpath leading to a rundown housing complex. He went on ahead to scout it out."

"Copy."

"Should I remain at this 20?"

"Yes, stay there. Other than these cranes, I see no signs of civilization at my location. This housing place sounds like our best bet for contacting the inhabitants. We'll come to you."

"10-4 good buddy. Seth on the side." Jesse grinned, wondering if Seth had learned the CB lingo on his own or by watching some trucker movie from thc 70s.

By the time Lundy and Anna returned, Narleen had sufficiently recovered. Together, the group hurried to join up with Seth and Max. When Max saw Narleen coming, he ran to meet her. Although Jesse wanted to hear Max's scouting report, he waited, giving the couple time to talk privately. A few moments later, Max approached the others, holding Narleen's hand. First, he thanked Miss Holley for treating his spouse. Then he updated Jesse about the housing settlement: "I noticed about a dozen dwellings. No movement outside. Perhaps the residents have retired for the night. I suggest we approach with caution, tell them we are travelers seeking shelter for the night, which is true, and play it by ear. I would prefer not to draw my Gladius unless there are no other options."

"Let's hope they don't have ray guns or we're toast." Seeing worried faces on his colleagues, he apologized for his ridiculous comment. "I was only trying to lighten the mood with a little humor. Sorry, guys." *Get serious Jesse; you're their leader.* After scratching his chin several times, he offered a more constructive analysis of Camayah. "From what I've seen thus far, this world is pretty desolate: no trees, no foliage, no greenery, just sand, rocks, and rusty red hills in the distance. The area appears scorched, as if burnt by an unnatural fire."

"Yeah, like somebody nuked it." Seth cupped his hands and then opened his fingers to mimic an exploding bomb.

"I sure hope not." Trying to involve others in the discussion, Jesse asked, "Well, Reverend, what do you think?"

"I don't reckon such things. During my time on earth, we didn't have atomic weapons. I concur, though; this place is a wee bit desolate. And those ruins where we first landed are similar to the ones at Onnie Pass in Eskaonus. I wonder if the structures were part of an abandoned temple or other unsanctioned facility. Nothing remains except busted foundations and discarded equipment. More of a trash heap than anything else. Me thinks we should gather a couple lads to search around for more clues."

"Later perhaps. Right now we gotta find a place to stay for the night."

"Don't forget water," added Holley. "We didn't bring any. I'm not sure about you guys, but I'm getting thirsty." Each person affirmed they felt the same cravings. "And Narleen should probably have something to eat. She lost most of her last meal after we portaled here."

"Alright, folks, let's go knock on one of those doors and ask about room and board."

"Will we be able to communicate with the Camayahnite people?" Holley asked.

"I think so," replied Jesse. "Last time we traveled off-heaven, the Holy Spirit bridged the language barrier with a miracle similar to what occurred on the Day of Pentecost. It made it possible for us to understand them, and they, us."

"Aye, the incident is described in Acts 2:6 as I recall."

"Thanks, Rev. However, we still had to learn their local customs and terminology. The latter was a bit challenging."

"Dudes, quit yapping about it. I say we go find out."

CHAPTER 7

FIRST CONTACT

The group cautiously approached the first home in the housing complex. Anna knocked on the door while the others gathered behind her. Jesse felt she would be less threating than a person carrying a sword, who stood over seven feet tall, like Maximus.

After the third knock, a man opened a thin metal door. His yellowish eyes widened as he stared at the unexpected visitors. "Leetqu, come see; we have people from Sector Five, seven of them. They must be migrating." He opened his palms and said, "Joyful dusk to you."

A slender woman with long graying hair came forward and offered the same greeting and hand motions, adding, "Please do come in before the quawners drag you off. They are more prevalent during nightfall."

Annabelle duplicated the open-palm gesture, and replied, "Joyful blessings to you."

The man smiled. "I guess inhabitants from the southern sector use different greetings. It's fine with us. However, don't let Security hear you respond with the word *blessings*. Religious fanatics use that term and it's forbidden." With concern showing on his face, the man kept peering outside as he visited. "My name is Rekis and this is my bond, Leetqu. My offspring, Rauteira, is sitting at the table trying to build a datatop. She is savvy for a girl sixteen stages old." Rauteira glanced up and waved, then returned to working on her project. "You are welcome in our abode, but you really must come in now. The quawners are surely stalking about." Heeding the second warning, the collective hurried through the entry, and the man closed the door behind them.

Their home seemed more like a small apartment. A table, surrounded by three makeshift stools, filled the center room. Two side cubicles without doors branched off the main area. Several open closets lined the walls. There was no kitchen area, restroom, or stove. One wall had a small counter attached, holding several jars and other items that looked like scrap from a junkyard. A crystal hung down from the ceiling, giving off a greenish glow. No windows anywhere.

Rekis was tall, over six feet, yet slender, as if malnourished. He tied his long black hair, which contained white streaks, in a ponytail on the left side. Rauteira reminded Jesse of a typical high school student from earth. All three residents wore the same reflective clothing.

"How is the Sector Five assimilation coming along?" inquired the man. "We've heard the southernmost region is lagging behind the others due to an infestation of quawners. Migrants report the RIFTs and transport portals haven't been finished. What about the datastream communications? Are they operational?"

Not having answers for those questions, Jesse stalled. "Sorry, we haven't been following the expansion while traveling."

Not satisfied with Jesse's reply, Rekis tried a different query. "Airship fare is quite expensive for laborers, so we assume this is why you journeyed north on foot. Have you been traveling for many dawns?"

"Yes, quite a few. I lost count." Jesse felt his answer was essentially true if he included the two trips to Eskaonus.

"Sorry to interrupt, but one in our party needs water," explained Holley. "In fact, we're all very thirsty."

"We have no liquid here or food items. The Burning destroyed everything: resources, vegetation, and animals. Only the quawners survived by burrowing deep underground. I'm sure you already know this and are perhaps testing us," pressed Rekis. "Are you S2 agents?"

"No. Dealing with this heat has . . ."

Thinking Jesse was referring to the extreme heat in the flame pits, Rekis replied, "Mining Triverphol for fuel is dangerous and our homemade suits don't offer much protection from the scalding temperatures. Sooner or later everyone gets infected and their eyes turn yellow. Triverphol Sickness has taken its toll on many of us. My bond has early-stage symptoms. If the condition worsens, they will terminate her to stop the spread. Some in this sector have already been terminated this phase because they contracted the Disease or were suspected of being fanatics."

"We are sorry to hear about your losses." Holley stepped in front of Jesse, allowing him a moment of reprieve from all the questions.

"Little can be done." Rekis frowned and slowly shook his head. "We have one Hydru tablet left. Although we were saving it for an emergency, you're welcome to it."

Leetqu walked to the closet, opened a small tin box, removed a greenish-blue pill, and gave it to Holley. "I hope the person you mentioned will benefit. Sorry, the rest of your party will have to wait till dawn. We swallowed our doses of Hydru and Tycozide at nightfall, so we are already hydrated and nourished. On the morrow, my bond and I will earn more gelts digging in the flame pits. The going rate is ten gelts per dawn in this sector. If you skip the pleasure pills, in a few dawns, you'll have enough gelts to purchase Tyhydru and Dapferon tabs. They last longer. The current prices are posted in the RIFTs."

"I realize you are hungry and thirsty." Leetqu's odd yellowish eyes revealed compassion as she spoke. "Try to sleep the best you can and report early to RIFT III. If you explain that you are migrating from Sector Five, the S1 will probably assign you a temporary DIN. Rauteira is going there at dawn for this event's *Indo*. She can lead the way. Right now, though, we should rest. It is going to be another hot dawn and difficult workday." Leetqu and Rekis repeated the joyful dusk phrase, then hurried to their chamber, pulling a tattered silver curtain across the doorway.

"Sorry, travelers." Rauteira's pastel blue eyes sparkled as she spoke, her voice pleasant, her demeanor, sympathetic. "We only have three sleeping pads. You'll have to bed down on the floor." She grinned at Seth, bowed to the others, and strolled into her chamber, pulling the curtain shut. The group waited until they heard the man snoring before they gathered in a circle on the floor to discuss the situation.

Seth whispered, "A friendly family except their world is freaky strange."

"Aye, I wonder what these quawner creatures be. They sound dangerous."

"The recruit and I can investigate tomorrow, make a few inquiries. They can't be all that tough." Max patted his sheathed Gladius.

"Let's hope not. Anyone else have something to add?" asked Jesse.

"Apparently, there's no food or water here. I have no idea how they make these supplements or the science behind it." Holley pulled the hydration pill from her satchel and studied it. "Little wonder this family is malnourished. Since there's only one tablet available, I think Narleen should have it."

"No, I'll be fine."

"As your doctor, I disagree. You're dehydrated from the recent bout of vomiting." She handed the Hydru tablet to Narleen. "Swallow this. You need to stay hydrated since you're . . ." She stopped mid-sentence, hoping no one noticed her near slipup about Narleen's pregnancy. "Since you'll benefit more than us." *Whew, I hope Max wasn't listening too close.* She opened her medkit and located an antiemetic tablet. "Take this one as well. It will lessen the nausea."

"I think we should do as the woman advised and get some rest." Jesse placed his satchel on the floor to use as a pillow. "We can formulate plans in the morning after we visit this RIFT place."

The team spread out across the crowded floor in uncomfortable sleeping positions. Annabelle could see distress on their faces and wanted to help. She took out her nyeflute, reviewed the tablature, chose an arrangement, and began playing a tune. The music sounded sweet and soft, similar to a pan flute. Within seconds, her associates were asleep on the floor. She remembered Abdiel saying the songs wouldn't affect the flutist, just those who heard them. He mentioned one exception, but obviously this melody wasn't it. "Well, at least they won't struggle with hunger and thirst all night." She leaned against the wall. Her throat felt as dry as a cracker, her stomach grumbled. She closed her eyelids and tried to sleep.

CHAPTER 8

RIFT III

The sound of someone closing the front door awakened Holley. She heard muffled noises coming from Rekis and Leetqu's quarters and noticed the curtain drawn open. Assuming they were already up, she entered to ask a question. Leetqu stood in front of a cabinet facing the wall; her backside revealed she was naked. Holley averted her eyes. "I'm sorry, ma'am, I didn't realize you were unclothed."

Leetqu twisted her neck slightly to the left without changing her position. "We take our clothing off for sleeping. Being undressed is preferred after nightfall. We assumed you did the same last dusk."

"No, we kept our clothes on." *This is one custom I'm not adopting.*

"That is one's choice. There is no shame, either way." Still facing the closet, Leetqu removed her silvery outfit from the middle shelf. "How may I assist you this bout?"

"I'm wondering where the washroom is located."

"We have none. Hydru tabs keep us hydrated and our skin clean. See." She turned around and Holley noticed Leetqu had yellowish rashes and blisters covering her legs, chest, and forearms. Although she worked as a nurse practitioner and occasionally saw patients in the nude, she was still embarrassed and felt awkward staring.

"It's okay to look. This is what Triverphol Sickness does. It's not contagious at this point."

Gaining her composure, she replied, “I have something in my medkit that’ll help with those rashes and blisters.”

“Are you a healer? I didn’t realize their knowledge survived the Burning.”

“Not really. However, I do have experience with first aid care.” She removed the medkit from her satchel, located one of the two bottles of Helixzon that Mender Ottaar provided, and handed it to Leetqu. “Rub this on the affected areas. The salve probably won’t cure your infection, but it might resolve the skin deformities.”

“That would be wonderful. If Security ever finds out I contracted the Disease, they’ll start monitoring my condition and if the symptoms worsen, I’ll be sent to Termination.”

Holley apologized again for entering her quarters unannounced, pulled the curtain shut, and quietly departed. By then, the rest of the outfit had stirred and were milling around the table.

“If I don’t get hydrated soon, this old Scotsman is a goner.”

“Me too, Preach.” Seth grabbed his throat with both hands and made a choking motion. “I’ve never been this thirsty in my life, hungry too. Hope those goofy pills work.”

The discussion stopped when Leetqu emerged from her room, dressed in her jumpsuit. She handed Holley the empty bottle and thanked her for the salve. “You better hurry to the RIFT and get registered. The waiting line gets crowded by halfdawn. Rauteira is leaving for *Indo* now, so she can lead the way.” With open palms, she added, “Fair dawn to you.” Leetqu grabbed a forked digging tool by the door and raced out to join her bond at one of the nearby mining operations.

As the group exited their host’s residence, they could see the ruins where they had landed and a nearby mining operation with crews hard at work. One laborer handled the crane, dipping a bucket into the flames to withdraw a glowing liquid. He emptied it into metal barrels. Several worked inside the pit, removing rocks. In the distance, a cluster of laborers raked the ground. Others gathered small balls of material near large craters.

The newcomers followed Rauteira to RIFT III. When they

drew near, the party heard yelling and noticed an individual running away. Several men were following him, firing devices that made zapping noises and emitted yellow beams of light.

"What's going on, Rauteira?" Max asked. "Who are those men and why are they chasing this guy?"

"They're security forces, S2s who carry quispikes. The man they're hunting probably has the Disease, late stage, and they want to stop him before he spreads it to others. He could also be a discontent or religious fanatic. If infected, Security will take him to Termination. If a discontent or fanatic, he'll first be confined in Holding and later, taken to our Programming Center for processing."

More yellow lights erupted from the stunners until one beam hit the runner in the back. He dropped to the ground, remaining motionless. The S2s gathered around, bound him with ties, and started to drag him away, heading north.

"He must have been infected," Holley noted. She remembered what Leetqu said about those who have the Disease. It bothered her to think the same fate awaited Rauteira's mother and others mining Triverphol. She needed to find a cure for these people.

Suddenly, three creatures appeared, climbing out of dark holes in the ground. They moved quickly, spraying a clear liquidy substance at the S2s. Security dropped their captive and began firing their stunners at the spider-like beasts. It had little effect. In fact, it seemed to agitate them. The security forces were quickly overrun. Nearby laborers dropped their digging tools and scattered in every direction. Anyone sprayed with the venom, collapsed, seemingly paralyzed. The creatures picked up the three security personnel in their fang-like mouths and returned to their underground hollows. It was over in mere moments.

"Jeepers!" Seth stared spellbound at the monster spiders. "What were those creepy things?"

"Quawners, of course. Don't you have them in Sector Five?" No one in Jesse's collective answered. "In this sector, we're infested with them. They have impervious outer skins. None of our stunners can stop them, let alone kill them. They spit venom to immobilize their prey. Since quawners prefer live food, they left the stunned runner on the ground, determining he was already deceased. Their attacks usually come with little notice and afterwards, the creatures drag their victims into their dens, and they're never seen again."

"Freaky, what's the best defense?"

"Run!" She shook her head as if the answer was obvious.

"Sounds like a good rule, recruit," teased Max. "If all else fails, RUN! Maybe you should make it Rule Number Four."

"I will if you will."

"Although I would love to stick around and listen to this amusing banter, I have *Indo*. If I'm late for class, they'll penalize my parents by taking away two gelt credits. Check in with the S1 at the counter. I gotta go." Rauteira presented her open palms, smiled at Seth, and rushed inside.

Jesse gave the rally command by circling his finger. His team gathered around him and followed Rauteira into the RIFT. The facility contained a lobby, counters with screens, a long hallway, cubicles, and several kiosks. A security guard at the first counter, shouted, "Hail to the programmer." The newcomers responded with the same phrase, and then extended their open palms like Leetqu showed them. "Stop, we don't use such rituals here. Advance and place your finger in the scanner."

Jesse moved forward and inserted his right index finger into the slot indicated. "No, not the right, the left." He switched hands and tried again. "You don't have a Data Identification Number. You must be from Sector Five. We've been getting a lot of laborers migrating from the south. The lower areas haven't been assimilated yet."

Jesse knew better than questioning the terminology, but the thought still crossed his mind: *like the Borg, huh?*

"Assimilation! What kind of nerdish term is that?" spouted Seth.

The S1 appeared perturbed at the teen. "Shouldn't you be in *Indo* with the other children?"

"I'm not a child," Seth insisted.

"Fine, wait your turn. Otherwise, I'll send you to Holding till you learn to mind your tongue. And yes, the term for sectors connected by the datastream is assimilated. Sector Five isn't online yet. Our security and programmers are working on it.

Serious quawner issues down that way." Returning his attention to Jesse, he said, "I can register your crew with temporary DINs. You're first."

"Name?"

"Jesse."

"Residence?"

"None yet."

"Okay Jesse, your code is L342. Wear this ID band on your left wrist. You must have an official residence in this sector. There are very few openings at this interval. We'll probably have more housing available next event after Security sweeps the area for discontents and fanatics. In the meantime, you'll have to make do."

"Your wristband will allow ten gelt credits for three dawns, which includes free portal travel to our moons. On the fourth, you will be required to have a permanent DIN inserted into your left finger and work for your gelts."

"Our nourishment and Cradphenanill dispenser is over there." He pointed across the room toward the rear. "Prices are posted. Pleasure cubicles are down the hall. No more than three per chamber. Come early because the places fill up fast during latedawn."

"Concerning labor, we offer mining for precious minerals, digging for Criunite crystals, and gathering Foeca. I suggest joining a Triverphol operation. We have them on our three moons as well. Check with the S3s onsite."

The S1 started processing Maximus for a DIN while he talked to Jesse. "If you have security or coding experience, there may be other options. I understand our Programming Center is seeking data coders. You'll find it five ticks to the northwest. And Security at RIFT I is shorthanded. Their facility is located four ticks north, two ticks past Termination. This big guy should give it a try. At seven marks tall and over 300 masses, the SL might hire him, even without an interview."

"The Transport Portals and Airship Dock are ten ticks away. You could also try there. Holding always needs extra Security if one can find their hidden entrance. It's a couple ticks west of Programming. If any of you are qualified, ask for an interview. Unless your friends procure a security or programming position, they'll be assigned to our digging and mining operations." With Max's registration completed, the S1 started with Seth.

"Name?"

"Seth."

"Your code is L344. Next."

Anna stepped forward. As the S1 registered the remainder in line, he continued talking. "Concerning benefits, programmers and Security have reserved housing and earn unlimited gelts for themselves and their families. It's a better situation, except you'll have to submit to a limited programming session before being hired. If my SA finds out you are troublemakers, you'll be reprogrammed right off, a complete wipe. It makes life easier for us. Being an obedient drone ain't all bad." The S1 let out a bellowing laugh, followed by several more. "Rules and charts are posted on the walls. I suggest you become familiar with them. Next?"

While the final three in line were processed for their temporary IDs, Max walked the hallways to explore the premises. Jesse wandered around, studying the charts. On a side partition, he found a posting about the RIFT. It appeared to be an acronym.

RIFT

Reho (Recreation): Pleasure cubicles

Indo (Instruction): Rules, regulations, general education

Feyo (Feeding): Nourishment supplies

Taeo (Taxation): Registration, accountability, work assignments

Since Security didn't appear to be watching him, he pulled out his journal to log an entry:

<u>Entry Thirteen</u>

Arrived in Camayah. Max and Narleen came with us. The transport made her sick, but Holley treated her. She seems to be doing fine. First contact was with a local family. They were wary, yet helpful. I plan to press them for more information tonight. We visited one of their RIFT facilities. RIFT is an acronym for Recreation, Instruction, Feeding and Taxation. In regard to Feeding, it's a misnomer. This world has no food or water. The inhabitants use nourishment pills to survive. This place has huge six-legged creatures called quawners. They may be a problem. No other animals. They perished in an event called the Burning. No vegetation either. Hope to learn more about what happened here. Plan to split up and do some investigating this afternoon. Being watched. Gotta go . . .

Jesse quickly tucked his journal into the satchel as two security personnel approached. They stopped, looked, and then moved on without inquiring as to what he was doing. When Max returned from checking out the premises, he wore a frown on his face.

"Anything wrong? What did you discover?"

"On the main level, there are two closed stairwells, one leading up and the other down. I didn't see any classrooms. However, there are many cubicles lining the hall on both sides. Most are empty, but several are occupied, the doors closed. As I passed by, I heard disgusting sounds coming from inside. Ones I remember all too well from my days as a Roman soldier. People in those chambers are involved in an orgy. Such activities are vile, unrestrained, and involve numerous forms of depravity."

"I would assume those are the pleasure rooms the S1 mentioned. I want no part of it."

"Neither do I, sir."

In the rear, Jesse and Max located the dispensary that the guard mentioned. "I'm so thirsty and hungry, Max, I can hardly function. Let's figure out how to operate this kiosk before we faint." Jesse held his wristband near the ID scanner and the screen popped on indicating his code L342, a balance of ten gelts, and the pill costs.

<u>Nutrition</u>
Tycozide: 3 gelts
Dapferon: 6 gelts
<u>Hydration</u>
Hydru: 3 gelts
Tyhydru: 6 gelts
<u>Pleasure</u>
Cradphenanill: 1 gelt

He touched the screen for Tycozide and Hydru. Two tablets

rolled into a slot. One was reddish-brown, the other greenish-blue. He popped both into his mouth and swallowed them. The effects were almost immediate. His dry throat eased, and his stomach felt full, as if he had just eaten a three-course meal. The screen showed a four-gelt credit. Max flashed his wristband next. His code was L343. He followed the same procedure to obtain his nutrition and hydration tabs.

After completing their registrations, the other five joined Jesse and Max around the dispenser. Max explained how to activate the screen and procure the necessary nourishment.

Seth was last to use the kiosk. "What do these Cradphenanill cubes do?"

"Ya don't wanna to know, kid," Max replied.

Having received their DINs and taken their nourishment for the day, the group headed for the exit. "This place makes me sick," Jesse whispered. "I can hardly wait to get outside."

CHAPTER 9

INVESTIGATIONS AND DISCOVERIES

Once outside the RIFT, the team discussed splitting up to investigate the various facilities in Sector One. Max offered to probe their military forces. "Since the S1 thinks I would qualify to work for Security, I'll trek north to RIFT I and make inquiries."

"What if you run into quawners?" Narleen asked. "They are hostile and unpredictable."

"I'll pull my Gladius and make short work of them. From what I've seen, Camayah's stun devices are ineffective. However, old-earth weapons like swords might be good deterrents; even projectiles launched from a sling could make an impression." Narleen smiled at his humor, but also to indicate she had received her spouse's hint. She opened her satchel and pulled out her sling to inspect the pouch and finger loop on the cord. Scanning the ground for small, rounded stones, she gathered a handful, dropped them into her carrier, and placed her sling on top for easy access.

"Jess, I'll check out those mining operations," offered Annabelle. "The ones we passed earlier. I'll keep my radio on channel two so we can stay in touch." Although Jesse agreed with her choice, he urged her to use extreme caution, especially around the area where they had sighted the quawners.

"Me thinks I'll wander over to their Programming Center and see what's what."

"Okay, Reverend. Better take our spare transceiver. It's set for channel four. Keep me posted."

"Aye, count on it."

"Who wants to scope out their Termination Facility?"

"I will," Holley replied. "I'd like to learn what's done there and why the sick are exterminated instead of being cured."

"You're on channel three. Don't hesitate to use your radio." Holley acknowledged with a nod of her head.

"How about you, Seth? Any ideas?"

"Yeah, JW. I'll drop by the Airship Dock for a look-see."

"It's a long hike, over ten miles away. In this arid climate, I don't—"

"No worries. I plan on using my hoverboard. I'll be there in a flash. My talkie is set for channel one. Let ya know what the vibes are."

"Seth, can you give me a ride to the Transport Portals?"

"Sure can, Narleen. It's a two-person board. I can drop you off on the way."

"Great, then I'll pick the portals for my assignment."

"Alright, this covers all the main facilities except Holding, so I'll take that one. I'm still on channel five. After gathering intel, let's meet back at Rekis and Leetqu's place." The colleagues agreed and departed to begin their investigations. It was earlydawn.

Max walked with Holley to the Termination Facility, waited until she entered the facility, and then continued north at a forced march. Making good time, he approached RIFT I in under an hour. The building was similar to RIFT III, yet smaller in size. "Hail to the programmer!" shouted the S1. "Present your DIN." Without responding to the greeting, Max placed his wrist ID on the scanner.

"It says your code is L343, name Maximus, migrant from Sector Five, temporarily assigned to RIFT III." The S1 was about to clear Max when he noticed an irregularity. "Wait, there's a *hold*." He unstrapped his contact stunner. "Stay where you are."

Sensing trouble, Max pulled his Gladius, keeping it at the ready by his side. From a rear cubicle, a man who had been watching the encounter approached the counter. "I was notified on the datacomm you might pass this way. My name is Cndrek. I'm the Security Leader over this sector." The SL sized up the newcomer, noting his height of seven marks and muscular build. Cndrek entered his passcode to remove the *hold* from Max's data file. "I will handle this one. You're dismissed." The S1 hooked the bospike to his belt and moved down the hall, disappearing through an entryway.

"Are you interested in a security position?"

"Thinking on it. I have questions, though."

"No doubt. My queries, however, come first." Max sheathed his sword. "Is that digger yours?"

"It is."

"Short answers and to the point, I like it." Cndrek moved closer to examine Max's scabbard. "Unique tool and carrying case. Do you remember where you found them? Which ruins? Both appear ancient, pre-Burning era."

"Given to me as a gift."

"I see. If you take a position with Security, you won't need a tool for digging minerals. Perhaps we could make a deal or trade."

"What deal?"

"Let me ask a few more questions before I decide. Are you proficient with weapons?"

"Most."

"Can you command a squad of Security?"

"Not a problem."

"You passed. I will consider advancing you to the position of Security Assistant. As my SA, you'll not be programmed and will retain your name, unlike the lower ranked S1, S2, and S3s, who only have ID numbers."

"Are there other SAs under your jurisdiction?"

"Yes, I have one in RIFT II. Her name was Raetila. Like her, you will have no gelt restrictions. Bonds and offspring qualify for unlimited gelt stipends each phase, and they're not required to work. You'll have living quarters in a RIFT of your choosing. Each facility has four levels. The main floor has a *Taeo* counter, *Feyo* kiosk, communication terminal, *Indo* classrooms, and *Reho* pleasure cubicles. Upper levels house personnel and their families. The basement contains storerooms with technology, power modules, and assorted commodities, including a repair shop for fixing stun weapons and data equipment."

"Security forces receive Floksillin and Ploksillin vaccinations; the latter gives you partial protection against the Disease. And we have durable protective suits, not like the one you're wearing that's pieced together from discarded solar sails."

"Much to consider. First, I must speak with my bond."

"Your temp ID expires in three days. You better decide by then or my offer is off the counter, and you'll be conscripted to mining."

"Understood. You will have my answer soon. Fair dawn to you, sir." Max trudged out the exit and departed. On the return trip to Rekis and Leetqu's residence, he scouted the nearby areas, avoiding contact with security patrols.

At the mining site, Anna counted dozens of laborers in silvery jumpsuits, digging and removing a variety of rocks while the crane handler dipped his bucket in and out of the flaming pit. Others raked the ground nearby or gathered a milky substance around craters. An individual carrying a stunner approached her. "Hail to the programmer." Annabelle responded with the same greeting.

"Present your DIN." She held out her wristband ID. The security guard scanned it with a handheld device.

"It says your code is L345, name Annabelle, migrant from Sector Five, temporarily assigned to RIFT III. What do you want?"

"I was told to report to the S3 for an interview."

"Busy now. Come back next dawn." Anna began walking away. "Wait, do you have mining experience?"

"I've done a little digging in my day."

"Here's my situation. We have shortages due to laborers being infected with the Disease. I lose at least two workers every event. We have openings to mine minerals inside the flame pits, dig for Criunite crystals, or gather Foeca. You don't get to choose the assignment; I do."

"Acceptable. When's a good time to conduct my interview?"

"I just did. If you're interested, tell your RIFT, obtain a permanent DIN, locate a digging tool, and report to me before your temporary ID expires."

"Thank you, sir. I'll come again."

"Doubtful. All you migrants say the same thing. More likely, you'll be terminated by next phase. Move on, I'm busy." The S3 turned his head and noticed one of his laborers standing idle. Without warning, he fired his trispike. A beam of green light stunned the laborer, and she fell into the Triverphol pit, perishing in the flames. "Lazy old woman. Good riddance!"

Anna was horrified yet said nothing.

Seth unfolded his hoverboard. He positioned himself in the front and checked the foot controls while Narleen stepped on behind him. He pressed down on the activation pedal and off they went, speeding toward the Airship Dock and Transport Portals. The craft flew through the air mere inches above the ground. As they approached their designated areas, Seth leaned a hard left, turning his board around, concerned at what he saw.

"Breaker, breaker. This is Seth. Do you read me, JW?"

"Yeah, I got ya. What's the situation?"

"There's a bunch of those creepy crawlers over here. One of them popped out of a hollow and sprayed venom at us when we passed over. The goo almost hit us. I had to turn a 180 at the last second to avoid the other beasties."

"Better abort."

"10-4. But first we're gonna scout the area past the Airship Dock. I see dudes roaming around digging for something. Gonna park my board and rap with them before we scoot."

"Copy. Don't take any chances, especially with Max's wife."

Grabbing the radio from Seth, Narleen replied, "I'm fine, Jesse. Seth is being careful. What did you find out at Holding?"

"Not much. The place is locked up tight. Looks like a prison facility. Security posted in the towers. No entrance that I could see. I'm heading to the residence now. Meet you guys there later. Stay safe. Jesse out."

Meanwhile, Lundy entered the Programming Center and

strolled up to the counter.

"Present your DIN." Lundy complied. "Your code is L348, name Lundy, migrant from Sector Five, temporarily assigned to RIFT III. What's your business, old fellow?"

"I've come to talk with the head honcho."

"If you mean the Program Master," replied the P2, "he sees no one. The PM is always busy."

"How about another chap?"

"The Program Assistant is occupied."

"Too bad, I'm an experienced coder. Me thinks I'll take my skills elsewhere."

"Wait an interval." A person approached the counter from a side cubicle. "My name is Ahboen. I'm the PA for this facility. How much coding experience do you have?"

"More than any of your lackeys." *Better at language ciphers too.*

"I might be interested. Come back next dawn for an interview. If you qualify, I'll consider a P1 entry-level position. It comes with unlimited gelt credits, housing in our center, and other benefits."

"Aye, sounds reasonable. I'll see if my schedule allows."

"It better! If you don't show, Security will hunt you down and conscript you to Triverphol mining or confine your sorrowful face in Holding as a discontent, pending termination. You have three dawns to decide."

Lundy waved an acknowledgement and departed, sporting a sarcastic half grin. *What a bampot!*

"Holley to Jesse. Come in please."

"Go ahead Hol. What did you find out?"

"Following my DIN screening, the operators gave me a short tour, thinking I possessed the required expertise in genetics or medical research. I only told them I had experience as a medtech." His radio registered static as the signal faded. Jesse checked his transceiver to see if he turned it off my mistake. A moment later, her transmission continued: "Jesse, this place is both an execution facility and crematorium where individuals are terminated, and their bodies processed for chemicals. We have to do something about this."

"We're gonna try. Glad you discovered the facility's hidden purpose. The angels spoke about a great deception. Sounds like this may be part of it." Jesse paused, trying to recall Uzziel and Chesedel's exact words.

"Jesse, are you still there?"

"Sorry, just thinking. Are you returning now?"

"Yes. In fact, Max has been waiting to escort me."

"Copy that. See you both soon. Stay safe."

Rauteira was home from *Indo* by the time everybody arrived. She was working on her datatop project; old parts lay scattered across the table. After exchanging greetings with her, the group began reporting their findings. Seth spoke first. "Narleen and I were almost chomped by those black, six-legged bugs. If she hadn't hurled stones from her sling, we would have been goners for sure. The projectiles distracted the biggest one long enough for us to escape. Once we circled around, we spotted additional ruins in the distance, directly north of the airships. We stopped and talked to a few dudes who were digging holes and raking the ground." Seth began to pace around the table, disgust showed on his face. "You know, these locals have to scrounge for everything they have. This society doesn't provide anything—no clothing, supplies, household items, work tools—nothing."

In the middle of his report, Rekis and Leetqu entered through the door, having finished their labors at the flame pits. Anna thought she heard them mention Yah worship. The two grew silent, realizing they may have been caught discussing an unlawful and forbidden topic.

"Do you mean Yahweh?" Anna asked.

Rekis and Leetqu immediately dropped to their knees, faces touching the floor. Rauteira arose from the table and joined them.

CHAPTER 10

GARDEN MEETING

While Uzziel waited for elChesed to appear for their scheduled meeting, he watched a company of saints gather around the Tree of Life to pick fruit. Heavenly inhabitants found the taste sweet and refreshing. The skin was purple, the shape of a mango, except slightly larger and rounder. The fruit contained life-giving properties, and the multicolored leaves on the tree promoted healing.

Those who consumed a piece would place the leftover pit on top of the Walled Terrace. They realized that everything in heaven had a purpose, even a discarded pit. Whether the seed pits were gathered later by an angel or simply disappeared, no saint knew for sure. Such issues were never a concern in heaven.

The produce vendor had already filled his cart and was on his way to Straight Street to set up his display. Others were swimming nearby in the River of Life, enjoying the pure waters that always flowed crystal clear.

Uzziel and elChesed met often to embrace their friendship and discuss how best to implement God's plans for eternity. This time, however, the Cherubim wanted an update about the situation on Camayah.

"I hope I didn't keep you waiting," said Chesedel, as he materialized in front of Uzziel. "I was over at the Hall of Records, reading Jesse's incoming scroll messages to prepare for our consultation."

"Apology unneeded. Like I often say, there are no such

things as delays in a timeless eternity." Uzziel glanced around the perimeter, searching for a quiet spot. "This area seems a bit crowded at the moment. I suggest we move to a more secluded space. The Garden of Prayer should work." In a flash, they both disappeared.

Central Heaven contained three gardens: meditation, supplication, and prayer. The Garden of Prayer lay along Straight Street, across from the Gold Pearl Gate. It featured circular marble benches, spaced between trees and bushes to offer solitude as individuals prayed or read Scripture scrolls. Each bench allowed entrance through a small opening in the circle. The two angels stepped inside one and sat down facing each other.

"Yes, this is much better," Uzziel remarked. "It's been a busy time, not only in heaven but on the earth as well. After the Arrival, things have escalated. Soon, the Lamb of God will start opening the seven seals. This is the beginning of countless sorrows, a time of great tribulation."

"A time many have been dreading."

"For some, yes. Others are looking forward to this period. It's more like birthing pains, necessary, painful at the time, yet essential for delivering God's new kingdom and revealing His purpose for the redeemed. Which brings me to our little band of *Abrahams*." Uzziel folded his wings behind his back and adjusted his flaming sword, still sheathed at his side. "What have you learned about the outreach to Camayah?"

"Jesse has added two entries: Twelve and Thirteen."

"Go on."

"As we expected, the team detoured to Eskaonus. Jesse is seeking assistance from his former colleague, Maximus, who remained there."

"Heaven allows the freedom of choice, even for us angels," reminded the Cherubim.

"And Satan made a poor one, as did those who followed his rebellion."

"Sadly, this is true." Uzziel stood and unfolded his wings. "I have much to attend elsewhere. Please just summarize what Jesse wrote in his journal."

"Of course." Chesedel unrolled the scroll he brought with

him and scanned it for details. “In Entry Twelve, Jesse gives Maximus an overview of our assignment to Camayah. At first, he declines. But when Narleen, his wife now, insists that he help, Max relents. Apparently, his spouse is going with him. I didn’t realize such transferences were possible.”

“As long as she stays connected to him during transport, she should be able to portal with the others.”

“Your depth of wisdom in these matters never ceases to amaze me.” Chesedel glanced at the scroll again. “In his next entry, Jesse confirms the entire group arrived safely in Camayah. It seems this futuristic world has suffered a cataclysm called the Burning, which has destroyed much of the land. There is no food or water on the planet, so the inhabitants use supplement pills to survive. All animals perished in this disaster except a species of dangerous creatures called quawners. Jesse says the mission is proceeding well, and they plan to split up and do more investigating. He also reported Holley’s medical experience has already been helpful.”

“I knew she would be an asset. Anything else of importance?”

“No, I believe I’ve covered most of it.”

“Thank you, elChesed. Let’s meet again when you have further updates.” The Cherubim vanished. Chesedel tarried for a while in the garden to meditate and pray, then he likewise popped away, entering the unseen realm.

CHAPTER 11

ENLIGHTENMENT

"Please rise. We are not deities to be worshiped, just people not unlike yourselves." The family didn't budge. Jesse gently tapped each shoulder, hoping the three would respond. When they finally looked up, he motioned for them to get off the floor.

"But you know His name," Leetqu replied as she stood. "You must be the *sent ones* our provost believed would come one dawn and rescue us. Instead of the usual greeting with open palms, she crossed her arms over her chest, bowed her head and said, "Blessings to Yah." After standing, Rekis and Rauteira repeated the same mantra.

Ignoring Leetqu's comment and unique greeting for the moment, Jesse inquired, "Who is this provost you mentioned?"

"He is the only spiritual leader known to have survived the purge. His name is Malmach and his bond is Trikernae. We call her pravost. Both escaped two stages ago, along with a handful of believers. They are in hiding on one of our moons. We haven't heard from them since. The provost always taught us that one dawn, Yah would send emissaries to aid us. Malmach believed Yah had not forgotten us. Are you those messengers?"

Without providing an exact answer, Jesse replied, "Well, we did arrive from a high kingdom with a charge to locate the faithful and resolve corruption."

"I knew it. The interval your group stepped through our door, I felt something was different. Your odd language and lack of understanding about local happenings concerned me. I now realize why you were hesitant to reveal yourselves. You must surely be the foretold heralds."

Rekis continued where Leetqu left off, providing additional insight. "Anyone who doesn't follow the RIFT's tenets is considered a discontent or religious fanatic. They are apprehended and remanded to Holding. Next comes reprogramming, except it usually doesn't take with believers, so they're sent to Termination. Most of us have given up hope for having a better life. Can you relieve us?"

"We're gonna try. I think we should first locate your provost and pravost, including the surviving believers. With our temporary DINs, we have access to the Transport Portals for two more dawns. In the morning, I mean morrow, we can organize teams to explore your three moons."

"They're called Vilmieah, Ethade, and Easteapia."

"Thank you, Rekis." Trying to sound optimistic, Jesse added, "If they're there, we'll find them! Right now, though, please tell us more about Camayah and the circumstances behind this purge. It might assist with our pursuit."

Rekis and Leetqu glanced at one another, trying to decide who should tell the story. Rekis nodded his consent, and she began. "Our planet developed flight, stages ago, not to the outer atmosphere, just local voyages using airships, which deployed solar sails once the crafts achieved orbit. Their crews explored our three moons and built transport portals connecting them to Camayah. We had science and healing centers, Rift facilities, and religious temples. There were liquid lakes and rivers, flora, even trees. Then the Burning came."

"What was this Burning?"

"The scientists weren't sure, nor why it happened. They speculated it might have been a chemical disaster, a blending explosion, or an unknown event in the outer atmosphere. Only those who were in a Rift or science center survived. Those facilities were shielded and constructed to endure thermo-disasters, as were the portals. A few residents entered our emergency shelters in time. Some of those lived. I was one of them, a child offspring. The quawners survived by burrowing deep underground. Our world perished that dawn—hydrew, crops, animals, and nearly all our inhabitants—fried into nothingness in less than ten intervals. Unshielded structures and homes crumbled into ruins."

It was as if Jesse's question unleashed years of pent-up emotions. Leetqu's story came spilling out, raw, unrestrained. Jesse and his cohorts remained silent and let her continue.

"Early survivors scoured the ruins for materials to rebuild their homes, construct furniture, find substances, and make tools. They had no TPCs for power or lighting, just green crystals like the one hanging in our home, which my bond found while digging in the hills. Criunite is our only means of light."

"While we scrounged the ruins for everything, programmers, operators, and Security lived in abundance in their facilities. We made our protective clothing from pieces of discarded solar sails, while they maintained countless reserves in storage, tucked away prior to the Burning."

Jesse was unsure if he should ask another question. It might open the equivalent of a Pandora's Box. Although just a mythical tale from earth, he decided to chance it, hoping his query would release the deep hurts and allow healing to begin. "What happened to your leaders?"

"Most died in the Burning, others perished afterwards. With no government, a leader called the Program Master rose to power. He converted the Rifts into RIFTs, changing their purpose. New rules were instituted and security forces established to enforce them. Those who questioned these actions were termed discontents and imprisoned."

"The PM turned our science building into the Programming Center. Instead of being community places, the RIFTs became taxation hubs and pleasure venues. Emergency protocols were instituted. With no food or liquids, researchers formulated nutrition and hydration tabs from various chemicals and substances. Triverphol was mined to produce TPCs. Those who gathered it became ill. Operators erected Termination Centers to handle the spread of the sickness and to process deceased bodies for nutriments. Pleasure pills were promoted as recreation. Our populace soon became addicted. The more they consumed, the viler their actions became."

"The world I identified with as a child offspring no longer

exists. Most of my friends are either dead or reprogrammed as drone laborers. Yah worship is forbidden, replaced by hailing the Program Master. Even talking about one's former belief is unlawful, punishable by termination." She wept with tearless eyes. "I could go on if you want me to."

"No, I think we get the picture. Sounds like your inhabitants have suffered enough."

"Thank you for listening to our plight. After saying nothing for many stages, talking about it has helped. My heart feels unburdened for the first time in ages."

"And hopeful," added Rekis."

Jesse stood silent for the longest time, studying the faces in the room. "As promised, we will visit these moons on the morrow and do our best to locate your spiritual leaders and their displaced followers." Sensing the bout was late and with everybody exhausted, the conversation finally wound down. Before heading to their quarters for sleep, Rekis and his bond offered the Yah blessing again.

Anna duplicated their cross-your-heart gesture, replying, "Yahweh hasn't forgotten . . ." She stopped in mid-sentence as if listening to an inward voice. Words formed in her mind. She felt led to speak them aloud.

"In the day of many sorrows, hope will arise like a winged nawmie rising from her nest. She will soar the heights and her hatchlings will follow her, free and unafraid. Liquids will be found in the hidden places. Soreseeds will be planted, food will be plentiful again, and goodness and compassion will rule the dawn." As soon as Anna finished, she noticed the family rubbing their eyes. Her teammates were also affected.

"Grand prophecy if I ever heard one." Lundy used his sleeve to wipe his nose.

Seth began sniffling. "Dudes, I told ya her words were anointed; her songs, too."

"Wow, Annie, that was . . . powerful." Jesse took a deep breath, then slowly let it out. "Do you know what nawmies and soreseeds are?"

"No, I've never heard those words."

"We have," Rekis responded. "Nawmies are birds that went extinct after the Burning, along with the other animals, and the once-abundant soreseed plants haven't grown here in ages."

"Only *sent ones* could discern these things or know about our hopes for restoration. You surely must be those people." Leetqu hugged Rekis and kissed him on both cheeks. He returned the gesture. Joy showed on their faces. "I'm sorry. My bond and I got carried away."

"We didn't mind," replied Anna.

"Rekis and I have much to consider, including your insightful words. However, with nightfall approaching, we must rest for next dawn's labors." Leetqu and her bond entered their sleep chambers and pulled the curtains. Rauteira stayed up and worked on her datatop. After thirty intervals, she put the half-completed device on a wall shelf and trotted off to her quarters.

After the family fell asleep, the collective sat on the floor in a circle and discussed their upcoming plans: "I say we visit RIFT III early, get our nutrition and hydrations pills, and then hit the Transport Portals."

"Jess, those portals are at least ten ticks away. In this heat, it will take five bouts to travel there, assuming the quawners don't get us first." Three other team members shared Anna's concern.

"Dudes, I can zip you there in a couple intervals on my hoverboard. It's a two-person board, but I'm sure it will carry three. And I can outrun those quawners any dawn of the event." As the group discussed the issues, they realized they were gradually incorporating Camayahnite terminology into their conversations.

Jesse scratched his chin as he considered assignments. "Okay guys, here is how we'll do it: Max and Narleen will search the first moon, Annie and I will handle the second one, and Seth and Holley the third. We can rendezvous at the portals when we're finished."

"What ya got for the old Scotsman?"

"Rev, I want you to stay here with your radio and monitor our progress."

"Aye, and while I'm at it, I'll see if I can help the young lass with her project."

"Good idea. Well, comrades, we have an early start next dawn. Let's try to get some rest."

Like the previous night, the advocates spread out across the uncomfortable floor. Anna took out her nyeflute and piped a song. The music was soothing. Afterwards, her partners had peaceful expressions on their faces. Her tablature indicated the tune released encouragement. The second song caused her colleagues to fall fast asleep.

When they arose in the morning, Rekis and Leetqu had already departed to labor in the flame pits. Since Rauteira didn't have *Indo* until next event, she was busy working on her datatop project; parts and pieces covered the table. After exchanging greetings with the teen, the allies walked to their local RIFT, presented their DINs, and obtained Hydru and Tycozide pills for the dawn. Now hydrated and nourished, they gathered outside. Holley handed her radio to Narleen. Seth kept his, and Jesse and Anna kept theirs. Each search party carried at least one radio. With the teams ready, Seth began delivering them to the Transport Portals, starting with Max and Narleen. Lundy returned to the residence, pulled out his binder of coding scrolls, placed his radio on the table, and sat down to assist Rauteira.

CHAPTER 12

MOON VILMIEAH

Seth dropped Max and Narleen at the Transport Portals, made a U-turn and returned to RIFT III, where his next passengers waited for a ride. Prior to entering the portals, Narleen organized her satchel, hiding the radio Holley gave her at the bottom and placing her sling near the top. She tucked the five rounded stones she'd gathered earlier into a side pocket. While his spouse repacked, Max studied the building's layout, noting a few strategic vulnerabilities. When Narleen finished, the couple strolled inside and presented their DIN wristbands. Behind the counter stood two S1s with bospike contact stunners strapped across their chests. The room was filled with flashing screens and power-control panels. Several cubicles branched off from the main area. Closed closets lined the walls. The transport platform sat in the middle of the floor.

After enduring another boring screening process, they requested a portal jump to Vilmieah. The two stepped onto the platform and stood in the circle indicated. Whirring noises sounded and intervals later, Max and Narleen materialized on a similar platform. Another S1 rechecked their DINs and pointed them to an elevator. They rode the lift to the lunar surface and walked outside. The red dwarf sun overhead cast a strange reddish glow over the area.

Moon Vilmieah appeared as barren as Camayah. No flora anywhere. Rocky hills filled the moonscape as far as the eye could see. Max counted five mining operations, the cranes busy removing flaming Triverphol. He and Narleen headed for the largest pit mine. The S3 yelled, "Hail to the programmer!" The couple responded in kind. "Present your DINs and state your business."

"We are interested in joining your crew," replied Max in a gruff voice.

"Good, we've lost too many to the Disease and need to replace them."

"Can we look around before we decide?" Narleen asked.

"Laborers get no decision on venues. You go where I put you. Got it!"

"We understand, sir."

"Fine, if you are stupid enough to tramp around these hills with quawners lurking at every crevice, go ahead. If you survive, come back and see me. I'll contact your RIFT and have you assigned to my crew. Now, get out of my way. I'm busy. I have a half-empty crate and three loads of fuel to deliver by dusk."

The couple followed the footpaths south until they ended. "Where do we go from here?" Narleen wondered. "There must be leagues of territory."

"Let's try those rocky hills to the west first, then turn southeast."

"Shouldn't I let Lundy know we arrived and our status?"

"Good idea, Nar. Give him a call."

"Narleen to Lundy." No answer. "Lady Narleen to Lundy MacBain." No reply. "I don't understand why he isn't responding. He's supposed to be monitoring the teams."

"Not a priority. We'll contact him later. Stow the radio for now and let's continue our search."

Max and Narleen scoured the southeastern regions for three spans and found nothing. Tired from hiking through the rugged terrain, they sat down to rest on a rocky rise, avoiding any nearby hollows. Max snuggled closer. "Are you still mad at me, Nar?"

"A little. You realize I love you, though."

"I was beginning to wonder."

"Maxie, this search could last for yarns, and I'm starting to feel queasy again. I think we better call it a cycle and . . . listen, do you hear those faint clicking sounds?"

"Yeah, lots of them. Not sure what they are." Scanning the low ground, Max noticed a cluster of quawners climbing out of holes on the lunar floor. Somehow, the creatures sensed their presence, rushed uphill, and surrounded them, stopping twenty paces away. "They've cut us off." Max unsheathed his Gladius and stood in front of his spouse. "I don't think I can defeat them all. And there's nowhere to run, assuming we could outrun them."

"Max, they're moving again, creeping closer." Instinctively, she pulled out her sling, loaded a stone from her satchel, twirled it around to build momentum, and released. It stunned the creature momentarily. The quawner spun around in a circle, probably wondering what happened.

"Nar, I don't think those stones are—"

"Wait!" She noticed a jagged green crystal lying nearby. She loaded it in her sling and set up for another toss. The projectile hit the spider beast between the eyes and dropped it to the ground.

"Quick, go find more of these crystals. Try the next ridge." She pointed to a green outcropping. "I'll keep them busy with stones from my carrier. Hurry!"

Max darted off and began prying at the vein of Criunite with his Gladius, easily breaking loose a large section. He smashed it into smaller pieces with his blade, grabbed a handful of crystals, and sped back to Narleen. She was gone. "Narleen . . . Nar, where are you?"

In the distance, he saw the cluster scurrying away. One of them carried his spouse in its fang-like mouth. One by one, the creatures disappeared into a large crater. He dropped the green crystals on the ground, raised his sword high over his head, and raced after the quawners at a dead run. *Battle frenzy* took hold of him. He felt invincible, strong as an ox. He had experienced this condition once as a centurion. On that fateful day, he battled fifteen barbarians by himself, defeating the entire group with a broken Roman pilum.

When he entered the hollow, his frenzy morphed into a *battle trance*. Normal time faded away, senses were heightened. He heard clicking sounds before the quawner spayed its venom at him. Since everything moved in slow motion, he avoided the attack. Another creature, more clicking, more venom. He sidestepped the clear liquidy substance and kept advancing, swinging his sword in all directions. Several quawners fell, wounded, their legs cut in half. Others retreated, escaping into the cavern. Max followed; the trance deepened. He felt no fear. Events were still occurring slowly, giving him time to react beforehand.

Green crystals lined the walls, providing light. Up ahead, he encountered seven cocoons. Most were torn apart; bones lay beneath them. More clicking, more venom sprayed. He easily avoided it. One cocoon remained intact. Below it laid a silver satchel. Being careful, he cut the webbed sack open with his sword and discovered Narleen inside, unconscious, partially covered with a sticky substance, her sling cord still looped around two fingers.

He checked for signs of life. Narleen was breathing, but barely. Max sheathed his Gladius, removed his spouse from the webbing, and balanced her over his shoulder, holding on with his left hand. His fingers felt numb from the venom. Max ignored it. He clutched her satchel in his right hand and ran. The cave smelled musty; the floor felt spongy. More clicking, more venom sprayed. He dodged it and kept running until he reached the entrance. Once he exited the crater, the frenzy and trance lifted. Time returned to normal.

Max carried his spouse in a northerly direction until he sighted the mining area. Narleen regained consciousness once they neared the Transport Portals. Still groggy from the effects of the paralyzing venom, Max offered her his arm in support as they walked inside and rode the lift to the first level. After Security scanned their DINs, he requested a jump. The couple stepped onto the platform; an interval later they were back on Camayah. It was latedawn.

CHAPTER 13

MOON ETHADE

Seth shuttled the next team to the Transport Portals and returned to the RIFT where Holley awaited. Jesse and Annabelle had agreed to search the second moon of Camayah. He carried a radio in his satchel. Anna's bag contained her nyeflute and the extra walkie-talkie. After being cleared to use the portal system, they stepped upon the platform. The S1 pressed his screen and the two dematerialized. Moments later, they arrived on Ethade.

Another S1 greeted them, saying, "Hail to the programmer."

Jesse and Anna responded in kind. "You know, Annie, this greeting is beyond monotonous. If you see a suggestion box anywhere, I'm gonna recommend a different one."

With a sullen grimace on her face, she agreed. "Any salutation would be better." The pair took the lift to the lunar surface and exited the facility. Once outside, they noted the same barren conditions on the moonscape as on Camayah. Jesse sighted five flaming pits and more cranes south of the portals. One person was stomping back and forth, shouting at the crews. He assumed the man was an S3 and decided not to engage him. Instead, they approached a group of laborers who seemed to be taking a halfdawn break.

Jesse and Anna offered the dawn greeting with open palms extended. The crew ignored them. "Excuse me. I'm Jesse, and this is Annie. We were wondering if you have seen a company of new people on this moon." No answer.

Anna moved closer and stood facing the oldest one. "What is your name, sir? Mine is Annabelle."

"Name is L127. I serve the programmer." She glanced at Jesse, who slowly shook his head. Next she tried the youngest laborer, a girl who looked like a teenager.

"Name is L212. I serve the programmer."

"Annie, we probably won't learn much from them. I assume these individuals have been programmed like Leetqu told us about."

"It's really sad, Jess. They're like mindless drones. Can't we do something? Is there a way to reverse this brainwashing and restore their identities?"

"Unknown. Perhaps Lundy can find a solution in his coding book. Right now, though, we better start searching."

The duo trekked north for two bouts and didn't see any sign of the lost wayfarers, just endless leggs of barren land, rocky hills, and craters. Searching in the extreme heat rapidly took its toll, and Jesse raised his hand, signaling for a halt. "Let's take a short break while I give Lundy a status report." He set the dial to channel four. "Jesse to Lundy." No answer. "Rev, are you there?" No reply. "What's that preacher doing? He's supposed to be monitoring the radio. Annie, can you try your walkie?"

"Annabel to Lundy, come in please." No answer. "Reverend MacBain, please respond." No reply, only static. She returned the radio to her satchel. "Maybe we are out of range."

"I don't think so. Abdiel told me these transceivers function at extremely long distances." Jesse checked his unit to see if the controls were set to multi-band. They were. "No apparent issues on our end. We'll contact Lundy later. Let's continue the search."

"If we split up," Anna suggested, "we can cover more ground before sunset."

"Not sure that's a good idea with these monster insects roaming around."

"What do you propose, Jess?"

"I don't know. Not a ton of good options. We don't have time for a full grid search. It would take stages to traverse the entire moon. With a random pattern, we could explore certain areas in hopes of finding them, assuming this moon is where the provost and his followers are hiding. When I served in the Navy, they also had what's called a zigzag search pattern. Although mainly used over water, the principle is similar. Here, let me show you." Jesse drew in the dirt with his finger to demonstrate how it worked.

"It seems a bit complicated to me. Maybe we better stick with the random idea. At least we would cover a few locations."

"Okay, we'll separate for a couple bouts. I'll go west and work my way south. You try east and do the same. Let's meet again below the mining area. Call if you discover a marooned party."

"What about the quawners?"

"Yeah, right. Hope we don't run into them. They seem to inhabit the lowlands near craters. Try to travel the ridges as much as possible. See you in a bout or two. Stay safe."

After searching numerous leggs of similar terrain, neither Jesse nor Anna found signs of the missing people. They connected below the mining area and called it quits for the dawn. On the way back to the portals, they noticed the mining area was empty, not a laborer in sight.

"Where did they go? Why would the crews leave in the middle of a workday?"

"There's the reason." Jesse pointed to black silhouettes scurrying around the portal facility. "The laborers escaped inside to avoid the quawners."

"How are we going to reach the portals and return to Camayah?"

"We may not live long enough to find out. Several of those overgrown bugs have spotted us, and they're heading this way. We better run for it!"

"Where to? These things are everywhere, and we have no weapons."

"What about your nyeflute? Do you think it might work against them?"

"Not sure. I can try a few arrangements. Plug your ears with your fingers so you're not affected." Anna played the song that causes sleepiness. No impact. The creatures moved toward them at an ever-increasing speed. Others in the cluster joined the frenzy.

She piped the tunes for confusion and temporary blindness. Nothing. She motioned for Jesse to uncover his ears. "Jess, I played three numbers. None were successful." She pulled the tablature scroll from her satchel and handed it to him. "Here, hold this up so I can read it. I'm gonna try one more."

"Should I plug my ears again to avoid the effects?"

"No, not for this one."

"Annie, I don't wanna rush you or anything, but we're about to be their next meal."

Feeling the pressure of the moment, Anna struggled with fingering the notes. Finally, the correct arrangement flowed forth, sounding uniquely celestial. The creatures stopped advancing and began wandering aimlessly, as if lost.

"What's happening?"

"I don't think they see us, Jess. I just fluted the invisibility tune."

"According to the angel, flutists aren't affected by their own nyeflute music."

"This must be the one exception Abdiel mentioned, since we are both hidden from their view."

"Well, keep doing it. Should I still hold the tablature for you?"

"No, I've memorized the notes. Tuck the fingering guide into my carrier. There are more songs to learn, so I better not lose it." While Anna continued piping the song, the two threaded their way through the middle of the cluster. The quawners seemed to sense their presence yet couldn't see them. Jesse and Anna safely entered the lift and rode it to the main level. When they approached the control room, she quit playing and returned the nyeflute to its holder. The duo appeared out of nowhere.

"Where did you two come from?" asked the S3.

"The lift," Anna advised. "And we've made a decision about the work conditions on this moon. Too dangerous." The S3 could hardly disagree.

They showed their DINs to the S1, stepped onto the platform, and transported to the planet, arriving at latedawn.

MOON OF EASTEAPIA

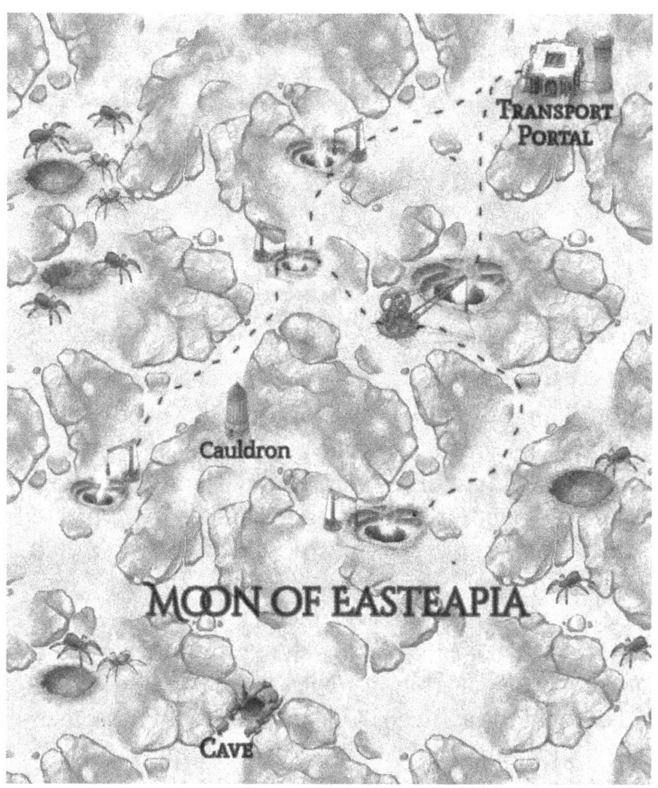

Camayah has three orbiting moons: Vilmieah, Ethade, and Easteapia. All are fictional places. However, all tangible places, whether known or unknown, were made by God.

"All things were made by him; and without him was not any thing made that was made" (John 1:3).

CHAPTER 14

MOON EASTEAPIA

Seth raced back to RIFT III, performing a 360 before stopping. "Come on Holley, hop aboard and let's book it; we have a moon to search." Seth checked the channel on his radio and placed it back into his carrier. Holley slung her medical bag across her shoulder and climbed on behind Seth. He pressed the foot pedal to engage the hoverboard, circled the RIFT, and then gunned it. They flew over the terrain like a speeding Indy 500 racer. Security patrols noticed the travelers and fired their stunners at them, but to no avail. They were moving too fast to hit. Laborers in the nearby pit mines acted like mindless drones that either didn't see them or didn't care. In less than five intervals, the pair approached the Transport Portals.

He brought his craft to a screeching halt, folded the board into quarters, stuffed it into his carrier, and together with Holley, entered the portal facility. They showed their DIN's, requested transport to Moon Easteapia, and stepped onto the platform. Seth sneered at the two S1s in the terminal who seemed to ignore them. "Dudes, are you gonna beam us up or not?"

A moment later, the duo arrived on a smaller platform. Another S1 greeted them with hail to the programmer and directed them to the lift. As they rode it to the lunar surface, Seth mused aloud, "Hey, Hol, this greeting of theirs is getting to be a real drag. Can't they use something different? How about what's crackin' or hang loose? Even flashing a high five would be better than this hailing the programmer rap." Holley grinned, enjoying

Seth's slanguage from the 70s.

Once on the surface, they scurried to the rear of the facility, not wanting to be seen by Security. Seth unfolded his hoverboard. "Let's do an initial loop around the area and then move out farther to conduct a circular search pattern, enlarging it as we go."

"You're the driver, Seth. Works for me."

"Cool, let's fly."

After bouts of searching and finding nothing except barren moonscapes with rugged hills and rocky lowlands, Seth parked his board on a ridge. "We better check in with the reverend. Why don't you give him a jingle while I hike to the top of the next slope and see if I can spot any signs of the provost or his followers?"

"Holley to Lundy." No answer. "Holley to Reverend MacBain." No reply.

When Seth returned, she advised him that Lundy wasn't answering. "Let me give it a try: Seth to Rev, ya got your ears on?" No response. "Come on, Preach, answer your phone." Only static. "I don't get it. He's supposed to monitor our calls."

"Hope he's okay. Should we contact the other two teams?"

"Naw, they're probably busy with their own searches. I'm sure Lundy's fine. He's probably busy reciting Scripture to Rauteira. Let's try one more loop around the area and then call it quits. It's getting late." Holley hopped on behind Seth while he adjusted the floorboard pedals. "Time to scoot. And watch out for quawners. I noticed a few roaming nearby on the last pass."

Seth conducted a final sweep before he turned his board toward the portals. Feeling confident, he cruised past a low hollow. "Whoops, incoming spider goo. Watch your balance, Hol. I gotta take some evasive action." Seth leaned right, then left. "Ha, they missed us. Just like riding a surfboard at Malibu, huh, Holley? Hol . . . hey Doc . . ." Seth glanced over his shoulder and Holley wasn't behind him on the board. *When did she fall off?* He circled around to find her lying on the ground. A huge quawner poised itself to grab her in its mouth.

"Rule Number One: Expect the unexpected." Seth pressed on the foot controls to accelerate. "Rule Number Two: Face your fears to overcome them." He drove his vehicle straight at the monster, hitting it broadside, knocking the thing onto its back. As the creature wiggled its six legs trying to right itself, Seth swooped down and parked his board to load Holley, draping her over the floorboard on her stomach. "Rule Number Four: RUN!" He took off and soared away, scanning the terrain for a safe place to descend. On the left lay an isolated area near a rocky hill; he maneuvered his hovercraft toward it and landed.

Immediately, he flipped Holley over. A clear substance covered her face. She wasn't breathing. Using his hands, he wiped it off. The substance numbed his fingers. *Must be the venom.* He checked the pulse in her wrist. Not even a slight beat. "Arrgh!" Opening her satchel, he removed the medkit. He rifled through the kit, looking for a mini-defibrillator. Not included. As a surfer, he'd seen swimmers stung by a Portuguese man o' war. According to lifeguards at the beach, its venom could paralyze and kill small fish. *If this spider goo is stronger, she might not survive.* He knew what to do. He began CPR. "Breathe Holley, breathe!" While he applied chest compressions and exhaled into her mouth, his lips turned numb from the venom residue on her face. He continued. Soon he could detect shallow breathing. He checked her pulse again. *Weak, yet there.* "Alright, Holley, keep it going. You got this girl."

He heard a grinding noise and turned around to see a large boulder moving, revealing an opening in the stone wall behind him. Seth expected a quawner. Instead, three individuals rushed out. Two picked Holley off the ground and carried her inside the opening. The third one asked, "Who are you?"

"I'm the cavalry. I've come to rescue you."

"Well, Cavalry. My name is Malmach. Welcome to our hollow, but you should come inside. The quawners are surely stalking about."

Seth left his hoverboard, grabbed Holley's satchel and medkit, and followed the man. Once inside, three people pushed the boulder across the exit to seal it.

"Your companion will be fine. She's been paralyzed by venom. My bond, Trikernae, will see to her recovery."

"Are you two the provost and pravost?"

"We are. Please have a seat, Cavalry; then tell us how you arrived here and how you discern who we are."

"Actually, my name is Seth. Cavalry is just a . . . well, an expression. My friend is called Holley."

"And your purpose?"

"Yeah, it's a long story."

"We have a few bouts until your companion regains consciousness. I will hear this story."

"Two folks on Camayah, Rekis and Leetqu, told us you're the preacher for their group and have been hiding on one of the system moons.

"So, you know Rekis and his bond?"

"I do. They're a cool couple."

"If you mean faithful, I agree. What else?"

"Since they hadn't heard from you guys in a while, we told them we'd try to locate you."

"And . . ."

"Here's the skinny: They believe we are sent from Yah to liberate your people and fix this corrupted world."

"Are you?"

"I don't understand your local prophecies. However, we do serve Yahweh."

"Yahweh! How do you know this name?"

"Many believers refer to Him as such."

"I see. Perhaps you are these heralds. If so, this would be wonderful news. As I consider the matter further, please take a walk with me. I have something you might be interested in seeing."

Seth shadowed the provost deeper into the cave. The tunnels smelled musty. Crystals in the walls and ceiling illuminated the interior, bathing it in a greenish glow. They wound through numerous passages, all leading downward. Unlike the gravelly paths near the entrance, the surface felt spongy, as if stepping on moss. They broke into an open area. Ahead of them, a patch of greenery appeared.

"Are those plants, or am I tripping?"

"No, they're real. We call them soreseeds. They come in various varieties: vegetables, maza, editable gourds, and shrubberies. The dark pink berries are my favorite. They are sweet and tart at the same time." The provost picked one and handed it to Seth.

"No thanks. Not right now. I've already taken my nutrition pill this dawn." *Pink berries; why does it always have to be pink berries?*

"Yes, I agree. Probably best to avoid real food when taking Tycozide." Malmach popped the berry into his mouth and smacked his lips, enjoying the taste.

"How to these things survive here?"

"The plants grow rapidly in the green light from Criunite crystals. More importantly, there's humidity in this locale. You can feel the dampness. Soreseeds usually require ground liquids, but they can also draw moisture directly from the air."

"One dawn, Trikernae was digging in the ruins of Sector One for salvage and happened upon the entrance to an old emergency shelter. Inside she found a pouch of soreseed sets. After we escaped the purge and discovered this cave, we planted them. Although only a small garden, it produced enough to survive on for the past two stages. The Dapferon our group accumulated before we departed only lasted two events."

"That explains food; what about drinking water?"

"If you mean hydrew, come see." The provost led Seth to a corner of the cavern. "We dug a shallow hole here. Moisture accumulates and runs down the wall to fill it. There is enough liquid for one ration per dawn for the seven of us. We believe the vapor seeps up from deep fissures and dissipates into the air. Although it's only speculation, we wonder if the quawners survived the Burning by retreating underground and digging holes to release the liquid. Due to the dangers involved, we haven't ventured out to explore their hollows. We stay away from the creatures, and for the most part, they leave us alone. Besides, they're unable to move the heavy stone covering our entrance, even though they have tried many times in past phases."

Malmach dipped his index finger into the pool and rubbed the precious fluid on his lips, savoring the taste. "Not sure if underground hydrew is only found here or if the other two moons have it as well. Our planet may also contain pockets of it in certain places."

"You know, preacher, I'm thinking." Seth walked over to inspect the half-full pool of emerald-colored fluid. "If Camayah has the same conditions and if there are more of those seeds around, you might be able to restore plant life on the planet."

"We believe the RIFTs might have soreseed sets in their secret lockers, along with other things that survived the Burning."

"If there's only one ration of water per day per person, how do you dudes wash or stay clean?"

"Once an event, we use leaves from the maza plants to clean our skin, and then we go outside to let the sunrays remove odors and impurities." Malmach picked a leaf and gave it to Seth. "It makes a good scrapper, too. Take one with you; it might come in handy." Seth added the leaf to his satchel. "We likewise hang our clothes in the sunlight to deodorize them, what's left of them, anyway. Our suits are fairly decrepit now."

"I have more questions; I would—"

"I'm sure you do, Seth, as do I, especially about where you come from. Let's continue this conversation later. I feel we should go back and see if your bond has recovered."

"Holley isn't my bond, just an associate. She is also a doctor."

"I thought all healers perished in the Burning, ages ago."

"She came with us from . . . um . . . a different realm."

"Interesting. Maybe you are the foretold ones. Time will tell. Shall we check on Holley's condition?"

Seth agreed, and the two returned to the central cavern. They found Holley sitting up, talking with Trikernae.

"Seth, you should hear their story. These seven people survived in this tiny cave after escaping unbelievable persecution. It's an amazing tale of faith and determination."

"It's not so tiny, Hol. There are lots of passages in the rear. At any rate, I would love to stay all night and rap, except we hafta dip out and report to our team lead about finding the missing believers. Do you feel you can travel?"

"Yes, but . . ."

"Hol, we'll devise a rescue plan and return soon." The stranded followers heard his comment, too, and smiled. Seth pulled his two-way communicator from his satchel. "In the meantime, we can stay in contact with this radio." He handed the unit to the provost and showed him the settings. "I will try calling you at daybreak on the morrow. Someone will need to go outside to use the transmitter because the signal will probably be blocked due to the thick stone interior." Seth retrieved the medical bag and handed it to Holley. Before moving toward the exit, he nodded to the pravost and said, "Leetqu and Rekis will be happy we found you."

Three individuals opened the entrance and Seth and Holley walked outside. The entire party of castaways, two women and five men, followed them. They stood in the entrance and offered arms-across-the-heart benedictions. Trikernae added, "Blessings to Yah," and then she and the others returned to their hidden cave and slid the boulder to close the entrance.

Seth inspected his shuttle and began to wipe away the excess venom residue from the floorboard with his maza leaf. "Before you do that, let me gather a sample for analysis." Holley scraped off some of the clear substance and put it in a sealed vial inside her medkit. "Okay, I'm ready." Seth finished cleaning off his hoverboard, discarded the leaf, and they climbed aboard. As soon as he adjusted their balance, the two took off and raced toward the portals. This time, Holley hung on tight to Seth. He brought the craft to a stop behind the facility and stowed it in his carrier. Together, they entered the facility and beamed back to the planet, arriving at nightfall.

CHAPTER 15

THE CODERS

Lundy had waited until the three teams departed to search the moons of Camayah before he headed to the host family's residence. Since Rekis and Leetqu's daughter, Rauteira, didn't have *Indo*, she stayed home to work on her datatop project. Lundy walked in, pulled up a stool, removed his binder of coding scrolls, and placed his radio on the table. She was expecting him.

"Well, lassie, how can I help?"

"Do you assemble data equipment?"

"Building processors isn't me specialty. I'm more of a translator of languages and expert in codex. My binder might assist you, though." Lundy slid it over to her.

She unrolled the scrolls and studied them. "This stuff is interesting: special access keys, coding procedures with diagrams and instructions, reverse programming, a series of lines with antidata symbols, and codes that negate other codes. There's even a section on how to build a dataframe called a CPU. Wow, very high tech. Some of this might be helpful once I get my device fully assembled." She replaced the material and slid the binder back to Lundy. "I've been building this thing for two stages, maybe longer. I've scrounged for parts in the ruins, even found a broken screen, which I repaired. Although it doesn't look like much, I believe it could operate if I had a power source."

"You mean a battery?"

"That's obsolete technology, but yes, such a cell could power it. Unfortunately, we are not allowed to openly possess energy modules. The RIFTs consider it a crime. Only Security, programmers, and operators may use them."

"Doesn't sound fair or make sense."

"Agreed. Our *Taeo* and *Indo* rules are despised by most laborers." With a sly grin on her face, she asked, "So, what did you have in mind?"

"This." Lundy handed his radio to Rauteira. "My communicator must have an operating gismo. Can we adapt it for use in your contraption?"

"We'll know in an interval." She turned the radio over, pried off the rear panel with a fork-like tool, and removed a cylinder. "This tube is probably your battery." After a little adjusting, she plugged it into the side of her datatop and tapped a dial on the circular base. The screen flickered several times and then turned solid. "It's active. I knew you were a *sent one*."

"Just call me Papa Lun. Since your computer works, what can you do with it?"

"Not much, really. I could program a game to play or organize my *Indo* lessons. However, if I had a datacomm unit, we could connect to the datastream and perhaps access a few systems at the RIFT."

"Does *Indo* or *Taeo* allow such actions?"

"No, one of many things they forbid." She began pushing symbols on her circular console. "I guess I'm a discontent like my parents."

"Tell me more about these comm thingamabobs."

"Basically, they're transceivers allowing dataframes to connect to the databand."

"Like being online?"

"Ancient terminology, but yes."

"Old Lundy has another idea. I was told this talkie, which we have partially disassembled, has multiband capacity. According to the designer, it can transmit and receive on any band or frequency. Maybe your datastream is another band wavelength . . ."

Before Lundy finished his thought, Rauteira grabbed the radio and removed a rectangular object with seven wires. She reopened her datatop, stripped all the colored wires on the gadget, connecting three to the screen and the other four to various pieces inside her device. She replaced the top panel and tapped the center dial to turn it on. The screen came to life. A line appeared and began to blink. "We're connected to the dataflow. Wow! It's asking for an entry code."

Lundy scanned his binder for passwords. "Here, try this one." He turned the scroll around and pointed to the one at the top of the page."

She entered: *open #7 release @ function #7 codex #7 end.* Almost immediately, the line cleared. *Code Accepted.* "We're in!"

"Can we access the Programming Center from here?"

"No, not Programming. Although we might be able to conduct low-security searches with valid passcodes, accessing the full system would require more energy than this little cell contains. I'd need a TPC."

"What's a TPC?"

"Triverphol Power Core. The modules come in three sizes: Large for mainframes, airships, portal systems, and cranes. Medium for programming terminals, most data equipment, and communications. Small for stunners, lighting, hand scanners, and minor devices. A small core will work."

"Where can we get one?"

"Not sure exactly. But I think the RIFTs have many such cores in their locked storage, along with other supplies they don't provide to laborers."

"If I were to find one of these secret lockers, how would I know what TPCs look like?"

"The modules have a viewing window that gives off a yellow flaming glow. They were developed after the Burning, using Triverphol and other chemicals. Triverphol is highly unstable and exposure to an open core causes the Disease." As Rauteira and Lundy visited, she continued to push symbols, bringing up different windows on her screen. "Forget about breaking into their storage areas. You'd be stunned before getting close and remanded to Holding."

"Me clan brothers may devise a solution when they return from searching your moons. In fact, they should be here soon.

While we wait, show me what types of searches are possible on your wee computer."

"Let's try a basic query." She entered *recent quawner sightings*. The reply came back *Nineteen*. She cleared the search and tried *recent detentions*. The screen flashed *Two*. "I'm wondering, Papa Lun, if your clan will be angry that I disassembled your talkie?"

"Aye, probably. At me, though, not you. It wouldn't be the first time I offended somebody. During my time on earth, I . . . well, never mind. It's nothing to ruffle one's feathers over. I'm sure our team will forget about it once they see what we built with the parts. Besides, we still have four portable transceivers."

CHAPTER 16

STRANDED AND MISSING

Max and Narleen arrived planetside. They exited the Transport Portals and walked outside to wait for the rendezvous. After seeing no one for a while, Max asked his spouse to try the radio. "Better check with Seth to determine his whereabouts or see if he's already recovered Jesse and Anna. If we have to hike, it will take five bouts to reach Rekis and Leetqu's place. It's at least ten ticks away, and we'd be traveling past sundown during quawner activity. I don't want to face anymore of those creatures this dawn."

"Me neither." She felt for her sling, finding the hurler but no stones. A quick scan revealed a few rounded rocks nearby, so she gathered a handful and dropped them into her satchel. Once she had restocked her projectiles, she took out her radio. "Narleen to Seth." No reply. "Seth, answer please." Nothing except static. "Maxie, I don't think these communicators are working properly."

"There must be another reason. Signal interference, or perhaps Seth turned his off."

"Should I try someone else?"

"No, let's move out. We have a long trek ahead of us. We already know Lundy isn't responding. As for Jesse or Anna, they can always contact us once they return to Camayah."

Meanwhile, Jesse and Anna materialized on the portal platform and went outside to meet with the others. It was latedawn, nearing nightfall. They waited for about thirty intervals. Nobody showed. Both used their radios: Jesse called Seth. No answer. Anna tried to reach Lundy's two-way, hearing only static. "I don't understand why these things aren't functioning. The units worked yesterdawn. I think they're broken." With a teasing tone, she added, "Maybe you should have asked for a candle lamp instead, like you did for the Eskaonus mission."

"Funny, Annie, real funny. You mean the one I busted in the hidden cave?"

"Just trying to lighten the mood."

Perturbed, Jesse bit down on his lower lip. "Why don't you check with Narleen? If she and Max don't answer, you might be correct."

"Annabelle to Lady Narleen." No reply. "Jess, this is getting—"

"Annie, where are you guys?"

"At the portals, waiting. Isn't Seth supposed to shuttle us to the residence?"

"That was the plan. Wait a moment . . . Maxie wants to speak to Jesse." Narleen held the radio up while Max talked into it.

"Sir, we tarried at the portals; made contact calls; heard from no one all dawn. Therefore, we decided to hike back. I estimate we're four ticks in front of you. We'll wait for you to close the gap. It'll be safer if we travel in a group, especially with twilight approaching. Leetqu said the quawners are more prevalent at nightfall. Besides, I have the only weapon." Narleen scowled and tugged on his sleeve. "Correction: Narleen also carries a weapon, her sling."

"We copy. On our way. Jesse out."

It was dusk by the time they reached Max's location. Fortunately, the first of Camayah's three moons had risen over the horizon and provided enough light to see as they traveled. Trying to avoid any obvious hollows, they approached the Programming Center. Skirting the facility, the weary partners continued in a southeasterly direction.

Seth and Holley arrived at the portals during nightfall and

waited for half a bout. Since no one showed for the rendezvous, Seth assumed the others had left on foot. With Holley clinging close, he sped off on his hovercraft to search for them. Seeing four silhouettes in the distance, Seth raced up and stopped alongside, scaring them half to death.

"Where have you been? Why aren't you answering your radio?" Jesse's tone revealed his frustration.

"I left it on the moon."

His anger escalated. "What? Why?"

"Don't blow a circuit, JW. I'll explain the whole thing once we shuttle you guys to Rekis and Leetqu's digs. They should hear the story, too."

"I'm sorry, Seth. I'm really tired and let my—"

"No biggie, forgotten. Who wants the first ride?"

"Can you take Nar?" Max asked. "She's still feeling nauseated. It's been a harrowing dawn for her." Annabelle was about to correct him when he added, "And for each of us."

Seth delivered Narleen and Holley, then returned for Jesse and Anna. Max was last. After Seth stowed his hoverboard, he and Max entered the house, finding Lundy and JW in the middle of a tense discussion. Seth decided to wait on sharing the good news about finding the provost and his followers.

"Are you serious, Reverend? You did what with your communicator?"

"Rauteira and I disassembled it and used the parts for her datatop."

Jesse's irritation rose again. "You knew you were to monitor our calls, right?"

"Aye, I made a calculated decision that having a computer was more expedient than your wee walkie-talkie." Lundy swiveled the device around so Jesse could see the working screen. "With her datatop, we can discover more about the current situation here, perhaps even hack into a RIFT or other facility. All we need is—"

"Excuse me for interrupting." Rauteira stood and turned off her datatop. "I'm concerned about my parents. They always stop at the RIFT for *Feyo* prior to coming home, and they're usually here by latedawn."

The dire situation quieted Jesse's exasperation about the

radio, allowing his empathy to return. "Could they be visiting coworkers?"

"No."

"Have they ever been this late?" asked Holley.

"Never."

"Then I'm heading over there to find them."

"I'll go with you, Holley." Narleen darted for the door. Max followed his spouse to the exit to join her.

"Max, please stay here and protect Rauteira and our colleagues," urged Jesse. "You are the only one with a sword. I'll escort the ladies."

"But sir—"

"We'll be fine, Max. Guard those in the house. I'll contact Anna at the first sign of trouble." And the three rushed out.

RIFT III was packed. People had formed a line in the hall, waiting for *Reho* cubicles. The crowd was raucous, high on Cradphenanill. The S3 of the facility stood nearby, monitoring the crowd, holding his trispike at the ready. S2s wandered the perimeter with quispikes at their sides. Jesse, Holley, and Narleen marched up to the counter and presented their DINs to an S1. "Good pleasures to you. Eager for a cubicle, are ya? Well, get in line. Some will open soon."

"Joyous dusk to you," replied Holley. "We're interested in locating two laborers."

"Sure, if there's room in their cubicle, I can work one of you in ahead of the others. Our limit is still three per chamber. Remember to take Cradphenanill tabs before entering." He glanced down at his screen. "I need a code number?"

"We're not here for—" Jesse put out his hand to stop Holley from revealing too much.

"Sorry, sir, we don't have her number," replied Jesse.

"I'll search our database. Name?"

"Leetqu."

"Ah yes, she's been remanded to Holding. L074 has the Disease and if her condition worsens, she'll be sent to Termination on the morrow." The two women gasped yet said nothing; Jesse's neck stiffened as he glared at the S1.

"What about her bond, Rekis?"

"Have a code number?" Jesse shook his head no. "I'll check. It says he has been remanded to Holding under suspicion of being a discontent. L075 is scheduled for reprogramming on the morrow."

The S3 wandered by. "Do you three associate with L075?"

"We sure do; he's our friend."

"Guards!" Instantly, three yellow beams of light struck the advocates and they fell to the floor, paralyzed, barely breathing.

"Bind them and carry them away to Holding."

"Now? Can't it wait until dawn?" inquired one of the S2s. "It's dangerous outside. Quawners are out hunting prey."

"That's your problem, not mine."

Another one asked, "What about their satchels?"

"Take those as well. Let their Security handle this situation." He turned to scan the crowds. "You S2s have your orders. Move out."

Several bouts later, when Narleen and the others didn't return, Max began to worry. "Okay, recruit, assemble your flying scooter. We'll scout the paths around the RIFT and then circle the perimeter. Little doubt they ran into trouble."

"Quawners, ya think?"

"Unknown."

"While you guys are out searching, I'll keep hailing them." Anna pulled out her radio and began calling.

Outside, three moons filled the horizon. One sat overhead, the other two on the right and left. "It must be latedusk. No sign of them anywhere," noted Max. "Let's make one more pass, then head back to see if Miss Anna made contact." Seth leaned left and looped around the RIFT before returning to the residence.

As soon as they entered the door, Anna notified them that neither Narleen nor Jesse had responded to her hails. "What are we going to do now?"

"The lass here has an idea," offered Lundy. "She might be able to access RIFT III on her datatop and search for general information."

Before they could comment either way, Rauteira had already logged into the datastream. "I found RIFT III, except I need another passcode."

Lundy opened his binder and pointed to three. "Try these and see if any work."

The third one released the *hold.* "We're in. Since I know my parents DINs, I will try those first." She entered L074, the code for her mother, and searched for updates. "It says . . ." Rauteira began to weep. "Mother has been remanded to Holding for contracting the Disease. She's scheduled for termination on the morrow." Rauteira quickly entered L075, the code for her father. "The search shows he was also remanded to Holding, under suspicion of being a discontent. He's scheduled for a reset session at Programming on the morrow." She continued crying. Without normal body liquids, there were no tears. "Help me, Papa Lun." Lundy put his arm around her, trying to console her.

"We'll obtain their release, lass. You can count on that."

"Bro, we gotta respond. Can't we storm the castle or something?"

Max paced around the table, sporting a stern face, rubbing his chiseled jaw. "Already working on a strategy, recruit."

"What about Narleen, Holley, and Jesse? Did anyone take note of their IDs?" Lundy asked.

"Their DINs are on their wristbands." Anna tried to cry, except no tears flowed. "I think Jesse's code number is close to mine . . . but I'm not really sure."

Recovering from the shock, Rauteira wiped her moistureless, pastel blue eyes. "Let me try a basic search for your friends." She tried several queries. "Nothing comes up by name. However, it indicates three migrants from Sector Five with temporary DINs were taken to the Holding Area for interrogation."

"Dudes, the bad cops got 'em all. And we better break them out of jail by next dawn."

CHAPTER 17

RAIDING THE RIFT

Discussion concerning the captives proceeded into latedusk. Lundy and Rauteira sat by each other at the table, entering codes and conducting searches on her datatop. Anna perched a stool across from them, studying her tablature and practicing finger positions for her nyeflute. Seth and Max paced around the table, opposite one another. Whenever Seth passed by, Rauteira glanced up at him. Although she didn't think anyone noticed, Annabelle saw her obvious interest in the blond-haired, freckled teenager. Every few circles around the table, Max stopped to see what Lundy had uncovered. On his subsequent loop, he paused to ask Anna questions about which fluted tunes would do what. Occasionally, he gripped Seth by the arm and led him to the corner to talk. Then the circle pattern began again.

Finally, Max stopped pacing and addressed the group. "I realize Jesse is our team leader. However, he's not available to plan the rescue for Rauteira's parents and our three colleagues. Therefore, I would like to carry on in his place. As a military commander, I suggest a three-part operation. First, Seth will transport Miss Anna and me to the RIFT where we'll obtain our Tycozide and Hydru for this upcoming dawn. It should leave us with enough gelt credits to purchase nourishment tablets for everyone else."

"Isn't this our last dawn for courtesy gelts?" Lundy asked.

"Correct. The morrow will be our third dawn. Afterwards,

we must begin working in their flame pits or go without."

"And we'll be required to have permanent DINs implanted in our fingers," reminded Anna.

"Well, laddies, I don't know about you, but this preacher ain't gonna allow a mark on me finger, nor on me hand or forehead. I've read Revelation, and I ain't taking any chances."

"Me neither, Preach."

Before the conversation became sidetracked, Max interrupted the DIN discussion. "Second, Anna and I will search the lower level for weapons and other items. She thinks one of her nyeflute tunes will mask our activities."

"Can you guys find a TPC?" Rauteira asked. She went on to describe the three types of power cores and their uses. "I only require a small one to run my datatop. With the extra power, I can delve deeper into the dataflow, which is essential for hacking purposes."

"We'll try, Rauteira." Max paused to see if there were additional questions or comments before proceeding. "Third, we will return and finalize plans to rescue those in Holding. If we have stunners, it will greatly enhance our chances of success."

"Shouldn't we try to get some sleep?" Anna rubbed her eyes and yawned. "The teams look exhausted from exploring the moons and dealing with quawners."

"Sorry, there's no time for that, Miss Anna. Much strategizing must occur between now and dawn. Besides, we have the second phase of our rescue to organize."

"I really think we should retire for the evening." Max ignored her suggestion. "Alright, since everyone is staying up till dawn, I'd like to practice my music if no one minds."

"Sure, just don't . . ."

She put her nyeflute away after playing the song that causes sleepiness. Lundy and Rauteira laid their heads sideways on the table with closed eyes. Seth dropped to the floor and curled in a ball. Max yawned several times, slumped over on his stomach next to Seth, and began to snore. "I told them they needed rest." Anna smiled to herself. She rose from the stool and wedged herself into a corner, wishing the tune had affected her as well. Like the others, she was exhausted. "I'll wake them in a few bouts. The rest will do them good." She closed her eyes and tried to sleep.

The following dawn, Anna roused the crew early. “Rise and shine, sleepyheads. It’s predawn; time for phase one.” The partners stirred, feeling refreshed. Rauteira lent her tote to Max so he could carry items confiscated from the RIFT and then joined Lundy at the table to conduct more searches with her datatop. Seth asked to borrow Anna’s radio before stepping outside to assemble his hoverboard. When Annabelle and Max were ready, he shuttled them to RIFT III and waited outside, near the rear of the facility.

Once the two went inside, Seth set Anna’s radio to channel one. “Cavalry patrol to Malmach.” He waited an interval and tried again. “Provost, are you there?”

“Is that you Seth?”

“The one and only.” He grinned to himself. “We ran into a couple planetside problems.”

“Explain.”

“Rekis and Leetqu were taken hostage by Security. They’re in Holding. He’s scheduled for reprogramming and she for termination. Three from our party were also captured.”

“Not good. Can anything be done?”

“Yep, we’re gonna break them out of jail. Got a plan hatched. Hafta postpone the moon rescue until we gather all our people.”

“Understood. We’re okay for now.”

“I’ll give ya a jingle on the morrow with the details. In the meantime, pack up and get ready to leave your digs.”

“Will it be safe to return to Camayah?”

“Hope so. Saving your flock is one reason Yah sent us here. Seth out.”

Maximus and Annabelle approached the S1 at the counter and presented their DINs. “Your wristbands expire at dusk, which means no more gelt credits. If you don’t secure jobs or join a mining crew, you’ll starve or die of thirst in less than one event.”

“Thank you, sir,” Max replied. “We have job opportunities pending.”

"Where?"

"At the Holding Area."

"They always need Security. I hear they're shorthanded."

"Good, then our prospects are promising."

"Since you're already here, why not enjoy a *Reho* session? All our cubicles are available at this bout. Let me know if anyone will be joining you two."

"Thank you, sir, perhaps later. We want to use the dispensary to purchase our nourishment tablets before leaving for Holding."

"Fine, move along."

After obtaining doses of Tycozide and Hydru, Anna and Max retained a twelve-gelt credit apiece, so they purchased nutrition and hydration pills for Seth, Lundy, and Rauteira, including two extra doses for emergency rations. They walked past the kiosk and located a stairwell marked Lower Level. Seeing the entry was locked, Max pulled his sword and pried it open. The noise alerted three S2s who came running through the hall with their quispikes aimed at them.

Before they could fire their weapons, Max plugged his ears with his fingers and Anna played the confusion tune. The guards began bumping into walls and into themselves. Afterwards, Anna motioned for Max to unplug his ears. Max stared at the guard's reactions and shook his head no. She nodded yes. He kept shaking his head. Finally, Anna gripped his arms and yanked downward, pulling his fingers from his ears. Max paused, waiting to see if he'd turn into a bumbling fool. Fortunately, he didn't. "I'm not sure how long these effects will linger on the guards," advised Anna, "so we better start searching for these secret storage compartments."

They raced downstairs and noticed dozens of storage units. More Security approached. "Halt or we'll fire." Max quickly plugged his ears and Anna played the same tune again. Like on the main level, the guards appeared confused and began bouncing off walls like pinballs. The duo dodged the men and approached the first entrance, only to find that it contained a keypad. Since they didn't plan on electronic locks, Max stuck his sword into the jamb and wiggled it. The door slid open.

The center space contained sealed crates, stacked halfway

to the ceiling. On the right and left were four cubicles, "Let's check the rooms first. We're looking for stun weapons and power cores." The first one held shelves of pristine jumpsuits, tools, and other gear. Max grabbed two suits, thinking they would offer more protection than the tattered ones Rekis and Leetqu wore. He folded and stuffed them into the tote. Finding nothing else useful, he moved on to the next place.

Anna entered a cubicle with dozens of open boxes containing nourishment tablets. She yelled out, "Max, they have nutrition and hydration pills in here."

"Take the extended-release ones."

She recognized the rounded, single-dose pills their group had been consuming. Bypassing those, Anna sifted through the various containers until finding oval tablets. She gathered three handfuls of Dapferon and Tyhydru. The white cubed ones, which she assumed were Cradphenanill pleasure pills, were left alone. "I retrieved at least a hundred nourishment tablets. Moving on now to search another area."

The third spot yielded data equipment, unusual technology, and TPCs. "Bingo. Just what Rauteira requested." Anna carefully removed a core no bigger than a fist and added it to her satchel.

In an adjacent room, Max found three lockers marked S1, S2, and S3, each containing shelves of stun weapons. The first section was stocked with bospike contact stunners. He left those alone. Wanting long-range weapons for the rescue, he snatched a quispike from the second locker and a trispike from the third. Max looped the gun straps across his shoulder and proceeded to the next location.

The final chamber held an assortment of things; none of them seemed necessary for the raid, except the glowing green crystals. Remembering that Criunite made an effective projectile for Narleen's sling, Max added about twenty pieces to his tote. On the way out, he noticed several rolls of bandages. Max took one, cut off two short pieces of fabric with his sword, and added the remainder to his collection of plunder.

Prior to leaving, Max unstacked the first row of crates and pried open the one labeled maza. Inside were three haversacks. He slit one down the middle with his Gladius. White kernels, similar to corn, spilled out. "These could be soreseeds. Those other crates must be filled with them." Anna seized a handful and dropped them into a pocket inside her satchel.

With their carriers crammed full of items, the pair departed the storage locker, leaving the door open. Max stuffed the pieces of fabric into his ears as they rushed out of the exit. The guards on the lower and main levels were still spinning in circles and bumping into walls. When they approached the front counter, the S1 drew his bospike and told them to halt. Anna played the confusion song once more. The man began to beat his head against the counter like a hammer driving a nail. Not looking back, they exited the facility, boarded Seth's hovercraft, and sped away to the residence.

CHAPTER 18

PRISON BREAK

Max and Anna rushed inside. Seth folded his hoverboard and followed them. The raiding party began unloading their seized spoils. Max unstrapped the two stunners and placed them on the table. Anna distributed nutrition and hydration pills to the others, keeping the extended-release tablets in her satchel. She gave the TPC to Rauteira. "Is this what you requested?"

"Exactly, thank you." After showing the core to Lundy, she began installing it into her datatop. As she worked, Max added the two jumpsuits to the tabletop. He kept the Criunite crystals and roll of fabric in the tote.

"These outfits are for your mother and father. They appear durable, and I hope they offer more protection against the harmful effects of Triverphol exposure. The RIFT had hundreds of them." She inspected the suits before taking them to her parent's quarters. When she returned, Max asked, "May I retain your tote for the rescue operation?"

"It's yours; I have an extra in my sleeping chamber." She gave the open-palm salutation, and then sat at the table by her datatop, tapping the dial to activate it.

Seth reset the channel on Anna's radio and returned it to her. "Thanks for the loan, kiddo."

"Well, are ya gonna tell me why you needed it?"

"Not now. Let's get our people back first and then I'll explain everything."

Anna puffed her lips and frowned at Seth, showing her displeasure. Max watched the exchange, yet said nothing.

While Rauteira reviewed Lundy's binder for passwords, Anna dropped a handful of maza kernels on the table by her. "Are these soreseeds?"

"I have no idea; I've never seen soreseed sets. My parents would . . ."

"Don't worry, lass; we be freeing your mom and dad soon." Lundy picked up the white seeds and placed them into a small metal container located on the wall shelf. "If these things survived the Burning, I'm sure they'll last a couple more dawns."

"Gather around, everybody." Max moved to the center of the room. "The plan for phase two is fairly straightforward. We enter the Holding Area, disable Security, locate and free the prisoners, and escape unharmed."

Max held up the two stunners. "Does anyone have experience firing weapons?"

"When I was a kid, my parents bought me a Red Ryder BB Gun. I was a pretty good marksman."

"Alright, recruit, you get the trispike. I think it has a longer range than the quispike."

"I'll take the other pea shooter."

"Do you know how to discharge a weapon, Reverend?"

"Me figure it out as I go." Max handed the quispike to Lundy and demonstrated how to hold and aim it.

"Finding the entry to Holding could be an issue. Jesse couldn't locate it. The S1 mentioned it has a hidden entrance."

"It's shielded," Rauteira responded.

"Can you release the shield?"

"I can try. I'm already logged into their system. If I can locate the correct dataflow and connect with a valid passcode, I can probably hack their security protocols and make the ingress visible. They will no doubt override my intrusion, so the entry may not be detectable for long, maybe an interval or two."

"Long enough."

"The access will likely have a keypad lock. Since those are set locally, I cannot help with that."

"Understood. See what you can do about the shielded entry.

We'll take it from there."

"Miss Anna." Max paused to formulate his next order before continuing. "Security will soon discover our earlier raid at the RIFT and tie it to this residence. Therefore, I want you to stay here with Rauteira. If they show, which I assume they will, play one of your nyeflute songs. She must not be captured. Without her efforts to release the shielding, we won't succeed." Realizing his comment lacked empathy, he added, "Your safety is important as well."

"I used the invisibility song on Moon Ethade. It kept Jess and me hidden from the quawners. Security at the portals didn't see us until I stopped playing the tune."

"Sounds like the perfect choice." He scanned the room and sensed doubt in his team. Having seen concerned faces on Roman soldiers prior to a big battle, he understood the anxiety his companions felt. Max unsheathed the Gladius and raised it high. "For Yahweh and victory!" The three advocates and Rauteira repeated the battle cry. He gave the shout two more times, waited for their response, and then slid his sword back into its scabbard. "Well, kid, it's time to storm the castle and free the captives. Get your hoverboard assembled and start shuttling our assault squad to the site. Drop us halfway between Holding and RIFT II. We'll approach the rest of the way on foot."

It was earlydawn when Max, Lundy, and Seth arrived outside the Holding Area. The red sun had already risen in the east. They positioned themselves about a hundred strides away, behind a low ridge, and waited.

"It doesn't appear she succeeded."

"Give the lass a wee bit of time, Seth. Hacking computers ain't easy peasy."

A bout passed and nothing. Suddenly, Max bellowed, "Look, the hidden entrance. The battle begins. Follow me!" The three stayed low to remain out of sight and crept forward, forming a line adjacent to the entry. The security guards didn't notice their approach. "Reverend, can you open this keypad lock?"

"I'll give it a go." Lundy tried several passcodes he remembered from his binder. "Sorry, none are working. Should I keep trying?"

"No, we're out of time. The shield is reactivating." Max thrust his broadsword into the bottom frame and pried with all his might. The door slid up. "You two concentrate on the four tower positions. I'll handle the Security in the yard. And try to find cover to avoid being hit by a light stream." Seth and Lundy leveled their lasers and placed a finger on the triggers. "Ready?" They nodded yes. "A sword for the Lord and for the captives." And the three charged into battle.

The yard erupted with the zapping sounds of stunner fire. Green rays rained down from the towers and yellow rays from inside the compound. One landed at Seth's feet. He did a forward somersault to avoid it and aimed his trispike at the farthest tower. A green bolt erupted from his weapon, striking the watchman in the chest. The man dropped below the railing.

Another burst flew toward Lundy so close it scorched the white hair on his head. Lundy dashed to the closest entryway and returned fire with his quispike, aiming at the nearest position. The yellow flash struck the tower too low, missing the sentry. Green and yellow bolts flared in each direction. The guard shot, and Lundy ducked. Lundy shot, and the guard ducked. After more misses, Lundy figured out the timing and the next time the watchman peeked over the rail, he scored a direct hit. The man fell forward, landing on a stoop before rolling off into the yard.

Meanwhile, Max charged forward. The *battle heat* consumed him. He felt strong, invincible. With every stride, the flow of action began to change. The *battle trance* followed. Normal time disappeared. Things began occurring in slow motion. A green shaft of light streaked towards him. He stepped aside. A yellow one followed. He easily ducked to evade it. More flashes, all avoided. The trance deepened; time slowed to a near standstill. Max held his Gladius out in front of his body. Whenever a beam flashed, he bounced it off his blade. Some ricocheted, landing on the ground; others hit the individual who discharged it. One by one, the S2s fell, most paralyzed by their own light beams. More flashes, more misses. A squad of S1s with bospikes raced forward, trying to reach Max. Their run appeared more like a walk. They were hardly moving. He avoided their attacks. Using his sword, he cut their bospikes in half, as easy as slicing butter.

Seth took aim and knocked out the third tower sentry. His next burst brought down the fourth. Lundy's targeting skills improved with each shot. He stunned the remaining S1s as they retreated with their broken bospikes. Soon, the yard was filled with motionless bodies. Seth and Lundy hurried to join Max in the middle of the compound. By the time they approached him, the trance had lifted. Normal time resumed.

"Bro, your moves were incredible. You looked like a Jedi warrior."

"Earth fables, recruit."

"After seeing you today, I'm not so sure."

"Are you okay, Reverend?" asked Max.

"I'm fine. Got me hair singed a bit on top."

"I'm proud of ya, troops, ya done good. You can join my Eskaonite militia any cycle." Max sheathed his blade. "Let's search the holds before Security sends reinforcements. Lundy, take the left. Recruit, on the right. I'll check in the center areas."

A few intervals later, Lundy reported, "These cells are locked."

"Same situation on my end, except I hear yelling inside one of the holds."

"Hang on, kid, I'll be there in a moment. First, I'm gonna check these other cells." Using his sword, Max pried open five holds. The sixth one contained five prisoners, each one gagged, with their hands bound behind them. He hustled inside and removed the restraints. He could see the relief on their faces. They started talking all at once. He put up his hand to silence them. "One at a time."

Narleen embraced him around his waist and wouldn't let go. "Maxie, you were right. I shouldn't have come. I'm really sorry—"

"Shush, you're safe now."

"I'm sure glad you volunteered for this mission," said Jesse as he rubbed his wrists, trying to get the feeling to return. "I thought we were goners." Holley waited her turn to speak. Rekis and Leetqu remained silent and listened.

"It was a team effort, sir. Lundy and the kid made the difference." Max sheathed his weapon. "You're the group leader, sir. What are your orders?"

"Carry on, Captain Maximus. We will follow your lead."

"Then I suggest we exit this facility as soon as possible. I have little doubt that more Security are on the way. We can debrief once we're safe."

"Max, they seized my medkit and our satchels. I think they're locked in the control center, where Security first interrogated us."

"Show me." Holley walked outside the cell but stopped when she saw the carnage from the raid. Bodies lay scattered across the yard. "They are only stunned," Max noted. "However, they won't remain unconscious for long. Therefore, we better hurry."

"Over here, bro," Seth yelled. "There's a dude in this one. He's banging on the door." Max dashed ahead of the others, pulled his broadsword, and pried off the lock. Inside, he found a man who wasn't bound or gagged.

"Who are you, sir?"

"My name is Runess. I've been remanded here for stages. I'm a Security Assistant." Instantly, Seth aimed his trispike and prepared to fire. Lundy came running, holding his quispike at the ready.

"I strongly suggest you explain. And make it quick and short. My associates have you targeted. Why are you a prisoner?"

"Like I said, I'm an SA. I supervised the Airship Dock in this sector. My crew and I were out exploring the southernmost hemisphere, and we saw something we weren't supposed to see. Afterwards, I made a full report to our SL and PM. They ordered us to be taken to Holding. My five-person crew was terminated. The PA tried to reprogram me, several times in fact, except it never took. Not sure why they didn't terminate me as well. Maybe it's because I was an SA. I don't really know. Death would have been better than being a hostage for two stages."

"Where are the other detainees?"

"Gone."

"Which means what?"

"It means they took them to Termination or Programming. Captives don't last long here. In fact, I heard Security moving a group through the yard three bouts ago."

While Max interrogated the stranger, the others caught up. "Is that you, Runess?" asked Rekis. "Your face is scarred, almost beyond recognition."

"Yep, it's me. Security tortured me so many times, I lost count. And they cut off my two thumbs, see." He raised his hands and wiggled the remaining fingers.

"You recognize this man?" Max asked Rekis.

"Yes, he's a Yah follower. We thought him dead."

"Alright, SA, you have two choices. Stay imprisoned or leave with us."

"Easy decision. I'm going with you."

"Max!" Holley pointed to a locked room. "This is their control center."

"Let's have a look-see." He used his heaven-made Gladius and cut the door apart with two blows. Inside were several locked cabinets. One by one, Max pried them open until he found the three satchels. He sheathed his sword and grabbed the carriers, returning the medical one to Holley, the others to Jesse and Narleen.

Jesse opened his satchel and rifled through it. "Everything is here. My radio, however, is in pieces."

"Mine is also damaged," added Narleen.

"How about your medkit, mender, anything missing?"

"No, it seems intact."

"Concerning those broken radios, Rauteira is a smart lass, and she might be able to reassemble them when we—"

"We're not going there, Reverend, at least not yet. The residence is probably under surveillance. I'm open for suggestions, though."

"Security never enters the ruins. They believe the place is haunted by the spirits who died in the Burning," advised Leetqu.

"Jeepers creepers. Is it?"

"Of course not, Seth."

"Good, cause I'm not doing any ghost busting on this trip."

"But the old emergency shelter is still there, buried under a pile of scrap. I'm pretty sure I can find the entrance."

"That's our destination then." Max surveyed the yard to

check the condition of the guards. A few were starting to revive. "Seth, ready your flying chariot. We best shuttle our people out of here." He turned to face Jesse. "Sir, confiscate several of those weapons. We may need them." Next, he glanced at Runess. "I assume you're familiar with stunners."

"All three types."

"Grab a quispike and trispike."

Seth soon had his board assembled and loaded with the first two passengers.

"Okay, troops," shouted Max, "time to retreat to the ruins and locate this shelter."

Seth made three more trips to get everyone. Max and Jesse were last.

From the control center, an alarm began to sound.

CHAPTER 19

HIDING

AS SOON AS the assault team departed, Anna bolted the front door. She realized that wouldn't stop Security, yet it might give her enough time to react. Rauteira busied herself trying to hack into the dataflow at Holding and disable the shielding that hid the entry. Two bouts later, using Lundy's data binder, she finally found a valid passcode. After entering it, she tapped *Release Shielding* on her screen. The reply line said *Accepted.* "This should give them a couple intervals before Holding discovers my intrusion. I hope Max, Seth, and Lundy can save my parents and your friends."

Anna's reply was cut short by a bang at the front door. "Someone's trying to force their way in. Quick, grab your datatop and stand by me." She pulled out her nyeflute and played the invisibility tune. The bolt she had placed across the front entry bent in half, and the door crashed in. Two S2s entered, carrying quispikes.

"See anybody?"

"No, but I thought I heard music prior to entering."

"You consumed one too many Cradphenanill tabs last dusk at *Reho*. You're hallucinating. Search the sleeping chambers while I check the shelves." A few intervals passed. "Well, partner, I'm waiting for your report."

"Nobody's here."

"That's fairly obvious." He held up two vintage jumpsuits and a tin of soreseed sets. "I found this contraband. Our SL will be intrigued when we show him this stuff." He packed the items into his haversack. "Let's go inspect these other housing units. We'll try here again at halfdawn." And the S2s stomped out.

Once Anna was sure the men were long gone, she stopped playing her flute and the two of them reappeared in the room.

"Should I close the door?" asked Rauteira.

"No, leave it as is. When the S2s return, we don't want them to become suspicious."

"How do you think the rescue is going?"

"Time will tell. All we can do is wait and remain hidden."

The group arrived at the ruins after being shuttled there on Seth's hoverboard. The rescue had succeeded, making them all fugitives. Leetqu and Rekis began searching for the abandoned emergency shelter while Max and Runess circled the perimeter to keep watch. Not knowing what signs to look for, Jesse and Seth followed Rekis; Lundy shadowed Leetqu. Narleen and Holley sat down by a crumbled section of wall.

"Mender, I'm feeling really nauseated. Do you have more of those . . ."

"Yes, I have three antiemetic pills left. Take one and save the others for later." Holley pulled out her stethoscope. "Let me listen to your heart and breathing."

"Can you hear the baby?"

"A little too early to detect a fetus with this device. If I had an ultrasound machine, maybe."

"Could you try, please?"

"Sure." Holley positioned the stethoscope on her belly and listened. "No detectable heartbeat, which is normal at this stage of development." Next, she placed the device on Narleen's chest and then on her back. "Breathe deeply, again. Good!" She returned the scope to her medical bag. "Your vitals are fine. Still, it's best not to overexert yourself."

"Easier said than done in our current circumstances."

"Agreed, but please try." Narleen swallowed the antiemetic pill and placed the other two in her satchel. "Did the prison guards provide nourishment tablets?"

"At dawn we were given hydration; nutrition was withheld."

Max walked past. "Is everything alright, Nar?"

"Yes, Maxie, I'm just resting and talking with the mender."

"I found it!" yelled Leetqu. "The shelter is over this way."

The flat, ground-level entrance was littered with pieces of metal scrap, torn solar sails, rocks, and debris. Working together, the men cleaned it off. The access cover was fused to the doorframe, as if it had been heat welded. After repeated efforts to lift the hatch, a crack developed. Max used his sword as a pry bar to open it the rest of the way.

The interior was dark and the air stale. Max entered first. He descended a flight of stairs and placed one Criunite crystal per corner. Green light allowed him to see the rectangular interior. The area was scattered with junk, yet large enough to hold fifty people. The group followed Max inside. Lundy and Rekis remained at the foot of the stairs, holding their stunners. The others gathered together into smaller bunches and talked amongst themselves.

Leetqu and Holley stood opposite each other. "May I see your arms, ma'am?" Leetqu pulled up her sleeves. Her Triverphol Disease had worsened. The yellowish blisters were cracked and oozing puss. Her skin showed decay in spots. "Do you have these conditions on other parts of your body?"

"Sadly, the Disease has spread. My bond told me there were additional rashes on my shoulders; some have blistered. I feel really weak, and I'm beginning to experience muscle spasms in my arms and legs. I'm probably contagious." Runess, who was standing nearby, stepped two strides backwards.

Holley whispered in her ear, "I don't believe this disease is spread through contact." She opened her medical satchel and withdrew a needle, scalpel, and a small container. "May I take a scraping from your arm to analyze? I also need a sample of your blood." Leetqu nodded yes. As soon as Holley had collected the sample and drew blood, she grabbed the last bottle of Helixzon from her medkit. *Should have asked Ottaar for more.* "I want you to put this salve on all your infected areas. I'm sorry the first treatment didn't last longer. This second application should reduce the skin deformities for the time being. Unfortunately, it won't reverse the infection. However, I hope your blood and tissue samples will help me develop a cure."

Leetqu began to remove her suit. "Wait a moment." Holley noticed the men staring in their direction. "Gentlemen, a little privacy, please." Other than her bond, the men turned to face the wall. After Leetqu stripped off her clothes, Holley rubbed a quarter of the healing salve on her back to cover the rashes, and then handed the remainder to Leetqu. She applied the rest to other infected areas on her body. A few intervals later, she redressed. "Okay gentlemen, you can turn around again."

"Isn't she contagious?" Runess asked.

"No! She is not. I'm not sure if Triverphol Disease is a sickness or condition. Either way, I intend to find out and develop a cure."

"There is no cure," replied Runess. "As an SA, I received Floksillin and Ploksillin vaccinations on a regular basis. Even some of our vaccinated Security became infected and had to be terminated to stop the contagion."

"This foolish termination practice must end. Whatever this thing is, it is not spread through contact." Holley's words were forceful, convincing.

"Hey, the doc knows what she's saying. Take a chill pill, Runess. No offence, dude, but I have important news to share that concerns everyone."

Seth moved to the center area. "Hol and I located the provost and pravost on Easteapia, including five of their followers. They were hanging in a cave, filled with glowing green crystals, just like those." He pointed to the ones in the corners.

Upon hearing the news, Leetqu embraced Rekis and kissed his cheeks. He returned the affection. Joy showed on their faces. They crossed their hearts with their arms and repeated the mantra, "Blessings to Yah." Runess forced a halfway smile.

"There's more. Their group found water, I mean hydrew, and they planted a vegetable garden inside the cave."

"With soreseeds?"

"Yeah, it's what Malmach called them."

"On Easteapia?" Leetqu seemed pleasantly surprised. "How much hydrew?"

"Enough for one ration per dawn. Malmach thinks there are

more liquids in the deep hollows of Easteapia and on other moons, maybe even in certain places on Camayah."

"Anna and I discovered a storage room full of seeds in RIFT III," interjected Max. "I suspect other facilities also have stockpiles of them. The crate we opened was labeled maza and contained white kernels, similar to corn."

"That's one of the soreseed plants," confirmed Leetqu.

"Here's the rub, dudes. I told the provost we would come rescue his flock next dawn."

"Seth, we have our hands full at present. I don't see how—"

"Bro, I gave them my word. Isn't this why we were sent here?"

"The kid is right," replied Jesse. "The angel told me our first priority would be to locate and protect the few believers who remain faithful."

"One must always honor their word." Max shook his head, regretting his comment. "It appears my judgment is skewed. Perhaps it would be better if I—"

"Step aside? No way! I asked you to come with us to Camayah. We depend on your expertise for strategic planning and operations."

"Thank you, sir. Then I suggest we return to the residence, check on the welfare of Miss Anna and Rauteira, and then plan a rescue mission from there." Max motioned to Lundy and Rekis. "Go outside and see how close we are to nightfall. It would be best to travel under the cover of darkness."

"Maxie, what about the quawners? Aren't they more prevalent during darkouts?"

Answering first, Leetqu replied, "It's true. Even Security avoids being outside after nightfall for the same reason."

"If so, this is the best time for us to depart. Security won't be watching the house, and we can approach unnoticed." Max scratched his chin as he pondered the best exit strategy. "Seth, can your hoverboard outrun these creatures?"

"As long as we don't stop for sightseeing. From here, I can transport two riders every five intervals. It'll be a cinch."

Meanwhile, back at the residence, Anna held her nyeflute and kept watch as Rauteira conducted searches on her datatop.

Security revisited at halfdawn and again during latedawn. Each time, Anna played her nyeflute to hide their presence. At nightfall, the same S2s conducted a final sweep of the premises.

"The door is still ajar. It doesn't look like the perpetrators have been here."

"Agreed. I think we're wasting our time; we could be enjoying *Reho*."

"Are you sure you didn't hear music as we approached the entry?"

"No. You better taper off on those pleasure pills. You're sounding paranoid. Check their sleep chambers again, while I give this place the once-over."

"Anything?"

"Nothing."

"We're done here. Did you bring sealer tape?"

"Got an entire roll."

"Good, seal the door and let's get out of here. It will be dusk soon, and I prefer traveling before the quawners leave their dens."

The S2s jammed the door shut, sealed it, and then headed for RIFT III. A quarter tick away from the facility, four silhouettes appeared. "Quawners!" The pair began firing their quispikes at them. The yellow beams did little to deter the creatures, so they hooked the stunners to their belts and ran. Venom sprayed. Moments later, they were being carried off in the mouths of two large quawners.

At dusk, the collective left the shelter and spread debris across the entrance to camouflage it. Seth began shuttling people, starting with Rekis and Leetqu. He picked up Holley last.

"Seth, see the hollow on the right. Stop there."

"You gotta be kidding, Doc."

"I'm not. Only for a moment. I want to collect a sample of Foeca."

"I have a bad feeling about this, Hol. Do you remember what happened on the moon?"

"Just do it. It won't take long."

"Wonderful, a fab idea! At the first sign of spider goo, though, we're dipping out." Seth shifted his weight, steered for the hollow, and brought his hoverboard to a rapid stop. Holley disembarked and quickly collected a sample of the sticky, milky substance. The moment she stepped on the board, Seth took off, banked left, and sped toward the housing units. He was about to make another snide comment when she whispered in his ear, "Rule Number One, recruit." Although he couldn't see it, she had a huge grin on her face.

CHAPTER 20

PLANNING

Seth and Holley entered the residence to a noisy discussion. "Close the door, Seth, and come join the conversation."

"In case you hadn't noticed, JW, the entry is broken. Looks like somebody smashed it open with a battering ram."

"According to Anna and Rauteira, S2s have been here four times to search the place. Besides bending the door, the men confiscated two protective jumpsuits and a tin of soreseed sets. They left prior to our arrival."

"Grab a handful of nutrition and hydration tablets." Anna pointed to the table. "They're extended-release tabs. One is Tyhydru and the other, Dapferon. Apparently, we won't be going back to the RIFT for nourishment. We're fugitives now."

As Holley and Seth stocked their satchels with supplements, the group continued their discussions. "Aye, like I was saying, someone should talk with this Program Master chap and see if he will listen to reason. And if he ain't gonna be reasonable, we should nip his precious center in the bud."

"Can we neutralize the Programming Center from your datatop?" Jesse asked.

"No, I don't think so," replied Rauteira. "You must have direct access to the mainframes at the center. And Programming is the most secure place in this sector or any sector."

"Alright, we'll table those concerns until after the lunar operation. This moon rescue is gonna be a doozy to pull off."

"What about Termination?" probed Holley. "How secure is that facility?"

"According to my searches, Termination isn't as secure as Programming. We may be able to hack in and impact their dataflow."

"Well, guys, we must do something. This place is killing people for no other reason than to use their body chemicals to make who knows what. I say crash their system."

"If you mean shutting it down completely, that could create a planet-wide panic. The facility produces nutrition and hydration tablets, Cradphenanill, and vaccinations like Floksillin and Ploksillin."

"What about inserting a computer virus?" Jesse wondered out loud.

"Another ancient tech term, but yes, we could disrupt the termination equipment with antidata. Papa's Lun's coding binder contains several such codes. I will discern more once I hack in."

"Okay, Rauteira, focus your efforts there and keep me updated on your progress."

"Can we cut off communication between the portals?" inquired Maximus. "It would help to mask our movements."

"Even if this were possible, it's not recommended. All communications run through the datastream, which includes the datacomm my device uses. "

"Can't cut the head off of the viper without killing the snake, eh?"

"I'm not sure what you mean, Papa Lun, but it would be counterproductive."

Jesse changed to a new topic. "Lundy thinks you can fix our two radios. We have all the pieces."

"That, I can probably do. Leave the parts here, and I'll try to reassemble them in between queries and searches."

"Hey, dudes, what about the rescue of the provost and his followers on Easteapia?"

"I've got a strategy, recruit. However, it will require a fast-moving assault team of five people." Max went on to briefly outline the plan: "First, secure the portals. Second, force the S1s to transport us to Easteapia. Third, liberate the believers and escape to the planet. And fourth, try not to get killed in the process." Max grinned at his own humor. No one else did. Ending on a serious note, he added, "Those volunteering should expect heavy resistance from Security and the chance of being captured."

"I'm not a soldier, Max, so I've decided to stay here," advised Holley. "Besides, I need to analyze Leetqu's blood and tissue samples to see if I can determine the origin of Triverphol Disease. Maybe I can develop a cure for it. I also have the substances I collected, which I want to examine. Both analyses are important."

"Resolving threats, health or otherwise, is part of our overall mission," acknowledged Jesse.

"And I would like Narleen to assist me." Although Holley didn't actually require a lab assistant, she requested Narleen, mindful of her pregnancy.

"I'm glad to stay and help the mender, except I know little about healing methods."

"Testing samples is simple. I'll teach you how."

"Good, that's resolved. Anyone else? Reverend?"

"I'm remaining with Rauteira to code."

"Annie?"

"I assumed I'd be staying here to play the invisible song in case Security returned. During my downtime, though, I would like to show Leetqu how to make slings from scraps of solar sails. She has several pieces in her sleeping chamber. According to Max, Narleen's sling and the Criunite we confiscated at the RIFT are effective deterrents against the quawners. It seems as if the glowing crystals have properties that can penetrate their hardened skins."

"Great idea, Miss Anna." Max handed her the Criunite from his tote. "Since you were the most accurate slinger in the Eskaonite militia, perhaps you can demonstrate the correct form as well." She thanked him for his praise and suggestion.

After much discussion and debate, the planning session concluded. The bout was late. At the end, Max enlisted Jesse, Seth, Rekis, and Runess for the assault team. While people milled about, Jesse took out his journal and summarized the main proposals:

Addendum

1. Holley and Narleen stay at residence and work on medical analysis.

2. Lundy and Rauteira hack into the Termination Facility.

3. Anna provides cover with her nyeflute songs and shows Leetqu how to make slings from solar sails.

4. Max leads an outfit to rescue the stranded believers. His squad includes me, Rekis, Seth, and Runess.

5. Dealing with the Programming Center waits until the believers are secured.

Before closing his journal, he added a log update:

Entry Fourteen

I haven't posted for several days, I mean dawns. A lot has transpired since my last entry: Two locals, Leetqu and Rekis, never returned home from working in the flame pits. When Narleen, Holley, and I went to check on their whereabouts, we were subdued and confined in Holding, a jail facility. Fortunately, Max and two of our party members stormed Holding and saved us before we were reprogrammed, or worse, terminated. This world is really messed up.

Seth and Holley located the missing Yah believers and their ministers on a moon named Easteapia. We have hatched a plan to remove them from their self-imposed exile. I asked Max to handle the military planning for this and other strategic operations. I don't think we would have been successful without him.

We only have two of the five radios in working condition. One was incorporated into a portable computer called a datatop. The other two transceivers are in pieces. I hope Rauteira, a tech-savvy teenager, can put them back together.

Since my journal entries are seen in heaven, I have a request. We need angelic intervention. As stated in the above addendum, Anna can protect us with her nyeflute songs, namely, the invisibility tune. However, we have no way to hide these exiled believers once we return them to their planet, which is complicated because Security now considers us as discontents.

There's an old emergency shelter in some nearby ruins. Lundy believes it was part of a destroyed temple complex. It does look similar to the ruins along Onnie Passage in Eskaonus. It would only be a temporary hiding place until we can sort things out. Just wondering if a couple of guardian angels can watch over the refugees? If not, we'll make do.

Busy day tomorrow. I better get a couple hours of sleep beforehand. I'm trying to project confidence to my colleagues, but inside I'm worried.

By the time he finished his entry, the family had retired to their sleeping chambers, and the others were settled on the floor, hoping to grab a few bouts of sleep before dawn. Jesse found an empty corner and joined them. Seeing their cramped conditions and fatigued faces, Anna played her favorite nyeflute tune. Within moments, everyone was sound asleep. Exhausted herself, she closed her eyes and drifted off to sleep. A dream sequence began. Strange images and names flashed through her mind:

Hungry forest, great wilderness, wandering traveler
Rivers flowing uphill, empty hollow, hidden city
Burning citadel, sinking ships, broken scepter
Worms in a hole, TREOW, little girl named AliRoot

CHAPTER 21

ANGELIC INTERVENTION

The fruit vendor had just set up his food cart and began arranging his wares. His mobile produce stand featured a rainbow-patterned canopy and the most delicious fruit in Central Heaven. Although his cart could be found on other streets, he preferred Straight Street, next to the Walled Terrace. A crowd of saints were leaving with handfuls of fruit when the Cherubim appeared. The vendor bowed to show his respect for a senior-ranked angel. "Greetings, Uzziel. You haven't graced my stand in a while."

Uzziel viewed the selections. "They all look so delicious. What do you recommend?"

"This one." He pointed to a purple-skinned fruit shaped like a mango. "Fruit from the Tree of Life, of course."

"Are they expensive?" asked the Cherubim with a grin on his face.

"No, they are free, like everything in heaven." Both angels laughed, enjoying the banter. "Tell me, Uzziel, how is this Jesse fellow and his outreach bunch fairing?"

"I'm waiting to find out. Chesedel should be here shortly with a report." As he spoke, a cluster of saints popped into view and approached the cart. As they made their selections, Uzziel stepped aside to give them room. He loved watching the saints enjoy the fruit that God had freely provided. Before they finished with their choices, Chesedel materialized on the other side of the street and walked over.

The guardian angel bowed. “Shalom, Uzziel.”

“And the same to you, elChesed. What do you have for me?”

“Jesse’s last journal entry. Some of it contains good news. A few things, however, concern me.”

“I see. Let’s stroll down Straight Street so we can talk privately.” Both angels nodded to the vendor before departing. “Start with the good news.”

“Jesse writes that Seth and Holley have located the spiritual leaders and five of their followers on a moon where they’ve been hiding due to persecution. The little flock is safe for the time being. Our envoys are planning a mission to liberate them from their self-imposed exile and return the faithful to their planet.”

“Please continue.”

“Due to an earlier incident, Jesse, Holley, and Narleen were captured and imprisoned in a place called Holding. Fortunately, Maximus and two cohorts freed them.”

“Overall, it’s a favorable report. And your concerns?”

“For one, Jesse has asked for angelic intervention.”

“Why?”

“He can’t protect his party and the provost’s congregation at the same time. He has requested guardian angels to watch over the local believers after they’re removed from the moon.”

“You indicated two concerns. What is the second?”

“This Easteapia mission sounds dangerous, even life threatening, and I feel unsettled.”

Uzziel stopped walking and turned to gaze into Chesedel’s eyes, reading his thoughts. “You wish to help them?”

“Since Jesse and the others are my charges, I feel an obligation.” Chesedel handed Uzziel a copy of Jesse’s fourteenth log entry. “There is additional information in the log, including an addendum summarizing their current situation and plans.”

The Cherubim studied both entries. “It says there is an emergency shelter the team plans to use following their rescue operation. Do you believe you can locate this shelter based on the information provided?”

“Yes.”

“Alright, I’ll authorize travel within the outer realms. Take two winged sentinels with you. I will summon them to meet you at the White Pearl Gate. None of you are to pull your swords for any reason. This is not our fight."

"Understood. We will follow the rules for angelic interactions."

"Good. I wish you Godspeed." And Uzziel vanished, leaving a golden trail of light behind him.

Once the Cherubim departed, Chesedel transported to Outreach & Supply. At the main counter, a clerk angel helped a line of saints with their choices. Abdiel stood by the side counter, sorting through merchandise. "Well now, elChesed, I haven't seen you in a while. How are your charges doing?"

Chesedel bowed, showing respect to a higher-ranked angel. "Jesse and his group are facing a few struggles on Camayah."

"So are the people on earth. I heard the Lord recently opened the second seal. But you didn't come here to talk prophecy, did you?"

"No, I seek wisdom and advice."

"Both are my specialties. What's on your mind?"

"Uzziel authorized outer-realm travel for me and two sentinels. We have been assigned to protect the collective and several local believers on Camayah. However, we must follow the rules of non-interference."

"Those rules can be tricky sometimes. What were the Cherubim's exact words?"

"He said not to pull our swords for any reason."

"Aren't all guardian classes authorized to protect believers and offer encouragement?"

"In most cases."

"And Uzziel had no other restrictions for you and the winged ones?"

"None."

"I would say you can still use your angelic powers to protect people, as long as you don't pull your swords to do it." Abdiel paused for a moment to answer a question from his assistant clerk. "I sense you have another concern. What is it, my friend?"

"Since guardian angels normally stay hidden, how do I let Jesse know his request for angelic intervention has been granted?"

"You mean without bending the rules. Hmm . . ." Abdiel paced around the floor, thinking. "I suggest leaving him a token. And I have the perfect item." Abdiel floated up to the tenth shelf, withdrew a small box, and returned. "Go ahead and open it."

"A candle lamp."

"Correct, except it's not just any candle lamp. It is the one Jesse took to Eskaonus."

"You saved it all this time."

"Well, time is relative in heaven, but yes, I figured it would be needed again. And this portable light is the one thing Jesse will recognize, even though he thinks he broke it. Place the lamp in a location he frequents. This way you're not revealing yourself, only leaving a gift. I'm sure he will get the intended message."

"Thank you, Abdiel. May Yahweh bless you."

"He always does. Godspeed on your assignment."

Chesedel popped over to the White Pearl Gate. The two winged sentinels were waiting, and together they entered the portal and departed. A bright light flashed, followed by the sound of thunder.

The three angels streaked through the heavens, unhindered by time, space, or dimension, and arrived in Camayah. It was predawn. The sun hung low, still hidden below the hills in the east. Now that Chesedel had entered the same domain as Jesse, he could hear his thoughts again. They flew to Sector Five and located the ruins Jesse described. A quick search revealed the emergency shelter. Although it was covered with debris, the entrance was easy to identify using their angelic powers of sight.

"You two are stationed here. Hide this entrance from intruding eyes." The protectors hovered unseen above the entrance and spread their wings downward. Instantly, the entryway disappeared, as if it never existed. Chesedel slipped inside and materialized. He noticed the four glowing crystals in the corners and smelled the stale air. He placed the candle lamp in the center of the floor and flipped open the lid. A flame burst forth, giving off a gentle, golden light. The fragrance of frankincense filled the room. *Ah, much better.* He entered the unseen realm again, passed through the ceiling, and faced the cherubs. “I will return after I check on our envoys and the exiled believers on the third moon.”

Chesedel flew to the housing unit where the advocates were staying. He entered their residence and found them asleep. The angel resumed his solid form. He approached Annabelle and whispered into her ear: “Annie, use the nyeflute confidence tune.”

She stirred momentarily and stared at him. “Chesedel, are you really. . .” He gently touched her on the head, and Anna closed her eyelids, falling into a deep sleep.

“Finish your dream, sweet one. Later, it will make sense.” Chesedel dematerialized, rose through the roof, and flew toward Easteapia. He found the cave where the provost, pravost, and their followers were hiding. He passed through the boulder covering the entrance. They were sleeping. Feeling confident he would not be discovered, he materialized in order to minister encouragement. When he finished with the seventh person, he returned to the invisible realm and exited the cave the same way he entered. Once outside, he noticed quawners crawling around the hollows and wondered what had happened to cause them to become so aggressive. They were not created that way.

He returned to Sector Five and hovered above the Transport Portals. Chesedel sensed the upcoming battle, but knew he was forbidden from intervening with his sword. Gazing past the skyline into the atmosphere, he noticed the rotation of the three moons around Camayah and their relative positions to the sun. He waved his hand, causing the largest moon to slightly increase its orbital speed. After one last look at the portals, he flew back to the ruins and thanked the sentinels for their unwavering sacrifice. “I’ll return as soon as I can.” The angel then entered the heavenly dimension, arriving at the White Pearl Gate, where Uzziel awaited elChesed’s report.

CHAPTER 22

MOON RESCUE

In the morning, Anna rose early to study her tablature scroll and found the tune she had dreamed about. She took out her nyeflute and played the confidence song. The effect was immediate. One by one, the collective rose from their slumber with determination showing on their faces. When Anna finished her song, she handed out nourishment pills to those who needed them.

Concerning stun weapons, Seth kept his trispike; Jesse and Rekis were armed with quispikes; and Runess and Max carried trispikes. Since Narleen was staying at the residence, Max gave her the extra stunner and demonstrated how to aim and shoot it. Although not involved in the foray, Lundy retained his quispike for protection.

While the five-person assault team readied their gear, Rauteira plopped down on a stool, powered up her datatop, and accessed the dataflow. Lundy stood behind her, offering suggestions and providing passcodes from his binder. Narleen sat on the stool next to Holley. She watched as Holley opened her medical satchel, removed the samples she had collected, and set up the portable testing device included in the medkit. Since the household only had three stools, Anna and Leetqu knelt on the floor to make slings.

Seth stepped outside to assemble his hoverboard and called for Max to come join him. "What is it, recruit? Having trouble with your board?"

"No, the thing is fairly simple to unfold and prepare for use. I wanted to talk privately with you about Runess. He may be an informant, planted by Security. I don't dig his vibes."

"I have the same concerns about this former SA, who now says he's our ally. Before the dawn is out, we'll discern his true colors. In the meantime, let's keep a close eye on him." They finished their conversation and went inside. Seth asked to borrow Anna's radio and Maximus gave the final briefing. He concluded with one last comment. "Like I said last dusk, we will take the portals first. Our subsequent moves will depend on the outcome. Sir, do you have additional comments?" Jesse shook his head. "Anyone else?"

"I do. A Scripture came to me mind last dusk in a dream. Deuteronomy 32:30 says that one shall chase a thousand and two shall chase ten thousand. Our rescue detachment has five chaps."

"Good word, Preach. I can relate."

The group stood and wished the raiders success. Rekis and Leetqu offered their open-palm salutations. Anna fluted the confidence song again. As with her other tunes, the melody flowed sweet and smooth. When she finished, the assault team marched outside, and Seth began shuttling them to the Transport Portals. It was predawn. The only illumination came from a lingering moon. Those who stayed behind continued to work on their projects and assignments.

Seth dropped Max and Runess near the backside of the portals, then returned with Jesse and Rekis. Thus far, no one had spotted them. Max held his sword at his side, leaving the trispike in his tote. The other four hid their weapons behind their backs. "Okay, squad, this is important. Don't stun the S1s. We need them to transport us to Easteapia. Let's hope our intimidation tactics work. If they don't, we have very few options."

They casually walked to the front and entered the terminal. There were two S1s on duty. One stood at the counter, the other by a monitor. "Present your DINs."

"DINs? DINs? We don't need no stupid DINs," quipped Seth.

"These are the discontents who attacked Holding," shouted an S1. "Halt or we'll stun you." The S1 at the counter darted forward with his bospike in hand. Max raised his sword and knocked it out of the man's hand. The contact stunner slid across the floor, out of reach.

"Max," yelled Runess, "the other S1 is using the comm link to send an alert." Maximus turned, swung his sword, splitting the monitor down the middle with one chop.

"If you don't want this to happen to your necks, I suggest you yield." The S1 standing behind the shattered display, unstrapped his bospike and tossed it to the floor. Both raised their hands in surrender.

Rekis and Max stepped upon the transport platform. Jesse stood guard at the counter while Runess aimed his weapon at the S1s. Seth removed Anna's radio from his carrier.

"Cavalry patrol to provost." No answer. "Malmach, you got your ears on?"

"This is Malmach. My ears are on my head. Why would I—"

"Never mind. Are your followers packed and ready to leave?"

"Yes. We don't have much to bring, other than ourselves and personal items."

"Stellar. I'll be there in a flash. Seth out." Seth handed the radio to Jesse. "You better keep the walkie-talkie. I'll use the other one to call you from the moon after we rescue the provost and his people." Seth joined Max and Rekis on the platform. "Alright, security dudes, three to beam up." Runess watched to make sure the S1 entered the correct coordinates. A moment later, gauges flickered on the equipment behind them, followed by a whirring sound, and the three disappeared.

"Alright, S1s. Sit in the corner and don't move a notch. Runess and I will be watching you." Jesse walked to the control room entrance and peeked out. What he saw alarmed him.

As soon as the three materialized on the moon platform, yellow beams flared and Rekis dropped to the floor. Seth ducked and fired his trispike twice, striking both guards. "I'm not sure that was a good idea, kid. With incapacitated controllers, there's no one to activate the portal for our return."

"Sorry, bro."

"Apparently, Security was alerted and waiting for us."

"Yeah, and they replaced the S1s with S2s."

Max peeked around the corner to see if more Security were lurking before he checked on Rekis' condition. He was lying on the floor where he fell, unconscious, with a bruised forehead. First, Max checked his vitals. "Good, he's breathing." Next, he retrieved Rekis' quispike and stowed it in his tote. "Not the best of circumstances, recruit. Still, it was quick thinking to use your stunner. Otherwise, we would have been neutralized as well."

"What's our strategy?"

"I'm thinking on it. We better retrieve the refugees before more trouble arises." Max sheathed his sword and withdrew his trispike. "I'll guard the door and tend to Rekis. I suggest you assemble your flying chariot inside the lunar lift. Once you reach the surface, take off and fly like the wind. We must assume there will be additional resistance from the mining site supervisors and their minions."

"I'm pretty sure Security can't hit me if I'm moving at full throttle. They haven't so far. I'll see you in a few with the crew."

S3s were waiting as Seth left the lift and began shooting at him. He maneuvered his hoverboard to avoid the green beams, circled left across the barren terrain, and then headed south for the cave. The provost, pravost, and their band of believers were waiting outside.

"Do any of you know how to use a long-range stunner?"

One woman raised her hand. "My name is Tawehna. Before my bond was terminated in the purge, he demonstrated the weapon to me. I can operate it."

"Hop on my board, Tawehna. We gotta clear the way, first. There are several S3s and a handful of S2s blocking our path to the portal."

"How do you determine their ranks?" Tawehna asked.

"Easy peasy. The S3s fire trispikes with green rays and the S2s shoot quispikes with yellow ones." Seth handed the trispike to his lady passenger. "We're gonna do a strafing run to take out the resistance." Glancing at Trikernae and Malmach, he added, "Everything is chill. Don't worry; your flock is gonna be fine. This isn't my first gig." He adjusted his footing to balance the craft for the additional rider. "I'll be back in a flash. Since there are six of you, it will take me three trips to get everybody to the portal lift. Hang loose."

Seth approached the Triverphol mining area and began circling, weaving around green and yellow streaks of light. "Aim for the security guards, not the laborers. Most of those are mindless drones who couldn't care either way."

"Whatever you say, *sent one*." Seth was about to correct her when he was forced to make a quick turn to avoid two laser beams. Now wasn't the time for explanations.

Eight passes later, all the Security was neutralized. "I guess my years of surfing paid off. This was easier than riding a gnarly wave through the pilings at Malibu Pier. They never laid a hand on us." Seth made a quick stop at the lunar lift and dropped off his first passenger. "On the main level, you'll meet an individual over seven-feet tall." Tawehna seemed confused at Seth's terminology. "I simply mean he's a big dude. He'll take care of you until I return with your bros."

With the groundfire eliminated, Seth took his time to shuttle the others. After they were safely delivered, he returned to the cave entrance to gather their belongings. The operation came off without a hitch. In a couple bouts, the seven believers and their gear were safe inside the portal terminal. Seth folded his hoverboard as he rode the lift to the main level. From the hallway, he entered the control room. Rekis remained comatose. Trikernae knelt by his body, tending to him.

"Provost, can I use your radio for a moment?" He reset the channel. "Seth to JW." No answer. "Seth to team leader, please reply." Nothing, except static. "If you can hear me, we have a problem, Houston. There is no way to return to the planet. The security personnel who operate the portal controls are out cold."

"Copy that, Seth. I'll have to get back to you. Runess and I are pinned down and taking heavy stunner fire." Seth heard zap, zap, zap, then static.

Meanwhile, at the residence, Holley used the portable lab included in her medkit to run tests. Narleen mostly watched, occasionally handing the doc various items she requested. Holley ran the blood and tissue samples from Leetqu through her device and recorded the results in an electric tablet. Triverphol Disease showed as an unknown type of radiation poisoning. Not a disease in the normal sense or a virus. The analysis indicated that even mild exposure to Triverphol caused the symptoms to appear. She tried various medications on the samples, retested, yet nothing worked as a remedy.

Holley considered using the healing leaves Ottaar had given her. However, she would need water as a reagent to dissolve the leaves and turn it into a viable serum, which she hoped could be administered by injection. A tea might work, but again, water was needed, and lots of it, especially if she wanted to treat all the infected residents in Sector Five, not to mention the entire planet. *How does one brew tea without water or a way to heat it?*

Lundy and Rauteira sat across the table and conducted searches on the datatop, trying out various passcodes from his binder, hoping to access the dataflow at the Termination Facility without setting off alerts to their intrusion. To Anna, it looked more like two friends playing a video game. The duo laughed as they worked. Rauteira made fun of Lundy's accent. Lundy teased her about her obvious attraction to Seth. At times, Rauteira treated Lundy like a long-lost grandfather.

Anna and Leetqu crouched on the floor adjacent to them. They were using Narleen's sling as a pattern to make more. Leetqu sliced strands of old solar sails using a sharpened piece of scrap metal, shaped like a knife. Anna used another one to cut four holding pouches. They poked holes in the pouches and tied the strands to them on each end. She placed a piece of Criunite in one and twirled it above her head. "Although these are crude, I think they'll work. Let's go outside and sling a crystal to test it out."

She stopped at the entry when she noticed two individuals approaching from the north. "Quick, pick up your things and gather around me." She darted to the table and collected the nourishment tablets. Leetqu recovered the slings and scrap materials from the floor. Rauteira snatched her datatop and placed it in her tote. Lundy stuffed his binder into his satchel and swung the quispike strap across his shoulder. Without sorting them, Holley tossed the medkit items into her doctor's bag. Narleen clutched the other stunner and grabbed her bag. Anna pulled out her nyeflute and began playing a tune. A moment later, two S3s burst through the entry.

"The seal tape is missing. Somebody's been here. Should I search the place for contraband?"

"Why bother. We're here to burn it down."

"Did you see any sign of the S2s who were sent here yesterdawn?"

"No, they're missing. Those two idiots never reported in to the SL. Never trust an S2 if it's an important task." Both men chuckled. "Alright, partner, let's get this done."

"How many Triverphol accelerants?"

"Three should do it. One in each sleeping chamber and a third in the main room. Set the timers for five intervals."

"With a triple charge, won't the adjacent housing units also catch fire?"

"Probably."

"What about the residents?"

"Most are gone, working in the flame pits already."

"There could be children at home."

"Not our problem." The partner placed the accelerants as directed. "Activate those charges and let's move out. I don't want to linger around when this place explodes into a flaming ball." And the men dashed out.

After the S3s departed, Anna quit playing her flute. "We must leave immediately."

"What about our personal items?"

"Sorry Leetqu, you and Rauteira will have to leave them. If we don't go in an interval, we'll all be killed. Take what you're holding and follow me."

"Where?"

"South, I guess. Hurry!" While Anna played the invisibility tune, the allies snuck outside. Five intervals later, Rekis and Leetqu's home erupted into flames. They heard the explosion as they ran.

Both men ducked behind the counter for cover. Green and yellow flashes filled the inner hall. Slowly, the security forces notched forward. "Jesse, set your quispike for continuous discharge or we're going to be overrun."

"How?"

"Instead of pulling the trigger backwards, push it forward." Jesse released uninterrupted blasts of yellow light, striking those who had broken into the command center. Although bodies started to pile up at the entry, the S2s and S3s slowly gained the advantage.

Runess followed suit, releasing continuous streaks of green light. Unexpectedly, the security forces withdrew and closed the main entry door. Jesse peered out from the viewing port. "They're retreating."

"More likely, Security is pulling back to set up a siege perimeter and wait us out."

"Since the skirmish has ended, we better check on our two prisoners."

"I just did," replied Runess. "Their bospikes are on the floor, except they're gone."

"How? Where?"

"Not sure. I assume they escaped. There is a maintenance tunnel on the left. The S1s probably snuck out during the fighting."

"Arrgh! Forget about them; right now, we need to get our people off the moon." Jesse pulled out his radio. "Jesse to Seth."

The reply was immediate. "Are you guys okay? I heard zapping noises before your call faded out."

"Yeah, we're fine. What's your status?"

"We retrieved the seven followers, but our gooses are royally cooked. As soon as we made the moon jump, we were ambushed. Rekis was hit by a laser. He's out cold, wounded too. I had to stun the two portal controllers. We got no way off this rock."

"Stand by." Jesse turned and asked Runess, "Can the moon portal be operated remotely from the planet?"

"Yes, except you must have an override code."

"You were an SA. Do you have one?"

"I did before I was captured. Not sure mine is active."

"Try it. Maybe it still works."

"If the code is accepted, it will only be valid for a couple moments. Once an intrusion is detected by the monitoring department, a local RIFT can have it disabled."

Using the radio, Jesse relayed the information: “Seth, have everyone gather on the portal platform. There’s a slight chance we can operate the lunar portal remotely. We’re gonna try a group transport, but we just have one chance at this.”

Seth replied, “Rule Number Three, JW.” Max smiled at the kid’s response, knowing where the rule originated. Max tucked his trispike into his tote, picked up Rekis, and slung him over his shoulder. Seth quickly gathered the others onto the platform. “10-99, we’re loaded and ready for transport. Let ’er rip.”

Runess entered his old security code and touched *Moon Override* on the screen. Gages flashed red; whirring noises filled the room. Instantly, ten figures materialized on the planetside platform. “Great, it worked; thanks, Runess. You just earned your pay.” Jesse switched his gaze to Max. “Well, Maximus Gallius, how do we get out of this one?”

Max strode to the viewport and stared outside. Dozens of security forces had surrounded the facility. “We’re trapped, sir; perhaps we should consider surrendering . . . wait, something is happening outside. Come take a gander.”

Jesse rushed to the viewing window. Although it was only halfdawn, the sky had darkened. “The moon is sliding across the sun. To me, it looks like a solar eclipse is developing.”

“Not possible! The next one isn’t due for phases,” Runess replied.

“Possible or not, it is happening,” argued Jesse. “If it’s a total eclipse, darkness may give us the advantage we need. Based on the ones in my homeworld, we’ll only have a quarter bout to escape. Runess, can you turn off the lighting from your display?”

“I’ll know in an interval.” Runess tapped a screen icon and the hub and hallway dimmed. Then he tried to cut the lights near the egress. The screen blinked, revealing a fifteen-interval countdown. “Sorry, we only obtained a temporary pause.”

“Long enough. Let’s gather in the hallway and prepare to leave during the umbra, when we will have a brief window of total darkness.”

“How are we gonna see?” several believers asked.

“We won’t, but neither will the guards,” replied Max. The group exited the portal control hub and entered the hallway.

Runess, Jesse, and Seth led the way, holding their stunners at the ready. Max went next, balancing the unconscious Rekis over his shoulder. The others followed, with Trikernae and Malmach bringing up the rear. Halfway to the exit, a side panel opened and the missing S1s crawled out, stood, and discharged yellow rays. Jesse and Runess returned fire, hitting both guards. During the encounter, one of the yellow beams struck Trikernae. She dropped to the floor, face down, unmoving. Malmach knelt beside her and gently lifted her head. She was still breathing. He cuddled her in his arms.

"Do you want us to delay so you can tend to her?" asked Jesse.

"No, let's stay with the escape plan." He lifted his bond off the floor and the party continued on to the outer exit.

"Good, it's not sealed." The hallway lights were off, and outside, the horizon was turning pitch black. "Okay, guys, are you ready? When the eclipse is full, follow me out of the exit. Don't make a sound, even if you trip or fall." Jesse held an index finger to his mouth. "No talking at all, not even a whisper." He chewed on his lower lip as he considered what else to add. "Use one hand to feel along the outer walls to navigate around the facility. Use the other to touch the back of the person in front of you. Those carrying the injured, do the best you can to stay in formation. Once we reach the backside, we will make a run for it. Seth says there are ruins to the north. That is our destination."

By the time they reached the rear of the facility, the shadow covering the sun slipped away. Daylight slowly returned. With Max carrying Rekis and Malmach holding onto Trikernae, the outfit raced forward. After a tick, they slowed their pace.

Jesse kept checking to see if they were being followed, yet there were no signs of pursuit. Apparently, Security believed they were trapped inside the portals. He wondered if their successful escape was pure luck or something more providential.

CHAPTER 23

THE SHELTER

At late dawn, the escapees approached the ruins. Exhausted, they stopped by a collapsed wall to catch their breath. Rekis and Trikernae were still unconscious, so two of the refugees from the moon located a torn section of solar sail and covered them, giving their injured comrades a little respite from the heat. Malmach moved over to tend to them. Maximus, Jesse, and Seth rested for a few intervals, and then stepped aside to confer privately with each other.

Max spoke first. "We were fortunate, sir, the eclipse occurred when it did."

"Yeah, real lucky or maybe it was something else."

"Like what, dudes?"

"Not sure. I think it was more than a convenient coincidence. So, Captain Maximus, what do you propose now?"

"Our options are limited, sir. However, I suggest we shuttle everyone to the emergency shelter as discussed last dawn, wait until twilight, and then deploy out scouts to check on our colleagues at the residence."

"What about security patrols?" Jesse glanced over his shoulder to look for any movement in the distance. "They'll be hunting for us once they discover we're not at the Transport Portals."

"I'm pretty sure I can circle around the barren areas to avoid them," Seth interjected. "It will take longer to reach the hiding place, but it'll be safer."

"Alright, kid, put your hoverboard together and start making trips. Begin with those who have stunners so they can establish a perimeter."

"Runess and I have weapons. We'll do it," offered Jesse.

"Sounds good. I'll stay here and guard the others while Seth makes his shuttle jaunts. After a defensive perimeter is set, we can transport the wounded, then the others. Trikernae and Rekis are immobile, so they must be carried. Their recovery time can vary, depending on the number of stuns they received.

"Hopefully, it will be sooner rather than later."

"With eleven dudes, not counting myself, it will take six trips."

"Thanks, Seth." Jesse patted him on the shoulder. "I'm sure glad we have a speedy craft to ride. I'll go explain the situation to the others."

By nightfall, Seth had delivered the last person to the southern ruins, and the group began searching for the shelter. "Max, do you see the hatch?" Jesse asked. "I know we covered it with debris; the ingress should be around here somewhere." As soon as Jesse and Max drew closer, the two sentinels raised their wings, revealing the entrance. "Here it is. It appeared out of nowhere. Strange!" Several of the men cleared away the rubble. Max opened the doorway and Jesse entered first, followed by the others.

In the middle of the room sat a lit candle lamp, giving off a gentle glow. The interior no longer smelled stale; a sweet fragrance permeated the air. Jesse strode over and picked up the lamp to inspect it. The vessel looked exactly like the one he had on Eskaonus. Max and Seth noticed it immediately. "JW, that's your candle lamp, but I saw you throw it at the knowledge tree in the hidden cave. The thing shattered to pieces. How did it survive?"

"As I've said many times, things from heaven are eternal." Max withdrew his Gladius and waved it in a circle. "Like this blade, even if I could break it, I don't believe it would remain damaged for long. The same goes for your oil lamp." He sheathed his sword and glanced around. The glowing crystals caught his eye. "I guess we no longer require Criunite for lighting." Max collected the crystals from the four corners of the bunker and stuffed them into his tote. "May need these for the slings that Miss Anna and Leetqu are making."

Jesse replaced the candle lamp on the floor and climbed the steps. Once outside, he scanned the area, seeing nothing. "I know you are here, someplace. If you're listening, I appreciate the support." The two winged ones smiled, yet remained in the unseen realm. Jesse waited a moment, then descended the stairs and closed the hatch.

"Sir, with the sun nearly set, the kid and I better check on the members we left behind at the residence. Perhaps we should all relocate here for the dusk. Since Runess has a trispike, he can secure the entrance until we return."

"I have a stunner, too, except I don't think weapons are necessary. I've got a feeling we'll be safe here. I believe the candle lamp was a reply from heaven."

"It may well be. At any rate, we'll be back soon."

As Seth and Max neared the housing area, they noticed puffs of black smoke filtering into the air. The area had a metallic, burnt smell. Drawing nearer, they discovered that Rekis and Leetqu's dwelling was half melted. Two adjacent homes were also destroyed. The other units in the complex remained intact, although covered with blackened soot. People wandered around outside, looking confused. Seth brought his hoverboard to a sudden stop.

Max hopped off the floorboard and dashed into what was left of the abode. Seth followed. "Bro, there is no way they could have survived this blaze."

Heartbroken, Max cried out, "Help me look for their remains." They conducted a quick search, finding nothing other than ashes and melted debris. Max dropped to his knees, overcome with emotion. Seth stood by, saying nothing. Several moments passed before Max arose, slowly shaking his head in disbelief. "Seth, please go check the other units and talk to those who are displaced. I'm gonna circle the vicinity; if our companions escaped beforehand, maybe I can find their trail."

"Max, I don't think . . ." He cut his comment short. "Sure, I'll do that." Seth approached a man and women who were roaming in and out of a melted structure. "Excuse me, folks. Have you seen the neighbors from the adjacent apartment? There were four women, a teenager, and an older guy."

"We serve the programmer," said the man. The woman gave the same reply. Realizing the conversation was going nowhere, Seth scurried on and found a young child standing alone by a burnt house.

"Excuse me, little girl. Do you know what happened here?"

"Security arrived. Ten intervals later, my home was in flames. I was outside playing with this doll." She showed him a handmade figurine. "Mother made it for me from scraps found in the ruins." She tucked it under her arm. "I can't find my parents. Have you seen them?"

"No, I'm sorry, I . . ." Although Seth wanted to say more, he couldn't find the words. He moved down the complex, knocking on the doors of other units. Their responses were similar. Either they said hail to the programmer, or I serve the programmer. Some offered no reply at all. Finding little success, he walked back to his board and waited for Max.

A couple intervals later, Max came running by. "Seth, did you out find out anything?"

"Not really. Max, I am so sorry—"

"I have no time for remorse. Activate your flying cart and let's conduct a full search. I've already covered the local vicinity. We'll increase the perimeter and circle this entire sector. They can't be dead. They just can't be."

They searched for one bout before Seth brought his board to a stop. Dusk covered the land. "Bro, we better head back. It's getting late and the others—"

"I understand the priorities, recruit. Try three more passes. This time, fly farther south. If we see nothing, I'll call off the search and we'll return to the bunker."

On the final pass, six silhouettes appeared in the moonlight. "Quawners!"

"I don't think so, Seth. Move in closer." Max drew his Gladius in case his assumption was wrong.

They found six figures huddled together in a cluster. "Max, it's them. They survived." Seth stopped in front of them. "Any of you dudes thumbing for a ride?"

"I almost fired my stunner at you," informed Lundy. "We thought the shapes racing toward us were either quawners or Security." Anna and Narleen, who had been twirling their slings, put them aside. Narleen rushed toward her spouse. Max sheathed his sword, hopped off the hoverboard, and met her halfway. They hugged each other repeatedly, not wanting to stop.

"Rule Number Three, huh, Max."

"That's right, kid." Maximus reluctantly released Narleen's embrace. "If we don't quit or lose heart, we will reap good things."

"Aye, we're happy you didn't give up on us."

"Truthfully, Reverend, we almost did. The situation felt pretty hopeless. I'm glad we kept searching." Realizing the urgency, Max changed the focus. "Seth and I noted the damage at the residence. We can listen to the details later; right now, though, we better move everybody to the safe haven." Max unsheathed his Gladius. "Start shuttling, recruit. I will stay here and keep watch. Pick me up last."

When the guardians beheld the first two individuals dropped off by Seth, they lifted their wings and revealed the hidden hatch to the refuge. Leetqu and Narleen pounded on the entry. "Open the door; it's us," shouted Narleen." The hinges creaked, and Jesse emerged, along with Runess. "Seth is bringing the others. Long story, but everyone's okay." The men waited outside for the remainder to be delivered. Seth and Max arrived last, and one by one, the group entered the chamber, closing the entry behind them. The angels again lowered their wings to hide it.

Anna and Lundy noticed the candle lamp in the middle of the floor as soon as they entered. "Jess, isn't that your oil lamp from Eskaonus? I thought you broke it?"

"I did. You all saw me toss it against the cloned tree in the hidden cave. The lamp shattered into pieces."

"Me thinks it be the same vessel. Why is it here?"

"I wrote in my journal we needed divine assistance. I believe the candle lamp is a sign my request has been honored. If so, then cherubs are keeping eyes on this sanctum and those of us inside."

Narleen stepped forward for a closer look and waved the air in front of her nose. "I've smelled this fragrance before."

"Aye, that Chesedel is a sly one."

"Who is this person?" asked Malmach.

"Not a person," corrected Anna. "He's an angel of Yahweh."

While several believers discussed the matter among themselves, Holley and Leetqu walked over to see Rekis. Rauteira joined them. Holley checked his vitals and inspected the bruise on his forehead. "He may have a severe concussion."

"Rekis received a stun, as did my bond, Trikernae. Those effects should wear off soon," advised Malmach.

"This explains their comatose conditions. Concerning his concussion, let's keep a close eye on it. If additional symptoms appear, such as headaches, double vision, or nausea, I'll have to treat him." She noticed fresh rashes on Leetqu's face and arms, yet said nothing about it, not wanting to alarm the group. "When your bond wakes, Leetqu, he should avoid strenuous activity."

"Thank you, healer. I will make sure my bond complies."

"You said it was a long story," reminded Jesse. "Let's hear the recap." Anna and Narleen explained the fire and running for their lives. Jesse and Seth responded by detailing the events of the moon rescue. After a couple bouts of rehashing the dawn's events, the collective gathered into smaller subsets. The provost sat by his bond and whispered words of encouragement as he braided her gray hair into a long ponytail. Jesse, Max, Seth, and Runess gathered in a corner to discuss which actions to take next. Lundy, Anna, and Narleen joined the believers as they debated the topic of angels and compared religious dogma. Holley continued making the rounds, diagnosing health issues and visiting with their comrades.

Finally, Anna stood. "Dear friends, it's been a harrowing time for each of us. I think we should take a dawn off. Enact a type of Sabbath. In my land, it was a day to pause and reflect on spiritual matters. And not work."

"No work at all?" asked the provost.

"For the most part, yes, although people were allowed to do certain things and travel short distances. The whole idea was to rest. It's what we need more than anything else. I'm sure our rescue operations can wait at least one more dawn. And if what Jess said is true, then we have divine protection in this place."

"What about finishing the projects we started earlier?" inquired Holley.

"We are not under bondage. I'm sure that finding cures, conducting datatop searches, cutting patterns for slings, and tending to loved ones are allowed. I'm merely saying we would benefit from a little downtime."

"I agree with Anna. I'm wiped. This dude needs a siesta."

"Annabel is wise in these matters. And me bones are plum tuckered out. I could use a short break. What about you other laddies?"

Most of the party agreed. Max frowned, revealing his disappointment. Still, even he understood the importance of resting one's troops prior to a big battle.

Anna opened her satchel and passed out Dapferon and Tyhydru to those who required nutriments. "I suggest you find a nook to bed down in before I play my nighty-night song." The Yah followers had no idea what she was talking about but believed she was a *sent one*, so they complied with her request.

Moments later, everyone was sound asleep. Anna tucked her nyeflute into her carrier and crawled into a corner. Exhausted herself, she closed her eyes and slowly drifted off to sleep.

CHAPTER 24

DAY OF REST

The collective had grown to eighteen individuals. In addition to the original party of seven envoys, it included Malmach, Trikernae, and their flock of five followers; Rekis, Leetqu, and their daughter, Rauteira; and Runess, the former SA.

In the morning, the group awoke refreshed. Rekis and Trikernae had recovered from being stunned, at least enough to sit upright. Unfortunately, the bruise on Rekis' forehead was worse, turning dark purple overnight and doubling in size. Both the pravost and Rekis noticed the odd-looking lamp in the middle of the floor, giving off a golden glow. Without going into detail, Jesse offered a brief explanation, which they seemed to accept. Afterwards, he introduced the moon refugees to the six people they hadn't met. For the next few bouts, the allies intermingled and got better acquainted. Since they agreed to make it a day of rest, the comrades split into smaller cells.

Max and Narleen huddled in a corner and snuggled, whispering to each other. Occasionally, a short giggle was heard. Anna and Leetqu sat together and continued making slings, adding eight to the four they completed last dawn. Rauteira conducted searches on her datatop while Lundy watched. Holley sorted through her medkit, reorganized it, and pulled out her testing equipment. The provost and pravost sat quietly and watched the others. Rekis laid his head in Leetqu's lap and fell back to sleep. Seth joined the moon refugees and entertained them with a story about a huge shark and needing a bigger boat.

Jesse reclined against the rear wall and wrote in his journal.

Entry Fifteen

Our team is resting today. Anna calls it a Sabbath. Not an actual one, since several are working on projects. Holley is analyzing samples and substances, searching a cure for Triverphol Disease. Lundy is coding, and Anna is making slings. Max, of course, is strategizing.

During the moon rescue, we ran into all sorts of problems. Eventually, we retrieved all the exiled believers. When it seemed like certain disaster, a solar eclipse occurred, and we escaped during the darkness of totality. Several locals were hurt by stunner fire, a type of laser beam, but they're recovering.

We all returned safely to the shelter, where I found a heaven-made candle lamp, just like the one I took to Eskaonus. Lundy and Anna believe it's the same one. Whether it is or isn't, the intended message is clear. Heaven heard my appeal for angelic intervention. Although I can't see any angels, I believe they are keeping us safe. I say us, because everyone is staying in the emergency bunker now. The residence we were living in was burned down by security forces. The fire almost killed six partners, but with the help of Annie's nyeflute, the group escaped in the nick of time. With the addition of the seven believers from Easteapia, our collective has grown to eighteen.

We're having a planning meeting later, probably tomorrow, to see what can be done about the Programming and Termination facilities. We want to stop the practice of brainwashing, called reprogramming, and the senseless killing of unhealthy individuals for their body chemicals. Those issues seem overwhelming.

Please thank Chesedel for me. I assume he was the one who left the candle lamp. Besides being an encouraging sign, it will come in handy for light. And it makes this dingy place smell nice.

After Jesse finished, he put his journal away and walked around, interacting with the newcomers. Narleen slipped over to visit with Trikernae and Malmach. Since she was a vice-leader and they were pravost and provost, the three had a lot in common, being mentors in their respective societies. Maximus paced through the refuge, pausing sporadically to scratch his chin. Seeing a frown on Holley's face, he stopped to inquire why.

"Tell me, mender, how is the research going?"

"I'm frustrated, Max. I have tested the tissue scraping and blood sample from Leetqu several times. No matter what I try, I can't find a cure. And to make matters worse, I examined Leetqu earlier and her skin rashes and lesions have returned. She's so weak, she can hardly move, and her muscle spasms are escalating. I'm afraid our friend will die soon unless I find a permanent solution for this Triverphol Sickness. Many residents will. Perhaps even us if we contract it."

"What about Ottaar's healing salve?" wondered Max.

"I already gave Leetqu the two bottles of Helixzon I brought with me. It only provided temporary relief."

"How about the healing leaves?"

"I've considered them. I have a small bag, maybe five or six leaves and a few half pieces in my medkit. However, I need water as a reagent to formulate a serum for testing. I could try brewing a tea like Ottaar does, but then again, it would require water, not to mention a heating stove."

"I may be able to assist with your water request."

Seth wandered by and joined the conversation. "What's happening, Hol? Did your analysis reveal anything nifty?"

"Nothing on the cure for Triverphol Disease. Nevertheless, I learned a few things from the venom sample I collected from your hoverboard. It is a hallucinogenic, similar to LSD, except it's a narcotic with paralytic properties. This is how the creatures immobilize their prey."

"Spider goo is a bummer, for sure."

"Well, there's more. I analyzed the sticky substance I collected near those hollows, which the locals call Foeca. It has the same properties as quawner venom. If Foeca is being added to make Cradphenanill, I can see why the tablets are so pleasurable and addictive."

"Drugs are a bad trip, man. My friends used to take acid. It's wild stuff. Messes with your brain."

"So does Foeca. It's a psychedelic but also a strong narcotic. I believe it to be quawner excrement."

"You're kidding. You mean the stuff is dung?" Seth grimaced, scrunching his face. "I guess we're not only dealing with spider goo but spider poo as well."

"Correct. Here's the good news, though. I might be able to reformulate the venom or Foeca to work as a deterrent or anesthetic. But we would need a way to deploy or spray it at the creatures."

"Let me think on it," Max said. "I may have a few ideas for a delivery method."

"Hey, Doc, do you have something in your medical bag for cabin fever?" Seth grinned, enjoying the jest. "Everybody around here is sick from restlessness."

"I've got a suggestion," replied Anna as she strolled past. "How about a song?"

"I'm down for it. What about you, bro?" Max only shrugged his shoulders. "Gather around, dudes. Annabelle is gonna do a song for us. Her music is always chill."

Anna moved to the center of the room by the candle lamp. "This ballad was written by a boy named David who tended sheep. For those who don't know, sheep are furry, four-footed animals that are gentle creatures. Whereas some call this the shepherd's psalm, it's really a story about a lamb's confidence in his keeper."

She began her medley with a nyeflute prelude. Max quickly covered his ears. Jesse did too. Anna stopped and lowered her flute. "Don't worry guys, this one I composed myself. It won't cause confusion or other wayward effects." She raised the flute to her mouth again and resumed playing. Her piping of notes filled the air with mellifluous music, as quiet as a precious whisper. Then she added the words:

The LORD is my shepherd; I shall not want.
He maketh me to lie down in green pastures:
He leadeth me beside the still waters.
He restoreth my soul:

(Nyeflute Selah)

He leadeth me in the paths of righteousness for his name's sake.
Yea, though I walk through the valley of the shadow of death,
I will fear no evil: for thou art with me;
thy rod and thy staff they comfort me.

(Nyeflute Selah)

Thou preparest a table before me in the presence of mine enemies:
thou anointest my head with oil; my cup runneth over.
Surely goodness and mercy shall follow me all the days of my life:
and I will dwell in the house of the LORD *for ever.*

Anna ended the arrangement with a final interlude. During the verses, the candle lamp's flame grew brighter. The sweet smell of frankincense became stronger and more fragrant. Unknown to Anna, her composition also released Shalom, the peace of God. After her vocal ended, the lamp returned to its normal size.

"Aye, a good one, Annabel. Psalm 23 is one of me favorites."

"Is the Lord you mentioned in the last stanza, called Yah?" Trikernae wondered.

"Yes, I believe it's one of His names. He has many others, too." As a discussion about divine names and titles unfolded, Max opened the hatch and peeked outside. He noticed two moons: one rising, the other setting. "It's nightfall. Apparently, our little Sabbath break has officially ended. Alright, recruit, time to make a night run."

"Where to?"

"One of the hollows."

"Dude, I don't think—"

"Worried about quawners, are ya? We might see a few. Can't let them stop us. Our task is to find water for the doc, and I think I know where we might get some."

"Are you talking about hydrew?" inquired the provost.

"I am." Max removed the trispike from his tote and leaned it against the wall. "Won't need this thing; stunners aren't effective against quawners."

"Perhaps this bucket will help if you locate fluids." Malmach handed Max a pail made from scraps of solar sails. "We used it to draw liquid in our cave. It only holds a few cubes, maybe a half beaker."

"Thanks, provost." He folded the pail in half and stuffed it into his tote. "Let's go, recruit. Better leave your stunner here. It will get in the way." Seth pulled the weapon out of his satchel and placed it next to Max's trispike.

"What if we run into those creepy crawlers?"

"Hopefully, most have left their dens by now. In case we meet a few, ya better grab one of the slings Anna and Leetqu made, and a few chunks of Criunite."

"Max, I don't think going outside during dusk is a good idea," interjected Jesse. The other team members listened to the exchange between Max and Jesse, not offering advice one way or the other.

"Sir, if we don't find water so the mender can develop a cure, Leetqu is gonna die. Isn't our mission to save people?"

"It is."

"Am I not overseeing strategic operations?"

"You are. Nothing has changed."

"Good, then we're going." He glanced at Narleen as she pressed her lips together. Her face showed concern. "Don't worry, Nar, we'll be fine. I have the kid with me." He slapped Seth on his back and smiled. "Okay, recruit, let's move out. I'll give you the briefing on the way."

"Rule Number Two, right, bro?" Seth tucked a sling and three green crystals into his carrier.

"Exactly." And the duo departed the shelter, closing the hatch behind them.

CHAPTER 25

SEARCHING FOR WATER

Once outside the shelter, Seth began assembling his hoverboard. The moonlight provided good visibility. While Max waited for the recruit to finish, he scanned the area. Not seeing any movement, he climbed on the transport behind Seth. After adjusting the controls, Seth asked, "Which hollow?"

"Head east. We'll explore the one next to RIFT III."

Their conversation continued as they cruised along: "What if we encounter Security?" wondered Seth.

"They should be inside their facilities at this bout, concerned about running into prowling quawners."

"Shouldn't we be as well?"

"Maybe, but we have no other choice if we hope to locate water." Max pointed at a cave on the right. "Stop at the entrance." Max disembarked and peeked inside. "Looks clear. Hopefully, the creatures have left their den."

"What's the plan, if you have one?"

"I always have a plan, recruit. Take it slow at first, being cautious. If we hear the quawners—"

"Hold on. What do you mean if we hear?"

"The creatures make a clicking sound prior to spraying their venom. That should give you time to react. At the first click, we best outrun them. How fast can you travel through the tight curves in this cavern?"

"I guess you've never seen me surf the breakers in California. I can thread my way through a rocky shallow, riding a gnarly wave, while doing a hang ten."

"Then I should feel confident." Max slapped Seth on his back and laughed. "From here on out, though, let's keep our voices down." He stepped back aboard and gave the hand signal to advance. The duo entered the hollow and followed the tunnel until Max whispered, "Stop here for a moment."

Seth slowed his hovercraft to a crawl. He pulled out his sling and loaded it with a crystal. "Did you hear some creepy crawlers?"

"No." Max kept his voice low. "I just want to collect more Criunite. This area is filled with it." He jumped off the board and strode to the wall. Max withdrew his Gladius and pried off a large vein. He smashed luminous crystals into dozens of smaller pieces and added them to his tote.

"Bro, you're making too much noise. Quawners, remember?"

"I'm done. We may need these green projectiles before our little outing is finished." He handed Seth several handfuls. "Alright, recruit, stow these crystals with your sling and let's move out."

As soon as they turned the first bend, clicking noises echoed through the tunnel. "Gun it! Now's the time to show me your surfing abilities." Seth pressed on the foot pedal, banked to the left, and then sped forward, barely avoiding two sprays of venom. He weaved around curves and through the straightaways at top speed. They continued the pace until they approached a series of hanging cocoons. "Stop here, kid."

"Dude, I got a bad feeling about this."

"I won't be long. Keep your sling at the ready." Max inspected the five webbed sacks. Below two of them were a pile of bones. Quispikes lay beside the remains. "S2s, no doubt." He wasn't interested in their stunners. The protective suits, however, drew his eye. "These are the same ones I confiscated at the RIFT." Max grabbed both outfits and stuffed them into his tote.

Seth wandered around behind him. Nearby, he spotted a small tin box. Inside were soreseed sets. "I think this container came from the residence. It has the maza seeds you and Anna discovered at the RIFT."

"It would appear the S2s who searched Rekis and Leetqu's

home didn't fare too well afterwards."

"Neither will we if hang here too long."

"Agreed." Max scanned the vicinity, sniffing the air several times. "This section smells musty, and the floor feels spongy. I think we're getting close to water, I mean hydrew. Let's keep going." They climbed back onto the hoverboard and flew down the tunnel. At the junction, Seth veered right. He continued the same pattern at subsequent forks, until they approached an open area where the tunnel ended. In the middle of the cavern was a pool of emerald-colored liquid. Large insect footprints surrounded it. Foeca littered the area.

Seth parked his vehicle and the two disembarked. They stepped carefully on the moist ground, trying to avoid the Foeca, and approached the pool. "Water! Lots of it. You nailed it, bro."

"So it would seem." Max dipped Malmach's bucket into the liquid, filling it about half full. We better . . ." before he could finish his statement, a cluster of quawners approached, making clicking sounds.

"Duck, Max, incoming spider goo." The first spray missed. Seth pulled out his sling and launched a crystal. The creature spun in a circle and collapsed. Max pulled his sword with one hand, hanging onto the bucket with the other. Seth whirled more crystals—all hitting their marks. Within moments, five quawners lay on the ground, incapacitated, no longer a threat.

"Let's fly, kid. We best not be here when they wake."

"Wait an interval. I hafta plant these maza kernels." Seth stowed his sling and raced over to the pool, circled it twice, scattering the seeds along the banks.

"Why did you do that?"

"Because I think they'll grow in the damp soil, under this greenish light. They flourished in the provost's cave on Easteapia." He placed the empty tin in his satchel.

"Perhaps someday we'll revisit this place and discover your garden." Max chuckled at his quip, then sheathed his blade and climbed aboard the flying shuttle. Seth soared through the passages, banking left, then right. "I hope you remember the way to the entrance, kid."

"Me too." As they approached the cocoons, Seth seemed more certain about their direction. Twenty strides past the webbed sacks, the duo encountered more creatures, but they were moving too fast to be hit by their venom. Once outside the hollow, Seth made a beeline to the emergency shelter. The third moon had dropped below the horizon, causing the dusk to be darker than normal.

Even though the bout was late, everyone was still up, waiting for Seth and Max to return. Suddenly, the hatch flew open, and the midnight adventurers entered. "We found hydrew." Max placed the pail in front of Holley. "Will this work for water?"

From her medkit, Holley removed a sterile glove. She slipped a hand inside and dipped her finger into the fluid, bringing it to her mouth for a taste. "It's water, I think, or something similar." Others in the group gathered around to see the discovery.

"And there is more where this came from," added Seth. "The provost's assumption was true blue, I mean green. There's still liquid on this planet, except it is buried deep underground."

"So, mender, can you make a healing leaf serum with this fluid?" wondered Max.

"Hope so. I've never created one, but I'm sure there's a process outlined in my medical manual. I'll have to study it."

Seth chimed in, "What about making a tea like Mender Ottaar does?"

"For tea, a stove is required and a kettle to simmer it in. We have neither."

"Really, Hol, you mean you don't know?"

"What?"

"How to make sun tea." Seth handed the tin box to her. "Use this little container for a teapot, add water, toss in a few leaves, and put it out in the sun for three bouts. You'll have tea the natural way. My buddies and I always made a batch whenever we went surfing."

"You're a genius, Seth." She skipped over and kissed him on the cheek. His freckled face turned red with embarrassment.

"No, I'm just a surfer who loves sun tea."

"I'll make a batch at daybreak and set it outside to steep. We should know by nightfall or the next dawn if the mixture will cure the Disease. I'm so happy I could kiss you again."

"That's okay, Hol, once is enough." Seth sheepishly backed away, his face still flushed.

"Exciting news about locating water," Anna said. "However, it's late and I think we could use some rest. Sounds like a busy dawn on the morrow."

"For me it will. I'm brewing up a remedy." Holley grabbed the pail of hydrew and placed it in the corner. She laid her satchel on top to cover it.

Max, Jesse, and Runess conferred among themselves before adding, "And we have important missions to organize."

"Excuse me for interrupting your important busyness," said the pravost. "I'm wondering if Anna could play her sleeping tune again."

"Not needed this evening, Trikernae. With all the tired faces, I'm sure people will fall right to sleep."

"I want you to, Annabel. After your wee tune, I got the best snooze I've had in ages."

"Me too," said Narleen. "I love your music. It's so calming, and the next cycle I awoke refreshed."

"Yeah, play it again, Sam, I mean Ann." Jesse smiled at Seth's constant use of clichés.

The collective spread out across the barren floor. Soon, everybody was sound asleep, all except Annabelle. She watched as her friends slumbered until she could no longer keep her eyelids open.

CHAPTER 26

THE CURE

Holley and Seth rose before the others. She filled the metal tin with hydrew, took out one of the healing leaves, cut off the tip, and added it to the container. It held sixteen cubes of liquid, about two cups. She left the remaining fluid in the pail, hoping it wouldn't evaporate too quickly.

Seth raised the hatch, and the two went outside. It was predawn; the sun had peeked above the hills. They could already feel the heat rising. "Where should I put it?"

"Anywhere sunlight can warm it." Seth pointed to a gap in a collapsed wall. "Over there looks decent."

"I wish this tin box had a lid."

"Or a kettle top." Seth spotted a small, tattered piece of solar sail, half buried in the rubble. He pulled it free and wiped it off. "Here, use this. At least it will keep the dust out."

"Good idea. How long does it take to make sun tea?"

"Three to four hours on earth. Let's check our batch at halfdawn. That should give it enough time to steep." And together they returned to the bunker.

Inside, the collective had awakened. Lundy and several others were watching Rauteira piece together radio parts. Jesse, Max, and Runess sat in a circle talking. Trikernae still felt ill from the effects of being stunned, and the bruise on Rekis' forehead had tripled in size. Their respective bonds tended to them while they rested. The others were quietly visiting or walking around the cramped shelter to stretch their legs.

"Narleen and I are going outside to practice twirling stones," informed Anna. "Anyone care to join us and learn how to use a sling? We have ten extras, and they seem to be good deterrents against quawner attacks." Five of the believers raised their hands. Anna distributed the slings and demonstrated the proper way to hold and twirl them. "We aren't using our supply of crystals for practice, so you'll need to gather a handful of rounded rocks." The group followed the two women outside and began tossing stones at the forty-lenn range.

Holley plopped down in a corner and opened her doctor's manual to read about making serums and vaccines. She wondered if hydrew's properties were similar to water and if it could work as a reagent to develop a viable antidote. Mostly, she waited for her healing tea to brew in the warmth from the sun.

Seth paced around the bunker until Rauteira caught his eye. She was trying to reassemble their two radios. He stopped in front of her. "Can I help?"

"Yes, I'd appreciate the assistance. These communicators are in dozens of pieces. I'm having a little trouble sorting out which items go with which radios. The security guards tore them apart like ignorant fools."

Seth sat beside her, surveyed all the parts, and wondered why he even offered to help. He was only trying to be friendly. "What do you want me to do?"

"Provide tools when I ask for them. That way, I'll finish sooner."

"Where did you get those tiny gadgets?"

"I made them from scraps of metal I found in the ruins. Pass me the joiner." Rauteira pointed to a mechanism that looked like tweezers with miniature hooks on the ends. "Now, the puller." She indicated an instrument similar to a miniature crescent wrench. The assembly process continued in much the same fashion with Rauteira attaching parts and Seth handing over the tools.

"Seth, can I ask you a few questions?"

"Sure, ask away."

"Is the healer your bond?"

"No, we're simply good friends."

"But she kissed you on the cheek." Seth's face flushed red. "In our sector, if one person kisses the other on a cheek, it means they're prebonded. After they become bonds, like my mother and father did, couples are allowed to kiss one another on both cheeks. Well, of course, other things too. That's how I came into being."

"Hol's kiss was a show of appreciation, nothing more."

"I see. Then you're not prebonded with anybody?"

"No, why do you ask?"

"Oh, just wondering." She pointed to another implement. "Please give me the threader."

"The Camayahnites sure have interesting customs."

"Most are good ones. Are you aware I can bond with someone in two stages? I'll be eighteen."

Not knowing how to respond, Seth said, "Really."

Jesse wandered by, unaware their conversation had become awkward. "How are you two doing? Have you been able to fix our walkie-talkies?"

"All repaired." Rauteira showed both to Jesse. "Although they're assembled correctly, I recommend testing them first. I can make adjustments if necessary."

Jesse checked the channel settings. "All seems to be working fine. Thanks, Rauteira." He placed the units into his satchel.

"Seth assisted me."

"My thanks to you both."

"Since Papa Lun's radio was incorporated into my datatop, I can't remove it without deactivating my device. I still need the band selector to connect to the dataflow. It serves as my datacomm actuator. I'm using the battery, too."

"That's okay. Four communicators are sufficient. And since we require your datatop for searching and coding, leave those items installed." Jesse turned to walk away, then stopped. "What's the word on accessing the Termination Facility?"

"Papa Lun and I think we can temporarily disable the termination cubicles. The operators, however, will probably discover our intrusion and undo the hack soon thereafter."

"How long?"

"Not sure, perhaps two dawns. We plan to use a

sophisticated antidata code from Papa's Lun's binder."

"Will they be able to track your datatop to this location?"

"Unlikely. I applied a masking program."

"Can't the plug be pulled on that whole wicked place?" asked Holley.

"If you mean shutting down the complex, the answer is no. This can only be done by the OL or OA on location."

"I guess we can't just walk in there, not yet anyway. That concern will have to wait." Jesse appealed to Holley, who nodded in agreement. "Alright, you and Lundy go ahead and disable those execution chambers."

At halfdawn, Holley went outside and retrieved the sun tea. The tiny piece of healing leaf had turned the fluid orange. "Time for the moment of truth." She gave the brew to Leetqu. "You get the first drink."

Leetqu took a sip. "Interesting taste, not bitter at all." She returned the tin to the doc.

Holley noticed the level was almost the same, so she passed it back. "Because you have the Disease, you should consume a larger amount." Leetqu downed several more mouthfuls. "Good, I think you ingested a sufficient dose. You're next, Rekis."

He swallowed a single gulp. "Thank you, healer. Since there is a little remaining, can Trikernae have a drink? She's still feeling the effects of being stunned."

"Sure, she's more than welcome."

Trikernae only drank a little. "I'm grateful, *sent one*." Before handing the container back to Holley, she poured a couple drops on her bond's head and rubbed the liquid into his bald scalp. "Malmach used to have long black hair. Maybe the orange mixture will help." Everybody laughed at the thoughtful yet ridiculous idea.

Holley glanced inside and noticed some at the bottom. "Who wants the last swig?"

"I'd like to try the tea," replied Runess. He drained the last of it and licked his lips. "It does taste sweet."

"We should know the results soon, maybe this eve or in the morn." Holley sat the empty tin in the corner by the pail of hydrew. "I have enough water to make one more batch of tea or develop a test serum, but first I have to read up on vaccine development. Thanks for participating in this trial." She offered the open-palm salutation to show her appreciation. "If this process works, we may have a remedy for those infected with Triverphol Sickness."

Malmach climbed the steps and lifted the hatch. With repeated usage, the rusted hinges worked much easier, allowing one person to raise it. He peeked outside, seeing it was nearing nightfall. "Annabelle, since it's not dusk yet, can you sing another one of your ballads?" He rejoined his bond on the floor. "Both Trikernae and I find encouragement in the words and your music."

"Yeah, Annie, do another one." Everyone agreed with Seth, except Max who merely shrugged his shoulders.

"Fine, if you insist, I'll try a medley this time." She pulled out her nyeflute. "These words come from Psalm 27:5–6, a holy book from my land." She began by playing her prelude, a composition she now called the Shalom tune.

For in the time of trouble he shall hide me in his pavilion:
In the secret of his tabernacle shall he hide me;
He shall set me up upon a rock.

(Nyeflute Selah)

And now shall mine head be lifted up above mine enemies round about me:
Therefore will I offer in his tabernacle sacrifices of joy;
I will sing, yea, I will sing praises unto the LORD.

(Nyeflute Selah)

"This second one is from Psalm 63. Although I sang it on the first night in Eskaonus, the words are even more fitting for Camayah."

O God, thou art my God; early will I seek thee:
My soul thirsteth for thee,
My flesh longeth for thee,
In a dry and thirsty land, where no water is.

(Ending Interlude)

The candle lamp reacted the same way it did previously, except this time the flame sparkled while it glowed. The provost stared as the flame doubled in size. "I've never seen anything like this. It's truly a marvel."

"A wee bit more than that," Lundy replied. "It's the anointing."

CHAPTER 27

THE BRIEFING

As soon as the songs ended, the entire group gathered in a circle to make plans for the next mission. They discussed various strategies to enter the Programming Center and how to confront the PM without being stunned or captured. After listening to input from the collective, Jesse, Max, and Runess stepped aside to confer among themselves. When they returned, Maximus commenced the briefing.

"Since we have three trispikes and four quispikes, we can arm up to seven people for the assault team. Five individuals have already been chosen. They are Jesse, Seth, Lundy, Runess, and me. Miss Anna is part of the team, but she's equipped with a sling and nyeflute. I need at least one more volunteer, preferably a shooter."

Malmach raised his hand. "I'll go."

"I'm sorry, provost," lamented Jesse. "We can't take the chance you'll be captured or terminated. You and the pravost are probably the only two spiritual leaders left alive on the planet. We cannot allow your lives to be put at risk. Although I appreciate your willingness to serve, prudence dictates you remain here." Malmach frowned with disappointment. Trikernac smiled, relief showing on her face. "Since you have one of our radios, we can keep you updated as the operation unfolds."

"I'll join the outfit," offered Rekis. "This is my battle as much as anybody's."

"You are a good soldier," Max admitted, "but unless your

head wound heals by dawn or the doc clears you for duty, you'll have to sit this one out."

"I'll be fine." He marched around the room to show off his prowess. "I'm feeling so much better after drinking the tea."

"Doc?"

Holley caught up to Rekis and examined his bruised forehead. "I'll recheck his concussion in the morn and advise you." She returned to her spot by Narleen before adding, "I feel it's in our best interest if I stay behind to formulate a serum for the Disease. I also hope to develop a quawner repellent. Narleen has offered to assist me."

"Jesse and I already assumed this would be your choice, and Narleen's too," replied Max. "Mender concerns have a high priority, as does your research."

Tawehna raised her hand.

"Yes, ma'am. Do you have a question?" asked Max.

"No, I am volunteering for the assault unit."

"I'm sorry, ma'am. We require a—"

"Hold on a second, bro. This lady is one of the moon refugees. She helped me rescue the others by single-handedly stunning an entire squad of Security. She's an excellent shot with a trispike. We gotta have her on the team."

"Alright, Tawehna, you're in. The kid is a good judge of character. We will make weapon assignments later. Moving on to the actual operation, here is our four-phase strategy:"

"First, approach the Programming Center under the cover of darkness. Second, secure the entrance and disarm Security. Third, detain the programmers. Fourth, locate the Program Assistant and enlist his help in confronting the Program Master. If the PM won't hear our concerns and make changes to better the lives of his people, we may have to consider a system-wide shutdown. Lundy can handle that."

"Not in this wee life. Me learned a few things from my coding binder and by watching Rauteira, but not enough to program or hack a computer mainframe. Only Rauteira has such knowhow."

"Papa Lun's words flatter me, and his assessment of my ability is accurate. Therefore, I request to be a part of this undertaking."

"Sorry, that's impossible. It's too dangerous and you're a child," Jesse insisted.

"I'm almost the same age as Seth and he's going." Rauteira looped her arm around Seth's arm. "Besides, he will protect me." Seth raised his eyebrows and tilted his head to one side. He wanted to respond yet remained silent.

"I will defend my offspring as well," added Rekis, "if you allow me to participate."

"Max already said you would have to wait until—"

"Aye, me also." Lundy interrupted Jesse and stood next to Rauteira in a show of support. "If talking to the PM doesn't yield results, then you will need her expertise to access the system mainframes."

Jesse looked at Max, Rekis, and Lundy. All three were nodding their heads. Ignoring their responses, he stomped around the shelter, mumbling to himself. Suddenly, he stopped. "Okay, Rauteira, you can go. If the PM is not receptive, you may be our only hope for a successful outcome." Turning to face Seth, he added, "She's your responsibility. You are to stand by her side at all times during this operation. If at any point her life is in danger, load her on your hoverboard and escape to the shelter. Nothing is to happen to her."

"Understood, JW. I'll keep her safe."

"And Rauteira, do you promise to stay close to Seth and follow his every command?"

She grabbed his arm tighter and stated, "I do."

Jesse walked toward the rear, mouthing the words, "If this goes squirrely, may God help us all." He didn't think anyone noticed his silent muttering.

When he passed Anna, she whispered, "He will."

Jesse paused and stared at her. "Do you hear my thoughts, too?" She just grinned.

Max cleared his throat and motioned for Runess to come forward. "We'll conclude this briefing with a report about the Programming Center. It's your turn, SA." Runess took a knee in front of the group and began:

"Programming has five levels. The first one contains the main entry, service counters, comm terminals, and a security detachment of S1s who only carry contact stunners. Floor two includes reprogramming cubicles, workstations, and research labs. Personnel on this level are not armed. The third has housing for the programmers and their family members. Level Four contains the PA's office and residence. The top section is where the PM lives and works. His quarters are probably shielded. No one I've met has ever been inside."

"Is there additional intel on this facility?" asked Jesse.

"Nothing pertinent, other than mentioning the lower levels have underground storage. I believe those areas also contain design and repair shops for technology. However, I've never been there since it requires clearance from the PM or PA."

"That's the lay of the land, recruits. We have an early start on the morrow. We will conduct a final briefing prior to daybreak. Joyous dusk, everyone." Max stepped aside, stretched out on the floor, using his tote as a pillow, and closed his eyes.

The colleagues knew the eve-time routine: find a comfortable place to bed down and listen to Anna's favorite tune. Moments after she played her nyeflute, the people were sound asleep. Anna moved to a corner and leaned her head against the wall, hoping to get a few bouts of shuteye before predawn.

As she slept, odd images plagued her dreams:

Faceless man, two women weeping, tearless eyes
Ancient crater, emerald clouds, pools of liquid
Flying arks, strange animals, silent noises

CHAPTER 28

PROGRAMMING CENTER

Several bouts before dawn, the group awoke to prepare for the raid at the Programming Center. Holley made the rounds to check on the conditions of those who consumed the healing-leaf tea. Leetqu's rashes were gone, and Rekis' bruised forehead was healed. Trikernae felt stronger as well. Runess' two thumbs had begun to grow back. Even Malmach's balding scalp showed new hair growth.

Max gave the final briefing. He summarized the mission goals and informed everyone that Holley cleared Rekis to join the assault team. Jesse collected the four communicators and redistributed them for the mission. As the lead, he kept one. The other three were given to Seth, Anna, and the provost. Max tore up the bandage roll in his tote and handed two pieces to each member to use as ear plugs in case Anna played a nyeflute song during the raid.

Concerning armaments, Max, Seth, and Runess were equipped with trispikes. Lundy and Jesse retained their stunners from the previous dawn. Max returned the quispike that Rekis had dropped on the moon, and Narleen passed her weapon to Tawelma. As for other measures, Seth checked his supply of projectiles for his sling. Anna did likewise. Since Max preferred using his Gladius, he stowed his trispike, placing it inside his carrier. Rauteira packed her datatop and the coding binder. The crew was ready, as much as they could be.

Before the comrades departed, Leetqu gave her cross-your-heart salutation. The entire collective returned the gesture. Malmach offered a brief prayer to Yah, asking for His safety and blessing. Lundy shared a verse from Romans 8:28 about all things working together for good to those who are called. Anna played the confidence tune on her nyeflute. Then they opened the hatch and went outside.

Predawn was still two bouts away. A half-moon hung in the sky, providing enough light to see the surrounding terrain in shadows. Seth shuttled the team to the Programming Center, dropping his riders behind the facility. With two passengers each time, it took three trips to move the assault party. The fourth transport held Anna and Rauteira.

Once everyone had arrived, the group snuck around the side of the structure. Prior to entering the front entrance, Anna fluted the invisibility tune.

"Did you see the entry open by itself?"

"Yeah, I already asked the maintenance crew to check the keypad. I think there's something wrong with the locking mechanism. You better go close the ingress before a quawner comes in."

"I hope you're kidding." The S1 raced over and manually shut the two doors. "Hey, did you hear music when they first opened?"

"You're working too many late bouts. Fortunately, this dusk shift is almost done. Afterwards, we can head to *Reho*. I have my Cradphenanill tabs ready to go. How about . . ." Suddenly, nine individuals materialized out of nowhere. Six of them were aiming stunners at the S1s. One person held a sword; the other carried a flute. A teenage girl stood nearby.

Max glared at the apparent boss. "I suggest you and your entire squad stand down. Do it now!" Instead of giving an order to his five fellow S1s, the guy rushed forward with a bospike in hand, trying to stun Max. Tawehna fired her quispike and a beam of yellow light knocked the man to the ground. "The rest of you have two choices," Max declared. "Either surrender or get stunned." The five guards tossed their weapons on the floor and raised their hands. "Good choice."

Lundy and Rekis gathered their bospikes and stowed them

behind the main counter. “Runess, is there a place to detain these individuals?” inquired Jesse.

“Yes. Down the hall on the right are twelve holding stalls. The programmers use them to secure discontents prior to reprogramming. The entries have latches on the outside.”

“Perfect.” Jesse carried the unconscious man while Lundy and Rekis marched the others to the first stall. The men were directed inside. “Don’t make any trouble. We will have somebody nearby, keeping watch,” admonished Jesse.” He bolted the door, and the partners returned to the foyer to find Max giving out orders.

“I need sentries on this exit.” Tawehna, Lundy, and Rekis stepped forward. “Thanks for volunteering, legionnaires. You three are my reserve detachment. Try to find heavy objects to barricade the doors and then set up a defendable perimeter.” Max approached the keypad and studied it. “Is there a way to disable this device?”

“I can have it jammed in a couple moments,” replied Rauteira. “Come on, Seth, you can help me.” She grabbed him by the hand and led him behind her. She pulled out Lundy’s binder from her tote and flipped through it, searching for a passcode. In less than an interval, she had the keypad disabled. She looked at Max. “It’s done.”

“Good job, guys.” Max glanced around the foyer. “Seth, I want you to remain here with Rauteira and keep her safe.” He observed Anna standing by herself. “Miss Anna, stay close to the reserve force in case a nyeflute song is warranted.”

“I have my sling, too.”

“Right. Hopefully, neither one is required.” Max pointed his sword at the passageway. “The rest of you, follow me upstairs. We are the advance force.” Trailing behind him, Jesse and Runess climbed the steps leading to the programmer’s area. As soon as they exited the stairwell and entered Level Two, they noticed three programmers sitting at their workstations.

“One is the P3 supervisor,” advised Runess. “The others are P2s.”

“Who are you? You don’t have authorization to be here,” shouted the P3, as he rose to his feet. “I’m calling for Security.” Runess and Jesse aimed their stunners. The supervisor cringed and sat back down. “Please don’t hurt us. We’re unarmed.”

“Then don’t touch your datacomm screens.” Max lowered his Gladius. “Where are the rest of the programmers?”

“A few P1s are readying the cubicles for a group of discontents who will arrive at earlydawn for reset sessions. Everyone else is probably asleep in their living quarters.”

“Alright, P3, move across to the corner and sit. Have your two associates join you.” The men gathered by a nook in the wall and plopped down on the floor. Max assigned Runess to guard them while Jesse rounded up the other ones. He returned with three individuals: two males, one female. “Sit with your friends and don’t twitch a muscle,” ordered Max.

“What do you suggest we do now?” Jesse asked Runess.

“Let me talk with the P3 first. Then we should take them to housing and post a guard.” Runess walked over and pulled the P3 aside. They spoke for several intervals before he returned. “The P3 said he will cooperate and promised to make sure the programmers remain in their apartments, along with their bonds and offspring.”

“Do you think we can trust him?” Jesse studied the P3’s face, looking for tells.

“Yes.”

“How so?”

“Hiehew is a Yah believer. Thought I recognized him when we entered this section. I wasn’t sure until I posed a couple questions. It’s been ten stages since I’ve seen him.”

“Okay, programmers, we’re moving to Level Three,” bellowed Max in his deep voice. “And don’t try anything foolish or you’ll be stunned.” The advance unit marched the six detainees to the third floor. “Go to your residences and stay there. I want no trouble.”

“I’ll make sure everybody complies, sir. You can put your digger away.” Max half-nodded and sheathed his sword. After the five programmers left the hall and entered their chambers, Hiehew made a crossed-arms gesture to Jesse and Max.

“What did you tell him?” asked Jesse.

“That you and Max were *sent ones*. I also showed him my severed thumbs and explained how they had miraculously grown back.” He held them up. “See, they’re almost full length; I even have thumbnails."

"I guess we'll have to trust this guy to keep his people confined until we—"

The radio crackled. "Seth to JW."

"Go ahead Seth. What is it?"

"We're under attack by the bad dudes. A ton of Security just arrived and positioned a mining crane at the front entrance. It has a wrecking ball attached, and they are swinging it, trying to break in the doors. The entry will be smashed open in a few intervals. I've got no way to leave with Rauteira. We're surrounded."

Jesse briefly conferred with Max and Runess. "Max says to reposition the reserve unit to Level Two and establish another perimeter. Try to hold them off. Once a defensive posture is gained, escort Rauteira to Level Three and wait for further instructions. The P3 on the third landing is sympathetic to our cause and has offered to keep the programmers and their families confined to their quarters. If you discover our trust is misplaced, use your stunner to resolve the situation."

"10-4. Understood."

"And if the approach is clear, please call to the provost and update him on the situation. We're at the third level, moving to the fourth to confront the PA. Jesse out."

The reserve outfit dashed upstairs moments before the front doors crashed open. After arriving on Level Two, they pushed a tall cabinet to the middle of the room and tipped over desks and chairs to create a barrier. Anna stood behind the cabinet. Tawehna, Lundy, and Rekis knelt behind the desks and aimed their weapons.

"Should I stay and assist with the defense?" asked Seth, as he readied his trispike.

"No, we have this covered." Saving her limited supply of Criunite crystals, Anna loaded a stone into her sling. "Get Rauteira to safety." Seth grabbed Rauteira's hand and the two bounded up the steps. As soon as they left, the pair heard the zapping echoes of stunner fire.

Green and yellow beams flew past the defenders. They ducked and returned fire, knocking out several attackers. More

Security stepped in to take their places. Anna peeked around the cabinet, released her first projectile, and ducked for cover. Repeating the same tactic, she loaded another and continued flinging stones in rapid succession. More attackers dropped.

"We're not gonna hold them at bay for long." Anna slung another stone, hitting the nearest attacker in the forehead. "There's too many of them."

"Should we retreat?" asked Lundy as he fired off two beams of yellow rays.

Expecting a rushing maneuver, Tawehna switched her quispike to continuous discharge and released a series of uninterrupted blasts. Five guards went down, but more scrambled in to replace them. "*Sent one*, we're being overrun."

"Quick, everybody plug your ears with the fabric Max gave you." Anna waited for them to comply, stowed her sling, and withdrew the nyeflute from her satchel. She played the confusion tune. A moment later, the attackers dropped their weapons and began bouncing off the hallway walls. Some spun in circles, bumping into themselves. Others had blank looks on their faces, not knowing what to do. Anna motioned for her three comrades to remove the earplugs. "We must reposition. Follow me and keep your weapons at the ready."

As the four hustled up the stairs, Anna pulled out her radio. "Annabelle to Jess."

"Go ahead Annie. What's the situation?"

"Security overwhelmed us, and we had to abandon Level Two. The attackers are responding to the confusion tune, so it bought us a little time. What are your orders?"

"Check on Seth and Rauteira. If everything is secure on their floor, continue to Level Four. We'll meet you there."

Seth and Rauteira entered the residential ward and approached an individual who was standing alone in the hallway. Seth aimed his stunner. "Are you the programmer dude?"

"I am."

"The P3 who's helping us?"

"Yes."

Seth lowered his weapon halfway. "Why? What's your angle?"

"Before I respond, I desire a truthful answer. Are you a *sent one*?"

"He is," responded Rauteira. "And Seth is very brave."

"Give me the real skinny, programmer, without the jive-talk. Are you for us or against us?"

"For." The P3 crossed his arms over his chest. "As a Yah believer, the mind wipe didn't succeed. They couldn't reprogram me or take away my identity. I've remained a secret believer ever since. My name is Hiehew."

"Alright, Hiehew, sounds like you're cool." Seth tucked his trispike into his satchel. "What's the lowdown here?"

"This section is locked down. Most of the programmers and their families believe we are conducting a drill. A few suspect something is amiss. Regardless, the people will stay in their apartments until I give the all clear."

Seth pulled out his radio. "Cavalry patrol to Malmach." Static, no reply. "Seth to provost, do you have your ears on?"

Malmach chuckled, "I do. I seldom remove them. What's the mission status?"

"We took the first level but had to abandon it when Security breached the doors. The second is under attack. I'm on the third. The advance dudes are ascending to the fourth to confront the PA. Rauteira is safe. I met a secret believer named Hiehew. He'd make a good addition to your fellowship. The bummer news is that we are surrounded with no way to escape."

"What can I do?"

"Have your followers say a prayer for us. 10-10, Seth."

Max, Jesse, and Runess entered Level Four, finding the doorway open. The area contained a workstation with two monitors. One screen was blinking with a faint red light; the other appeared to be turned off. There were cabinets on the right and a hallway on the left, which led to a side chamber. The door was closed. While the advance force searched the office, the reserve unit arrived. Anna entered first, followed by Tawehna, Lundy, and Rekis. No sooner had they stepped into the room, when a side door opened, and a heavyset man sauntered out.

"Hail to the programmer." He walked to his workstation, sat in a chair, and propped his feet upon the desk. "I've been expecting you. I just received a datacomm message about a band of discontents that raided Programming. Your efforts will fail. In fact, the facility is being surrounded, even as we speak."

"That's Ahboen, the Programming Assistant," confirmed Runess.

"Greetings, SA. I thought I recognized you. Weren't you in Holding, pending termination? Well, no matter. By dusk, all you discontents will be reprogrammed or terminated." The PA reached for the second screen.

"I suggest you keep your fingers away from the screen." Max placed a hand on his sheathed Gladius and patted it.

Ahboen laughed. "What are you going to do, stop me with a digger tool? You're too late. Security will be here momentarily."

"Annie, check his living quarters," Annabelle nodded to Jesse and rushed inside. She discovered two young women, both naked, their hands bound behind their backs. They wore neck collars attached to each other with a metal cord. Their eyes were half-shut as they struggled to stand upright. Anna closed the door and returned to the office space.

"Jess, there are two ladies in there. They're unclothed, bound with cords, and appear to be drugged."

"Ah yes, those are my *Reho* women. They probably overdosed on Cradphenanill tabs."

"*Reho* women are pleasure servants. Most are held against their will," advised Runess.

"Annie, help them get dressed and take off their restraints."

"Gladly. And I'll tend to them until the effects from those pills wear off." Anna returned to the chamber.

"Well, PA, you're out of chances. I strongly suggest you help us." Jesse aimed his quispike at Ahboen's chest.

"And if I don't, you'll stun me, right?"

"He might, but I'm considering a more permanent solution." Max's demeanor changed, his face grew stern, his eyes narrowed. He withdrew his sword and held the blade against Ahboen's neck.

"Calm down. Put that digger away. There's no need to lose your head."

"I was thinking it might be you who does."

"I'll play along. What do you want?"

"To see the Program Master."

"He sees no one, not even me."

"How do you talk with one another?"

"Through the datacomm. In fact, I received several messages already this dawn. One dispatch was about your pitiful assault."

Max glared at Ahboen and then turned to address Jesse. "Sir, can you and Runess lift this stubborn PA to his feet? We are moving to the top section. Lundy, you're with us. Tawehna and Rekis, stay here and guard this landing."

The advance team climbed the passageway and entered Level Five. All they saw was an empty hallway and a keypad on the wall. The area was shaped like a miniature pyramid. No obvious doors.

"So, where is the entrance?"

"It's shielded."

"Enter the code and drop the shield." Max pressed the blade tighter to Ahboen's throat. "Now!"

"Okay, okay, but you'll never get in. The door opens from the inside. Only the PM can release the lock."

"Quit stalling. Enter the code before one of us loses their head. And it's not gonna be me." The PA shuffled over to the pad and punched in a series of symbols. The entry slowly appeared.

A moment later, Max jammed his Gladius into the side doorframe . . .

CHAPTER 29

CONFRONTATIONS

Using his sword, Maximus pried with all his might. Slowly, a crack developed. He continued to wiggle his Gladius until the opening was large enough to squeeze his fingers into the gap. Jesse and Runess joined the effort. After much pulling, the door finally slid to the left. The Program Assistant stood by and watched, curious about what lay inside, but fearful in disobeying the Program Master's order to never enter his quarters. While Lundy held a stunner aimed at Ahboen's back, the PA notched closer to the entrance and took a peek.

The PM's chambers contained a workstation, large monitor, an empty chair behind his desk, and a side cubicle on the left with a closed door. A massive mainframe stood in the middle of the floor and rose upward, touching the apex of the pyramid-shaped ceiling. Various dials and multi-colored blinking lights dotted the monstrosity.

Not seeing the PM in the main enclosure, Max yelled, "Quick, check the sleeping area. Don't stun him, though, we need him coherent." Jesse and Runess raced to the door. Since it was unlocked, they opened it cautiously and entered. A moment later, the two returned.

"Nobody's inside, just an empty apartment." Runess appeared befuddled. "No furniture, no belongings, not even a bed."

Ahboen walked into the bedroom, followed by Lundy. "Well, PA, where is your Program Master?" inquired Jesse in a strained voice.

"I have no idea. I communicated with him thirty intervals ago."

"Is there a transport portal in this place?"

"No platforms I can see. I don't understand it. The PM should be here. If he departed his quarters, he'd have to exit through my level." Ahboen wandered over to the monitor screen. "It shows the alerts he sent about your raid. The Program Master must be here, somewhere."

"Unless the laddie is an invisible man, he ain't present."

Jesse pulled out his radio. "Seth, are you there? Please reply."

"10-2, JW. What's the scoop on Level Five?"

"Undetermined at this time. How are things on the third landing?"

"Hunky-dory. Is the PM dude gonna cooperate?"

"That may be an issue. You and Rauteira better get up here."

"10-4. We're on our way."

Jesse switched to channel two. "Jesse to Annie."

"Go for Annabelle."

"Hey, Annie, what's the situation on Level Four?"

"All secure here. No hostiles. I think they're still dealing with the confusion song I fluted on the lower level. The two intoxicated ladies are lucid now and decided to stay in the PA's residence until it's safe to leave the Programming Center. I advised them to never be tricked into offering their services to Ahboen or anyone else. And to quit taking pleasure drugs. They agreed."

"Good. Thanks for seeing to their welfare. Seth and Rauteira are on their way from Level Three. Once they arrive, try to bar the entry door, and then move everybody to the top level."

"Is there a problem?"

"Not sure at this point."

"Okay, we'll be there shortly."

"Copy." Jesse switched to channel one. "Calling Malmach. Are you there?"

"Yes, *sent one*." Jesse had quit trying to correct the label Malmach assigned him and his team. "What's the situation? Did you find the Program Master?"

"Not exactly. We are in his compartment, except he isn't here. Maybe Rauteira can hack into the mainframe and locate him. Not a lot of time to chat right now; the circumstances are complicated and somewhat fluid. Will update you when I can."

"Understood. I'll ask those in the shelter to keep praying for your safety and success."

"Thanks, Jesse out."

The reserve group arrived and crammed into the tiny space. Jesse motioned for Tawehna and Anna to come closer. "Can you two relieve Lundy? He's been watching the PA to make sure he stays out of the way until we need him." The women pulled Ahboen aside and marched him to a corner. Released from guard duty, Lundy stowed his weapon and joined Rauteira by the mainframe. "Rauteira, can you try to access the PM's computer?" asked Jesse. "We need to determine his whereabouts or other pertinent information."

"On it." She sat down in the chair. "Papa Lun, read me the passcodes from your binder. We'll enter them one by one to see if any unlock the system."

Concerned, Max kept eyeing the exit. "I want a couple people with stunners to watch this entry."

"We'll do it." Rekis and Runess scrambled across to the stairwell and assumed defensive postures.

Max continued to pace the floor, glancing at every nook, thinking out loud. "We gotta have an escape plan if this mission stalls."

Rauteira tried all the passcodes from Lundy's binder. "Only one of these works. It opens a history file, but most of the data is missing. There are no phases or stages, just a general timeline." Jesse moved closer to see the screen:

The Burning: cause undetermined, probable stellar event, animal life perished, hydrew evaporated, vegetation and crops destroyed, few survivors.

Council of Twelve chosen: nine scientists, three leaders.

Triverphol mined for power.

Deadly sickness arises.
Dataflow fixed.
Substitute nourishment developed.
Programming Center reorganized.
Sectors established.
RIFTs reorganized, security protocols required.
DINs mandatory for all residents.
Gelt credits instituted.
Deity worship banned.
Holding Area built for discontents and fanatics.
Termination Facility required for processing chemicals.
Council of Twelve accused of treason and terminated.
Program Master becomes new leader.

"Is there nothing else?"

"No, all other historical entries were redacted or never entered."

"Hmm . . . Are we able to disable this computer or use the datacomm to send messages?"

"Sorry, the system is blocking my queries and commands. A correct password is required."

Jesse crossed his arms and began tapping his foot. "Well, PA, do you have the passcode?"

"No, only the PM has the master code. I doubt you'll be able to hack in without it."

"Papa Lun, can I see your code binder for an interval?" Rauteira flipped through the scrolls twice. "What is this dotted box on the back of the last page? It's blank."

"Let me take a gander." Lundy studied the outline. "I have no idea."

"Dudes, hand it to me." Seth examined the empty space. "You know what I think? This box might contain invisible ink. When I was kid, my friends and I wrote secret messages with lemon juice so nobody could figure out what we were saying. We pretended to be secret agents, like in the James Bond movies."

"Get to the point, recruit."

"Yeah, right. Anyhoo, if you use heat, the hidden message should appear."

"We don't have a heat source in this—"

"Hold your horses, laddies." Lundy began rubbing his fingers rapidly across the empty box. The friction created warmth and a few moments later, a line of code appeared. He smiled. "Try this one."

Rauteira entered *# 777 < y – e – s – h – u – a > release*. She touched *Send* on the screen. Instantly, the monitor screen cleared. A directory appeared. "We're in."

"Find out what you can. I'll be right back." Jesse hurried out of the room and approached the stairs where Rekis and Runess stood watch. "See or hear anything?"

"All's quiet."

"Keep a close eye out. We are pretty much trapped in here." Jesse returned to the main chamber to confer with Max. "Any ideas how to get out of this place?"

"I'm working on it. We have a handful of options, but most of those are bad ones. We may have to force a confrontation to escape. Such a strategy is—"

"Hey guys, I found something really interesting," shouted Rauteira. Other than Rekis, who stayed to guard the hallway, the team members gathered around the monitor. Even Ahboen moved closer to view the screen.

"Apparently, the Counsel of Twelve employed an automated program to maintain dataflow communications. The program gradually grew in power and took over the entire system. It spread false data on the Counsel and ordered Security to imprison and terminate them. There's no one who oversees this place. No Program Master. Never has been. This mainframe is running everything, controlling all the data.

"Oh man, I've seen this movie before. It never ends well. You mean the programmer dude is AI?"

"What's that?" Ahboen asked.

"Artificial Intelligence," replied Anna. "This world has been duped."

"Ya think?"

"What do you want me to do, Jesse?" Rauteira continued to enter commands, pulling up additional information.

"Shut the thing down. No wait. Can we send out a planet-wide dispatch?"

"I believe so."

"Set up a comm link while we work on the message. So, what do you have to say now, Mr. PA?"

"I feel stupid for—"

"You are." Jesse cut off his answer. "Here's the crucial question: Will you help us? People know who you are. Perhaps they'll listen to your appeal. In case you're undecided, the correct answer is yes."

"Sure, I'll try."

"No tricks or you'll be sorry. Do you understand?"

"What do you require of me?"

"Total cooperation." After a short discussion, the party decided on a series of messages. "Rauteira, I'll dictate the alerts to you; put them out in the name of the Program Assistant." Jesse glared at the PA. "You got a problem with that?" Ahboen shook his head no. "Good!"

Alert 1: *Discovered the Program Master is a fraud. He does not exist.*

"How can we tell if there's a response?" Jesse asked Rauteira.

"It should show on the datacomm."

The group waited for several intervals. "Anything?" probed Jesse.

"Nothing."

Alert 2: *The PM is a runaway data program, not a real person.*

No replies.

Alert 3: *RIFT's are ordered to stand down and withdraw security forces from the Programming Center.*

No responses.

"Can we stream pictures or add a video link?"

"Absolutely. There are four image recorders." Rauteira pointed to devices in each corner.

"Your turn, PA. Step in front of this camera and make a verbal appeal. I want your face shown across this whole planet. And afterwards, we will upload a video of the interior, showing the PM's empty abode, the mainframe, and all of us." Jesse tapped Runess on the shoulder. "Please stand next to the PA. Some people may recognize you as being a Security Assistant from the Airship Dock. The rest of you gather behind Runess.

Alright, Rauteira, run the live feed."

"This is Ahboen. You know me. As you can see, I am standing in the PM's residence at the Programming Center. He is not here. Never has been. He is not a real individual. We've been betrayed—me, most of all—and I am ashamed to have fallen for this deception. By my side is Runess, the former SA in charge of the docks. He has been reinstated and promoted to SL." Surprised and more than a bit distrustful, Runess maintained a blank expression, not confirming or contradicting Ahboen's pronouncement. The PA put his arm around Runess and drew him close as if they were best friends. "And now, consider these following images."

Jesse motioned for Rauteira to begin the video. When it ended, the PA spoke again. "All RIFTs are hereby ordered to stand down. Unless there is compliance, all gelt credits for Security personnel will be deleted."

Rauteira kept her eyes glued to the display. Finally, a message popped onto the screen, followed by others:

RIFT I, will comply. This is Cndrek, SL for Sector One. I'm ordering the RIFTs in my section to stand down. Security forces are to return to their facilities . . . I just noticed the big guy in the feed. If he wants a job as my SA, have him stop by and see me.

Raetila, SA from RIFT II. We're standing down.

RIFT III, standing down.

Welcome back, Runess. Airship Dock awaiting your orders.

RIFT VII, standing down.

RIFT X, standing down.

Transport Portals, will comply.

Security at Holding, standing down.

RIFT XIII, all personnel have yielded.

The replies kept coming. Rauteira stood and grabbed Seth by the arm. "It looks like all the RIFTs are reporting in, including the new one from Sector Five. Nothing yet from the Termination Facility."

"We'll deal with Termination on the morrow," replied Jesse. "Okay, Maximus, now what?"

"Somebody oughta call the provost and give him an update. Then we best leave this place. But first, Rauteira should delete the complete database."

Overhearing the conversation, Rauteira entered an antidata code from Lundy's binder. It took several intervals, but it eradicated the program, including secret files and backups. After the screen cleared, she sent another code to overwrite the entire partition. "It's done. The PM has been terminated."

"What about me?" asked Ahboen.

"You're coming with us. You can grab your things on the way out. On the morrow, you can help us deal with Termination. Sounds like they're going to be a problem."

"Alright, troops, let's start working our way through the levels. And keep your stunners at the ready. There may be rogue Security still hanging around." Following Max, the allies exited the room and descended the steps, heading to Level Four. Tawehna and Anna walked behind Ahboen, gently nudging him along.

CHAPTER 30

UNDOING THE DAMAGE

The group entered Level Four. Anna checked the PA's sleeping quarters and discovered it was empty. The two women Ahboen had confined and drugged were gone. While the PA gathered personal items from his workstation and chamber, Jesse pulled out his radio to contact the provost.

"Jesse to provost, come in please."

"Malmach here. What's the situation? Favorable, I hope. Seth called earlier and said your team was surrounded and asked us to pray."

"I'm glad you did. Some things have resolved. Others are pending. No one was hurt in the operation. I can't wait to tell you the whole story. Right now, though, we have to wrap things up and depart this facility. Should be at the shelter by nightfall."

"Any surprises?"

"Yes. Several you will hardly believe. I'll explain later. Jesse out."

"Alright people, we are moving down to the third section." The partners descended the stairs and entered the residential ward. Hiehew was standing in the hallway as he promised. No other individuals were present.

"What's the situation here, P3?"

"The programmers and their families are in the living quarters, awaiting the all-clear. Most of them believed it was only a drill. I didn't try to correct their perception."

"That was probably wise." Jesse lowered his weapon and

slung the strap over his shoulder. "Give them the release signal, then choose two trustworthy programmers and follow us to the next landing. There's work to do." Three intervals later, Hiehew returned with two associates, and the party moved on to Level Two.

"The security forces are gone, Jess, including those who were stunned in the earlier skirmish," noted Anna. "The confusion tune must have worn off, and they left." Being vigilant, Max posted Runess and Tawehna at the exit to keep watch, just in case the situation changed.

Jesse gathered the others in a circle around him. "Listen up, folks. Time to undo this brainwashing, starting with the programmers."

"It's not possible," stated Ahboen. "Once someone's identity has been wiped, it can't be restored."

"Incorrect, sir," Hiehew replied. "Files on those who have been reprogrammed are stored in our database. Reversals have been done before, mostly to repair errors in the identity wipe."

"Can you do it, I mean, restore a mind?" Jesse asked, as he pointed to his forehead.

"I've never seen the process myself. Perhaps if I had—"

"I can help," Rauteira interjected. "Papa Lun's coding binder describes many processes. We should be able to adapt them for correcting the damage."

"I'm not sure you should stay here, Rauteira. The current situation is untenable."

She grabbed Seth's arm. "Seth can protect me." A squinted face indicated Seth felt awkward with the arrangement.

Lundy raised his right hand. "I'll watch the lass."

"As will I. She is my offspring."

Jesse chewed on his lower lip as he pondered his reply. "This reversal process may not work, and even if it does, it could take a while to deal with the kinks."

"We have extra sleeping quarters available upstairs," advised the P3. "If your specialists are allowed to help me, I will see to their needs. And we have comfortable beds."

"You know, laddies, old Lundy is tired of sleeping on hard surfaces. I'd appreciate a wee cot to put me head on."

"Hmm." Jesse strode about in a circle, trying to make up his mind. *Decide, Jesse; they're watching you.* "Alright, Rauteira, because your father and Lundy have promised to stay here with you, it should be fairly safe."

"I will remain, too. My assistance might be required."

"Sorry, Ahboen, not gonna happen. I doubt you've had a come-to-Jesus moment."

"What's that?"

"A change of heart." Jesse stopped pacing and stared at the PA. "Until I discern your true intentions, you're with us. Besides, I'm counting on your cooperation at Termination."

"If Preach and Rekis are hanging, I can go with you guys, right?"

"I'm sorry, Seth, I gotta leave you here. Your quick thinking, courage, and adaptability are invaluable. I'm sure Max would agree."

"I do. The kid is the best recruit I've ever had. And I've trained hundreds."

Jesse continued, "And you have a radio, so you can provide regular updates on this mind-restoration progress."

"You can cut the psych, dudes; I'll stay."

"Excuse me for interrupting," said Runess, "but I would like to return to the Airship Dock. Since I'm a supervisor again, I may be of more value there."

"Sir, if Security has recalled their forces, I would like to tag along with Runess, at least for a dawn or two. If you let us borrow a communicator, we can keep in contact."

Anna removed a radio from her satchel. "Max can have mine." Having never operated one, Maximus turned it over in his hand a couple times to examine it, and then stuffed the device into his tote.

"How are you gonna get there?" pressed Jesse.

"Walk. It's not far. We should be there prior to nightfall."

"What do I tell Narleen? I'm sure she's expecting to see you."

While Max hesitated, Runess answered the question. "Tell Narleen her bond will pick her up in an airship in the morn. I'll give the two bondmates a short tour of the northern sectors. If you need them for whatever reason, I can fly them back within bouts. And they can room in the captain's cabin. It will be like another bondedmoon."

Max smiled, intrigued with the idea, realizing he had been inadvertently ignoring his spouse. "Sounds tempting. Due to our mission priorities, I haven't spent much time with Nar."

"Have you ever sailed in a ship?"

"Several times. I rode the waves in Roman galleys and once in a Bireme."

"Never heard of those types. Our airships sail the skies, not liquid waves, and if outfitted with solar sails, the heavens."

Max nodded to affirm his interest.

"First, let's see what the situation reveals on Level One," advised Jesse. "If everything is secure, you two can depart for the docks."

"Before you leave, you better take these projectiles for your sling." Seth gave Annabelle a handful of Criunite from his carrier. "These glowing crystals are a quawner's worst nightmare."

Seth watched longingly as his friends scurried downstairs, leaving him behind. "Don't worry Seth; I'll keep you company," consoled Rauteira, as she gripped his arm even tighter.

The main area appeared empty. The front entrance was smashed apart, doors crumpled, debris scattered across the floor. Maximus checked behind the side counter and in the hallways. "No one's hiding." He raced across to the holding cubicles where the S1s were detained. The door was unbarred and the captives gone. "It may be a trap," warned Max.

"I don't think so, but keep your stunners at the ready." Jesse peeked outside, seeing no one. "The way looks clear. Okay, Max, you and Runess are released. It seems the military part of this operation has concluded. Now it's time for diplomacy."

"We'll rendezvous next dawn, sir. And don't say anything to Nar about the airship. I want it to be a surprise."

"Will do." Runess and Max offered their farewells, marched through the exit, and turned north. Jesse, Anna, Tawehna, and Ahboen followed them out and headed south. It was latedawn.

A few bouts later, Jesse's party approached a series of

hollows. They circled left to avoid them. By nightfall, they were in sight of the ruins, and the travelers quickened their pace, keeping their eyes glued to the horizon. The group was unaware that a cluster of quawners had tracked them at a distance, once they passed the hollows. Anna heard faint clicking sounds and stopped to listen. That's when she noticed silhouetted shapes racing toward them. "Quawners!"

Jesse and Tawehna aimed their stunners. "Those weapons won't stop them." Anna pulled out her sling and loaded a piece of Criunite. "Get behind me and try to avoid the venom." More clicking sounded, followed by sprays of venom. Ahboen ducked, barely avoiding being hit.

Anna launched a crystal at the closest creature. As the quawner dropped to the ground, she loaded another crystal and released it. Four more tosses in rapid succession subdued the rest of the cluster. Afterwards, six quawners lay sprawled on the ground. Three were still moving their legs, yet all were disabled, no longer a threat.

Jesse stared at the aftermath. "Wow, Annie. I forgot how effective you were in Eskaonus with your sling."

"Seth taught me the basics. Speed and accuracy came with practice. I can teach you the form if you're interested. I have five extra slings."

"Thanks, I'll think on it." *I'm sure she meant later*. "Well, gang, we better reach the emergency shelter before these creatures awake and renew their assault. The ruins are only a quarter tick away."

The group ran the rest of the way, opened the bunker's hatch, and entered. Everyone was eager to hear what happened. Jesse gathered them around him. First, he detailed the mission results and then introduced Ahboen. He let the PA explain how a maintenance program assumed control after the Burning and became the Program Master.

Needless to say, the allies were shocked by the revelation and had many questions. Ahboen answered their queries with long drawn-out replies, always justifying his innocence. When Jesse corrected the PA's story with the actual facts and his complicity in the matter, Ahboen sneered at him. Jesse responded with a stern glare.

Narleen broke the tension when she asked, "Where are the others?"

"Seth, Rekis, Rauteira, and Lundy are staying the dusk at the center to begin the process of deprogramming individuals," advised Jesse.

"What about Maxie?"

"Oh yeah, Max said to tell you he'd see you at firstlight. He has a surprise for you."

"Like what?"

"All I can say is you two will spend a little quality time together." Narleen frowned, disappointed, wanting to know what Jesse meant, yet relieved her spouse was safe.

"So tell me, Holley, how did the research projects go?"

"I successfully developed a healing remedy, except I need additional hydrew to produce more. And Narleen and I created quawner bombs, made from Foeca. It's what we named them, anyway. We rolled the mixture in sand to give it weight and let it dry in the sun. These small projectiles contain the same compounds quawners use to paralyze their prey. If a creature is hit near its eyes or mouth, the released compound will cause them to sleep for bouts. The effect is similar to a general anesthesia. We can demonstrate the process on the morrow. It's like throwing a dirt clod. It explodes on contact."

"Sounds really interesting." Jesse yawned and rubbed his eyes, trying to remain attentive. "Sorry, guys, I'm wiped. It's been a harrowing day, and I need to hit the sack soon. I suggest we all find a place to bed down."

"You mean I'm sleeping on the hard ground?"

"That's right, PA. Just like the rest of us. Your dawns of luxury are over. And in the morn, you and I are heading to Termination to resolve that situation."

"Can I come along?"

"Yes, Hol, I was hoping you would. Being our medical expert, you are the best advocate for this task. Since this is a diplomatic undertaking, we don't wanna scare the operators by arriving with a large crowd. I think a team of three should be sufficient. Besides, we'll have the PA with us, or should I say, the former PA."

"What do you mean former PA?"

"We will discuss your position status later."

"What's the plan?" wondered Holley.

"I don't have a specific one other than to determine the facts and resolve them. *Maybe I dismissed Max too soon?* Either way, those termination cubicles are going offline, permanently." Jesse moved to a corner and tossed his satchel on the floor. "No more questions; it's time for rest. Some of us have a busy schedule on the morrow. Joyous dusk everyone."

CHAPTER 31

TERMINATING TERMINATION

At predawn, the hatch to the shelter opened, and Max and Runess entered. Other than Narleen, everyone else was still asleep. She ran to Max and gave him a huge hug, followed by a series of kisses. "I worried when you didn't return with the others."

"Sorry, Nar, I felt obligated to go with Runess after the mission concluded at the Programming Center. He planned to travel by himself to the Airship Dock and—"

"I forgive you, just don't do that again." Their conversation awakened the others in the bunker. Slowly, they arose, stretched their stiff muscles, and began to move around. "Jesse said you had a surprise for me. What is it?"

"Come and see." Taking her by the hand, Max led her up the steps. Outside sat an airship. The craft had a silvery canopy, inflated like a blimp, with a long boat-like carriage below it. The ramp was lowered. "We're going on a little sight-seeing trip with Runess and his crew. Let's gather your things." When the two reentered the shelter, they noticed Jesse, Holley, and Ahboen huddled in a circle, talking with Runess.

"So, what are you three doing this fine dawn?" Runess asked.

"We're headed to the Termination Facility to visit with the Operational Leader," replied Jesse. "Certain changes must occur at this facility. Not sure to what extent until we scope out the situation and get truthful answers. Specifically, I plan to ask why the OL didn't respond to our queries. We're bringing Ahboen with us to help negotiate."

"Instead of walking to Termination, let me give you three negotiators a lift. Our ships are real fast. They are equipped with Triverphol-powered engines, so I can have you there in less than five intervals. And I'll hang around if you think there's gonna be trouble."

"No, just drop us off. This is a diplomatic endeavor. Besides, Max is looking forward to some alone time with his spouse. I've been pushing him pretty hard, ever since we arrived in your sector. I don't care to delay their special trip; they both need a break."

"No disagreement there. As soon as I finish with their tour, perhaps I can interest you in taking one with me. There is a landmark in the southern hemisphere I think you should see."

"If time allows, I'll consider it. I'm a sailor, myself. Served on a number of naval ships in my time. I flew in a couple aircraft, too."

"Then you'll fit right in with the crew." He cracked a half-smile. "Time to shove off."

Jesse and Max left their stunners in the shelter. Holley and Narleen grabbed their satchels, offered their farewells, and along with Runess, the group of five exited the shelter and boarded the airship. Anna, the provost and pravost, and several believers followed them outside to watch the ship lift into the air. After it departed, they returned to the bunker and closed the hatch.

Four intervals later, the airship landed outside the Termination Center and Jesse, Holley, and Ahboen disembarked. Max peered over the rail and asked, "Should I stay until things are secured."

"No, we have this. You two enjoy the excursion. Since you have a radio, I'll contact you if we run into complications." Jesse and Holley waved goodbye and entered the facility, with Ahboen leading the way.

Immediately, the Operational Leader confronted them. "Hail to the Program Master."

"There is no PM," replied Ahboen. "I sent dispatches yesterdawn asking you to stand down. You never replied."

"You are mistaken, PA. I hear from the PM every dawn. He is alive and well."

"No, he is not. He never existed. The PM is a data program gone awry."

"So, you say. Regardless, I have no intention of stopping our processing here. In fact, we've been having a little trouble with the termination cubicles. Because of a malicious hack, they've been offline. We finally reactivated them this dawn. Since our Operational Technicians are behind with their quotas, they plan to terminate a group of discontents before halfdawn, including those infected with the Disease."

"Stop killing the sick," shouted Holley. "I have a cure for them."

"Who are you to order me around?"

Before Holley could respond, Ahboen held up his hand to stop her. "She is a healer from Sector Five, and I believe she has developed a vaccine for Triverphol Sickness."

"Doubtful. There is no cure. Even our Floksillin and Ploksillin vaccinations are only partially effective." He looked across the hall at a bunch of OTs who were waiting for instructions. "If that is all, I have much to do this dawn."

"Am I to understand you are disobeying my direct command?"

"Yes. In fact, you're probably a discontent, yourself. You and this so-called healer should leave now, lest I add you both to our disposal schedule." As the OL turned to leave, Jesse whispered something in Ahboen's ear.

"OL!" Ahboen yelled. "You're relieved! You no longer run this facility. Who is next in command?"

"I am, sir. My name is Layshura. I'm the Operational Assistant."

"Okay, OA, I'm placing you in charge. This healer is your liaison. You will follow her directions and answer all her questions. And the same goes for Jesse, her associate. Do I make myself clear?"

"Yes sir. What about the OL? Shall I have him terminated?"

"No, place him in a holding cubicle and lock the door. We will deal with his disobedience later."

"How may I assist you, healer?" Layshura asked.

"My name is Holley. I am a medical research specialist. For now, you can answer a few questions about this facility." She strolled across to the counter and studied the monitor screens. "What do you do with the chemicals removed from deceased individuals?"

"We add them to various products we produce, namely Cradphenanill."

"You mean pleasure pills?"

"Correct. We take Cradphen, a whitish crystal, and grind it into power. Then we mix the powder with Foeca and add processed body chemicals to produce Cradphenanill cubes. It's one of our most popular tablets."

"Consequently, innocent citizens are murdered to make drugs."

"Well, I wouldn't put it that way, but yes, it is part of the process."

"This is no longer acceptable. You will stop making these tabs." Although Holley's eyes revealed sorrow, her face reddened with anger. "Do you add bodily substances to create hydration and nutrition pills?"

"No, those processes use—"

"You can explain your formulas later. What about vaccinations?"

"Body chemicals are also included in vaccines."

"These practices will stop this dawn. You'll disable all extermination cubicles and delete the data about those procedures. Can this be done from your mainframe?"

"Yes, healer, but I don't see why—"

"Do as she says," advised Ahboen. "Explanations will be forthcoming. Will any of your OTs be opposing these changes?"

"No, they'll obey, as will I. If the PM and his polices have been lies, we must adapt accordingly."

Ahboen began tapping his foot as he glared at Holley. "I hope we are finished now."

"Hardly," interjected Jesse. "There's more on the docket. Even though I haven't mentioned this to anyone yet, the Council of Twelve needs to be reestablished. I plan to hold an organizational meeting at the Programming Center." He turned to face Layshura. "Can we send invitations from your terminal?

"Yes, it's connected to our datacomm."

"Good. You're hereby invited to represent this facility and be one of the twelve, if this is agreeable?"

"It is. I'd be happy to serve. I feel changes are warranted and so do many of the operators who work here."

"What about me?" Ahboen asked.

"You are also slated for a councilmember position. This legislative body will include people who represent the laborers, programmers, Security, and Yah believers. Since the PM's government was a sham, a reformed one is warranted. I will help get it organized."

"I'm not sure involving religious fanatics is a good idea. Their worship has been banned."

"No longer." Jesse paused, scratched his chin, pondering his next requests. "Layshura, please forward dispatches requesting that Security Leaders from each sector attend. The meeting will commence on the morrow, earlydawn, at Programming. I suggest the SLs travel by airships, so no one is delayed. And make these communiques from Ahboen. I want to see the confirmations before I leave the facility."

"Should I send those messages now or wait until we decommission the cubicles?"

"Do them first, and then you can proceed with the healer's instructions concerning shutdown protocols." Holley nodded her permission to Layshura.

Jesse walked over to the workstation and watched as Layshura entered the dispatches. Within a few intervals, the replies arrived on the screen. "All sectors have confirmed, sir."

Jesse thanked her and slipped outside to contact Max on the radio. "Captain Maximus, do you read me?"

Instead of Max, Narleen answered. "Go ahead, Jesse."

"How do you like sailing the skies?"

"Oh, it's wonderful. I've experienced nothing like it. On Eskaonus, we only have sea-bound ships. Thanks for asking, but I'm sure you contacted us for a different reason. Let me hand the radio to Maxie."

"Sir, is there a problem?"

"No, not at this point. I'm merely calling with an update. I've scheduled a meeting to discuss forming a new Council of

Twelve."

"I'll return immediately."

"Please don't. You and Narleen enjoy this dawn and dusk. However, I would like both of you and Runess to attend this meeting. It's scheduled for the morrow during earlydawn at the Programming Center."

"We'll be there."

"See you soon. Jesse out."

He changed radio channels. "Jesse to Seth."

"Read you loud and clear, JW."

"How are things going over there?"

"Thanks to the Rev's coding binder, Rauteira and Hiehew are making progress. They've begun reversing mind wipes, starting with the P1s.

"Ready for a break?"

"Yeah, in more ways than one."

"Great. We're almost finished at Termination. Can you give us a ride to Programming?"

"That's a big 10-4. Be there in a flash."

Jesse returned to the main counter where he found Holley huddled behind a monitor, watching Layshura enter data commands. "Ahboen and I are heading to Programming. Are you gonna be okay here?"

"Yes, the OA has guaranteed my safety and a place to stay for the dusk. Since there are lots of procedures to enact, this shutdown could take bouts. I will see you on the morrow for the meeting. She has requested an airship to bring us both."

"Perfect. You can brief me next dawn on the results." He glanced at the PA. "Well, come on, Ahboen, we're leaving."

"I can stay here and help."

"Not a chance. I'm keeping my eyes on you for a while. Let's move out. You and I are taking a little ride on a flying scooter."

When Jesse arrived at Programming, he marched Ahboen upstairs to Level Two where the deprogramming was underway. After listening to the P3's report, Jesse asked if there was extra room in housing for ten additional guests. Hiehew replied, "More than enough. Allow me to show you one of our living chambers. They hold four occupants, and we have dozens of vacant units."

Jesse stepped inside the apartment and inspected it. Feeling satisfied with the accommodations, he pulled out his radio. "Malmach, do you copy?" Static noises. "Provost, are you there?"

"Of course, where else would I be?"

"Yeah, right." Jesse grinned to himself. "I'm sending Seth over to shuttle everyone to Programming. You'll be sleeping on beds this dusk instead of hard floors. Gather your things. And ask Anna to bring my candle lamp."

"Since we feel safe here, why the sudden change in venue?"

"There is a planning meeting scheduled for the morrow to establish a Council of Twelve to govern this planet. I need our friends and advocates present ahead of time. You, the pravost, and several others are being invited to serve on this council. I will explain more when you arrive. Jesse out."

CHAPTER 32

COUNCIL OF TWELVE

Jesse arose early, feeling renewed. It was the first comfortable night in a week of dawns. He hoped the others in the collective felt the same way. He flipped on his candle lamp and pulled out his journal. Although Jesse really didn't need the light to see because his bedroom had its own lighting, he enjoyed the sweet fragrance his oil lamp produced.

Entry Sixteen

I'll start this entry with the big reveal. The esteemed leader of this planet, known as the Program Master, is a fraud. He never existed. He, or rather I should say it, was a maintenance program gone awry. This planet was being run by artificial intelligence. After a cataclysm befell Camayah, this so-called PM emerged and instituted changes based on lies. I'm not sure how the devil fits into all this, or if he does, but I am reminded of the Scripture that says Satan is the father of lies.

Our team pulled the plug on this deceptive program, creating an opportunity for a replacement government. Accordingly, we hope to reestablish the Council of Twelve, the ruling body the Program Master program eliminated when it took over. We will offer guidelines to this new council and perhaps, point them in a better direction.

In other news, the moon rescue was a difficult operation yet successful. On a subsequent mission, Max and Seth found water, what the residents call hydrew. It lies deep underground. Since this is an advanced society, I will suggest they pump it to the surface. We also believe the RIFTs have stockpiled seeds. It wouldn't take much to restore vegetation on the planet, at least in certain places. Perhaps this dead, arid place can be terraformed.

Lundy and others are trying to undo the programming forced upon residents to erase their memories and control their minds. Holley developed a cure for an unknown disease using healing leaves. And Runess, a former airship captain, wants to show me something in the lower hemisphere.

We transported everyone from the shelter to guest housing at the Programming Center, so I guess we no longer require angelic intervention. Never saw a single angel, yet I felt their presence. Thank Chesedel or whoever came to support us.

I have a difficult meeting to chair and expect contention from several of the citizenry invited to serve on this board. I'll be sharing practical and spiritual solutions. What happens thereafter is on them. Free choice, right? Besides, it's their planet, not mine. I pray the meeting ends well. If it does, I'm gonna take Runess up on his little airship tour. I plan to ask Seth and Annabelle to join me.

He returned the journal and lamp to his satchel and went down to Level One. A large table had already been set up with twelve chairs. Other seating lined the walls. The hall was crowded and noisy. Some were milling about; others were already seated. There were five people Jesse didn't recognize, which he assumed were the SLs from the five sectors.

Seeing his team already present, he gathered them around him and motioned for the provost to join the discussion. Jesse outlined a tentative agenda for the meeting and explained their subsequent plans. With those strategies in mind, he collected and redistributed the radios. Max, Holley, and Lundy each received one. Jesse kept the fourth. "We'll stay with the preset channels." With a grin on his face, he added, "Reverend, hang on to the radio this time." Once the party entered the main area, the chatter ceased. Jesse stood in the center of the room and began:

"First off, let me clear up a matter. Certain residents are calling us *sent ones*. I did not invite you here to debate religious prophecies, but to restore a fallen governmental system. What I can tell you is this: Our group of seven envoys portaled here from a different realm. Whether we are the *sent ones* your spiritual leaders expected, I cannot say. Such discernment often comes with time. Right now, we have other pressing matters, namely, the reestablishment of the Council of Twelve."

"Since there are only twelve spots around the main table, you should all move to allow the delegates a seat. I have appointed leaders to represent all the factions on this planet. The Council will include SLs from the five sectors. They'll represent security concerns. Cndrek, from Sector One will be the SSL or Senior Security Leader. The other four will report to him." The SLs took their places, sitting next to one another.

"Rekis and Leetqu are spokespersons for the laborers. Malmach and Trikernae will be spiritual advisors. Layshura, the Operational Assistant, is representing the Termination Facility, which has been renamed the Health Center. Ahboen, the former PA, and Hiehew, the P3 supervisor, will speak for the Programming Center, under its new name of Science Center." Those who were identified filled in the remaining seven seats.

"Before we continue, I will entertain a few comments."

"As the second in command to the Program Master, I should be the leader."

"I'm sorry, Ahboen, there will be no PM or PA positions unless the Council appoints them. Nor will there be kings, dictators, supreme rulers, or otherwise. The twelve members are free to decide on changes as soon as certain agendas have been implemented. Since your whole legislative system has been a sham and most polices, corrupt, our goal is to help you get things back on track. After that, this board can run matters as they see fit."

"Any questions?" Eight individuals raised their hands. "Sorry, folks, I didn't realize there would be so many. To stay on point, we will respond to your questions as we go along. I hope our presentations will deal with most of them. First to speak is Holley, our medical expert, who some call *the healer*."

"Since there is much to cover this dawn, I'll try to be concise with my report," stated Holley. "The termination cubicles have been closed and are in the process of being disassembled. Accordingly, the Termination Facility has been renamed the Health Center to better represent its purpose. Your operators will no longer slaughter people, sick or otherwise, and use their body chemicals to make pleasure pills and ineffective vaccines."

Several hands went up. "Please allow me to finish. This facility will continue processing nutrition and hydration tablets until more natural nourishments can be instituted. Maximus will discuss those issues when I'm finished. Moreover, we have developed an innovative process to cure Triverphol Sickness as well as other diseases. Thus far, the test results show a hundred percent efficacy. However, for both replacement nourishment and medical treatments, we need hydrew."

"There is no hydrew on this planet," stated Cndrek. "It evaporated during the Burning."

Max approached the table, carrying a small pail. "You are misinformed, sir." He plopped the pail in front of the SSL. "There are about eight cubes of emerald fluid remaining in this bucket. Our doc used the rest to make an antidote for Triverphol Disease by adding a special ingredient from her medkit."

"And it works." Leetqu stood and rolled up her sleeves. "My whole body was covered with rashes and decaying skin. I also had muscular degeneration and weakness, a sign of late-stage progression. Security discovered I had contracted the Disease and scheduled me for termination. Fortunately, Holley's antidote cured me. I have no symptoms at all."

"And we can make more cures, for which the doc requires water, I mean hydrew."

Cndrek peeked inside and passed the pail around to the other SLs. "Where did you get this liquid?"

"Deep in a quawner cave, and there is more where this came from. In fact, I believe most hollows have pools of hydrew. All you gotta do is go get it."

"If you are correct, and I have my doubts, how do we enter these dens and not be killed by the creatures?"

"I'm glad the SSL asked." Max reached into his tote and passed out slings to the five SLs. He likewise placed a small chunk of Criunite and one of Holley's quawner bombs in front of each. "Your stunners have no effect on these beasts, whereas these twirling devices can launch projectiles that do." Max snatched a piece of Criunite. "This luminous crystal can penetrate the hardened skin of a quawner and disable it, allowing time for a person to escape. We know this because we have successfully used this method numerous times."

Next, Max selected a quawner bomb. "This projectile is made from Foeca. It's rolled in sand to give it weight and then dried in the sun to give it hardness." Max waved to his spouse. "Nar, please come demonstrate the technique."

Narleen approached the table and curtsied to Cndrek. She loaded a bomb into her sling, twirled it around three times to build momentum, and released it. The councilmembers ducked as it flew overhead. The projectile hit the far wall and exploded into tiny fragments. "If that had been a creature," explained Max, "it would have been put to sleep for bouts. Our doc has analyzed this substance and she can tell you more about it."

Holley stepped forward again. "Foeca is quawner excrement." Puzzled faces around the table led to murmuring. "It has the same properties as the creature's venom. Both substances are hallucinogens with paralytic properties. Little wonder this sticky ingredient is added to Cradphen to make pleasure pills. And if I may, since I have the floor . . ."

"Go ahead, Holley," Max replied.

"Be advised that the making and distribution of Cradphenanill tabs has been halted. Besides using quawner dung, operators are adding elements processed from terminated human beings. This killing of individuals for their body chemicals must stop." The murmurs erupted into complaints. Hands were raised to ask questions. A few were shouting. "I'm sorry. There is no other—"

Jesse interrupted Holley before she said something that might derail the meeting. "The committee can debate this decision later. Max, carry on with your report."

"As I was saying, hydrew still exits on the planet, deep underground."

"You want us to risk our lives to enter quawner dens just for a couple drinks of liquid?"

"The risk would be minimized with the use of slings and projectiles. There is, however, a better solution. Our team leader will elaborate."

Jesse moved to the front, paused for a moment as he

gathered his thoughts. "Making endless trips into quawner hollows is not tenable. Even so, this is an advanced society, and I'm sure you can figure out a way to drill wells to access the hydrew and pump it to the surface. Furthermore, I'm aware the RIFTs have numerous crates of soreseed sets. Is this not correct, Security Leaders?" The five SLs reluctantly nodded their heads. "Thank you for your honesty. With this surplus, I suggest this commission develop plans to sow those seeds around sources of hydrew and grow crops again. Not only will you have liquids and actual food, you may be able to terraform your planet with vegetation in certain places."

"What else are these RIFTs hiding?" Trikernae stood to her feet, her eyes revealed anger.

Max answered, "I know for a fact they have stockpiled protective suits and numerous containers of nourishment tablets, not to mention tools and other supplies."

"You mean the RIFTs have protective outfits lying around while laborers search the ruins to make theirs out of scraps!" Rekis pounded his fist on the tabletop to show his displeasure. "I think these jumpsuits should be provided free to every worker."

"This is one of the things the assembly must decide," enjoined Jesse. "I also recommend supplying these laborers with proper diggers and equipment."

"And double their gelt credits," Rekis added.

"I concur. As legislative overseers, you can do many things to better the lives of your citizens. I'm imploring this committee to debate all these matters and vote on solutions. A simple majority carries the motion. If there's a split decision, Malmach's vote breaks the stalemate."

Jesse cleared his throat before continuing. "Although we have already discussed most of the situations and circumstances demanding attention, I will repeat everything for the sake of clarity. And I suggest data records be kept for future reference."

1. There is no PM. Never has been. The Council of Twelve is again the representative government for this world.

"And policy changes are warranted."

2. Reprogramming to take away a citizen's identity must stop. All mind-wipes, whether partial or complete, will be reversed.

"Reversals cannot be done," shouted one of the SLs.

"Yes, they can. In fact, the restoration process is underway for programmers at the Science Center. The laborers and operators are next, then Security. If you will please allow me to continue without interruptions, I will try to answer your concerns at the end."

3. Reho pleasure chambers will be decommissioned.

"Allow the displaced to use them as temporary residences until proper housing can be established."

***4.** Develop plans to drill for hydrew, plant soreseed sets, grow crops, and restore vegetation.*

***5.** Laborers shall be given protective gear and their wages increased.*

"I recommend doubling or tripling their gelt credits."

***6.** Excluding weapons, the RIFTs surplus storage will no longer be hoarded. Distribute those items to the needy.*

"Residents shouldn't have to dig in the ruins for the basic things required for living."

***7.** The processing of Cradphenanill cubes will cease.*

***8.** Religion will no longer be unlawful. Yah worship is allowed.*

"I suggest the Holding Area be converted into a religious center."

***9.** Nutrition and hydration pills are to be phased out once natural products are available.*

***10.** And lastly, no more hail-to-the-programmer greetings.* The hall erupted into laughter.

"Most of the other issues have already been presented or discussed. Holley will be the liaison for the Health Center. She will work with their operators to supply the cure to each sector. Lundy will be the contact person for the Science Center. He, Hiehew, and Rauteira will oversee the restoration of people whose lives were ruined due to reprogramming. And Max and Narleen will visit the RIFTs to make sure they're opening their stores for the locals. Transportation has been offered to them by Runess, who is the new SL over the Airship Dock. Are there any final questions or comments?" The provost raised his hand.

"Yes, Malmach, what is it?"

"Whether you and your friends are the foretold ones or not,

I feel we should thank you for saving our world." More affirmations arose from the crowd, including applause.

Jesse motioned for the clapping to stop. "We are only servants, not saviors. It will be you, the Council of Twelve, who accomplishes this endeavor."

"Anyone else?"

"Yeah, if the big guy is still seeking a job, I can use him," added the SSL.

"Feel free to talk with Maximus about his availability."

"Last call?" The room went silent. "This meeting is adjourned. Your respective liaisons will advise you. I've been invited on a tour of your planet by Runess, and his airship is waiting. Anna and Seth are accompanying me." Jesse offered a deep bow, followed by the open-palm salutation. "Fair dawn to you." The gesture was returned by everyone except Ahboen, who slouched back in his chair, crossed his arms, and scowled.

Jesse, Anna, and Seth exited the hall with Runess leading the way. Max, Narleen, Holley, and Lundy followed behind them. "Since you have radios," reminded Jesse, "I would like to receive regular updates while we are away."

"How long be ye gone?"

"Runess said it was a five-dawn trip, one way, depending on the travel speed. About ten in total, I guess." The four climbed the boarding ramp, spread out across the foredeck, and waved goodbye to their friends. Slowly, the airship lifted into the sky, made one circle around the Science Center, and then flew south.

CHAPTER 33

SILENCE IN HEAVEN

"And when [the Lamb] had opened the seventh seal, there was silence in heaven about the space of half an hour. And I saw the seven angels which stood before God; and to them were given seven trumpets. And another angel came and stood at the altar, having a golden censer; and there was given unto him much incense, that he should offer *it* with the prayers of all saints upon the golden altar which was before the throne. And the smoke of the incense, *which came* with the prayers of the saints, ascended up before God out of the angel's hand. And the angel took the censer, and filled it with fire of the altar, and cast *it* into the earth: and there were voices, and thunderings, and lightnings, and an earthquake" (Revelation 8:1–5).

Chesedel stepped out of the Hall of Records with copies of Jesse's recent log entries. Heavenly inhabitants were walking the streets and footpaths as usual, except none were visiting, laughing, or singing. In fact, there were no sounds anywhere. The prayer gardens were filled with saints, more than normal, yet he heard no prayers being said, not even a whisper. Even the bubbling Fountain of Life made no noise. He rushed to the Throne Room. The always-open doors were closed. He knew what it meant.

The time of many sorrows had come. Tribulation was unfolding. The seventh seal had been opened and heaven would remain silent for half an hour. Seven trumpet calls would follow. Since Uzziel was in the Throne Room with the other seven cherubim, he decided to wait with Jesse's update. Chesedel tucked entries Fifteen and Sixteen into his blue sash. Feeling the Cherubim would want him to take the initiative, he popped over to the White Pearl Gate, pictured Camayah in his mind, and departed through the portal. Although a bright light flashed, no thunder was heard. All sounds in heaven were muted.

He traveled through the outer regions and arrived in Camayah. Remaining in the unseen realm, he flew to Sector One and passed by the ruins where the two winged ones hovered above the shelter. The sentinels looked as the guardian soared overhead but kept their wings lowered, hiding the hatch to the bunker.

When Chesedel approached the Science Center, he noticed Lundy working with two programmers and a teenage girl. The hall was filled with residents waiting to have their minds released from the brainwashing forced upon them. Next, the angel traveled north and located an airship carrying Maximus and Narleen. They were headed to Sector Two. Chesedel circled around and passed over the Health Center where he found Holley discussing medical procedures with several operators. Sensing no problems at any of the facilities or danger to his wards, he moved on.

Being in the same realm, the guardian could now hear Jesse's thoughts and quickly discerned his location. He flew south and located the airship carrying him, Annabelle, and Seth. All three were safe, which was his main concern as a protector. Finally, he returned to the ruins and materialized in front of the winged ones. When elChesed entered the seen realm, the two angels also reappeared. They folded their wings and drifted to the ground to stand next to their fellow servant. They bowed, showing respect to a higher-ranked angel.

Chesedel responded with an appreciative nod. "Are the people gone?"

Answering in unison, the sentinels replied, "Yes, they left recently. None have returned. Seth shuttled the entire group and their belongings to the Programming Center."

"The name has been changed to Science Center," advised Chesedel.

"That seems more fitting."

"Your assignment on Camayah is complete. Thank you for keeping everyone safe. We should return to heaven immediately."

"Is there urgency?"

"Indeed, the Great Tribulation has begun. The Lamb just broke the seventh seal and silence has filled the heavens. Soon the cherubim will begin blowing their shofars."

"Then we are needed there." The sentinels spread their wings and lifted off the ground.

"I concur. We must hurry."

The three reentered the unseen realm and departed. Moments later, they arrived in heaven as the first trumpet announced a judgment. "The first angel sounded, and there followed hail and fire mingled with blood, and they were cast upon the earth: and the third part of trees was burnt up, and all green grass was burnt up" (Revelation 8:7).

Chesedel raced to the Throne Room. The doors were open again, and Uzziel was walking down the steps. He held a shofar in his right hand. Six other cherubim with shofars followed him. Uzziel had tears in his eyes. They all did.

CHAPTER 34

THE AIRSHIP

"Alright, travelers, let me introduce my aircrew," Runess said. "We have Jawhawtu, the midmate, and Uewba, our rowmate. Normally, I staff a five-person outfit, but since we are carrying extra fuel and passengers, I could only keep two seasoned sailors. Both are loyal deckhands. Anna, you'll take the quarters next to Uewba. You'll find her an experienced navigator. And Seth, you can hang with Jaw. As our engineer, he's the hand who keeps our engines running. In fact, I am asking both of you to shadow your counterparts and learn the rails, but first, stow your gear."

"What about me?" Jesse asked.

"You're staying in the captain's cabin with me."

"I suppose you'll want me to swab the decks?"

"As former sailor, I guess you know the routine. The mop is in the corner." Runess grinned, hoping Jesse realized he was kidding. "For now, though, I would like you to follow me. We'll start with a tour of my ship. With a smaller crew, there'll be plenty of work for each person. Therefore, consider this cruise, part pleasure, part work. At times, I will need all hands on deck. Let's go see *Old Bella*; she's a beauty."

"Aye, aye, skipper," Jesse said with a smile, followed by the salute he used in the Navy. Runess led Jesse down a flight of stairs to the lower berth. "We have six sleepers, three to a side. The stern contains the engines. Seth and Jaw are probably across the hallway tending to them. The hatch on the left leads to the nether deck. It is our fuel hold. We also keep our equipment stored there."

"What kind of equipment?"

"Solar sails, which we no longer use since these airships haven't made orbit in ages, spare engine parts, and a weapons locker. Let's head topside." The two climbed the staircase to the flight deck. "My cabin is in the bow. Those steps on the starboard side lead to the navigator's post. Anna is already up there with Uew, learning how to steer this flyer."

"I have a few questions about these floating ships."

"Figured you might. They're probably the same inquiries Max had. Let's move into my quarters and talk a bit."

The captain's room contained three viewing ports, a workstation with one monitor screen, two hammocks attached to side walls, and three stools in front of the windows. "The nether hammock is yours. You can stow your gear in the corner. The navdata and datacomm are on my terminal. Later, I'll explain how those operate." Noticing Jesse's facial expressions, Runess could tell he was eager to learn more. "Pull up a seat and I'll answer those questions."

"What are these flying boats? They look like a mixture of zeppelin and spacecraft."

"I don't know what either of those crafts be. However, I can give you a brief history on our floaters. We had a huge fleet of them, over a hundred, and they were much larger in size than this one. Some held forty souls. The aircrews explored the upper atmospheres and our three moons. After transport portals were built, most of the larger vessels were decommissioned."

"Mothballed them, huh? What then?"

"The Burning came. Since the docks were not shielded, those port facilities were destroyed, here and on the moons, along with the entire fleet. Since the transport portals were shielded, they survived and are used solely for off-planet travel."

"This Burning sounds pretty terrible."

"The catastrophe occurred before my era. All I can tell you is what I've heard. In the aftermath, smaller ships like *Old Bella* were built. We currently have twenty. Each sector has at least three. Sector One has several more."

"Can your rebuilt crafts still fly the upper atmospheres?"

"In theory, yes. We carry solar sails aboard."

"If these vessels travel in space, how do you survive in an airless void? Do you use spacesuits?"

"I'm not sure what you mean by space, but all air is breathable: on our planet, in orbit, across the moons, and all areas in between. Ancient airship commanders never explored past the orbits of our three moons, so I have no idea what lies out there in the outer atmosphere, nor does anyone else."

"I see. What kind of power? Fission or fusion?"

"Your terms are unknown to me; I'm a simple sailor, not a technician. As I understand it, our specialists experimented with splitting miniature elements. Those tests, however, yielded unfavorable results. The process was deemed too dangerous when it destroyed several facilities within a quarter sector. Later on, scientists invented a blending process, which was less hazardous."

"Sounds like cold fusion."

"Again, I don't understand your terminology, yet it really didn't matter in the end. The Burning decimated the blending facilities, killed the researchers who worked in them, and destroyed data records. The process was lost."

"I'm sorry to hear that. Something similar occurred in the place I lived as a child."

"And where was that?"

"Earth."

"Your reference is unfamiliar to me." Runess leaned back and propped his feet on the spare stool. "Any other questions?"

"Yeah. Just wondering what gives these sailboats their lift?"

"Light air, of course. Prior to the Burning, power was made in blender facilities. Now it's produced in cauldrons. After the Event, we had no energy for many stages, until Triverphol was discovered beneath the surface. Pit mines were dug to remove it and cauldrons built to process it. These Triverphol plants produce three main products: TPCs to power our equipment and devices, gas that gives floaters their lift, and liquid fuel to run our engines. Triverphol is highly toxic and flammable, so we use protective suits to—"

A whistle sounded. "Cap, we are approaching the docks in Sector Five."

"Alright, Uew, take us in. I'll send a datacomm message and request a docking bay. Sorry, Jesse, we'll have to continue this conversation later." He touched the screen on his monitor and activated the ship's intercom. "This is the captain. All parties report to the flight deck." Uewba and Jawhawtu scrambled into position. Seth and Anna followed, not quite sure what to do.

Jesse rose from his stool. "What's going on? Why are we stopping?"

"We are landing to take on three barrows of fuel. We'll hold up here until dawn. Although airships can travel at dusk, it's safer to fly during dawn bouts."

By latedawn, the refueling was complete and Runess led his crew down the ship's ramp into the dock facility. There were several rectangular tables in the main hall, lined with benches. Individuals sat elbow to elbow. Some were yelling at one another, pounding their fists on tabletops. Others stared at the person across from them with stern, poker-like faces. Most were laughing.

Jesse tapped Runess on the shoulder and asked, "What's the ruckus about?"

"It's Guet, a strategy game played by crewmates to pass the bouts. Each player takes a color and starts with ten pieces." To Jesse, the pieces looked similar to wooden Tinkertoys, except they were made of metal. There were thin rods of different lengths, round objects, squares, triangular and oval shapes, and an eight-sided dice. "It's played on a table or floor in a circle, no board, with three to seven players. Guet can last several bouts or dawns. Let's join a game. It takes a while to learn the rules, but I think you guys might enjoy it."

"I hope you don't mind, Runess," Anna said with a sigh. "I'm not really interested in learning a new game. I'm returning to my quarters."

"Do you want my navigator to escort you?"

"No, I'll be fine. Just need a little downtime. I plan to compose a few songs on my nyeflute, and if there are adverse effects, I think it would be safer if no one else were present."

"Probably a good idea. I've seen what your tunes can do."

Jesse and Runess took seats at the shipmaster's table with

three SAs who were in the middle of a friendly disagreement on tactics. Seth joined Jaw and Uew at the midshipmen's table. The games went on until latedusk. Afterwards, Runess thanked his fellow sailors for a good time and headed back to his ship, followed by Jesse, Seth, and the deckhands.

"Guet is totally cool. A mix of RISK and checkers. I'm sure I'll do better next time."

"Well, that's good, Seth, because we play it every dusk." He pounded on the rail to garner everyone's attention. "Off to the sleepers with ya. We have an early start on the morrow and four more dawns to get where we're headed."

"And where are we headed?" asked Jesse.

"South. Most of the territory is an unexplored wasteland."

"Can you share the specifics on our destination?"

"Not yet. You'll find out soon enough. Be patient. Oh yeah, from here on out, we go dark. I don't wish to be tracked through datacomm communications."

"Do you expect trouble?"

"Not sure. Last time it didn't turn out too well for me and my shipmates, so I'm being cautious. Besides, not everybody agrees with your Council of Twelve appointments or suggested agenda."

"Like who?"

"Mainly, Ahboen, the deposed PA, and Raetila from RIFT II. I've also heard complaints from the SAs in Sector Three. Therefore, I'm disconnecting from the dataflow until we return to Sector Five. You can use your radios for communications. I'm pretty sure they can't be tracked." Runess raised the ramp to secure *Old Bella* for the dusk. "Sorry to cut this conversation short, but we better get a couple bouts of sleep before dawn. Time to hit the hammocks."

At predawn, the airship left the dock and flew south, across an arid, barren, and windless terrain. Temperatures were extremely hot, especially in the middle of the day. Jesse estimated them to be over 110 degrees. For the next three dawns, the routine was much the same. The craft would land at halfdawn. Runess collected rock samples and searched for minerals, while the crew checked the canopy for leaks. If any holes or cracks were discovered, they would be patched immediately. According to deckhands, they could ill afford to lose airlift this far away from a dock.

Jesse followed Runess and helped him haul things back to the hold. If he hadn't heard from Lundy, Max, and Holley, he would contact them for updates. Once the maintenance checks were completed, Seth unfolded his shuttle and gave rides to the midmate, rowmate, and Anna. About thirty intervals later, the crew reboarded, and the flight continued.

At nightfall, the airship stopped and hovered at the sixty-mark elevation. Occasionally, a cluster of quawners scurried by, glanced at them, and then continued on their way. After first moonrise, Runess pulled out Guet and the game began. Anna watched for a while, then excused herself and returned to her quarters to practice her nyeflute. By the third moon rise, the game ended, and everyone tromped off to their hammocks. In the morn, Runess dispensed Tycozide and Hydru tabs from his chest and the party continued their flight. The temperatures cooled slightly the farther south they traveled.

On the fifth dawn, *Old Bella* approached a distant mountain. Runess sounded general quarters and took out his magnifier to take a peek. He handed the viewer to Jesse. What Jesse saw surprised him.

CHAPTER 35

SURPRISES

As Jesse adjusted the magnifier, the image came into closer view. Floating over the mountain were puffy, emerald clouds, shaped like little cotton balls. "Is this cloud-covered peak what the authorities fretted about?"

"Partly, but I think they were more concerned with that." Runess pointed at three dots off the port bow.

Jess swung the magnifier to the left and refocused. "Those could be birds. And they're heading toward the summit."

"I believe they are called nawmies. They were supposed to be extinct, along with the other animals that perished in the Burning."

"Can I see?" asked Annabelle. She peered through the binocular-type device. "The larger speck is leading two smaller ones."

"Dudes, it's just like the prophecy Anna gave when she said hope will arise like a winged nawmie to soar the heights with her hatchlings. I say we follow them to see where they are going."

"I concur. Uewba, set our course for those dots in the sky." As the vessel closed in, the crew could see the birds without a viewer. The craft approached the summit and stopped. "Before we get too close, let's circle this peak and see what we can determine," suggested Runess. They made one pass around and hovered the airship near the rim. The mount had high ridges and a depressed interior, filled with greenish mist that obscured their view.

"It appears to be a crater with a rectangular shape." Jesse borrowed the magnifier, except he couldn't see through the mist. "Can we fly inside there?"

"Not under power. Too dangerous. We might crash into an unexpected plateau or tear a hole in our air canopy by hitting a jagged cliff. We could try drifting lower. Perhaps we can punch through the cloud cover enough to see what's down there."

Old Bella slowly dropped in elevation as it passed through low-lying clouds. Finally, the view cleared, and the crew beheld a long valley inside the depression, with small lakes of hydrew scattered everywhere. Trees, bushes, varieties of soreseeds, and other types of vegetation dotted the flat terrain. The place was teaming with animals.

Jesse leaned over the rail. "Is there a way to record this?"

"Already am. The imagers were turned on during our descent. We normally use them for surveillance. This craft is equipped with four. The feeds are being piped into the ship's datacomm, so we are capturing this entire event." He motioned to the rowmate and pointed. "Set her down by the green pond on the portside."

"There must be hundreds of animals trapped in here. Any idea how they survived the Burning?" asked Jesse.

"Not really. On my last and only trip to the southern hemisphere, I spotted this mountaintop, the emerald clouds, and a few specks moving across the horizon. When I filed my report with the SL, I was rebuked, imprisoned, and my crewmates terminated. I've always wondered if those specks might be nawmies, but I had no idea a mini-biosphere existed. I'm as amazed as you are. I thought everything evaporated in the Burning. Apparently, that's not the case for Camayah's lowest latitudes. Maybe this hollowed-out crater shielded the vegetation and species, and over time, the animals multiplied, and the flora thrived."

"Out of sight, man!"

"I agree, Seth. It's wonderful!" Anna lifted her hands in praise. "Now the hills shall sing, and the trees clap their hands."

"At this point, I believe even that might be possible." Runess grinned. "Either way, we better get a survey. I want teams to spread out and explore this area. Get me estimates on the number of animals, types of flora, soreseed varieties, and anything else of interest. Gather samples of vegetation and a couple beakers of hydrew. And break out the weapons; everyone should carry a quispike or trispike. We don't know how these creatures will react to people."

"I prefer not using a stunner. I have my sling and nyeflute. They'll keep me safe."

"Alright, Annabelle, I can't force you, although I strongly suggest you carry a weapon for protection. I'm staying aboard to edit the image data. The Council of Twelve will demand proof of this discovery. Get going, shipmates. I'll expect your reports in a bout." Runess watched as Jesse, Seth, and Anna hurried down the ramp, followed by his two deckhands. Four carried stunners.

The group made several trips to the ship to offload the samples. Leaves from plants and branches from trees were taken below to the hold and stacked in rows. The soreseed vegetables and fruits were put into bins. One bout later, four party members returned with their final observations. Seth recognized some plants, having seen several of them growing in the provost's cave on Easteapia. Since Uewba and Jawhawtu were born after the Burning, they knew little about the previous wildlife or their names. All such data was destroyed in the calamity, so they provided the skipper with animal descriptions instead. Jesse added helpful information about the soil and flora. Runess summarized their reports and entered the findings on his datatop:

Two hundred fifty land animals, various sizes, exotic, largest is twenty marks tall.

Fifty-five distinct animal species.

At least thirty birds, including nawmies.

Dozens of insect types, half are winged variety.

Lush vegetation: trees, plants, and soreseeds.

Four lakes of hydrew, two springs.

Moderate temperatures.

After the rowmate and midmate finished with their reports, they stood at the rails to observe the animals wandering around the vessel, seemingly unbothered by an airship or their presence. Uew asked, "Have you seen Anna?"

"She's inspecting a pool of hydrew," replied Jaw.

Overhearing their conversation, Jesse interrupted, "Which one? There are several."

"Not sure. I saw her walking toward the northern section of the valley. Or was it eastern? I was busy counting animals, so I really didn't pay close attention."

"Come on Seth, let's split up and check both areas." Seth ran north, and Jesse raced east. Since the explorations hadn't encountered any real danger, the captain assumed Anna was simply taking her time. Runess continued to edit the image feeds, making a short presentation to complement the data the crew collected. He hoped to depart by halfdawn for the return trip.

Seth found Annabelle kneeling in front of a pond, swishing her hands in the hydrew. "What are you doing, Anna? We're leaving soon."

"I'm just checking this pool of water. I see movement under the surface. I think it may contain fish or other swimming creatures." She pointed to the middle. "Look, there's goes another ripple."

"Cool, but we better make tracks. JW is worried about you." As they turned to leave, Seth yelled, "Quawners!" Two creatures eyed them and approached. Seth pulled out his sling, loaded a green crystal, and began twirling it. Annabelle removed the nyeflute from her satchel.

"Hold on a minute, Seth. They don't seem to be rushing us. Let's stay and watch them."

"I'm not sure that's a good idea. What if they hit us with spider goo?"

"If they threaten us, I'll play my invisibility tune, and we'll disappear."

The quawners approached the pool, stopped for a drink, and then ambled on toward an outcropping of vegetation growing underneath a leafy tree. They started to nibble the bushes.

"These quawners aren't carnivorous; they are plant eaters." Anna inched closer.

"What are ya doing, Anna?"

She plucked a branch from a nearby tree and approached the smallest one. "I'm gonna feed it. I think the big one is a mother and the other is her baby."

"Annabelle . . ."

"I'll be fine." She extended the limb and watched as the creature consumed the leaves. The larger quawner seemed unconcerned. Next, Anna stepped closer and petted the little one on the leg. The mother watched yet made no hostile moves. "These quawners are non-aggressive, and I have a theory."

Seth lowered his sling, keeping the projectile in the pouch, ready to launch it if the situation turned squirrely. "I'm listening."

"When the Burning destroyed the vegetation on Camayah, which was the quawner's food source, they turned carnivorous to survive. And later, out of necessity, became aggressive to protect their underground water supply. The ones in this locale were shielded from the cataclysm, flourished, and remained docile." She motioned to Seth with two fingers. "Come here and pet the baby one."

"Think I'll pass."

"What happened to Rule Number Two?" Keeping his distance, Seth shrugged his shoulders. "Oh, never mind." Anna gave the youngling one last pat on the leg and turned to face Seth. "Let's head back to *Old Bella*. I want to add this encounter to my report." By the time the two arrived, Jesse was waiting with a concerned look on his face.

"Everything okay?"

"Sorry, I was delayed. I checked out one of the ponds and noticed ripples under the surface. Not sure if they were fish or other aquatic life."

"Hydrew creatures, most interesting." Runess stepped out of the captain's cabin, holding his datatop. "Any other important discoveries?"

"Yeah, one. There are quawners here."

"What? Did they attack you?"

"No. In fact, they're passive, even friendly."

"I find this hard to believe."

"It's true, man, every word. Anna even fed and petted one." Seth went on to describe the entire incident in detail. Afterwards, Annabelle related her premise about the creature's evolution.

As they talked, Runess entered the encounter into his datatop. "I'll include your observations and conclusions in my final report. Too bad we don't have images for documentation." He tucked the datatop under his arm. "Right now, though, we need to prep for flight. It's a five-dawn journey to return to civilization."

"Is there a way to get there sooner?" pressed Jesse. "Increase engine speed or travel during the night? I hafta tell the Council about these findings as soon as possible."

"I don't recommend flying at dusk. Perhaps I could push the engines and gain an extra dawn. It would still require four to reach our destination."

"Dudes, what about space travel? Haven't you ever seen the movie where a commercial airliner malfunctioned and accidentally attained orbit? Without gravity, the plane moved more rapidly."

"Would an orbital maneuver get us home faster?" Jesse asked.

"Such excursions haven't been attempted in ages."

"Is it possible?"

"Yes, but to do so, we'd have to burn up most of our reserve fuel to achieve orbit, deploy old solar sails, and navigate the upper atmosphere, which I've never done, and then attempt reentry with limited fuel or none at all."

"If those actions were successful, how much time?"

"Less than a dawn." Runess glanced at his deckhands. They were nodding their heads.

"I'm down for it." Seth flashed two thumbs up.

"What about you, Annie? Any reservations?" Jesse raised his eyebrows and took a deep breath while he waited for her impartial reply.

"None. I believe the operation will work because Yahweh is on our side."

"It seems my team is willing to chance it. Well, skipper, it's your call."

"I'm probably a fool for trying this maneuver. And we may all die in the process. Still, I've always wanted to fly one of these crafts into the upper atmosphere." He leaned against the port rail and stared at the horizon. "Okay, mates, secure the hold, break out the solar sails, and batten down the hatches. Lower the port and starboard booms and attach the sails. Navigator, set course for the sky. Engineer, give me your best possible speed. Let's see if we can make orbit."

CHAPTER 36

ORBIT

The ascent to the upper atmosphere consumed their fuel reserves. There was just enough remaining to attempt one controlled descent. Once in orbit, four solar sails were deployed, two from each boom. Immediately, the reflective sheets captured light from the sun and began pushing the craft forward, slowly at first, increasing its speed as the photons bounced off the sails. Uewba performed several tacking maneuvers to steer the airship and make course corrections, much like a catamaran pilot does to change directions in the wind.

The sights from orbit were incredible. As Jesse peered over the rails, he saw a patchwork of colorful red hues. Vast deserts stretched out in all directions. The terrain reminded him of the Painted Desert in Arizona, which he had visited twice during his life on earth.

Since the vessel had a dawn of smooth flying ahead, the crew set up Guet on the deck and began to play. Having observed the strategy on numerous occasions, Anna decided to join in as one of the players. Instead of lasting for bouts, the game ended quickly after Anna made a surprise move with one of her pieces to win the game. She couldn't tell if Seth and the two deckhands were frustrated because an inexperienced player bested them or were feeling weary from recent activities, but the three of them stomped off to their quarters. A few moments later, Anna followed them to her compartment. She sat in the corner and practiced her nyeflute for a while and then climbed into her hammock to sleep. After Jesse helped Runess stow the game pieces, they slipped over to the port rail to watch the rising of a distant moon.

"When will we arrive in Sector One?"

"At the rate we're traveling, I would estimate less than a dawn. Fifteen bouts at the most. In the meantime, enjoy the view. I'm heading to my cabin to finish editing the image feeds and add them to my report. Your presentation should be ready by the time we land at the Science Center."

"Thank you, Runess. I think these discoveries will shock the populace. In a good way, I hope." Jesse went below to check on Seth and Anna and then returned to the foredeck. He contemplated the recent revelations, how they influenced the mission, and his next course of action. *Maybe I should hear a few updates first.* He pulled out his radio.

"Jesse to Max, do you copy?" He tried two more times before getting a response.

"Hi Jesse," replied Narleen. "Maxie is talking to the SL from Sector Four. Can I take a message for him?"

"I'm just calling for an update."

"I can provide that. We have been visiting RIFTs to oversee the distribution of supplies. Most are compliant, opening their stores, supplying tools and materials to upgrade the living conditions for residents. Laborers now wear protective jumpsuits, not the ineffective homemade ones. The *Reho* pleasure chambers have closed and are being used as temporary housing for displaced families."

"Great. Sounds like things are changing for the better. You said most RIFTs are compliant. Which ones aren't?"

"Mainly, RIFT II. Raetila, the SA, is not being very helpful."

"I see. Check with the SSL and ask him to intervene."

"I'll let Maxie know. Anything else?"

"Only that we are returning sooner than expected. I plan to meet with the Council of Twelve on the morrow at the Science Center."

"I thought you were going to be gone ten cycles. Did you cut your airship voyage short?"

"No, we finished our tour and are currently traveling the

upper atmosphere to arrive ahead of schedule. It's quite a view from here. At any rate, I have critical information to share with the delegates, and I want you and Max there."

"I will relay the information. We'll see you in a cycle."

"Jesse to Holley, come in please." Not getting a reply, he assumed she was busy. *Too bad these things don't have voice messaging.*

"I'm here, Jesse. Sorry for the late reply. I was in the middle of an experiment."

"Something good I hope."

"Looks promising. We've been working on a better way to administer the antidote for Triverphol Disease. Although I developed a vaccine formula, it would require a large supply of syringes to inoculate this entire population. We don't have those. And making healing tea for the masses isn't practical. However, Layshura, the Operational Assistant, had an idea."

"Go on."

"We are using the excess stock of nutrition tabs and dipping them in concentrated batches of healing-leaf tea. Once the pills dry, they have an invisible coating. We have already coated a thousand of them. Test results show they will cure the Disease. I think they'll also provide lasting efficacy. And it only takes a small flake from a healing leaf in a batch of tea to be effective. In fact, we have already started delivering pills to this sector."

"Where are you getting all the water, I mean hydrew, to make these batches?"

"From quawner dens. During our stay at the emergency shelter, Narleen and Anna handed out slings to five believers and trained them on their use. Led by Tawehna, this group has been entering the hollows and returning with hydrew every dawn. They sling green crystals to repel the creatures, thwarting their attacks."

"And no one has been hurt?"

"None. Here's what's interesting, though. One of the pools of hydrew had maza growing along the banks. And you'll never guess what else."

"What?"

"Tawehna said the creatures have been eating it."

"Aha. Kinda confirms Anna's conclusions about quawners."

"Which is . . ."

"It would be better to let Anna explain her assumptions in person. Right now, please contact Narleen. She can fill you in on our current location and situation. We'll arrive on the morrow to convene with the Council, and I would like you and Layshura to attend and share what you've done."

"Acknowledged, we'll be there." Holley paused for a moment to listen to a comment from Layshura. "Oh yeah, I wanted to mention the overstock of Cradphenanill at this locale has been destroyed. When those who were addicted have fully detoxed, I think they will be happier. Life should be more than seeking pleasure from an intoxicant."

"I couldn't agree more. Sorry to cut this conversation short, but I have one more call to make. I'll see you soon. Jesse out."

"Jesse to Lundy. Hey, Rev, do you copy?"

"Aye, I hear ya loud and clear."

"What's the latest from the Science Center?"

"Me got good news and bad news."

"Start with the good."

"Well, we've been rounding up mindless inhabitants and running the deprogramming protocols. Hiehew and Rauteira are overseeing the restoration process. So far, hundreds of people have had their identities returned, not to mention their memories. They are no longer saying they serve the programmer or other daft nonsense."

"Wonderful, keep it going."

"Here's the bad: Ahboen, the former PA, hasn't attended the scheduled committee sessions. He's been holed up in his quarters with the door locked. Security broke it down yesterdawn and discovered he was gone. They said it looked as if he packed in a hurry. Things were strewn across the floor and one of his datatops was missing."

"I wasn't sure where his loyalties lay. Now we know."

"Two programmers saw him leave the center in the middle of last dusk but didn't make inquires or try to stop him."

"Hmm. Contact the SSL and ask him to conduct a search."

"I already did. No leads yet."

"Okay, thanks for the updates. We are arriving on the morrow. We will deal with the Ahboen situation then."

"Why so early? I thought you'd be gone a wee bit longer."

"Narleen or Holley can fill you in on those details. In the meantime, contact the remaining councilmembers and arrange for an emergency meeting. I've already informed the others on our team. And one more thing."

"Aye."

"Invite Tawehna and her squad of slingers to join us. I need to thank them for their bravery."

"Me get everything handled."

"Much appreciated, Rev. See you at predawn. Jesse out."

Twelve bouts later, *Old Bella* touched down at the Science Center and the six explorers disembarked. Eleven councilors were sitting around the conference table, waiting.

CHAPTER 37

RESOLUTIONS

"Thank you for getting here on short notice. What I have to share is not only important, it's critical for the survival of Camayah. Before we hear progress reports, we need to discuss the absent councilmember. Has anyone seen Ahboen?"

"The former PA has not attended any of our committee sessions," responded Cndrek. "Two dawns ago, I went to check on his welfare and found his office locked. My security team broke down the door and discovered empty quarters. His personal items and one of his datatops were missing. During questioning, Raetila confirmed that he entered her RIFT during the past dusk. Ahboen had urged her to go with him, but she wisely declined. Yesterdawn, Lundy asked me to conduct a search of the area."

"Were you able to determine his whereabouts?"

"Yes and no. My S2s found a satchel three ticks east of RIFT II. It contained miscellaneous items, clothes, and a datatop—all belonging to Ahboen. The bag had traces of quawner venom on it."

"I see. Please continue the search and keep the board apprised. In the meantime, we should appoint a replacement member. I suggest Runess. He could represent airship and portal travel, an important faction I neglected to include the first time." Jesse waited for the murmuring to stop. "All in favor, raise your hands." The vote was unanimous. "Runess, please take the twelfth seat."

One by one, the delegates gave their reports:

Cndrek reported that RIFT I had converted a mining crane into a drilling machine and located hydrew. A crew had begun pumping it to the surface. Other RIFTs were following suit.

Hiehew detailed the Science Center's progress in reversing forced programming, thereby allowing the identities and memories of hundreds of residents to be restored.

Representing the Health Center operators, Layshura shared their success in creating an antidote for Triverphol Sickness and the current distribution schedule.

Sensing it was time for a break, Jesse paused the meeting and asked for Tawehna to come forward. "I want to thank Tawehna and her group of brave souls who entered quawner dens and retrieved pail after pail of hydrew. Because of their efforts, Holley and Layshura had enough liquid to develop an innovative process to administer a cure for the Disease, which as I understand it, also provides a lasting immunity." Nods of gratitude and clapping filled the hall as the five heroes returned to their seats along the wall.

When the session resumed, Malmach and Trikernae outlined their plans for converting the Holding Area into a religious center. Rekis and Leetqu explained how the laborers were better equipped and their gelt credits increased. The other SLs updated the Council on the closure of the *Reho* cubicles and the release of supplies from their storage areas.

The reports continued for several bouts, followed by discussions, and then votes to accept or deny motions. When it seemed like all the business had been dealt with or tabled, Jesse asked Runess to stand and give his presentation.

Runess detailed the discoveries made at the southern pole while projecting the corresponding images on an eight-mark viewer. As he talked, Jawhawtu and Uewba carried in flora samples and stacked them on the floor. The majority of the councilors were shocked, including several of the invited guests. Many questions ensued.

"Are you sure the birds were nawmies?"

"Where in the south?"

"Any inhabitants?"

"Actual trees with leaves?"

"Did you really see misty green clouds?"

As soon as Runess fielded the last question, Jesse took over the chairmanship again.

"Interesting developments, to say the least. Mindful of this relevant information about your past, I suggest you begin terraforming your planet by pumping out the hydrew and replanting vegetation and crops. Afterwards, the inhabitants can switch from nourishment pills to actual food and water."

"Concerning quawners, why not try domesticating them? If you give the creatures a plant-based food source and do not infringe on the territorial hydrew supply, you may find they become docile beasts. Perhaps airships can ferry the more aggressive ones to a moon and allow them to have their own refuge. Once habitable areas are established, you'll be able to relocate animals from the south and repopulate the northern sectors."

"It's not possible to transport large animals to a location that's a thousand leggs away, let alone to a moon. Whether they're quawners or otherwise."

"That's a cop out." Seth rushed over to the SL who made the comment. "A dude named Noah did it. He built an ark, moved a bunch of animals to a new location, and resettled the earth. And he didn't have the techno-knowhow you people possess."

Jesse followed up, "Well, Runess, is it possible?"

"Indeed. Our airships have the ability to reach the upper atmosphere, which by the way I just accomplished yesterdawn with *Old Bella.* And we can build larger vessels like the ones we had prior to the Burning. If the Health Center can figure out a way to sedate these animals, we can shuttle them as far as our airships can fly."

"We can use the Foeca formula Holley developed for her quawner bombs," advised Layshura. "It would put the quawners to sleep for bouts at a time. Other creatures as well. And from what you described, the animals in the southern hemisphere are already passive."

"One problem solved." Jesse walked over to the pile of vegetation on the floor, grabbed a handful of samples, and randomly spread them across the main table. "Take a close look and ponder the possibilities. I'm sure there are countless situations the Council of Twelve can resolve if they work together. We leave everything in your hands. You can have a better world that espouses faith, hope, and compassion or return to a dystopian society, filled with injustice, the pursuit of pleasure, and deception. The decision is yours. We pray you choose the former."

Jesse motioned for his team to join him. "Our group is leaving on the morrow. Therefore, we bid this body a heartfelt goodbye with a saying often used in our realm: Godspeed." It was near nightfall by the time the meeting ended. The seven envoys left the hall and climbed the stairs to Level Three where they planned to spend one last night in the residential ward. In the morn, they would gather with their collective of friends and allies to offer final farewells.

CHAPTER 38

FAREWELLS

The team spent the dusk at the Science Center, each member in his or her own room. Before retiring for the night, Jesse placed his candle lamp on the floor and flipped the lid to release the flame. He sat on the bed and watched the gentle glow while he gathered his thoughts. One bout later, he opened his journal.

Entry Seventeen

The first meeting of the Council of Twelve went well. I got them started by appointing delegates to represent the various factions on this planet. I outlined the main issues facing them and gave the membership proposals to consider. Afterwards, Anna, Seth, and I departed in an airship to their south pole. This is where the revelations began.

Apparently, native flora and most of the animal species survived the Burning, which had devastated the rest of the planet. We discovered a shielded crater containing its own little biosphere. It wouldn't take much to reestablish life here, if they pump water to the surface and plant soreseed vegetation. Then animals could be reintroduced in the middle and northern sectors. Over time, the inhabitants may be able to terraform their entire planet.

Regarding our mission goals, we accomplished most of them. The believers were freed from their moon exile. The practice of reprogramming an individual's mind to take away their will and identity has been halted, and the process is being reversed. Other changes are underway, too. Most importantly, Yah worshipers are free to practice their religion without the threat of being imprisoned or killed. The deceptions that plagued this world have been exposed, and because of Holley's efforts, a terrible disease now has a cure.

We plan to depart Camayah and return to Eskaonus after we thank the people who supported us. This has been an exhausting assignment for all involved. My colleagues deserve a break, so we're going to spend a couple days in the Lower Realm to recuperate. As for me, I look forward to a moderate climate, lush greenery, and attending a banquet with actual food and drink.

If I have learned anything during these last two outreaches, it is this: Eternity is not about us and what we want. It's about helping others, not only with spiritual concerns, but with practical ones.

Jesse closed his journal, turned off his candle lamp, and snuggled under the covers. In the morning, he arose early, removed the quispike from his satchel and leaned it against the wall. He slipped out of his silvery jumpsuit, laid it on the bed, and dressed in his clothes from Eskaonus. He detached his ID wristband, placed it on the nightstand, and repacked his carrier, keeping only his journal, lamp, radio, and a handful of nourishment tablets. Taking one last glance around his room, Jesse descended the stairs to Level One, and waited for the others.

At predawn, his associates and those who were allies began shuffling in for the final gathering. As per Jesse's instructions, the team members had left their DINs and stunners in their quarters and dressed in their off-world clothing. While the group visited among themselves, Rauteira and Seth snuck over to a corner to talk privately.

"So, you're really leaving this dawn?"

"Yep, almost time to book out of here."

"May I ask a favor before you depart?" She stepped closer and took a hold of his hand.

Instead of releasing her embrace, he allowed her to hold on. "Sure, what is it?"

"I know we are not prebonded, but I would like to kiss you

on the cheek." Seth studied her eyes, sensing sincerity. "When Holley did that, you said it was only a show of appreciation, nothing more, not a sign of a relationship or bonding. You were simply good friends."

"Yeah . . ."

"Well, because you're a friend, I would like to share my appreciation for what you have done to help my family and our planet."

"I guess that would be chill." He turned his face, and she gave him a small peck on the left cheek. "Am I allowed to return the appreciation?"

"Oh, yes, would you?" He bent over and reciprocated on the opposite cheek. Her face flushed red. She smiled, released her grip of his hand, and trotted off to join her parents who were talking with Max and Narleen. Seth followed, trying to act nonchalant. He didn't realize that Max, Narleen, and Rauteira's parents had been watching the encounter.

"Hey, recruit, any news to report?" Max grinned.

"Uncool, bro, don't ask."

As soon as the last guest arrived, Jesse moved to the center of the hall and gathered everyone together in a circle. He noticed joyful faces and a few sorrowful ones. "Okay, folks, I appreciate you being here to see us off. Does anybody have a farewell message to share?"

"Me, I suppose." Lundy gazed at Rauteira with saddened eyes. "You have been like the granddaughter I never had. Me thinks I'll miss you most of all. Please keep the coding scrolls as a keepsake. Besides, you understand this data language better than I do. And one day, I mean dawn, when you need a special code, look for it in my binder and reminisce."

She ran up to him and wrapped her arms around his waist. "I love you, Papa Lun. I will never forget you." Lundy wept moistureless tears of joy

"I would like to thank my assault units." Max pounded his fist across his chest. "It's been an honor to serve alongside you."

"Layshura, carry on the work at the Health Center." Holley opened her medkit and removed a small bag. "I'm leaving these healing leaves with you. Remember, it only takes a tiny piece, brewed in hydrew, to be effective. Use the cure wisely."

"Thank you, healer. I will cherish this amazing medicine."

"Malmach and Trikernae, you are the only spiritual leaders on this world," Anna said in a sweet, cheerful voice. "Never relinquish your ministry or doubt your calling. For in due season, you will reap good things, if you don't quit or lose heart. Isn't that right, Jess?" Jesse nodded, recalling the day Max shared Rule Number Three with him on Eskaonus.

More appreciations followed: some from the collective, others from the residents. Jesse waited until everybody had their say and then offered a final word. "I also wish to thank our supporters. We could not have accomplished half of what we did without you. And now, it is with a heavy heart, I bid you farewell."

"Will we ever see you again?" inquired Leetqu.

"I've been asked this question before. Perhaps one dawn, we will meet in a different realm, an eternal one. Until such time, let me give you the reply a wise mender gave me: Dayrise will bring what it brings."

"Alright, team, let's join hands." The people in the hall backed away, not knowing what to expect. "Reverend, will you do the honors?"

"Aye, just think where you want to be and you're . . ." A flash of light, a rumbling sound, and the seven vanished into thin air.

After a few moments, someone said, "I told you they were the *sent ones*."

CHAPTER 39

BACK ON ESKAONUS

As Ottaar walked out her front door, she felt a slight shaking, followed by the sound of muted thunder. The mender turned around and rushed back inside in time to see seven figures appear out of nowhere. Six were standing; one was kneeling on the floor, holding her sides, struggling with a series of dry heaves. “Lady Narleen, are you okay?”

Max lifted his spouse off the floor and carried her to the settee. Holley went over to offer her assistance. The others gathered around Narleen. “I’m fine, just a little queasy. Give me a moment to catch my breath.”

“I’ll put on a pot of tea. It will help settle your upset stomach.” Ottaar hurried across to her kitchen, filled a kettle with water and placed it on the stove. She sprinkled in a handful of Anatora leaves, covered the kettle with a lid, and left it to simmer. When the mender returned, she noticed the condition of the other team members. “Sir Jesse, your party looks like they haven’t eaten in yarns. Their faces and bodies are emaciated.”

“We haven’t. The place we visited didn’t have food or anything to drink, only nutrition and hydration pills.”

“Hmm . . . let me set out some real nourishment. I have yestercycle’s kin, dried antaloop, and berry juice.” She returned with two platters. With another trip, she brought cups, plates, and a large pitcher of yarm. “I’m concerned about the weight loss in such a short period of time. This group is little more than skin and bones, except you, Lady Narleen. It appears you have put on a bit of weight, maybe a quarter stone. And you're feeling queasy? How long have you been nauseated?"

"Twenty cycles."

The mender glanced at Holley who nodded back. "I see. Does Max know about your condition?"

"Know what?"

"No, I haven't told him yet. I was waiting until we returned."

"What condition?"

"Now's a good time as any."

"Nar?"

"Alright, since Holley already knows. I should probably tell everybody else."

"Knows what?" Max's impatience turned into frustration. His jaw tightened.

"That your wife is pregnant," Holley replied with a smile. "You two are going to have a baby in about seven months."

"Are you sure?"

"Little doubt, Captain," confirmed Ottaar. "Congratulations to you both!"

"Nar, why didn't you tell me?" He sat on the settee by Narleen and wrapped his arms around her.

"You needed to focus on your assignments and not get sidetracked worrying about me. We were on Camayah for at least seventeen cycles, and if you were distracted for even one of them, the mission might have ended in failure. I would not be the reason for that."

"Really, seventeen?" Ottaar's eyes widened. "You guys departed one cycle ago. I assumed you changed your minds and returned."

"Dudes, you mean we have only been gone one day, I mean dawn, I mean cycle. Arrgh! With all these location changes, I'm getting confused about which calendar to use."

"Yes, Seth, your group left yestercycle at firstlight."

"Strange. For us, it was much longer . . ." Jesse paused to count the elapsed timeframe in his mind. "Are you sure we haven't been gone seventeen cycles?"

"No, just one," insisted Ottaar.

"Wow, I guess time really is relative."

“Isn’t time the same everywhere?

“Apparently not. I’m not sure I understand the concept myself.”

“We can discuss the date differences later. Right now, you need actual food in your stomachs, especially yours, my Lady. You have two mouths to feed, and I don’t mean your spouse. Sit down and fill up your dishes. I’ll fetch the tea for Lady Narleen. The rest of you can have yarm.”

A knock sounded at the front door. “Mender Ottaar, do I have permission to enter?” asked Phauch, the Militia Chief. “I am looking for Captain Maximus. Lady Saephira thought he might be here. I have an urgent dispatch to deliver.”

“Your captain is here. Come on in.” Phauch darted through the entry, bowed to show respect, and handed the message to Max.

“This dispatch is vague. Please elaborate.”

“The Postal Tower received a flyer message a span ago. It says half of the fleet at Bayegulf is missing. For some reason, they never returned to port after their fishing expedition.”

“I’m sorry, Nar. I have to leave. I wish—”

“Go! I understand. You are the Captain of the Militia. I would expect nothing less.”

“Chief, after everyone breaks their fast, escort Lady Narleen to Residential Hall.”

“It will be done, sir.”

“Menders Ottaar and Holley, will you please see to my spouse’s welfare?” Both women nodded in agreement. “Good, then I will meet everybody at the nightrise banquet.” And Max raced out the entrance, heading toward the mail tower.

“The ships may have run into foul weather or tarried at sea to catch a bounty of tarkks.” Ottaar wandered over to the door and closed it. “Either way, the crews should be home soon.”

“Let’s hope so,” responded Anna. But in her heart, she felt the reason for the delay was more sinister.

Cast of Characters

Abdiel (AB-dye'l): High-ranking angel. His name means servant of God. He manages Outreach & Supply in Central Heaven.

Ahboen (ah-BOW'n): Program Assistant (PA), mixed loyalties.

Annabelle Altshuler: Also called Anna, Annie, and Annabel. Messianic believer, anointed songwriter, musician, raptured saint.

Bio: Annabelle was born in Ghana. When her parents died, a Jewish family in England adopted her. She attended their synagogue, and later, a messianic fellowship where she had a charismatic experience. Soon thereafter, God started giving her prophetic dreams and spiritual songs, which certain folks in her congregation didn't appreciate. They asked Anna to keep those revelations and songs to herself or leave. After praying for wisdom, she decided to move on. Soon thereafter, the Rapture occurred.

Bolgog (BOWL-gog): Senior Commander in the Guards. He later became the de facto leader of the Upper Realm when Lord Eddnok disappeared.

Calrin (cal-RIN): Teenager from Beayama, harpoon angler, friend of Seth.

Chepho (CHE-foe): Militia Lead in the Lower Realm.

Chesedel (CHESS-a-del): Official name is *elChesed.* Faithful messenger, Jesse's guardian angel. His name means mercy of God.

Cndrek (KUHN-drek): Security Leader (SL) for Sector One, stationed in RIFT I. Later promoted to Senior Security

Leader (SSL).

Eddnok (ED-nock): Lord Eddnok, deposed ruler of the Upper Realm, former magistrate in Briacap.

Bio: Eddnok is self-centered, cunning, helps those who are faithful to him, and turns on those who are not. He consumed fruit from the cloned knowledge tree and embraced evil. He was last seen entering the Lost Forest.

Flissae (FLISS-ay): A prostitute who worked for Eddnok. Currently hiding in Tabahir.

Fruit Vendor: Angel who operates the mobile produce stand in heaven.

Gelr (GEL'er): Former Upper Realm commander who defected to the Lower Realm. Promoted to Captain of the Safeguards by Lady Saephira.

Hiehew (HI-hue): Programming Supervisor (P3), secret Yah believer.

Holley Rossie: Also called Hol, Doc, and healer. Former nurse practitioner, recent resident of heaven.

Bio: Holley worked in an emergency care facility on earth before she arrived in heaven. She regretted not going to Eskaonus with Jesse and the team. Later, Holley realized her healthcare knowledge was why she was chosen for the first outreach. A medic would have been advantageous, considering the dire conflicts the team encountered. When presented with another opportunity, she joined the second outreach to Camayah.

Jawhawtu (jaw-HAH-too): Also called Jaw, airship midmate, engineer, young man.

Jesse Walt: Also called Jess, JW, Sir, and Brother Walt.

Served in the Navy, former police officer, chosen as team leader, raptured saint.

Bio: After high school, Jesse enlisted in the Navy and became an MP. When he got out of the service, he took a position as a small-town police chief. Due to an unfortunate DUI accident, the department forced him to resign. He had trouble finding work until a convenience store hired him as a clerk. Jesse is inquisitive, caring, and sometimes conflicted. He enjoys journaling. After the Rapture, he was asked to lead a group of envoys to Eskaonus, and then later to Camayah.

Layshura (lay-SURE-ah): Operational Assistant (OA) at the Termination Facility. Promoted to Operational Leader (OL).

Leetqu (LEET-kue): Inhabitant of Camayah, married to Rekis, her daughter is Rauteira.

Lucifer: Also known as Satan, the devil, and son of the morning.

Lundy MacBain: Also called Reverend, Rev, Preach, Master Lundy, and Papa Lun. Scottish minister, Bible scholar, language translator, missionary, martyred saint, resident of heaven.

Bio: Reverend Lundy ministered for many years as a pastor. He lived in Scotland 400 years ago. One day, he encountered a mob of agnostics who didn't care for his preaching. They pulled knives and killed him. His soul emerged in heaven. He spends his time in prayer and meditating on Scripture.

Malmach (maul-MOK): Spiritual leader in exile, called the provost, married to Trikernae. He is hiding on a moon in the Camayah system with other Yah believers.

Maximus Gallius: Known as Max, Maximum, Maxie, and the big guy. Roman soldier who found faith in Christ during the first century, longtime resident of heaven.

Bio: Maximus was a Roman soldier, a centurion, in charge of ninety men. He worshiped the false god of war, Mars. While away on an eastern campaign, barbarians raided his hometown. They killed everyone in the village and raped his beloved, Cassia, before murdering her. His plans for marriage and children ended. He grew distraught, bitter, and angrier by the season. Then one day, Max met a fisherman who told him about the one true God. He and several of his legionnaires accepted His Son as Savior and were baptized. Later, Caesar discovered their new allegiance to the Christ and put the group to the sword. Max awoke in heaven. He currently abides on Eskaonus.

Melmandus (mel-MAN-dus): Former Captain of the Militia. Perished in a rockslide.

Membarb (MEM-barb): Woodsmith in Beayama, friend of Ottaar.

Menarbat (MEN-ar-bat): Called the Tracker, former overseer of provisions in Beayama, traitor. Last seen entering the Lost Forest with Eddnok.

Nanlon (nan-LAWN): Owner of the Copper Rail Tavern in Tabahir. He is the barkeep, cook, and housekeeper. His son works in the stables.

Narleen (NAR-lean): Lady Narleen, Vice-leader of the Lower Realm, assistant magistrate in Beayama, married to Maximus.

Bio: Narleen served as Saephira's lady-in-waiting in Beayama before being promoted to Vice-leader of the Upper Realm. She is trustworthy, compassionate, supportive of others, and sometimes impetuous.

Operational Leader: (OL) at the Termination Facility, unnamed, disobedient. Replaced by Layshura.

Ottaar (OH-tarr): Mender in Beayama, medic and physician. Promoted to Mender of the Realm by Lady Saephira.

Phauch (PAW'sh): Militia Chief in the Lower Realm.

Preaverca (pray-VER-ca): Former postal overseer in Beayama, traitor. Last seen entering the Lost Forest with Eddnok.

Program Master: (PM), supreme ruler of Camayah, identity unknown.

Raetila (ray-TILL-ah): Security Assistant (SA) from RIFT II.

Rauteira (rah-TEER-uh): Tech-savvy teenager, daughter of Rekis and Leetqu.

Raydoo (RAE-do): Teenager from Beayama, harpoon angler, friend of Seth.

Rekis (REE-kis): Inhabitant of Camayah, married to Leetqu, his daughter is Rauteira.

Runess (ROO-ness): Former Security Assistant (SA) over the Airship Dock. Imprisoned at the Holding Center, accused of being a discontent.

Saephira (sa-FEAR-uh): Lady Saephira, Leader of the Lower Realm, senior magistrate in Beayama.

Bio: Saephira is the magistrate of Beayama and leader of the Lower Realm. When her parents died, she inherited their leadership roles. She was betrothed to Eddnok of the Upper Realm with the hope of creating an alliance between the two warring provinces. Before the wedding, Saephira discovered Eddnok only desired her as one of his concubines, so she declined the arrangement. She is wise, discerning, and honest.

Seth Cahir: Also known as recruit or the kid. A teenager, athletic, marathon runner, rock climber, loves all outdoor sports except surfing. Accepted Christ as his Savior during the Jesus People Movement in the 1970s, resident of heaven.

Bio: Seth loved outdoor sports like rock climbing, surfing, and biking. One day in Malibu, he was floating past the breakwater, waiting for a ten-foot wave, when a great white attacked him, biting his surfboard in two. He made it to shore, swimming, but the shark chased him all the way in. Afterwards, he swore to never enter the water again. Then one day during a bike ride, Seth was run over by a drunk driver, which paralyzed him from the waist down. Later, the doctors discovered a cancerous brain tumor. When they tried to remove it, he started hemorrhaging. He died in surgery and awoke in heaven.

Tawehna (tah-WAY-nah): Middle-aged woman, experienced with stunner weapons, one of seven Yah believers hiding on the third moon.

Trikernae (TRY-ker-nay): Spiritual leader in exile, called the pravost, married to Malmach.

Uewba (YEW-baw): Also called Uew, airship rowmate, navigator, young woman.

Uzziel (use-ZI-el): Called *the Cherubim*, high-ranking cherub angel, carries a flaming sword. His name means strength of God.

Waubush (WAH-bush): Former Captain of the Safeguards. Perished in battle.

Winged Ones: Sentinel angels.

Yhmim (yah-MIM): Deposed Vice-leader of the Lower Realm, traitor, serving a lengthy prison sentence.

GLOSSARY 1

CENTRAL HEAVEN

CENTRAL HEAVEN

Locations and landmarks in Central Heaven are speculative. Notwithstanding, several are based on Scripture, others inspired by tradition.

"But as it is written, Eye hath not seen, nor ear heard, neither have entered into the heart of man, the things which God hath prepared for them that love him" (1 Corinthians 2:9).

KEY PLAYERS

Abdiel (AB-dye'l): High-ranking angel. His name means servant of God. He manages Outreach & Supply in Central Heaven.

Chesedel (CHESS-a-del): Official name is *elChesed.* Faithful messenger, Jesse's guardian angel. His name means mercy of God.

Fruit Vendor: Angel who operates the mobile produce stand.

Lucifer: Also known as Satan, the devil, and son of the morning.

Uzziel (use-ZI-el): Called *the Cherubim*, high-ranking cherub angel, carries a flaming sword. His name means strength of God.

Winged Ones: Sentinel angels.

CHERUB ANGEL OR CHERUBIM

Cherub or cherubim in the plural form are celestial beings. They serve God and follow His will. The cherubim were first introduced in Genesis: "So he drove out the man; and he placed at the east of the garden of Eden Cherubims, and a flaming sword which turned every way, to keep the way of the tree of life" (Genesis 3:24). Although their biblical descriptions vary, cherubim are thought to have wings and carry fiery swords.

Before his rebellion and fall from heaven, Satan was a cherub (see Ezekiel 28:11–15).

HEAVENLY SALUTATIONS

Peace to You, Shalom, Blessings, Precious One, Beloved, Favored Ones, Dear Ones, Maranatha, and Godspeed.

LOCATIONS AND LANDMARKS

Dwelling Places: Housing for the saints.

"In my Father's house are many mansions: if *it were* not *so*, I would have told you. I go to prepare a place for you. And if I go and prepare a place for you, I will come again, and receive you unto myself; that where I am, *there* ye may be also" (John 14:2, 3).

Fountain of Living Water: A wellspring in Central Heaven that disperses the waters of life. Sometimes called the Fountain of Life.

"And he said unto me, It is done. I am Alpha and Omega, the beginning and the end. I will give unto him that is athirst of the fountain of the water of life freely" (Revelation 21:6).

"And the Spirit and the bride say, Come. And let him that heareth say, Come. And let him that is athirst come. And whosoever will, let him take the water of life freely" (Revelation 22:17).

Fruit Cart: Vendor's mobile produce stand on Straight Street.

Hall of Records: A storage facility where all the records and histories from the beginning of time are kept, including the Scroll of Life, scrolls of works, and all other related documents. The Hall of Records also contains a scroll room where residents can access Scripture, prophecies, hymns, poetry, and other writings to study, read, and enjoy. *Note: In biblical times, books were generally in the form of scrolls.*

"And I saw the dead, small and great, stand before God; and the books were opened: and another book was opened, which is *the book* of life: and the dead were judged out of those things which were written in the books, according to their works" (Revelation 20:12).

Judgment Seat: *The place where Christ delivers judgments and hands out rewards.*

"For we must all appear before the judgment seat of Christ; that every one may receive the things *done* in *his* body, according to that he hath done, whether *it be* good or bad" (2 Corinthians 5:10).

Orientation: An informational center to help with directions, suggestions, and guidelines for new arrivals. The facility also carries starter kits and offers a wide selection of clothing.

Outreach & Supply: A place to requisition materials, tools, musical instruments, Bibles, Torahs, and other items appropriate for use in heaven.

Patriarch Plaza: The most popular plaza in Central Heaven. It has a lecture podium and unlimited seating.

Paths of the Patriarchs: All interconnecting footpaths in Central Heaven.

Prayer Gardens: Special gathering places set aside for solitude and prayer. Some theologians believe certain biblical references or terms might foreshadow landmarks found in heaven.

GARDEN OF MEDITATION (Philippians 4:8): Located on Straight Street.

GARDEN OF PRAYER (1 Thessalonians 5:17): Junction by Damascus Road.

GARDEN OF SUPPLICATION (Philippians 4:6): Corner of Charity Street and Narrow Way.

Pearl Gates: The pearl gates are traditional names for entries, passageways, or portals into heaven. They are based on descriptions from Revelation 21:12–21, which mention twelve gates made with twelve single pearls. Each gate contains the written name of one of the twelve tribes of Israel. The three gates below are hypothetical.

GOLD PEARL (Matthew 13:45–46): Pearl of great price.

ROSE PEARL (Song of Solomon 2:1): Rose of Sharon.

WHITE PEARL (Isaiah 1:18, Revelation 2:17): White represents purity, newness, and forgiveness.

River of Life: A river with life-giving properties.

"And he shewed me a pure river of water of life, clear as crystal, proceeding out of the throne of God and of the Lamb" (Revelation 22:1).

Everything will live wherever the river goes (see Ezekiel 47:9).

A river went out of Eden and watered the garden (see Genesis 2:10).

Streets and Roads: Thoroughfares to various locations in Central Heaven and elsewhere. Some theologians believe roadways in heaven, like streets, are foreshadowed in Scripture.

DAMASCUS ROAD (Acts 26:12–13).
FAITH AVENUE, HOPE LANE, AND CHARITY STREET (1 Corinthians 13:13).
NARROW WAY (Matthew 7:14).
STRAIGHT STREET (Acts 9:11).

"And the street of the city *was* pure gold, as it were transparent glass" (Revelation 21:21*b*).

Throne Room: The place where the Ancient of Days resides.

"I beheld till the thrones were cast down, and the Ancient of days did sit, whose garment *was* white as snow, and the hair of his head like the pure wool: his throne *was like* the fiery flame, *and* his wheels *as* burning fire" (Daniel 7:9).

"After this I looked, and, behold, a door *was* opened in heaven: and the first voice which I heard *was* as it were of a trumpet talking with me; which said, Come up hither, and I will shew thee things which must be hereafter. And immediately I was in the spirit: and, behold, a throne was set in heaven, and *one* sat on the throne" (Revelation 4:1, 2).

Tree of Life: Ancient tree that grows and flourishes by the River of Life.

"In the midst of the street of it, and on either side of the river, *was there* the tree of life, which bare twelve *manner of* fruits, *and* yielded her fruit every month: and the leaves of the tree *were* for the healing of the nations" (Revelation 22:2).

"And out of the ground made the LORD God to grow every tree that is pleasant to the sight, and good for food; the tree of life also in the midst of the garden, and the tree of knowledge of good and evil" (Genesis 2:9).

The fruit did not fail nor did the leaves wither. Leaves were used for medicine and fruit for food (see Ezekiel 47:12).

Tree of the Knowledge of Good and Evil: Current status and location unknown.

"But of the tree of the knowledge of good and evil, thou shalt not eat of it: for in the day that thou eatest thereof thou shalt surely die" (Genesis 2:17).

"And the serpent said unto the woman, Ye shall not surely die: For God doth know that in the day ye eat thereof, then your eyes shall be opened, and ye shall be as gods, knowing good and evil" (Genesis 3:4, 5).

Waiting Line: An overflow area where people wait to appear before the Judgment Seat.

Walled Terrace: Scenic walkway in Central Heaven adjacent to the River of Life.

GLOSSARY 2

ESKAONUS

ESKAONUS

Eskaonus is a fictional world or place. However, all tangible worlds and places, whether known or unknown, were made by God.

"Through faith we understand that the worlds were framed by the word of God, so that things which are seen were not made of things which do appear" (Hebrews 11:3).

"Hath in these last days spoken unto us by *his* Son, whom he hath appointed heir of all things, by whom also he made the worlds" (Hebrews 1:2).

"And I saw a new heaven and a new earth: for the first heaven and the first earth were passed away; and there was no more sea" (Revelation 21:1).

OVERVIEW OF ESKAONUS

Eskaonus (Es-KAY-nohs) is an offworld planet or place with two provinces: Upper Realm in the north and Lower Realm in the south. It has two seas, one landlocked. Other continents or landmasses, if they exist, are unexplored.

There are no suns or moons. During the day, a glowing light similar to an aurora borealis shines forth until fading into a gloomy twilight. Afterwards, nighttime takes over followed by total darkness. Residents use torches during these darkouts.

The humid southlands have rivers, farmlands, and abundant plant life. The arid northlands are mostly barren with limited resources. Tall exotic trees called cottlepines cover the forests. Most animals are larger than those living on earth. Some have similar sounding names. Predator fish known as tarkks inhabit the lakes and lower tributaries. Slimy eels swim the rivers. Four-footed creatures with long hairy manes are used for riding and pack animals. The locals call them kacks.

Eskaonites harvest berries, maize, root vegetables, squashes, and mushrooms. Their main diet is fish from harpoon angling, but they also hunt for bush varmints and antaloops. Foods are heavily spiced to preserve them. Families generally eat two meals a day: one in the morning and a hearty dinner banquet after twilight. Drinks include various flavors of tea, yarm beverages, and kunakk.

KEY PLAYERS

Bolgog (BOWL-gog): De facto leader of the Upper Realm.

Calrin (cal-RIN): Teenager from Beayama, harpoon angler, friend of Seth.

Chepho (CHE-foe): Militia Lead in the Lower Realm.

Eddnok (ED-nock): Deposed ruler of the Upper Realm. Whereabouts unknown.

Gelr (GEL-er): Captain of the Safeguards.

Maximus Gallius: Captain of the Militia, married to Narleen.

Menarbat (MEN-ar-bat): Called the Tracker. Whereabouts unknown.

Nanlon (nan-LAWN): Owner of the Copper Rail Tavern in Tabahir.

Narleen (NAR-lean): Vice-leader of the Lower Realm, married to Maximus.

Ottaar (OH-tarr): Mender of the Realm, medic, physician.

Phauch (PAW'sh): Militia Chief in the Lower Realm.

Preaverca (pray-VER-ca): Former Postal Overseer. Whereabouts unknown.

Raydoo (RAE-do): Teenager from Beayama, harpoon angler, friend of Seth.

Saephira (sa-FEAR-uh): Leader of the Lower Realm, senior magistrate in Beayama.

Yhmim (yah-MIM): Former Vice-leader. Incarcerated for past crimes.

Although the Eskaonites have forenames and surnames, the latter indicating their family heritage, they prefer using first names only.

LOCAL GREETINGS

Good dayrise: Good morning
Good nightrise: Good evening

TIMES AND SEASONS

Firstlight: Predawn, also called morning twilight
Twilight: Time before nightrise
Morrow: Tomorrow, as in on the morrow
Dayrise: Daytime or morning time
Nightrise: Evening or nighttime
Darkout: Midnight or later, darkest part of the night
Darkness: Middle of the night
Dark, the: Short form for darkout
Day: Short form for dayrise
Night: Short from for nightrise

Yestercycle: Yesterday

Forecycle: Later morning
Midcycle: Noon or around noon
Aftercycle: Afternoon
Postcycle: Late afternoon
Latecycle: Later afternoon, nearing twilight

Moments: Minutes
Span/Spans: Hour/hours
Cycles: Days
Periods: Months, sometimes as undetermined
Yarns: Years, as in a few or many yarns
Ages: Long time, many years, long ago
Eons: Centuries, extensive periods of time, past eras

DISTANCES AND MEASUREMENTS

Leagues: Distance, approximately 10 miles, sometimes as undetermined

Paces: One pace = 3 feet (used for height, width, stride, and distance)

Stones: Weight

Hands: One hand = 4 inches, 18 hands = 6 feet (mainly used for height)

Comparisons: Tall as a cottlepine. Strong, big, or wide as a kack.

MILITARY AND ARMIES

SOUTHERN PROVINCE

Militia, the: Lower Realm soldiers

Safeguards, the: Lower Realm tower guards, watchmen, and gatemen

Captains: Senior officers in the Militia or the Safeguards, similar to Colonels

Militia Lead: Junior officer, similar to a Lieutenant

Militia Chief: Commissioned officer with authority like a Sergeant Major

Militiamen: All soldiers, ranked or unranked
Gatemen: Keep or entryway sentries

NORTHERN PROVINCE

Guards, the: Upper Realm soldiers

Commanders: Common designations for any officer in the Guards
Senior Commander: Command rank officer, similar to a Colonel
Commander: Middle rank officer, similar to a Major
Sub-Commander: Junior officer, similar to a Lieutenant
Squad Leader: Non-commissioned rank with authority like a Sergeant
Guardsmen: All guards, including officers, sentries, warders, and sentinels

PLANTS AND ROOTS

USED IN TEAS AND MENDER REMEDIES

Anatora: Flowering plant, mild tranquilizer
Azollie: Spiny root, stimulant, similar to caffeine
Helixzon: Oily plant, used to make healing salves
Netherute: Root, pain reliever, promotes sleep
Soaproot: White porous root, antiseptic qualities
Utondra: Antidote for yarm berry poisoning

VINEYARDS

Kunakk Vineyards (kue-NACK): Trellised vineyards near Nakk Village. The grain pods are cultivated by local vinedressers who grow, harvest, and produce a beverage called kunakk.

Yarm Vineyards (Yah'rm): A farm collective raising yarm berries. The bushes are tended by vinedressers in nearby Ritwell Village who ship the berries throughout Eskaonus to create juices and fermented drinks as well as fresh desserts.

Cities and Villages

Bayegulf (BAY-gulf): Port city, sailors, fishing, shipping center, allegiance to Lower Realm, city mender.

Beayama (bee-YAH-ma): Capital of the Lower Realm, non-fortress, militia headquarters, trading center, commercial shops, woodshop, metalworking, forges, city mender.

Briacap (BRY-uh-cap): Capital of the Upper Realm, fortress, large battalion, nearby mining operations, metalworking, woodshops, forges, alchemist, city mender.

Cali Village (CAL-lee): Lower Realm settlement, fishing at Mista Lake and along the Cali River, village mender.

Falein Village (FAY-leen): Lower Realm settlement, fishing at Falein Lake, farming, bush varmint hunting in the Neutral Lands, village mender.

Midvill (MID-vill): Neutral city, allegiance to Lower Realm, trading center, small militia garrison, city mender. The city straddles the middle of the boundary lines.

Nakk Village (NACK): Upper Realm settlement, vinedressers for Kunakk Vineyards, small garrison, no local mender.

Ritwell Village (RIT-well): Lower Realm settlement, vinedressers for Yarm Vineyards, fishing along the Gemous River, bush varmint and antaloop hunting in the Heill Void, no local mender.

Tabahir (TAB-uh-her): Nonaligned city in the Neutral Lands influenced by Briacap. Commerce comes from taverns, lodging, and brothels. Trading, smuggling, and bush varmint hunting. Lawless vicinity, no local mender.

Wilderness and Deserts

Blighte, the: Western badlands, barren, deadly hot, dry, no plants, no animals, inhospitable.

Heill Void (he-EL): Also called ***the Void***. Arid desert, sand dunes, windy, sparse vegetation, large spiny cactus, herds of antaloop, dens of bush varmints. Located southeast of the Nae Wilderness.

Nae Wilderness (NAY): Also called ***the Nae*** and ***the Wilderness***. Mostly unexplored, dangerous, borders the Lost Forest. Settlements are rumored to exist in the east. Explorers and trackers seldom travel more than a league into the region. Those who do, seldom return. The Nae is lifeless and desolate. It has no flowing water except in the southern part where the Gemous River intersects with the Heill Void.

Northern Expanse: Parched wastelands, scorching temperatures, unexplored.

Southern Expanse: Uninhabited region south of the Gemous River, chilly climate.

Mountains and Summits

Birgo Summit (BUR-go): Second highest elevation in Eskaonus.

Colrath Mountains (COAL-rath): Highest mountain range, red rocky shale, three abandoned mines, borders the Blighte on the west and Narmoot Forest in the south. Notable mounts are Gaulmore Peak and Birgo Summit. No minerals.

Gaulmore Peak (GAUL-more): Highest elevation in Eskaonus, south of the Northern Expanse.

Mnnie Mountains (MIN'nee): Southern mountain range, steep cliffs, deep dry canyons, ancient ruins, fresh water spring.

Closest rivers are the Cali and Gemous. Veins of tin and copper are scattered among the ridges.

Narnj Mountains (NARN-jay): Second highest mountain range, located north of the Lost Forest and west of the Hallet Sea. It has two working mines with major deposits of tin and copper ore.

Onnie Passage: (ON'nee): A pass through the Mnnie Mountains with steep cliffs and deep canyons.

Outlook Point: An overlook area by the Gemous River that lies east of Yarm Vineyards and south of the Lost Forest. Last familiar landmark before entering the Nae Wilderness and Heill Void.

MINING OPERATIONS

Dig, the: Copper mine in the Narnj Mountains.

Pit, the: Tin mine in the Narnj Mountains. Ore from both mines are taken to Briacap to be smelted and forged into bronze.

Red Drop: An abandoned mine in the Colrath Mountains. The dig collapsed and buried the miners inside. Later became a graveyard memorial.

Surface Mining: The Mnnie Mountains have small veins of tin and copper on the exposed ridges. The ores are transported to Beayama for processing.

FORESTS

Lost Forest: A large forest of cottlepines bordering the Nae Wilderness. It earned its reputation because people who entered the dense interior and were never seen again.

Narmoot Forest (NAR-moot): A sparse forest below the Colrath Mountains. Half the trees are dead or dying. Most of the ones growing in these woods are strangely deformed.

Seas and Oceans

Hallet Sea (HAL-let): Northern landlocked ocean, surrounded by steep mountains and the Northern Expanse wastelands, unexplored.

Nether Sea (NETH-er): Southern ocean, port access, harpoon fishing, coastal sailing.

Lakes

Falein Lake (FAY-leen): Shallow waters, docks, boats, harpoon angling, net fishing for eels, water supply for Falein Village.

Mista Lake (MISS-tah): Deep waters, docks, boats, harpoon angling, net fishing for eels, water supply for Cali Village.

Rivers, Springs, and Wells

Cali River (CAL-lee): A tributary of the Gemous River with an upper fork. Supplies water to Mista and Falein lakes. The river is teaming with river eels.

Dry Well: An abandoned well near Briacap, one of many that dried up after the Event.

Gemous, the (GEM-oh-us): Main river system of lower Eskaonus. It runs through the Heill Void and into the Nae Wilderness with a lower fork branching from the Nether Sea. The waters contain endless schools of slimy eel and migrating tarkks.

Hidden Springs: Mineral spring near the Narmoot Forest.

High Springs: Artesian spring located in the Mnnie

Mountains along Onnie Passage, non-alkaline.

Trobell Springs (TRO-bell): The main water source for Nakk Village and Briacap.

Yarm Springs (Yah'rm): A deep well near the Gemous River. Yarm Springs is the main water source for irrigating the nearby vineyards.

OTHER LOCATIONS

Boundary Lines: Northern and southern borderlines separating the provinces.

Neutral Lands: Formerly called the Disputed Lands. An area between the Upper and Lower Realms. Barren, lawless, and overrun by bush varmints.

Farmlands: Found entirely in the Lower Realm. They grow maize, varieties of gourds, starchy roots similar to yams, and vegetables.

Ruins, the: An ancient settlement in the Mnnie mountain range, origin unknown.

ITEMS AND INFORMATION

Alchemy: The forerunner of chemistry based on the supposed transformation of matter. Alchemists attempted to convert base metals into gold, discover universal cures for disease, and develop elixirs to prolong life.

Apothecary: An archaic term for a person who formulated and dispensed medicines. In addition to providing herbs and remedies, apothecaries offered general health advice to their patients. They also sold their ingredients and medications to other practitioners.

Antaloop: Deer-like animal with four horns. Numerous

herds inhabit the Heill Void along the Gemous River. They are hunted for their tender, sweet-tasting meat.

Breaking Fast: First meal after fasting through the night, more commonly known as breakfast.

***Bush Varmint**:* A three-legged, hopping creature with one front leg and two hind ones. Similar in size to a large jack rabbit, except the bush varmint has short ears and a long bushy tail. They live in burrows in the Neutral Lands and Heill Void. Cooked or stewed varmints are a popular entrée in the northlands.

Cottlepines: Type of evergreen pine tree with oak-shaped leaves on their branches instead of needles. They grow to a towering height.

***Dallups**:* Mushrooms in Eskaonus. They flourish in the southern lands, propagated by seeds instead of spores. The larger ones keep the patch full by spreading their seeds during darkout. Residents only harvest the middle-sized dallups. The caps are shaped like little Christmas trees, pointed at the top with green gills underneath.

Glifstring: An eight-string musical instrument, half guitar, half harp, which never needs tuning. It comes with a shoulder strap.

Homing Flyers: Fast flying predatory birds able to navigate at night and used to deliver messages. They are the size of a large raven with a smooth underbody and grayish fuzz-covered wings.

Hunting Mushrooms (or dallups): A courting ritual. Generally employed by women as a way to meet interested suitors.

Laddie: Scottish slang. Although often associated with men or boys, in the past, laddie was used as a nickname for women or girls. In the plural form, laddies, like guys and dudes, can also refer to a mixed group. Some consider the name gender-neutral.

Kacks: Four-footed creatures with long-haired manes used by the locals as mounts and pack animals. They are good swimmers, fast runners, hardy, and can travel for long periods of time without drinking water.

Kin: Crispy baked bread made with maize. Considered a main food staple.

Kunakk: Dark, frothy, liquor produced from vine-ripened grain pods cultivated in the Kunakk Vineyards. The distilling process makes the drink highly intoxicating.

Maize: An orangish-brown vegetable, similar to corn, grown on stalks in the farmlands below the southern boundary line. The dried kernels are ground and used to make kin.

Rule Number One: Always expect the unexpected.

Rule Number Two: Face your fears to overcome them.

Rule Number Three: In due season you will reap if you don't quit or lose heart (see Galatians 6:9).

Sentinels: Upper Realm soldiers who function as lookouts, sentries, or watchmen.

Settee: Two or three-person couch similar to an ancient Roman lectus. Used for reclining and sometimes as a spare bed.

Slimy Eels: Slimy eels, also called river eels, are greenish, non-predator fish that spawn in the seas before they migrate upriver into the lakes where they can grow to over ten-feet long. Anglers catch them with hook and line or by netting.

Tarkks: Predator fish found in lakes and the lower forks of rivers, similar in size to great white sharks or killer whales. The sea varieties are huge, growing to over a hundred feet.

Tarkkies: Juvenile tarkks, smaller but still large, about the size of a twelve-foot shark.

Tijvah: A Hebrew word for hope, expectation, and possibilities. It also refers to a rope or cord, which comes from a root word meaning to bind together, collect, expect, or wait upon. Common expression: hope is a rope.

Warders: Upper Realm soldiers who function as security guards, jailors, or stockade custodians.

Yarm: A drink made from the yarm berry, a grape-sized, pinkish berry harvested from bushes in the Yarm Vineyards. Yarm is a lightly fermented drink, which is usually diluted with water for children and adolescents. It's the preferred beverage in both realms.

FORTIFICATIONS

Alure: Access pathway in battlements (see wallwalk).

Battlement: A type of parapet on top of a rampart with spaced gaps that allowed the launching of projectiles from shielded positions (see crenels and merlons).

Citadel: Fortress or strongly fortified building or structure.

Crenels: Gaps between the raised sections (*merlons*) in parapets, battlements, or fortified towers. Defenders were able to observe and deploy weapons through the crenels.

Fortress: Stronghold with a military presence often included in a town or city.

Garrison Quarters: Where soldiers are housed and fed when on active duty.

Merlons: Raised sections between the gaps (*crenels*) of a parapet, battlement wall, or fortified tower. Defenders could hide behind the merlons for protection.

Parapet: Low retaining wall, often part of battlements, offering protection to defenders on the wallwalk behind it. A rampart was the main wall. The parapet was a lesser wall with a height ranging between chest-level and the top of someone's head.

Rampart: The main defensive wall in a citadel or fortified structure. It usually had a broad top with a wallwalk and parapet.

Stockade: Prison, holding area, or jail.

Wallwalk: Walkway running along the interior part of a fortified wall or parapet.

WEAPONS

Dagger: Handheld knife, shorter than a throwing knife, used in combat and for self-defense.

Fighting Staff: Also called a quarterstaff, battlestaff, and according to Max, *the persuader*. Wielded in sparring and combat. Common fighting techniques included lunge, strike (reverse, counter, or spin around), block, parry, sweep, fake, dodge, and deflect.

Gladius, the: A Roman medium length sword, double-edged, with a honed point suitable for cutting, chopping, and thrusting. The iron blade fit into a wooden sheath surrounded by either leather or bronze. Max's heaven-issued sword is patterned after the same basic design but forged with a superior metal of unknown origin. The edge was razor-sharp and the blade practically unbreakable.

Longbow: Although the longbow was commonly associated with the Celts in Wales, various ancient cultures employed them for hunting and warfare. Often made with yew but different woods were also utilized. The bow could shoot arrows over half a mile and were deadly accurate at 200 feet.

Sling: Ancient slings were constructed with a holding pouch connected to two cords. One cord ended in a loop, which slingers would slide over their fingers so when the other cord was released, the sling stayed attached to their hand. Rounded stone projectiles flung from slings could reach distances beyond 600 feet and had a high degree of accuracy at 150 feet.

Spears: The Guards used a red and black long-handled spear with a bronze point. It measured eight feet in length. Militia spears were shorter at six feet, unpainted and nondescript. Both types could be tossed like javelins. The accuracy range was between forty and fifty feet. Soldiers often carried two.

Swords: All swords from Eskaonus were bronze forged and tempered. The Guards preferred curved, single-bladed swords while the Militia wielded straight, double-edged ones.

Throwing Knives: Common weapons in both realms and carried in pairs. Depending on a person's expertise, thrown knives had an accuracy range of thirty feet.

BUILDINGS AND HALLS

Archives, the: Both Beayama and Briacap maintained a storage library with ancient documents, detailing their history and cultures, much of it vague and incomplete.

Great Hall, the: A building in Beayama with a large hall for public events such as banquets, exhibitions, and business meetings. It contained conference rooms and two kitchens.

Postal Tower: Also called the mail tower. The structure included a delivery room, residential quarters, a clerk's sorting desk, and roosts for the homing flyers. Cities staffed at least one tower for communications between communities. Villages used postal huts run by volunteers.

Residential Hall: Living quarters for Saephira and other governmental officials.

GLOSSARY 3

CAMAYAH

OVERVIEW OF CAMAYAH

Camayah (ka-MAY-ah) is an advanced world where science and technology have become the official religion. Other belief systems are unlawful. The followers or believers of such prohibited factions are persecuted, hunted down, imprisoned, and then reprogrammed. If the reset procedure is unsuccessful, the misguided citizens are terminated.

The pursuit and love of pleasure is the mainstay of most inhabitants, all except the believers who seek divine love and spiritual truth, but their numbers have been dwindling due to the purge. Some have escaped to the nearby moon to avoid capture.

Most of the populace perished in an event called the Burning. A past supernova from a distant sun may have caused this catastrophe, but the facts remain sketchy. After the disaster, Camayah became an arid wasteland. The few who lived, struggled to survive. Over time, the survivors developed into four classes of people: programmers, operators, security, and laborers.

Camayah's local sun is a red dwarf that emits a dim reddish light. Other planetary bodies, if they exist, have not been discovered. The planet has three orbiting moons.

PLANET AND MOONS

Camayah (ka-MAY-ah): System planet
Vilmieah (vill-MY-ah): First moon
Ethade (ETH-aid): Second moon
Easteapia (eas-tee-PIE-ah): Third and largest moon

KEY PLAYERS

Ahboen (ah-BOW'n): Program Assistant (PA), second in command.

Cndrek (KUHN-drek): Security Leader (SL) for Sector One.

Hiehew (HI-hue): Programming Supervisor (P3), secret believer.

Jawhawtu (jaw-HAH-too): Also called Jaw, midmate, airship engineer.

Layshura (lay-SURE-ah): Operational Assistant (OA) at Termination.

Leetqu (LEET-kue): Married to Rekis, daughter is Rauteira.

Malmach (maul-MOK): Married to Trikernae, spiritual leader, called provost.

Operational Leader: (OL) at Termination, unnamed.

Program Master: (PM) at Programming, supreme ruler, identity unknown.

Raetila (ray-TILL-ah): Security Assistant (SA) from RIFT II.

Rauteira (rah-TEER-uh): Daughter of Rekis and Leetqu.

Rekis (REE-kis): Married to Leetqu, daughter is Rauteira.

Runess (ROO-ness): Former Security Assistant (SA) for Airship Dock, prisoner in Holding.

Tawehna (tah-WAY-nah): One of seven Yah believers hiding on a moon.

Trikernae (TRY-ker-nay): Married to Malmach, spiritual leader, called pravost.

Uewba (YEW-baw): Also called Uew, rowmate, airship navigator.

GREETINGS

Hail to the Programmer: State-sanctioned salutation.
Fair Dawn to You: Good morning.
Joyous Dusk to You: Good night.
Good Pleasures: Salutation given to pleasure seekers.
Blessings to Yah: A religious greeting used by believers before being forbidden.

TIMES AND SEASONS

Interval: Minute
Bout: Hour
Dawn: Day
Predawn: Firstlight
Earlydawn: Midmorning
Halfdawn: Middle of the day
Latedawn: Afternoon
Nightfall: Twilight
Dusk: Night
Latedusk: Midnight or later
Event: Week
Phase: Month
Stage: Year, sometimes an event
Era: Undetermined period of time
Age: Century, long ago

Yesterdawn: Yesterday
Morrow: Tomorrow, later
Morn: Sunrise or morning
Eve: Sunset or evening

DISTANCE

Stride: Three feet
Tick: Mile
Leggs: Leagues or longer distance, sometimes undetermined

MEASUREMENTS

Notch: Inch
Mark: Foot
Lenn: Yard

WEIGHT

Masses: Pounds
Load: Ton
Crate: Twelve tons
Cubes: Ounces (fluids)
Beaker: Gallon (fluids)
Barrow: Fifty gallons (fluids)

DATA TERMINOLOGY

Assimilated: Facilities connected to the datastream
Beamed Data Transfers: Communications between portals, facilities, and airships
Data: All codes and information
Databands: Data channels
Datacode: Password or keyword
Datacomm: Communication device or pathway
Dataflows: Same as datastream
Dataframes: Small computers
Datapass: ID wristband or temporary DIN
Datastream: Flow of data
Datatop: Laptop
Data Systems: Computer programs
DIN: Data Identification Number or Data ID Number
Mainframes: Large computers

DINs

All inhabitants must have a Data Identification Number (DIN), which is needed for portal transports, airship travel, and access to the RIFT facilities. The code is implanted into the left index finger, which is placed on a scanner for identification. Temporary ID wristbands (datapasses) are supplied to migrants until they find a permanent RIFT and locate housing. Travelers between the five sectors are normally given three dawns to secure work and a three-dawn supply of nourishment tablets. If they are not employed by then, the courtesy pill supply and privileges are cut off.

Assigned DINs

L342: Jesse
L343: Max
L344: Seth
L345: Anna
L346: Holley
L347: Narleen
L348: Lundy

Radio Channels

One: Seth
Two: Anna
Three: Holley
Four: Lundy
Five: Jesse
Communicators are occasionally shared between members.

Stunners

Bospike: Contact weapon, carried by S1s.
Quispike: Short range, fifty lenns, yellow light beam, carried by S2s.
Trispike: Long range, ninety lenns, green light beam, carried by S3s.

Power

TPC: Triverphol Power Cores. The modules (or cells) have a viewing window that gives off a yellow flaming glow. The cores come in three sizes: Large for mainframes, airships, portal systems, and cranes. Medium for programming terminals, general data equipment, and communications. Small for stunners, lighting, hand scanners, and minor devices.

Supplements and Costs

Nutrition
Tycozide: 3 gelts (daily dose)
Dapferon: 6 gelts (extended release)

Hydration
Hydru: 3 gelts (daily dose)
Tyhydru: 6 gelts (extended release)

Pleasure
Cradphenanill: 1 gelt (rapid release)

Pill Descriptions

Tycozide: Round tablet, reddish-brown
Dapferon: Oval tablet, reddish-brown
Hydru: Round tablet, greenish-blue
Tyhydru: Oval tablet, greenish-blue
Cradphenanill: Cube, white

Locations and Places

Airship Docks: Docking areas for airships that provide travel to locations not connected by transport portals. Fares are expensive for locals: ten gelts per person. Security, operators, and programmers ride for free with unlimited usage. At one time, airships traveled to the moons and were equipped with solar sails.

Holding Area: A jail for discontents and fanatics while waiting for reprogramming or termination. Staffed by Security.

Housing: Living units for laborers. Most are built from metal scraps and secondhand materials found in the ruins.

Pit Mines: Underground cavities where Triverphol and other minerals or substances are mined.

Programming Center: Governmental complex for the planet. The center has five main levels. The first one contains the entry, service counters, comm terminals, and small security detachment. The second floor accommodates the reprogramming cubicles, work stations, and research labs. The third houses programmers and their family members. The Program Assistant's office and residence comprise the fourth level. The top section is where the Program Master lives and works.

RIFTs: Multipurpose facilities with numerical designations. All have the same basic layout. The main level includes an information counter, accounting kiosk, communication terminal, pill dispensary, classrooms for instruction, and recreation facilities. The two upper levels house Security and their families. Storage is found on the lower level. RIFTs communicate through beamed data transfers with other facilities, including airships and all portal locations.

The RIFTs are rumored to possess secret storage areas with various materials, technology, and certain supplies, which Security keeps for their own use. Being in protected areas, most technology and existing supplies were undamaged after the Burning. None of these items are shared with the residential laborers or their families. Each RIFT contains a repair room for fixing broken stun weapons and equipment.

RIFT is an acronym:

REHO (Recreation): Pleasure cubicles

INDO (Instruction): Rules, regulations, general education
FEYO (Feeding): Nourishment supplies
TAEO (Taxation): Registration, accountability, work assignments

Ruins: Remnants of buildings, former spaceports, and abandoned or destroyed temples. Broken objects and general debris are scattered throughout the area. Laborers scrounge these ruins for reuseable materials, pieces of solar sails, discarded relics, and any salvageable trash that can be used to make household items, tools, protective clothing, and other things needed for survival.

Termination Facility: An elimination center to terminate those who are un-programmable, deity worshipers, and any who have late-stage Triverphol Disease. Operators also oversee the production of nourishment tabs, vaccines, and Cradphenanill cubes.

Transport Portals: Travel hubs between connected locations on Camayah and the planet's three moons.

ITEMS AND INFORMATION

Airships: Floating crafts powered by Triverphol-fueled engines and equipped with solar sails for atmospheric travel.

Battle Frenzy: A mental state where combatants feel they have superhuman strength and are impervious to pain. Sometimes called *Battle Heat.*

Battle Trance: A condition of heightened senses where events appear to move slowly. The fighter sees things in slow motion, giving him or her time to react beforehand. Fear disappears. The person is focused. Time, itself, seems to linger. When the trance lifts, the flow of time returns to normal.

Believers: Yah worshipers.

Bonded: Married.

Bondedmoon: Similar to a honeymoon.

Burning, the: Also called the Event. A cataclysm that destroyed most of the planet. It may have been a chemical disaster, fusion explosion, or unknown supernova event. The cause was never determined. All flora and animal life perished. Water evaporated. Only a few individuals survived.

Caldrons: Processing facilities and storage for Triverphol.

Cradphenanill: Also known as pleasure tabs or cubes. They have narcotic properties that cause euphoria, increase desire, amplify sensuality, and inhibit self-control.

Crane: Heavy equipment with a bucket used to remove liquid Triverphol.

Criunite: A green luminous crystal that gives off light. They are found in Triverphol pits, exposed ridges in the hills, near hollows, and around ruins. Supplies are limited.

Diggers: Handheld mining and raking tools.

Discontents: People who disagree or reject the dystopian rules on Camayah.

Event, the: Also called the Burning. A past supernova from distant sun may have caused the cataclysmic event.

Fanatics: Derogatory name for religious followers.

Foeca (FOE'ca): Quawner excrement (dung). Called spider poo by Seth. Foeca is a sticky, milky substance found in round balls around cave entrances. It has narcotic properties.

Gelts: Digital currency.

Gladius: Max's heaven-issued sword, sharp, unknown alloy, unbreakable.

Hydrew: Liquids or fluids on Camayah, emerald-colored, similar to water.

Jumpsuits: Protective clothing.

Morning Sickness: The symptoms include nausea and vomiting. They usually begin after six weeks of pregnancy. Dry heaves are also common. Although the symptoms can occur at any hour, many women experience them in the morning, hence the name, morning sickness.

Nawmies: Extinct birds.

Nyeflute: A golden brown flute with carved intricate designs. The heaven-issued instrument fits into a tubular-shaped holding pouch with an attached shoulder strap. It comes with a fingering tablature for different songs or tunes. When played, the songs cause certain effects such as sleepiness, confusion, and invisibility. Others instill confidence, encouragement, and alertness. It's similar to a Celtic Boehm flute but slightly shorter in length.

Outer Atmosphere: Unexplored space.

Prebonded: Engaged, betrothed.

Quawners: Large spider-like creatures with six legs. They have tough outer skins and spit venom to immobilize their prey. These arachnids prefer to eat live food, namely people, so they usually drag their victims into their dens and wrap them in webs for later consumption. The beasts make unusual sounds, assumed to be signals, to communicate with others from their dens. The creatures are most active during the night. They use stealth to track their prey and clicking sounds when attacking. Quawners live in deep, underground burrows. Their hollows have luminous crystals scattered throughout the walls that give off a greenish glow.

Recycled Body Chemicals: A guarded secret, processed from terminated individuals, used in various pills and products.

Reprogramming: There are two types: limited (mind wipes) and complete (resets). The reset is an extensive brainwashing. It masks memories, replaces names with coded numbers, makes people more compliant, which turns them into nameless drones. The mind wipes for Security, operators, and programmers are less intrusive. They retain family histories and most memories. Those who have command rankings keep their names.

Solar Sails: A solar sail is a large reflective sheet that captures photons from a sun. These particles bounce off the sail, causing momentum, driving the sail and attached craft forward. Normally, they push the vessel away from a sun. But with a tacking maneuver, similar to a sailboat using the wind, the direction can be changed. Unlike spaceships that usually coast after reaching their maximum speed, crafts equipped with solar sails can continue accelerating.

Soreseeds: Soreseeds, also called soreseed sets, are a variety of plant types. Some germinate into corn-like plants called maza; others grow into shrubberies, edible gourds, and various vine or bush vegetables. The plants need ground liquids to survive, but can also draw moisture from the air during a misty night. Before the Burning, soreseed plants were the main food staples. Since all liquids evaporated in the catastrophe, soreseeds are considered extinct.

Supernova: Supernovas occur during the last moments of a star's life. The gigantic explosion can devastate nearby planets or an entire galaxy.

Tabs: Tablets, pills, sometimes called cubes.

Triverphol: A highly flammable liquid that is mined from the flame pits on Camayah and its three moons. The substance is processed and converted into light air, airship fuel, and power cells.

Triverphol Sickness or ***Triverphol Disease:*** Also called the Disease. The symptoms of infection are a yellowish rash, followed by blisters, then decaying skin, weight loss, weakness, muscular degeneration, and finally, death. During later stages, the sickness seems to spread to unaffected people and children. It has no known cure. Sooner or later, those who work around pit mines come down with this disease. Vaccination offers limited protection. Infected workers are considered replaceable by the PM. All people with late-stage Triverphol Sickness are terminated.

Upper Atmosphere: The area between planetary orbit and a moon.

Venom: A clear liquidy substance that quawners spray to immobilize their prey. It has paralytic and hypnotic effects.

Yah: Yahweh, God.

RULES

Rule Number One: Always expect the unexpected.
Rule Number Two: Face your fears to overcome them.
Rule Number Three: In due season you will reap if you don't quit.
Rule Number Four: If all else fails, RUN.

VACCINATIONS

Floksillin: Vaccine to prevent general diseases, seventy percent effective.

Ploksillin: Vaccine to protect against the effects of Triverphol Sickness, fifty perfect effective.

Vaccinations are only given to programmers, operators, and Security. Laborers are excluded. With no treatment options, if anyone becomes ill, the person is usually terminated before they infect others.

MINERALS, SUBSTANCES, AND MATERIALS

Minerals needed for hydration pills:

Liganol: Rock nodule containing Decanapron, dwindling supply.

Decanapron: Greenish mineral, extracted from Liganol.

Gluradol: Small oblong geode that contains Luqole, limited supply.

Luqole: Blue powdery mineral.

Ingredients used in nutrition pills:

Biocrisnite: Reddish mineral, abundant, processed to extract chemicals.

Plyenspur: Dark brown rock, abundant, processed to extract chemicals.

Substances required for vaccines:

Clignite: Crumbly yellowish mineral, rare.

Liganol: Brown powdery mineral, rare.

Recycled body chemicals.

Materials found in pleasure tabs:

Cradphen: Whitish crystal, abundant, runs in thick veins.

Foeca: Sticky opaque substance, abundant, added as a reagent.

Recycled body chemicals.

STAFFING, POSITIONS, AND RANKS

LABORERS: Common workers.

Laborers have no levels or ranks, only L plus their DIN. Their jobs include pit mining for Triverphol and other minerals or compounds, raking or digging for Criunite crystals, and gathering Foeca. Housing is not provided. Laborers must find their own living spaces or do without.

OPERATORS: Specialists who staff the Termination Facility. They produce nutrition and hydration pills, vaccines, and pleasure tabs. Operators and their families have residences at the facility.

Operational Leader (OL): Command position.
Operational Assistant (OA): Second in command.
Operational Technician (OT): Skilled operator.
Operators: Common name for all Termination staff.

PROGRAMMERS: People with coding experience who oversee the reprogramming of discontents and assist the PM with running the government. All programmers and their families live at the Programming Center.

Program Master (PM): Authority position, absolute ruler, never seen in public, name and identity are unknown.

Program Assistant (PA): Second authority position behind the PM.

P3: Supervisor, highest-ranked programmer, seniority.
P2: Mid-level position, moderate experience.
P1: Trainee.
Programmer: Common name for all programmers.

SECURITY: Guards who oversee security at facilities and mining sites. They carry DIN scanners and stun weapons. Security and their family members are provided complimentary residences in the local RIFT as well as other benefits.

Security Leader (SL): Command Position. Cndrek from RIFT I is the SL for Sector One.

Security Assistant (SA): Second in Command. Each RIFT has one.

S3: Supervisor, highest-ranked guard, armed with trispike.
S2: Mid-level position, armed with a quispike.
S1: Trainee, armed with a bospike.

APPENDIX

JESSE'S FORMER JOURNAL ENTRIES

Entry One

No changing of days, or nights, or light from the sun. Normal time continues on earth, I think. Here, it's basically one, long, everlasting day. Therefore, I'm calling this eternal era "the day after always," a day that goes on forever and ever.

I have not seen any little children or babies, only teens, who I would estimate to be around thirteen years old. A book I read once said people in heaven would be in their prime, yet I see a ton of older individuals, like Abraham, who looks to be the age described in the Bible. There are all ages here, just no little ones. If all the saints were thirty years old, it might feel like a cult or something. I plan on asking someone in the know about these matters. As for me, I look the same age I was before I arrived, except I don't need eyeglasses anymore or have a sore knee. And I feel strong and energetic.

Entry Two

Hope you enjoy the book. I made you a waterproof satchel to carry it in. Your pen is inside, full of ink, and ready to go. Take the journal with you. It may come in handy. I also recycled the old fruit pit I found on your desktop. Everything has a purpose here.

Godspeed, elChesed

Entry Three

Made it to Eskaonus. Rev. Lundy is missing. He didn't arrive with the rest of us. I'm getting a bit worried. We'll search for him in the morning. Built a shelter and made camp for the night. We are all feeling tired. Annie says she's a little sick to her stomach. Probably nerves. Hope things are better tomorrow. Will try to make contact with the Eskaonites and do some investigating. I don't want to give away our purpose, not until I know who's friend or foe.

Entry Four

Interesting couple days. Everyone poisoned by yarm

berries. We had no immunity. Search party from the southern lands found us and took us to local medic for treatment. Almost lost Annie. Attacked by assailants this afternoon. Not sure why. Concerning the evil, I haven't determined much. I think it concerns Eddnok and the northern lands. Big dinner tonight. Hope to find out more.

Entry Five

Dinner went OK. Gathered good intel. Expedition planned for tomorrow to see some old ruins. They may provide clues to what happened here and why there's no knowledge of God or belief system. Saephira thinks it may be an ancient temple. If so, why was it destroyed or abandoned? Need more facts. The leader has discerning dreams and seems open to spiritual matters. Not yet sure what evil lurks here on Eskaonus. Something, however, isn't right. We're all really tried. It's been a day. Praying for a restful sleep.

Entry Six

Really sleepy, so I'll make this entry short. Lots happened today. Discovered a buried scroll, must be old, yet it looks new, like the ones in heaven. The ruins are probably an old temple. How or why destroyed, I don't know. The answers might explain why there's no knowledge of God or religion here. Uncovered two carved symbols. They seem familiar to me. Starting to trust Saephira. Plan to tell her more about our purpose here, just waiting for the right opportunity. Preaverca hiding something. Lundy still missing. The rest of us are doing okay.

Entry Seven

Massive rockslide at ruins, many injuries, Anna paralyzed, townspeople dead, Lundy lost. It's all my fault. Guess I'm still a failure. I'm not gonna . . .

Entry Eight

Second day of red sky. Fewer windstorms. I imagine all of heaven knows about my failures from last night. Everyone in my group does, yet they continue to support me as leader. Not sure I would do the same. If someone is listening, all I can say is I'm sorry. I tried to erase my last entry, except for some reason, the ink is permanent. Couldn't tear out the page either. Max said things made in heaven are eternal. Apparently, this goes for my journal, the ink written thereon, as well as the satchel itself.

Chesedel told me heaven is the place of second chances. I pray there's a third one for me. I sure blew my first two.

Annie feels we will receive word on Lundy soon. I hope so. She exhibits an uncanny discernment in these matters. Annie also mentioned Chesedel visited her room last night. If so, that's wonderful. Miracle or otherwise, she's fully recovered. We are planning a rescue mission for Narleen who was abducted by the Upper Realm. Our answers lay there, I think, including the evil we were sent here to confront. Well, time for bed.

Entry Nine

Attempting a rescue mission tomorrow night. Hope to find Lundy and Narleen who are being held as prisoners and break them out of jail. Saephira hasn't pressed me on our purpose in Eskaonus, how we got here, or where we came from. I will probably share what I can tonight. Lord, grant me wisdom in this. Right now, however, everyone is focused on the night raid at Briacap. Praying for success and safety.

Entry Ten

Busy few cycles, I mean days, so I haven't been recording entries. Good news. We found and rescued Lundy, along with eight other prisoners who were being held captive by Lord Eddnok. He's as wicked as they come. I suspect Eddnok is behind the evil influence here.

Lundy translated an ancient manuscript that reveals a hidden cave with a mysterious treasure (attachment below). It might hold the answers we are seeking. He thinks we should focus on finding it. Me too. Except getting there is another matter. We'll decide in the morning.

Attachment

If treasure is what you seek then don't be meek, nor forgo the rift near the highest cliff. Buried deep within lies a secret twin of the richest gift known to gods or men. Take an uphill pace to seek a taste of wisdom sublime and power divine. So follow the trail to the mountains red, through the forest dead, past waters shed, and peaks that grow during daylight glow. Past ancient grave lays hidden cave where treasure awaits for a ruler of fate.

Entry Eleven

We may have discovered why evil has become so

widespread. The mysterious treasure appears to be a knowledge tree clone. According to Lundy, it produced forbidden fruit like the tree in Eden and even had a similar appearance. I'm not exactly sure how or why this occurred. Notwithstanding, we think Eddnok consumed the fruit, then ignored the good knowledge and allowed the evil knowledge to spread in his already corrupted heart. If so, many have perished because of his wickedness, including Falein Village, which is now in ruins. In regard to the hidden cave and what became of the knowledge tree, I haven't a clue. Chesedel may have the lowdown since he was present at the end. All we know for sure is the tree miraculously disappeared.

Our group helped rescue Narleen for a second time and restored Saephira to her rightful place as Leader. Most of the conspirators have been rounded up, all except Eddnok. Concerning other news, we were just invited to a planning dinner. I suspect we'll be asked to help participate in an effort to stop Eddnok before more of his wickedness takes root. Countering evil was one reason we came here, right? As for the second part, to bring the truth of God and His ways back to Eskaonus, we're still working on it.

This may be my last entry for a while. It's been a learning experience for all of us, especially me. I wasn't sure I could say this and mean it until recently, but thank you for sending us here. I look forward to finishing our mission, returning to heaven and sipping a cool drink from the Fountain of Life. The water here tastes like mud.

NOTE FROM THE AUTHOR

We sometimes assume life is the same for all created beings wherever they might exist—that individuals fit into the same mold, follow the same customs and laws, embrace the same plan of salvation, worship the same way, and end up in the same afterlife—or that spiritual warfare and physical conflicts no longer occur in the hereafter. Eternity may reveal this is not the case.

Concerning conflicts, a quick look through the Bible will detail much death and destruction endured by humanity. Some of those struggles are seen in Sodom and Gomorrah and in the violent clashes between Israel and Judah as they sought or rejected God's will. We should never assume that similar scenarios can't repeat elsewhere in God's infinite kingdom. Nor presume immortality merely involves floating on clouds as we play harps or that the final dispensation (Ephesians 1:10) means the Lord has completed His agenda. In regard to the latter, I believe our Creator has more to accomplish. And so do His redeemed.

God is the same yesterday, today, and forever (Hebrews 13:8), but His many worlds and realms, whether known or unknown, will not remain the same. Even our familiar cosmos will change. His new heaven and new earth (Revelation 21:1) will likely be distinctive, present new challenges, and offer opportunities for continued ministry. Redemption, after all, has an ongoing purpose, and eternity, an everlasting timeframe.

About the Author

Charles Earl Harrel is a Christian writer with more than 650 published works. His articles, inspirational stories, and devotionals have appeared in various periodicals and in forty-one anthologies. Charles is also a nine-time contributor to Chicken Soup for the Soul. He has written three books: *The Ministry of Divine Healing, The Greatest Moment,* and *The Day After Always*.

He pastored for thirty years, serving churches in California, Nevada, and Oregon, before stepping aside to pursue writing. Charles holds a doctorate in ministry. He and his wife, Laura, live in Portland, Oregon. They enjoy hiking, community outreach, and teaching from God's Word.

THE DAY AFTER ALWAYS (Book One)
Follow the intriguing story of five associates as they embark on a spiritual adventure to discover the possibilities and perils waiting in the time beyond time.

THE GREATEST MOMENT

One particular moment, surpassing all others, has been waiting since the dawn of time for its unveiling. This event is the greatest moment in the Bible. In this moment, God's greatest plan is fulfilled and our destiny revealed.

Made in USA - Kendallville, IN
89683_9781962168601
03.19.2024 2128